A Warrior's Mouth

Was she cursing him to the devil? Did this wee Campbell lass dare damn him? MacColla glared at her, trying to make sense of her strange accent. She seemed to be speaking English, but none like he'd ever heard. Her words were like the sharp claps of a barking dog. "Speak slow when you curse me."

He studied the movement of her mouth, trying to understand her words. Her lips were full and dark against the pale glow of her cheeks in the moonlight. He'd taste this Campbell woman, he decided suddenly.

MacColla kissed her. He'd wanted at first to be rough, but she was soft. So soft and sweet, his mouth gentled in the tasting of her. And, for a single moment, he imagined the lass kissed him back, her breath sighing into him, her mouth opening just enough for him to taste her, fresh and warm on his tongue.

And then, with a tiny growl, she caught his lower lip hard between her teeth and bit.

MacColla pulled away. She glared at him, bared her teeth, and exhaled with the measured breath of a prowling wolf.

He studied the wee Cam~~pbell~~ ~~woman before~~ him, and then strangely, inexplicably,

Berkley Sensation Books by Veronica Wolff

MASTER OF THE HIGHLANDS
SWORD OF THE HIGHLANDS
WARRIOR OF THE HIGHLANDS

Warrior
of the
Highlands

Veronica Wolff

BERKLEY SENSATION, NEW YORK

THE BERKLEY PUBLISHING GROUP
Published by the Penguin Group
Penguin Group (USA) Inc.
375 Hudson Street, New York, New York 10014, USA
Penguin Group (Canada), 90 Eglinton Avenue East, Suite 700, Toronto, Ontario M4P 2Y3, Canada
(a division of Pearson Penguin Canada Inc.)
Penguin Books Ltd., 80 Strand, London WC2R 0RL, England
Penguin Group Ireland, 25 St. Stephen's Green, Dublin 2, Ireland (a division of Penguin Books Ltd.)
Penguin Group (Australia), 250 Camberwell Road, Camberwell, Victoria 3124, Australia
(a division of Pearson Australia Group Pty. Ltd.)
Penguin Books India Pvt. Ltd., 11 Community Centre, Panchsheel Park, New Delhi—110 017, India
Penguin Group (NZ), 67 Apollo Drive, Rosedale, North Shore 0632, New Zealand
(a division of Pearson New Zealand Ltd.)
Penguin Books (South Africa) (Pty.) Ltd., 24 Sturdee Avenue, Rosebank, Johannesburg 2196,
South Africa

Penguin Books Ltd., Registered Offices: 80 Strand, London WC2R 0RL, England

WARRIOR OF THE HIGHLANDS

A Berkley Sensation Book / published by arrangement with the author

PRINTING HISTORY
Berkley Sensation mass-market edition / January 2009

ISBN: 978-0-425-22675-9

BERKLEY® SENSATION
Berkley Sensation Books are published by The Berkley Publishing Group,
a division of Penguin Group (USA) Inc.,
375 Hudson Street, New York, New York 10014.
BERKLEY® SENSATION and the "B" design are trademarks of Penguin Group (USA) Inc.

PRINTED IN THE UNITED STATES OF AMERICA

10 9 8 7 6 5 4 3 2 1

*In honor of all the Fitzpatricks, O'Donovans,
and Driscolls in my own family tree.
Warriors all—I can feel it.*

*With a special nod to my favorite Irishman of all:
James Patrick, my dad.*

Acknowledgments

I've been blessed with the Greatest Job Ever, and I'd like to express my heartfelt gratitude to those wonderful and talented people who help make it all possible, particularly Cindy Hwang, Stephanie Kip Rostan, and Leis Pederson. A thank you to Monika Verma too, as well as a special nod to all of the people behind the scenes at Berkley—you never fail to amaze me.

A tremendous thank you to Kate Perry, who is a dear friend, secret weapon, sparkling author, and expert on all things goal-oriented.

I'm also very grateful to Monica McCarty for all the sage advice, and for being the Julie McCoy to my Isaac, even though we never did get matching purple tracksuits.

I am indebted to Sharron Gunn, who graciously offered her support, expertise, and, most thrilling of all, my choice of archaic and modern Gaelic translations.

Thanks to Bella Andre for being an inspiration on all manner of life- and book-related matters. To Penelope Williamson for her wisdom, and for helping me get a critical scene just right. Also to Jami Alden and Anne Mallory for all those heartening deadline dispatches. And to Kalen Hughes for the busk.

Sincere thanks to my chief evangelists: Rudy Reyes, Ivan Wolff, Sue Goldstein, Joey Wolff, John Mackin, plus Michael, Connie, Jim, Patrick, the two Lisas, and, of course, Mom and Dad.

This whole project would've been impossible without

the loving support and understanding of my dear husband, Adam, and our two fabulous kids, who are still wondering when exactly mommy will be done with her book.

Sleep for a little, a very small while,
And fear nothing,
Man to whom I have given my love.

—FROM "DUANAIRE FINN," ANONYMOUS,
CIRCA SEVENTEENTH CENTURY

Warrior of the Highlands

Prologue

Campbell stared at the woman. She seemed an ill-used and wizened creature, despite the fact that she was likely not much older than his forty-three years. The moon's watery light picked out but a few white strands marbling her red hair, and yet her body was hunched into a rigid bow, fat and muscle stretched thin and tight on her bones.

He shifted. He'd have the woman get on with her ritual. His clansmen would look in horror at such black witchcraft, but the trepidation he'd initially felt was waning, and Campbell grew piqued with each passing minute. He resented sitting on the ground like some rustic, his back aching, with small rocks biting into his palms every time he adjusted his weight on the cold, packed dirt.

He tried to take her measure. It had taken coin aplenty to track the witch down, but her reserve planted the seed of doubt in his head: Was she truly one to be feared, or was she merely some shrewd carlin adept at parting men from their purses?

Though he stared openly at her, Campbell could get no more than a passing glance of her face full-on. Her eyes focused on a place in the far distance and didn't deign rest on him, always wavering ever so slightly as if she were blind, though he knew she was not. She moved in the darkness like a cat, and Campbell saw clearly how those who knew of such things told of witches choosing the detested animal as their familiar.

He would see if this Finola had powers. And he would burn her himself if she wasn't the sorceress she claimed.

Finola. His skin crawled. Campbell knew the name meant "white shoulder," and it thrust intimate and unwelcome images into his head. Fragments of ivory skin. The fall of red hair onto a pale shoulder.

He gave himself a shake. Perhaps it was the dark arts at work. Perhaps she had the power to shift shape into some fiendish consort for Lucifer himself. Unthinking, he spat into the ritual fire to exorcise such thoughts.

Finola's gaze shot up to meet his. The flames set her green and yellow eyes to glowing, and Campbell imagined he saw evil glimmering there, like an oily shadow sliding just beneath the surface. He'd hoped to catch her in a glimpse head-on, and now he just wished her to look away.

His voice cracked in the darkness. Anything to break the spell he felt chilling through his flesh down into his bones. "When will you begin, woman?"

The sinister glare receded like a retracting membrane from her eyes, and what was left was simply Finola regarding him with distaste. "You yearn for your enemy like a spurned child. Your impatience makes drudgery of a simple task."

He pursed his lips. *Impatience indeed.* There was a task at hand—he need not suffer the scoldings of some witch woman.

His clan harbored a long-running feud against Clan MacDonald. But it was Alasdair MacColla who'd raised the stakes, using his Royalist battles as an excuse to douse Scottish soil with the blood of untold numbers of Campbell sons.

And it was MacColla he'd destroy.

"I paid you good coin to help me ruin him."

Campbell's bravado was met with impenetrable silence. The witch merely set back to work, using her thumbs to mold the final touches on the clay figure lying before her. "You desire MacColla," she said finally. "And so here he is."

She leaned back to reveal a crude effigy, the reds and browns of the Highland earth packed together in a featureless, calico likeness of a man.

"The *corp creadha*. The clay body of your enemy Mac-Colla." She retrieved a handful of silken black strands from a pouch at her waist and systematically worked clumps into the crown of the tacky clay. "The hair of the sister recalls the man."

And then Finola struck fast, like a snake, reaching over to grab Campbell's hand, slicing his palm with a tiny steel blade.

"How dare—"

"You will silence your tongue, or I will exact your silence from you." For the second time, the witch's eyes met his.

Campbell's mouth went dry. The first traces of true fear seeped into him, shuddering up his spine, leaving his blood chilled in its wake. He would remember his purpose here. Remember what he was about. He was a man of stature who could kill this Finola with but a word. And he would use whatever it took—use *her*—to ruin MacColla once and for all.

She spoke again, but this time her voice was hollow, otherworldly. "We come in the night to a place where three streams meet."

Squeezing his hand with surprising strength, Finola pulled Campbell close to the *corp creadha*, drizzling his blood over the eye sockets she'd hollowed from the clay. "That the enemy sees the blood of your hatred."

Finola pulled a bone from the sleeve of her cloak, dull and yellow brown where the meat was scraped clean from the blade of a lamb's shoulder. "We place the *speal* upon the heart of your enemy." Firelight licked red shadows along the surface of the bone, placed on the torso of the clay corpse. "That the enemy feels the blade of your vengeance."

Power thrilled up Campbell's spine, dissolving his apprehension. He would strike the deathblow to MacColla and Clan MacDonald. The blade of his vengeance. Campbell gave a small smile at the sound of it.

She took tongs from the dirt at her side and began to extract charred river stones from the flames, placing them one by one around the effigy. "That the enemy burns in the flames of your destruction."

Aye, burn MacColla. Campbell would annihilate him. Their clans had feuded over land and power for generations. But with the war that now raged through Ireland and the Highlands, the rivalry had curdled into something venomous. Something murderous. *Burn.*

Campbell had rid the west of most of the MacDonald vermin. He'd imprisoned MacColla's father and brother, and though they roamed free now, he'd exiled the rest of the clan to Ireland.

But he'd underestimated the middle son. MacColla had returned for Campbell, sniffing him out like a dog, seeking his revenge. It was when he'd come to Campbell's own lands at Inveraray, savaging Campbell holdings and killing Campbell kinsmen, that he'd vowed to destroy MacColla once and for all.

But first he'd see him suffer.

Finola stiffened. With a sharp inhale, she rolled her eyes back and swayed, her breath coming in short pants. Rocking forward and back, forward and back, she intoned:

> *Cloaked in black of night,*
> *I call the elements. Hear me.*
> *By the blood of my enemy—*

Chanting and quaking madly now, she swept her hand over the clay crown of the corpse's head.

Grant me dominion over fire,
Grant me dominion over wind,
Grant me dominion over earth,
Grant me dominion over water.

Campbell was uneasy once more. That she'd taken his own blood for her ritual disturbed him, and his hand inched to the dirk at his side.

Uncertainty nagged at him, and dread that he'd stepped upon a path from which there was no return. It wouldn't sit well with his clan to know the lengths he went to. Black witchcraft was feared in the Highlands. He'd never known anybody who'd resorted to its use. Or at least none who'd confess to it.

But his noble Lowland peers, they'd simply have his head if they discovered he dallied in such devilish abominations.

I shall bathe in the lustral fire,
I shall bathe in pools of wine.

Her hands waved over the flames, sweeping the gray smoke to her breast. She cast palmfuls of dirt and water toward the fire and it hissed angrily, shooting plumes of ghostly white smoke into the night. Campbell hastily pulled a handkerchief from his waist pocket, covering his mouth and nose to protect his body from inhaling such evil.

I shall bathe in the tears of mothers,
I shall bathe in rivers of blood.

White sparks crackled out from the flames and whorled around them before winking into darkness. Campbell recoiled, looking around in panicked horror, his hand finally seizing the hilt of his weapon.

Finola stood suddenly, and the flames rose with her.

Campbell let go his dagger, whispering a prayer as he edged back from the fire.

The whites of her eyes filled her sockets and shone an eerie, translucent gray in the night. Her voice jumped higher, beseeching in a keening, inhuman voice,

Thine art the midnight beloved,
Thine art the black swan,
Thine art the prince of the night,
Hear me and grant dominion over the stars.

The witch fell to her knees and stared into the fire. Its hot, blue center swelled, and yet its crest split into what seemed like thousands of yellow tips, all licking and dancing in a frenzy. She leaned close, as if she would breathe the flames into her, to welcome the fire into her nose and mouth like a lover.

It was going too far. He'd stop the witch before she summoned the devil himself to them. Campbell reached his hand out, felt the heat of the flames and the damp of her sweat radiate to his fingertips. One slight movement and he could push the woman in, baptize her in fire as any witch should be. It was his moment to go back, to choose a different path than that of evil. Her body would burn, and none would know of Campbell's flirtations with the dark arts.

Eyes tearing, her thin, dry lips cracked into a smile. "I see," she whispered.

Campbell drew his arm back. He felt Finola's sudden serenity like a breeze in the night. And he found his own resolve. He would see as the witch saw. Use her powers just this once.

He'd wait for now. Her death would come in time.

Finola sightlessly took a wooden panel from the dirt. "So it is," she rasped, and began frantically muttering an incantation.

Her tiny dagger glittered silver white in the moonlight as she hacked and carved at the small square of wood. Untouched by the heat, she retrieved a chunk of charred kindling from the edge of the fire and used it to etch lines and circles on the panel. She worked quickly, as if in a trance, sketching with a loose arm shapes that slowly coalesced into figures.

"I call for you she who is most able to shatter MacColla." Finola slammed the wooden panel down before Campbell, and this time he didn't flinch. It bore the image of a large man with a woman by his side, smudged in shades of gray and black.

"I call the woman who would be his bride."

Chapter 1

Boston, Present Day

Haley rubbed her finger over the blade. Metal was a curious material. It assumed the body's heat, and yet would never be mistaken for a living thing. She turned it in her hand. It was the oddest weapon she'd ever laid eyes on.

Who was the man who'd held this? she wondered, projecting her mind to another time. Circa 1675, the catalog read. *Whose blood had it drawn?*

The filigree patterns at its base remained vivid, but the knife's edge was nearly serrated with corrosion. Though she knew it still had a bite, Haley couldn't resist tentatively scraping the pad of her thumb along the tip, and she gasped when it nicked her. She raised the cut to her mouth and breathed in the sour tang of steel that clung to her palm.

Another blade, sharper and colder, invaded her thoughts. It was years ago now but, in a single heartbeat, Haley was back. Reliving the moment that had changed her forever.

She fingered her scar, grazing lightly along it, as if it were some ghastly length of twine with the give of flesh beneath her fingers. The tissue had no feeling, and she could almost imagine it wasn't a part of her body. And yet she could never forget it. Would never forget that other blade, once pressed hard to her throat.

Her breath hissed sharply from between her teeth. Deep inhale, sharp exhale. *The breath sweeps the mind clear*, she could hear her father say. He'd been so helpful after the attack, using his experience and sheer will to pull his daughter back from the darkness that had enveloped her.

Just thinking of her dad brought a smile to her face. The love of her family had brought her back, but it had been her father's police academy training—leavened with some good old South Boston street fighting—that had helped Haley control the feeling of vulnerability that had paralyzed her.

Dammit. She really needed to figure out her dissertation, not get sidetracked by some weapon. She put the strange dagger back on the table and took a rubber band from around her wrist to pull her hair back tight. She'd come to the museum that day for inspiration, and Sarah had let her into the second-floor storage area to peruse what few artifacts they had that might be germane to a topic in seventeenth-century Britain.

Her advisor had threatened that Haley was in danger of losing her teaching stipend. She'd been in the graduate program for four years now, and though she'd managed to eke out a chapter here and there, she needed to establish her argument and finish the thing.

A thick hank of black hair slipped free and Haley roughly tugged her elastic out and pulled the coarse mass back into place. She needed a breakthrough to catch her advisor's attention. Something fresh. Something she could even milk into a journal article or two, and get the heat off of her for a little while.

Dr. Clark had just about lost his patience. Haley's interests in early modern weaponry didn't help matters, skewing, as they did, so dangerously close to what he considered military theory. And with a fellowship cofunded by the History Department and the Department of Celtic Languages,

Haley had no choice but to position herself as a pure Reformation-era Scottish historian. Period.

As much as she'd prefer studying old broadswords instead.

Muttering a very American expletive, Haley snatched the weapon back off the table anyway. She leaned back and, slouching low in the chair, stretched her legs out in front of her. It was gorgeous. And inexplicably buried deep in the museum's archives with so many other gems in the Harvard collection.

On the surface, it looked like a simple dagger. An elegant, though stout, dagger. But Haley had known instantly what she was looking at. It was what was known as a "combination weapon." Wary of gunpowder's unreliability, early modern arms makers created guns capable of multiple jobs. A spear that shot bullets. A hunting *trousse* with a small pistol flush against its machetelike blade. She'd once even seen an elaborate museum piece that was a sword, cane, hammer, and musket-rest all in one.

Many of the combination weapons were clunky—they would have been ostentatious displays of wealth, not something one would've relied upon for day-to-day hunting or fighting. But this one was stunning, extraordinary. It was only when she held it in her hand that she could sense the hollowness of the blade that would've served as the barrel of the pistol. And if the owner wasn't inclined to bullets, the tip of the knife could separate and shoot from the base like a lethal steel arrowhead. The flintlock mechanism that acted as cock and hammer was almost completely camouflaged by elaborate etching on the blade, and by the fine hounds' heads crafted at the T-shaped crossguard above the hilt.

Haley smoothed her palm along the flat of the blade, marveling at the intricate pattern. She shivered.

The air-conditioning must've clicked on. She set the dagger down and pulled her cardigan over her jersey dress, and was distractedly buttoning it to the top when she noticed it. Picking the weapon back up, Haley squinted closely at the hilt. She held it up to the light. Something was etched at the base, and it was unlike the filigree work on the blade.

She darted her eyes around the storage area. Seeing she was alone, Haley licked her thumb and smudged it along the bottom of the handle. Something was engraved there, but it was obscured by black tarnish. She huffed her breath on the metal and used the hem of her dress to polish it. The letter *J* appeared. And then *L. V. E.*

It was an inscription. "For J."

W-something-something.

Could it be "with love"? Who on earth would give their lover a dagger?

Haley roughly buffed the cap of the hilt to a dull sheen, pausing only with the ache in her arm. "For JG, with love from Ma . . ."

"Ho-ly crow!" she exclaimed as her phone vibrated to life, buzzing along the top of the table like an angry insect.

Putting her hand to her pounding heart, she glanced at the text message.

You're late. Get your butt over here.

Rolling her eyes, she muttered, "What, is the beer getting warm?" She stuffed her phone in her bag, gathered her notes, and with one last look at the dagger on the table, made her way out.

"Dr. Brawn," Haley said, leaning her elbows on the front desk and smiling broadly at one of the Fogg Art Museum's conservators.

"Dr. Fitzpatrick." Sarah Brawn smiled right back. They both knew they were still years from the coveted PhD, but they'd met in a first-year graduate seminar and, sharing a love of pizza and peculiar artifacts, had been friends ever since.

"I think I've got it. An idea for my dissertation," Haley clarified, seeing her friend's confusion. "Thanks again, by the way, for pulling that dagger for me. It helped get the juices flowing. Those combo weapons blow me away."

"Ooh, sock it to me. I assume you've got the title?" They enjoyed whiling away the hours contemplating grand titles for their as-yet completed dissertations, that being so much more fun than the actual writing.

She nodded enthusiastically. "Might to Power: British Firearms and the Forging of an Empire." Haley's tone was appropriately grand. "You know, how it was only with the rise of gunpowder that they were able to build an empire? That way I've got my focus on the seventeenth century, but I can also study all those cool old flintlock weapons."

"Hasn't that gunpowder thing already been done to death?"

"Hey," she said, feigning chagrin. "I'm still working on it."

"I mean . . . *nice!*" Sarah was thoughtful for a moment. "But *forging* really sounds more like a sword thing—"

Haley put up her hand to change the subject. "Meet up with us later?"

"Clan gathering?"

She nodded, pulling a long and well-worn scarf from her bag to wind around her neck.

"So that means it must be Sunday."

"Pigskin and pints at Paddy's." Haley smiled. "The countdown to the afternoon game's begun."

"You Fitzpatricks, you're like clockwork."

"Where football and my brothers are concerned? Yes." She scowled at the door as someone let themselves out and a blast of autumn air in.

"Don't you mean football, your brothers, and *sports bars*?"

"Yeah, yeah, and you're so above it all, right?" Haley readjusted her heavy canvas messenger bag, slinging it over her head and across her shoulder. "Come on, come out with me. I'll buy you a slice . . ." She elongated the word *slice* into as enticing a one as possible.

"Some other time, yes. Tonight? No. We've been over this. I am not interested in getting set up with one of the Fitzpatrick boys."

"Hey, we're good people!" Haley said, laughing. "And the Pats are playing."

Grinning, her friend merely waved her fingers in good-bye, nose already tucked back in her book.

❋

"Doc!" a chorus of voices shouted as Haley entered. Though far from being a fully realized professor, Haley's family had taken to calling her Doc the moment she began grad school. She looked around at all the welcoming faces, letting her eyes adjust. The place smelled of beer and fried things, and it brought a smile to her face. She may be in the ivory tower now, but she was South Boston through and through.

Three tall Fitzpatrick men were at her side in an instant, and two more waved at her from the table, beckoning with frosty plastic pitchers sloshing with whatever the beer of choice was that day. Sam Adams, if she knew her brothers.

The Fitzpatrick bunch took over Paddy's every week for the Sunday games, and was a fixture many other nights besides. Though the clan had grown to include some friends, a few cousins, one wife, two girlfriends, and the invariable men they tried to set their only—and baby—sister up with, the family resemblance among the siblings was unmistakable. The dark, wiry "black Irish" hair and pale skin with a perpetually rosy flush to the cheeks.

Daniel Jr., aka Danny Boy, clamped Haley into a hug, and the smell of fish filled her senses. She looked up and smiled into the eyes of her oldest brother. His hair was pulled back in a ponytail for his gig as a short-order cook in a seafood joint. Danny was tall and had a cleft chin. Haley couldn't understand how the most charming of them could be so completely single.

Colin and Conor, the twins, vied for a spot by their sister. They'd been the biggest troublemakers of all the six kids—*holy terrors*, her mother used to sigh—and now they were the most stable of the lot. One was married, the other might as well be, and they'd left their dates seated to come and scruff Haley's hair, take her bag, and unwind the scarf from her neck.

"C'mon, beautiful." Danny pushed his way back between their brothers to undo the top of the sweater still buttoned tight around her neck. "Loosen up a bit."

"A beer will help!" Gerry shouted from the table, raising his glass in a toast and flashing a wide, gap-toothed grin. His free hand fumbled with the crumpled pack of cigarettes he wasn't allowed to smoke inside.

"Yeah, Doc!" Jimmy shouted. He beamed at her from his seat, his arm wrapped tight around his girlfriend Maggie. Haley had to laugh at the sight of him—the tips of his ears already red with drink. They protruded almost comically from his head, accentuated by his buzz-cut hair, regulation cop just like Dad's. "Get in out of the cold."

"Yeah, it's colder than a nun's t—"

"Gerald Patrick!" Her father's voice boomed from the other end of the bar. "Jesus, Mary, and Joseph, boy. You kiss your mother with that mouth?" He approached Haley, a pint in one hand, a basket of curly fries in the other, and leaned down and bussed her on the cheek. "My day has greatly improved with the vision of you, darlin' girl. I'm glad to see your work could spare you of an evening."

More than forty years had passed since her dad had stepped off the boat from his native Donegal, but he'd never lost the warm Irish burr in his voice.

"And I take it Mom's at bridge night?" Even though they'd all stayed local, Haley's mother had been unhappy to see the last of her kids leave the nest and had taken up all manner of hobbies since. And their mother had been the only one surprised by how much fun she was having now.

"And where else?" Danny ushered Haley to a seat.

"Time to focus, people." Gerry poured himself another.

"Gerry has twenty bucks on the over," Danny said, glancing at the television.

"He's crazy." Conor looked at his sister intently. "What do you say? You've always been good at picking the line. Will the game go over fifty-four points?"

Haley took a deep pull of her beer while she considered. "Dallas hasn't gotten their running game going yet," she said with the same gravity with which she approached her scholarship. "I think it's going to be a shoot-out, so yeah, I'd side with Gerry on this one." She raised her pint to the brother in question.

"Listen up!" Jimmy reached over the table and stole Gerry's lighter from his hand. "Hey, attention, people." He clinked the old metal Zippo on the side of his glass. "I said shut up, you dips." Jimmy swatted the nearest brother on the head.

"What the—" Danny recoiled, and smoothed his hair back down into his ponytail.

"Apologies, ladies." Jimmy ignored Danny and nodded at the women. "But we have an announcement. Maggie, love?"

His girlfriend shyly pulled her hand from beneath the table. Directing her words to Haley, she said, "We were waiting for you to get here. I wanted you to be the first . . . the first to hear . . ."

"You'll have a new sister!" Jimmy shouted, and was at once drowned out in cheers and a few female shrieks.

"Really?" Haley leaned into her, genuinely pleased. "I've got to see the ring."

Colin spoke above the din. "And when are *you* going to make an honest woman of *yourself*, Doc?"

Haley didn't deign to give him a look, and merely kicked her brother beneath the table. She held Maggie's hand, shifting it under the light, setting the small diamond to twinkling. "Oh guys, it's beautiful."

Maggie's sweet face bloomed into a smile. Between the strawberry blonde curls that framed Maggie's delicate heart-shaped face and the six-two length of her swarthy brother, Haley couldn't wait to see what their kids would look like.

"And look," she wriggled her ring off and angled it up to the dim bar light. "Jimmy knew my size, and even inscribed it for me."

Haley took it from her, focusing on the tiny script. "James loves Maggie."

"The lout couldn't think of anything more creative," Gerry said.

"Shut up." Jimmy threw his brother's lighter back at him. "Her fingers are small."

"No." Haley frowned at them. "It's simple and perfect. It says it all." She turned to Jimmy. "It's lovely. Just perfect."

"Blessings, kids." Her father raised his glass in a toast. "May the road rise up to meet you . . ."

"Get comfortable." Gerry leaned low over the table and winked at Haley.

"May the wind be always at your back."

"And here we go," Danny muttered.

"May the sun shine warm—"

A roar erupted in the bar, and all eyes went to the TV screen. The Patriots had scored a touchdown, and soon everyone's attention was back on the game.

"*James loves Maggie*," Haley thought, warm inside at the thought of it. Jimmy was a good guy, he deserved every happiness. Her eyes were on the screen, but her mind began to drift.

Another, much older, inscription popped into her head. Just who would dedicate a dagger to their sweetheart? "*For JG, with love from Ma—*"

J. Not a lot of *J* names in Scotland. Haley wracked her brain. She decided it was safe to assume the recipient had been a man. Maybe John. Though, Scotland in the seventeenth century, the Gaelic version Iain more likely would have been used.

No, she thought, *he was in all likelihood another James, or Jamie*.

But *Ma* would be harder to pin down. You'd have Mairi, Malveen, Margaret, Marsali . . .

"*James loves Maggie*."

"Hey, Mag!" she heard Gerry tease. "Give your new brother some sugar."

"*Mag*."

"*With love from—*"

"Magda?" Haley exclaimed. The bar had fallen momentarily silent and everyone turned to her, but for Gerry, who was scanning the bar for whomever this new girl might be that his sister was greeting.

"Sorry. Just thinking." Haley hid her face in her glass as she took a big sip.

"You need to focus," Colin scolded her.

"You need to *will* them to win, Haley." Conor nodded somberly in agreement.

JG, she thought. *James Graham's wife was named Magdalen.*

But the dagger was dated 1675. Graham had been hanged at least twenty years before that.

She shook her head. She was grasping at straws.

JG could be any one of thousands of men.

But how many of those would have the resources to buy such an extravagant weapon?

"Hey, Doc." Gerry snapped his fingers in front of her. "Earth to Haley."

"I tell you, she needs to focus." Colin gravely shook his head.

"Huh?" Haley looked at them blankly. "Oh, yeah, yeah." Shifting, she stared blindly at the flat screen hanging in the corner.

Maybe the piece was misdated.

But it was a flintlock pistol. Anything prior to 1650 would probably have used a wheel lock mechanism.

"I have to go." Haley stood suddenly, screeching her chair along the sticky barroom floor. She was going to drive herself crazy. There was no way on earth that dagger had belonged to the famous war hero, hanged in Edinburgh in the middle of the seventeenth century. She needed to buff the rest of the thing off; she'd see it was Margaret or Marjory or Martha who'd given the strange gift, and then she could stop spinning out. She swore to herself she'd once and for all focus on her dissertation. Just as soon as she figured out this one little mystery.

Her pronouncement was immediately met with grumbling and dire predictions.

Danny stared at her in disbelief. "It's bad mojo to leave before halftime."

"You have only yourself to blame if they lose," Colin said.

"Aren't you going to celebrate with us?" Jimmy attempted, in the most masterful tack of all.

"No, really, guys, I need to chase something down."

"We'll only release you if you're referring to a male student in that school of yours." Gerry stretched his leg along the side of the table as if to halt her escape.

"Stop fooling around," Conor said, "and sit your butt down, Doc."

"Really. Sorry everyone." Haley reached over to give Maggie a big hug. "Welcome to the family."

"She's really leaving?" Conor asked his father in disbelief.

"God help her!" Danny shouted.

"Leave the girl be." Her dad nodded sagely. "She's got more important affairs to tend to than a mere football match. Our Haley knows what she needs to do."

Haley scampered back out into the cold, winding her scarf about her neck as she went, the sound of hooting, cheering, and teasing about "affairs" sounding at her back.

Chapter 2

The branches of the old rowan barely bore his weight as he scaled them, and yet the wind in the leaves made more of a rustle than MacColla. It was a moonless night and he felt his way, clinging closer to the trunk as the branches grew thinner and more fibrous with his ascent. Just as the treetop began to stoop with the burden, he saw the roof materialize from the darkness.

It was a ruinous old structure nestled among the trees, a stout, near-windowless tower house, despite its grand title of Inveraray Castle. During the day, wooden steps bypassed the ground floor to lead to the entrance via the great hall on the second story. As such, invited guests wouldn't have to endure the unsightly cellars and vaulted kitchen, and the uninvited would be denied entry when the staircase was retracted at night.

MacColla's laugh was low and quiet. He would, most assuredly, be considered among the uninvited, and yet the fools must've thought some removable steps to be adequate security, for there were no guardsmen to be seen.

There were no suitable windows to climb to from the

ground, leaving the roof as the second-best access point. He studied it from his perch. A dormer bearing a single door was the only thing that interrupted the silhouette of the sharp peak. A low stone parapet flanked a thin walkway along the roof's edge, presumably to prevent guardsmen from falling the five stories to their death. Faint starlight shimmered in small patches all around, captured by the night's dew.

Ah, and wet too, MacColla thought with a smirk. *'Tweren't simple enough to begin with.*

It was no matter. He'd risk life and limb without a thought to get to his Jean.

He heaved his weight. Perhaps it was a good thing after all that Campbell's lair was in want of windows. As it was, he'd be lucky if none heard the tremendous creak the old tree's bones moaned into the night.

MacColla leapt, hurtling his massive body through the air, crashing along the side of the roof and sliding down to land with an ungraceful thump on the narrow walkway.

He stood and drew his dirk from his belt. Speed and agility had been paramount, and he'd left his claymore behind. Brushing the leaves from his plaid, MacColla curled his toes and adjusted to the feel of the slate tiles, cold and damp under his bare feet.

He trained his eyes into the darkness, making sense of the terrain in the distance. The castle was nestled in Glen Aray, and the landscape was an almost impermeable black, punctuated only by the faint glimmer of Loch Fyne, a ghostly shade of dark silver in the far distance. He knew that squalid little huts clung to its banks in what constituted the village of Inveraray.

Certain now that nobody had heard his landing, MacColla made his way to the low entry cut into the dormer. "Och," he muttered, jiggling the locked door, "'twouldn't be that easy."

MacColla leaned on the stone railing and looked over the edge of the parapet. "I'll not be going down, I see." The nearest windows were a row of thin arrow slits over one story below.

He walked along the side of the ledge to where it ended, and looked around to the front of the tower. A small balcony was nestled in its triangular upper story. MacColla looked at the slick roof behind him, then again to the front of the building. Stones stepped inelegantly up to shape its peak.

"Nothing for it, then," he grumbled and, biting his dirk between his teeth, scaled the stacked and tapering blocks of granite until he was level with the small opening. Gripping the protruding stones between his thighs, he strained to reach the balcony. He grasped a crude stone banister in his hand and dropped, quickly grabbing on with his other hand as his body swung out. Heaving himself up and through such a tight space was awkward, and MacColla had to shimmy on his belly until he landed in a pitch-black upper chamber.

He forced himself to pause, despite his eagerness to rampage Campbell's so-called castle. She was close now. He could feel her presence, enduring God-knows-what at the hands of his enemy.

Just as his father had. His father who'd been held captive by this same man for so many years, in just such a tower, trussed like a savage. Campbell, who dared take another from Clan MacDonald prisoner.

MacColla hissed low in his throat at the thought of Jean. Frail, without guile, and lovely as the dawn, with shining black hair and a shy cast to her eye.

Lovely Jean. His sister.

He vowed he'd die at the hands of one hundred Campbells before allowing her to remain another day captive to the brutish bastard. Word was, the Campbell wasn't even in residence, and if the blackguard was fool enough to abandon his precious prisoner, MacColla would avail himself of the opportunity.

He stooped, walking the perimeter of the cramped attic room, tracing his hand along the damp stone as he went, shuffling a foot tentatively forward with each step to see with his body what his eyes couldn't make out in the dark.

The building would be in the old style—one-room floors connected by a spiral staircase—and it would do no good to announce his arrival by tumbling down the attic steps. Campbell's room would be on an upper floor, and would likely be empty. But he'd need to tread with care as he approached the lower floors. It was late, and MacColla hoped either sleep or drink—or perhaps both—would make easy work of dispatching his enemy's men.

MacColla wagered he'd find his sister in the cellars on the ground floor. Rather, it was where he *hoped* he'd find her. The guards wouldn't want to spend much time in the vaults beneath the castle, likely thick with rats, urine, and damp. If they used Jean even now, it was above ground that MacColla would find her, and he'd prefer finding his sister bound and untouched than being used for sport in the castle hall.

He sensed the opening in front of him, even before his toes slid over the lip of the first step. MacColla took his dirk in his left hand and felt his way down the tight spiral stairs that had been hacked crudely into the stone. He came to a landing and, shifting his dirk back to his right hand, gave himself a moment to let his eyes adjust to the fall of light and shadow in what was a much larger space.

Every floor will look this way, he thought, easily imagining the castle in his mind's eye. One of the lower stories would house whatever family Campbell chose to keep close, below that would be a great hall, and the kitchen and cellars would be on the ground level.

He scanned the room. A wardrobe, some chests, and a desk emerged from the shadows. It was well appointed, considering. This one would be the chief's then. MacColla spat in the direction of Campbell's bed, a gray hulk faintly illuminated by what was less a window than a rectangular hole to the outside.

MacColla continued down, opening his senses wide. Men were close, and he'd rather keep the benefit of surprise.

Eyes wide in the dark and nostrils flared, he was like a wild hunting thing, taking the measure of the floor below through pure instinct.

Distant snores. The quiet rumble of two men's voices speaking in a hush. Firelight licking at the bottom steps, too weak to cut through the black shadows of the stairwell. The charred bite of woodsmoke in his sinuses, overlaid with the sour tang of ale gone foul.

A voice jarred the relative calm. Much closer than the others. A third man, then, sitting just out of view of the staircase. MacColla crept down and into the orange firelight of the landing. Two sat at their ease in chairs in front of the fire, nursing their cups. The third sat on a small stool, his back to MacColla.

MacColla slid behind him and, for one strange moment, felt the rumble of the man's low laugh reverberate through his own chest as he slipped his hand around the Campbell's forehead, pulling him close to slit his throat.

The man's death was silent, but the scrape of his stool was not, and he soon had the attention of the other two Campbell clansmen. The taller one raised a call of alarm, but MacColla was unfazed.

He dropped their dead kin to the ground and stepped over him to assume a ready posture. He'd let the first move be theirs, as that was often when men made their fatal mistakes. Legs apart and knees bent, his arms held just up and out from his sides, MacColla was a stalking animal poised to pounce.

And the first to move was indeed the first to fall. The taller of the two Campbell men leapt forward, slashing his broadsword as he lunged toward MacColla. But MacColla caught him easily, seizing the man's sword arm with his left hand, and impaling the Campbell with his dirk.

The hush in the room was palpable, with a few grunts, heavy breathing, and the scrape of chairs the only things to echo off the stark stone walls.

He could see that the second man would pose more of a challenge, despite his much smaller size. The other Campbell man was fast, faster than MacColla, whose six foot six inches of brawn made him powerful but somewhat stiff when it came to combat in close quarters.

The Campbell kinsman didn't have a sword to hand so he jabbed at MacColla with a small dagger pulled from his boot. MacColla pulled back, but not fast enough to avoid the bite of the blade at his chest. The pain focused him, and he peeled his lips back into a snarl.

The Campbell pestered him with much hopping and a few quick feints and stabs of his small blade.

"Enough." MacColla slashed his dirk down and, standing so much taller, he easily caught the flesh at the man's collarbone.

The Campbell glanced at his bloodied shoulder and panic replaced what had been arrogance just a moment before. Frantic now in what he knew was a fight for his life, the man dashed to MacColla's unguarded left side, but before he could strike, MacColla flexed his arm.

Sometimes, he thought, *a man simply prefers his fists*. MacColla's bicep was a thick mass of muscle, straining like a rock against his linen shirt. He pulled back and swung, clubbing away his enemy's blade and striking him squarely on the jaw.

The sharp, clipped sound of pain shattered the focused quiet of the chamber, and MacColla's grimace turned into a smile. Flipping the dirk in his hand, he tucked the blade close against his forearm and punched the side of the man's head, his broad fist landing with devastating force across the Campbell's temple and ear. Deadweight fell with a crash that belied the man's small stature.

MacColla was primed now. He descended the stairs and came to the great hall. The snores he'd heard two stories up echoed off the cold stone. A low fire flickered, mostly a few angry embers casting amber light across the men strewn on blankets in front of the hearth. The acrid smell of piss and ale filled the room, and MacColla could tell he'd likely have no need to blood his blade further while these half-wits slept off their drink. In fact, he thought, looking toward the main door with a smile, he fancied that once Jean was safe in his charge, the two of them could even take the civilized way out.

The steps connecting the great hall to the floor below were wooden, rotted, and bowed with age. MacColla tread along the very outer edge, but it wasn't enough to avoid the complaining creak of old timber underfoot.

He paused and held his breath, then moved down in a swift, final burst. If someone had heard him, he'd face them head-on. Otherwise, he'd not tarry, wanting to get to his sister as quickly as possible.

The kitchen had a low, vaulted ceiling and stone walls covered in a decades-old veneer of oil and soot. An elderly woman slept curled close to the hearth. A few coals remained, smoldering amidst the thick blanket of black ash that had been the cook fire.

Some sort of lumpy, beige stew congealed in a cast-iron pot above it. *Potatoes.* MacColla scowled. His days in Ireland had cured him of the taste of potatoes forever. His grandmother had railed against the foreign, dirty little things. Swore up and down that a food not found in the Bible wasn't fit to be found on a good Christian table. She'd relented only after they'd sprinkled the ugly lumps with some holy water, and they'd been a staple with the MacDonald clan in Ireland ever since.

MacColla worked his way through two narrow pantries and a buttery before discovering the padlocked door. The lock was a rusted old thing, and he wasted a few minutes jiggling his dirk through the keyhole in an effort to spring it. Growing impatient, he finally just drew his arm back and sheared the hasp from the door with the butt of his weapon.

Jean cried out at the intrusion, and the sound near broke his heart. His sister stood in the pitch-black of a dank vaulted cellar, squinting and blinking her eyes rapidly to adjust to what was merely the faint ambient light of the kitchen.

Fury boiled in him.

"It's me, lass. Alasdair." He ran to her, lifting her easily into his arms, and the sight of the filth that soaked the hem of her dress made something in him snap. "Och, Jeannie . . . bonny wee Jeannie." Anguish tightened his voice as he scanned her body for signs of misuse.

She broke then, and her tears came in a shuddering rush. Jean tucked her face as tightly to him as possible, nuzzling into the crook of his neck as if she could close some fundamental breach between her life as she'd known it and what she'd just endured. Despite her shuddering body and staccato breaths, Jean's sobs were nearly silent.

The sight of his sister, broken in his arms and hiding her brave tears, hardened MacColla's resolve to a white-hot fury. The Campbell had disgraced his father, exiled his family to Ireland, and besieged his Highlands in a wolfish grab for power.

He'd once vowed to destroy the man. But now MacColla found he'd a taste for the blood of all Campbells, and it choked him like bile he needed to cleanse from his throat.

Chapter 3

"You still at work?" Haley hated talking on the cell phone and had to plug her other ear to hear the crackle of Sarah's voice over the intermittent rumble and screech of the subway.

"Yeah, I'm just finishing up. How's the game?"

"I left," Haley replied. "I'm headed back your way. I'm at Broadway Station now. Can you let me back into the storage area? I need to see something."

"You're still in Southie? Hale, I'm about to leave. The museum closed, what, an hour ago?"

"I'll be there in thirty, forty minutes tops, okay?" The inscription from that dagger spun in her head, and she knew she wouldn't be free of it until she checked it out again.

"From Broadway? More like forty, fifty minutes. Can't this wait til tomorrow?"

Haley let the question hang, hoping her friend would take pity.

"Okay," Sarah finally said. "I'll wait at the desk. Just knock when you get here. But I'm giving you ten minutes. Tops."

"You're the best. Be there soon." She flipped the phone shut and looked up. Her broad smile froze, then slowly bled from her face. Two guys stared at her, standing just too close to feel right.

The face of one was hardened into an accusatory stare. The other seemed slackened, by drugs or drink, his eyes half-lidded beneath his off-kilter ball cap. He nodded at her, as if they'd had some prior agreement. His mouth was open slightly, and Haley flashed back to the memory of two other men.

So many years ago now. They'd jumped her, on her way home from a late study group on the Quad. One hadn't bothered with Haley, intent on rifling through her purse and computer bag. She'd skimped for a year to buy that computer, but couldn't summon a care for the thing. It was the knife that had seared into her memory. The knife and the man who held it.

His mouth had also parted slightly, as if about to taste, hovering close over her face as he'd put his switchblade to her throat.

Ice prickled through her veins at the memory, and Haley sent up a silent thanks to the students who'd swept down Chauncy Street moments later. They'd been chatting and laughing, in their own world, never even seeing Haley. It had been enough to scare the men, though, sending them running back into the night.

But not before her attacker had rolled off her, dragging his blade in a shallow slice along her flesh as he went. Leaving her to feel the surreal warmth of her own blood trickling slowly down the side of her neck, dripping slowly onto the dirt.

She'd been an undergrad, an innocent sophomore then. A girl who'd never been scared of the dark. Rather, she used to love walking the campus late at night, thrilling at the dramatic shadows that played across all those grand brick buildings, those libraries and halls that had housed so many great scholars before her.

But Haley was innocent no more. That night, in that

moment, an exaggerated sense of how truly vulnerable she'd always been lodged in her like a tumor. A constant, festering thing that her body now harbored. She began training with her father soon thereafter. Weights, workouts, self-defense, with a rigor fed from the nagging sensation that she'd somehow escaped some worse fate. That, so far, she'd only avoided life's certain dangers by some strange fluke of the universe.

She'd been a history major, but her focus morphed into a morbid fascination with historical arms and battles. She delved headlong into the world of old guns and knives. Though they felt safe in their historical distance, those objects had nonetheless been designed for destruction. And it was as though, in studying a thing, she could cling to the hope of controlling it, of making sense of what had happened to her. Mastering it.

Just as she would master this situation now. She moderated her breathing, trying to slow the shallow hammering of her heart. It was her first brush with a potential threat since that night years ago, and she wouldn't let panic crush her.

She turned on her heel, clutching the strap of her bag tight across her chest, and walked to the other end of the platform. The T station suddenly seemed empty. She didn't know where everyone could be. She glanced down the tunnel: a homeless man slumped against the wall. Up the tunnel: a woman clutching tight to the plump hand of a young child, pretending not to see Haley.

She quickened her pace, and her footsteps echoed unnaturally loud off the white- and maroon-tiled pillars that studded the station.

They followed her, slowly. She could feel them. And she could hear the clink of the thick silver chain worn by the one with the hard stare, looped from his belt into his pocket.

Nearing the end of the platform, she stopped, pretending to study the route map hung on the wall. Her eyes focused on a bit of graffiti along the edge. Adrenalin rushed through her, jittering up the backs of her legs, humming at the crown of her head. She struggled to remember something, anything, her father had taught her about self-defense.

With great intent, she breathed hard from her diaphragm. Forced herself to concentrate on the workouts her father had put her through. Those methodical, deliberate movements they'd executed over and over.

Block, punch, sweep, back to center. Again and again until fighting had become as instinctive as breathing.

Heart slowing, Haley stood a little taller. She felt grounded, her feet connected solidly to the concrete beneath them. Legs solid, poised but loose.

The low rumble and clack of a distant train filled the tunnel. She felt the men recede. The subway screeched to a slow stop and Haley heard the whispered slide of the doors opening. Snippets of sound swirled around her. Conversations, the footfalls of people exiting the subway.

She turned and ducked into the nearest car, not quite sure if the foreign emotion heightening her senses was profound relief or disappointment.

❂

Still unsettled, Haley took the longer, better-lit route through Harvard Yard back to the Fogg. Despite herself, she'd jogged the whole way from the station, then banged harder than she'd meant to on the locked door.

"Easy, cowgirl." Sarah's baffled irritation was visible through the glass panes of the front entrance. She unbolted it and let Haley in.

"Seriously, Haley. Ten minutes tops" was her only greeting. Sarah quickly slid the bolt back into place. "It's not cool for me to be letting you in after hours. They'd have my hide."

Only a few scattered lights illuminated the interior. If she didn't already know the place like the back of her hand, Haley thought she'd be creeped out by the long shadows that crawled along the walls.

"Well, go ahead." Sarah nodded to the stairs. "I left it unlocked for you."

Eager to see the weapon once more, she took the steps two at a time. The door sealed shut behind her and it was like entering a vault. Because preventing dust and moisture was paramount, the storage room featured its own filtration system, and not much sound penetrated the windowless walls. For all Haley knew, she could be in a submarine on the bottom of the ocean, that was how disconnected she felt from the rest of the world when lost in thought in the archives.

Tossing her bag to the floor, she quickly retrieved the combination dagger/gun from its cabinet and sat at the table. She reverently unfolded the rectangle of lint-free cloth, and looked immediately at the hilt to study the inscription.

"For JG, with love from Ma—"

Sending up an apology to whichever museum gods might be looking on in horror, Haley buffed the inscription, this time using the thicker cloth it had been stored in.

Haley worked quickly. If Sarah caught her doing more than just eyeing the piece, it was *her* hide that would be had.

-g-

She glanced at the clock. Seven minutes before Sarah came knocking. But she had to know. She shook the ache from her hand, and rubbed with renewed vigor.

-da.

Haley gasped. *Magda.* "*For JG, with love from Magda.*" It could only be one couple. Not much was known about the woman, but James Graham was one of the most famous military heroes in Scottish history.

No. That was way too easy. James Graham had died on the gallows before this weapon was even made. Period.

But could she argue reasonable doubt? It might make for an interesting paper.

There were any number of women in the world named Magda. Though it wasn't a very Scottish name, there had to have been others. The weapon surely just belonged to some random nobleman.

She turned it in her hands. Stroked the filigree. It wasn't

just that it was a rare and gorgeous piece. It felt . . . important somehow.

What if?

People did survive hangings. She loved the old Scottish tales of people who'd somehow survived the gallows only to awaken confused and more than a little sore. Could Graham have somehow survived his own death, like "half-hangit" Maggie Dickson, who bolted upright from her cart, or James Spalding, who clawed out from his own shallow grave?

Apocryphal stories and historical truths were blended and swapped all the time. Especially in old Scotland.

No, there was something in her gut that told her. She didn't know how or why, she just *knew*. It had to be James Graham's weapon.

Overwhelmed by emotion and the knowledge of what she held, sudden tears pricked her eyes. To think that she held in her hands something that Graham might have touched, held, used so many centuries ago.

A thrill shivered up her spine.

The implications were huge. There were very few artifacts available from Graham's life, aside from his sword on display at the Montrose Museum in Scotland. His name was apparently inscribed on that blade as well, though she'd never been lucky enough to hold it in her hands.

The discovery of another artifact was tremendous. That it was such a rare and relatively pristine example of a combination weapon was icing on the cake. Personally identifying its provenance would bring Haley notoriety across a number of fields: European history, Celtic studies, military studies, museum studies . . .

Grinning, Haley sat a little straighter. She'd be at the top of her department for some time.

And that wasn't even the half of it. The weapon's date threw the timing of Graham's death into question. *Could it be that Graham didn't die when the history books said he did?*

Surely not.

She laughed. There was no way something like that could've been kept secret, from the king, the court, the nobles, the clans.

And yet here was the suggestion of proof. A weapon bearing his initials, using technology that wouldn't have been in place before Graham's presumed death. Or to be more precise, flintlock mechanisms like this were available in 1650, but only just. It had been a major innovation: to push back the powder lid and strike the flint at the same time. By midcentury, the mechanism was still too expensive to be widespread, and the much simpler wheel lock would've been preferred.

Tracing her finger along the elegant little flintlock, she grinned. If James Graham hadn't really died on the gallows, how that would rock the world of European history. And she could be the one to break the news.

She had it. She had her dissertation.

Even if her theory weren't true, she'd get a lot of mileage out of making the argument. She'd get going on a journal article that very night, set it up so she could use it as the intro chapter.

Haley scanned the weapon, jogging her mind for other ideas. There was no deep pitting near the pan, so that would mean it hadn't been fired much. She turned it over and examined the old, nearly vanished proofmark. Stamped on by the gun maker, it would've signified the weapon was up to his standard, had withstood a heavy charge of powder. She rubbed her finger into the indentation. The insignia looked like an *X* with a circle beneath. Possibly crossed swords and a sunburst? She'd need to dig deeper there. See if she could find similar examples, perhaps triangulate the date using the proofmark as a milestone in time. She might even be able to pinpoint it to a specific arms maker.

Though if she traced the weapon back and it turned out to originate prior to 1650, it would only disprove her theory.

Haley shook her head. She refused to think on that just now. Something in her gut told her she was right. It made perfect sense. James Graham had been a brilliant tactician;

he'd not have gone quietly to his death. Something—or someone—must have intervened. But what, and how?

She looked at the clock again. It was time to hustle out of there.

Beaming, Haley wrapped the precious weapon into its cloth and placed it back in the cabinet, double- then triple-checking that it was closed securely.

All the potential chapters took shape in her mind. She could see her argument clearly. And her title. *A Dagger, with Love: The Secret Survival of James Graham.* Or . . . *Flintlock: Resurrecting a Military Hero.* Or something. She'd drag Sarah out for a slice and they'd come up with something.

She bent to get her bag, then froze. A shadow flickered on the edge of her vision. Holding her breath, she remained still. Surely it was just her nerves on edge from what was turning out to be an eventful evening.

Silence.

She'd just imagined it then. A trick of her eyes, tired from straining all day under the fluorescent lights.

Haley stood. Her heart pounded suddenly, jolted to life as if by an electric shock.

There was something on the table.

"Sarah?"

No answer. She stepped closer. A dirty wooden panel sat in the middle of the table. It looked like a rough sketch of two people.

"What the—"

She called more loudly now. "Sarah?"

Her bag slipped from her fingers as she looked around. It wasn't like Sarah to just plop something on the table without saying hi. Haley had only turned her back for a minute. And she would've heard the door open anyhow.

Unless someone had been in the room all along, hiding.

A surge of panic focused her. Marshalling her nerves, she ducked around the table, peeked between the cabinets, looking in nonsensical places where no person could have fit.

She shivered.

Was it some sort of creepy joke?

Could Sarah be pulling her leg to get her back for having to stay late?

She picked up the panel. The smell of charred things filled her nose and turned her stomach. "Freaky," she muttered.

Etchings of runes and strange patterns had been crudely hacked along the edges of the panel. Haley brushed her thumb lightly along them, the wood raw and splintered where the knife had carved.

She blew the dirt from its surface. A man and a woman had been sketched with what looked like charcoal. Their features seemed like they'd been rendered quickly, loosely, picking up only the salient details. He was tall and broad, with wild hair and thick slashes of black for his brows. The woman was shorter, but not what you'd call small. She also had black hair, pulled back tight but for a hank loose over her brow. Haley tucked her own hair behind her ear.

She blew harder on the panel. There was something familiar about the woman. Squinting, Haley looked closer.

She cried out then, a single, sharp sound hitting the antiseptic walls. Her skin felt as if it was shrinking on her body, seizing her flesh into goose bumps all over, rousing the dust of thousands of hairs to stand erect.

The woman had a scar on her neck.

Haley's hand flew to her own scar, as if touching it would bring clarity to the image in her hands. Even though she knew it was empty, her eyes darted once again around the room. Was this supposed to be a picture of her? Was the man in the drawing some sort of stalker?

Haley had avoided touching the sketch for fear of smudging it, but she brushed it roughly now, trying to see it more clearly. Slivers of wood bit into her palm and she cursed, panic and anger and fear hammering through her.

Her head began to buzz, and she fought to stay focused. She wouldn't let the shock and adrenalin drown her.

The scar. There was something on the woman's scar.

She tilted the panel. Light hit it at an angle, winking briefly along the mark on her neck. She inhaled sharply. The scar was the dull crimson of spilled blood.

A tinny squeal lanced her eardrums. She shook her head roughly. *Stay focused.*

Haley was mesmerized now, compelled to reach tentatively from her neck to the woman's. Gingerly, she touched it.

The cool of still-damp blood was tacky beneath her fingertip.

The air around her seemed suddenly thick, humid and dense in her lungs. She felt a tug. *Fainting?*

Falling.

The blackness swallowed her scream.

Chapter 4

MacColla eased his sister to the ground and placed a kiss on her forehead. He put his finger to his mouth, motioning for her to stay silent.

He needed to get her to safety immediately, but leaving Campbell's tower house was proving a more daunting challenge than entering. He nudged the wooden entry stairs with his foot. They lay perpendicular to the open doorway, having been pulled haphazardly up and into the building at day's end. Lowering them back down without the aid of another man would make a noise fit to wake the dead.

He glanced at the three souls passed out from drink on the far side of the great hall. Even a houseful of drunken Campbells couldn't weather such a racket.

MacColla was leaning from the opening, assessing the long drop to the ground below, when he heard the crash. He spun to standing, dirk poised and ready in his hand, expecting to see a Campbell man.

Instead, a woman materialized before them, her white face ghostly in the darkness, dark gown fluttering at her legs as if a wraith in the night's breeze. Thick hanks of black hair hung loose around her face, blown gently along the sides of her cheek and full lips.

Their gazes held. Her eyes were gray in the ambient moonlight, transfixing him with the strange sensation that, if he only but focused a bit more, he could see forever in their depths.

The woman stumbled and he gave a start. Not an apparition.

She squatted to the ground, holding herself up on hands and feet like a wild creature. He stepped closer, straining for details in the shadows. The lass's dress stretched over her breasts and knees, baring a pale stretch of calf that MacColla couldn't help but note.

Not an apparition at all, but a Campbell. He'd been ogling a bloody Campbell.

"God spare me," he muttered, thinking he'd somehow bypassed a sleeping Campbell—one who'd managed to approach him unawares.

She slowly teetered to standing, and her dress continued to hug her body tightly. Though it exposed just a proper V of skin at her neck, it clung to modest swells at breasts and hips and thighs. Strange, low boots peeked from the hem, encasing her feet and lower legs in snug black leather. His gaze raked back up her body, then stopped, snagged once more by those strange, luminous eyes. He finally found his voice, hoarse and low. "*An e Caimbeulach a tha annad?*"

He walked toward her. "Answer me, woman. You've Campbell blood in your veins? A sister, is it?" He leaned down and grabbed her chin roughly, turning her face from side to side. She had strong features. Thick lashes framed wide eyes and a lush mouth compensated for her almost-prominent nose. Prettier than he'd thought a Campbell would be.

She tensed, and he felt the lean, firm muscles of her arm flexing in his hand. *And stronger too.*

Her skin was smooth and unlined, creamy next to what seemed a coarse halo of jet-black hair. "Nay," he said. "Not sister. Niece, then."

"*A bheil Gàidhlig agad?*" she asked haltingly. Her grammar was stilted, overly familiar.

"Aye, I speak Gaelic," he replied in English. "And what else?" He pushed her chin roughly from his hand. "But apparently you've strange notions of the *Gaedhealg* tongue."

He spared a glance to the men passed out by the fire, then MacColla squinted, studying her. "Where is it you're from?"

She leaned toward him, peering through the shadows. "You!" Terror lit her features like a torch. "You were in that . . . that painting. Who the hell are you?" She looked around frantically. "Where the hell'd you take me?"

Was she cursing him to the devil? Did this wee Campbell lass dare damn him? MacColla glared at her, trying to make sense of her strange accent. She seemed to be speaking English, but none like he'd ever heard. Her words were like the sharp claps of a barking dog. "Speak slow when you curse me."

He approached her. He saw spirit in those wide gray eyes, and he was compelled to look closer.

She shuffled back, arms askew as if to brace herself on thin air. The lass was shouting at him now, unintelligible words.

MacColla took her in once again, from head to foot. She was a well-proportioned one, of modest height and with just enough meat on her bones. If Campbell had a mind for kidnap, two could play at his game. If only he could understand her clamoring.

"*Air do shocair!*" he commanded, speaking over her. "Och . . . slowly now. I'd hear your curses . . ." He studied the movement of her mouth, trying to understand her words. Her lips were full and dark against the pale glow of her cheeks in the moonlight. He'd taste this Campbell woman, he decided suddenly. "Before I wipe them from your mouth."

He grabbed her, wrapping his hand easily around her upper arm. Though he'd pillaged in his day, MacColla was never one for rape. But a kiss? One kiss would be no crime.

The woman once again flexed her arm in his grip and he smiled outright. The feel of her solid flesh in his hand made his heart kick. Many a lass had offered themselves for a kiss by the great hero MacColla. But none such as this. This one had muscle to spare. *Interesting.*

Curse it, but he wanted a bloody Campbell.

He leaned down, closing the distance between them. The woman froze, like a hare paralyzed by the sight of the hunter's bow. A low laugh rumbled in his throat, so eager was he to taste her. His free hand clutched the soft flesh of her rump, pulling her toward him.

MacColla kissed her. He'd wanted at first to be rough, but she was soft. So soft and sweet, his mouth gentled in the tasting of her. And, for a single moment, he imagined the lass kissed him back, her breath sighing into him, her mouth opening just enough for him to taste her, fresh and warm on his tongue.

And then, with a tiny growl, she caught his lower lip hard between her teeth and bit.

MacColla pulled away. She glared at him, bared her teeth, and exhaled with the measured breath of a prowling wolf.

He studied the wee Campbell hellcat before him, and then strangely, inexplicably, he found himself laughing. These long years of exile, his father's imprisonment, his sister's capture—all a pall of waiting and dread that had clouded his vision for so long now. It was as if the veil had suddenly burnt to ash, kindling MacCòlla to life. A deep, freeing laugh exploded from low in his belly.

One of the men by the fire stirred.

He looked to his sister and the terror and confusion in her eyes made him remember himself. Clearing his throat, he nodded to Jean as if she'd communicated more than simply her silent, charged glare. "Aye," he whispered. "We must go from here."

He looked back down at the woman. "A bonny Campbell for my spoils," he said, licking the blood from his lower lip. It left a taste like rust on his tongue. He smiled wide at the lass then, knowing full well that the blood reddened his teeth.

He didn't need a man to help him lower the castle stairs after all, MacColla thought as he guided her to the entryway. He was of a mind to make the wee Campbell assist instead.

Snagging his hand in her hair, he cupped her head and guided her toward Jean. Despite the violence of the gesture, he tried not to hurt her—the ravaging of women was an ignoble sport. Though he'd half a mind to scare her into docility. He imagined he might need such tactics if he were to manage such a fiery soul as this one.

His aim was to use her for barter. The next time one of MacColla's Royalists found himself in a Campbell cell, this lass would be good to have at hand. Family members were the most effective bargaining chips.

He scowled. It was a lesson Campbell himself had taught, with MacColla's own father and brother as the example. He had handed over any number of his enemy Covenanters, all in hopes of trading for their lives. And if he'd had someone closer to Campbell's heart with which to barter? Perhaps he could've spared his father and brother so many long years imprisoned.

❈

What the fuck, what the fuck, what the fuck . . . The thought pinged through her mind like a loosed pinball.

Big man, black hair, those brows. And what the fuck was with her reaction to him? The first sight of him had sent an involuntary shiver through her. He'd kissed her, and her body had sent up a quick flare, pure animal reaction to the sheer size of him.

Haley shook her head to get rid of the memory. She'd get ahold of herself.

He was clearly the man from that hideous thing she'd found in the storeroom. Blood pounded in her fingertips, throbbing with the memory of that wooden panel, now gone from her hands.

Stark terror stole the breath from her lungs and the gush of adrenalin through her system dizzied her. Haley forced air into her paralyzed body. *Not a victim again. Not this time.*

She summoned her brothers' voices in her head. Their goading and their challenging. She heard them speak to her, girding her. *Man up, Hale.*

"Get the fuck off me." She tried to flinch her head from his grasp. His hand was mercifully gentle at the nape of her neck, though no less firm. The bastard just chuckled.

Who the hell was he? And what was with the Gaelic? Was he in her department at school? He'd surely been stalking her, but she'd never seen him before. How had he gotten into the museum?

Oh God. Sarah. Her panic turned to dread, a cold wash sweeping up from her belly. Was Sarah okay? If anything had happened to her, it was all Haley's fault.

"Where's Sarah? What did you do with Sarah?" She planted her feet hard, making him stumble slightly. He stared at her a moment and hatred surged through her. "Don't you speak English?"

"Aye, I've the English." He grasped her chin, pulling her face toward his. "Who's Sarah? Is it you've a sister hiding about as well?" The man looked around, glanced at his companion, and Haley registered the other woman for the first time.

Haley couldn't move her head much in his grip, but rolled her eyes as far as she could to study the woman. She seemed to be in league with the man. *What kind of scene is this?* She was slender and pretty, but Haley was gratified to see the girl also appeared to be a total wreck, her breath hiccupping, tears streaming down her cheeks.

"Who are you people?" she snarled, struggling in vain.

He ignored her, focusing only on his companion. "Easy, Jean," he told the woman in Gaelic. Then Haley thought he said, "We'll put down the stairs and be gone from here."

Stairs? Haley glared at them, trying to make sense of it. "Where are you taking me?"

"Alasdair," the other woman finally spoke, her voice a tremulous whisper. "The lass isn't right. She gives me the evil eye, even now."

The girl had meant not right in the head. Haley squinted hard at her. If there was any such thing as an evil eye, she'd summon it now for this simpering thing.

The man barked out a laugh, which seemed to distress his companion all the more. The girl seemed to yield before him, ceding all control. It annoyed Haley, made her want to stand up to him.

"Please." The girl spoke again, addressing only Alasdair. "Please just take me from this place."

His eyes softened when he looked at his companion, his fearsome mask melting into something kinder. A single-minded concern warmed his features, eased his full mouth.

Haley realized, startled, that he was . . . *handsome*.

And so completely focused on the girl's well-being. She felt a rush of inexplicable jealousy and glowered at her with renewed zeal, even as she thought how silly her impulse was.

She didn't need a man to look out for her. Haley was perfectly capable of looking out for her own damn self.

The girl's eyes widened. "Leave the lass be," she whispered. "She . . . She's . . ." Apprehension and sympathy both animated her features. "She's not right, Alasdair."

Haley could deal with apprehension. It was the girl's sympathy that pushed her over the edge. She tried to wriggle free from the man's grasp, hissing at his companion as she did so.

"Och, enough." He pushed Haley forward once more, toward what looked like a hole in the wall leading straight into blackness. "We must go, and now."

She wracked her brain to make sense of it. He must've knocked her out, but where had he taken her? It was like a castle. Had the freak taken her to some crazy McMansion outside Boston?

She looked around as much as her immobilized head would allow, expecting to see mounted animal heads and gaudy wrought iron fixtures. But the large room was mostly barren. There was just a crude dining table and a few men passed out by the fireplace.

She considered calling to them for help, but her eyes adjusted and she thought better of it. The dying fire highlighted the ragged halos of their matted hair, sticking out from soiled plaid blankets.

How had he gotten her there? She did a quick internal check. Nothing was sore, so he couldn't have knocked her out. He must've used chloroform or something. He'd surely had to drive far out of the city to have found this place.

Where the hell were they? Maybe somewhere near the Cape? A lighthouse maybe? She strained, trying to hear or smell signs of the sea.

He nudged her, bringing Haley to stand before the opening in the wall. *Oh God.* Was he going to push her out a window? The panic exploded again, dimming her vision, and Haley instinctively went into action, throwing her weight back, forcing her body away from the gaping blackness. She felt his hand grip her harder, but she frantically kicked herself backward, scuffing her heels along the stone floor. Her feet struck something hard and in her frenzy she noticed a wooden flight of steps like something from a theatrical stage blocking their path. Haley froze.

She tried to look again at the man's companion. *Useless*, Haley thought with derision. *Just standing there trembling.*

And then the surreal realization clicked. Her captors wore bizarre clothing, as if they'd just returned from some kind of historical reenactment. They were both filthy, her in a long gown, soiled black at the hem, him barefooted and in a kilt. And not like those dapper kilts and sporrans men wore at the Highland Games. This one seemed threadbare, winding around him, the end tossed haphazardly over his shoulder.

Oh shit. Dread chilled her. Haley couldn't say why, but their clothing set her already screeching internal alarms into high gear. She didn't know what these people were into, but getting kidnapped by a couple of Gaelic-speaking medieval history buffs didn't seem like something that bode well.

His hand on her neck was loose now. He kicked at the long, rickety staircase. *Typical man*, she thought with a disgust that cleared her head.

Calm. Calm. I'm calm. She did another internal check, forcing her mind and body to stillness. Her heartbeat grew regular. Her muscles felt juiced from the adrenalin, but no longer jellied from shock.

Typical man to underestimate a woman. She could get free. She'd have to jump. If that staircase represented their height above the ground, she only had about one story to fall. She'd have to roll her landing. Then run like hell.

She didn't give herself time to think. Haley tugged away from the man's hand and she winced, feeling a clump of her hair tear from her scalp. Leaping forward, she stepped one foot onto the edge of the stairs and vaulted into the void.

"*Ciod e . . . ?*" The cursed lass had flown out, black hair streaking behind her, like a crow loosed into the night. MacColla raced to the edge and looked down in time to see her hit the ground with a roll and take off running. "Och, Christ."

He looked to Jean and back out again. "Och," he growled once more. He grabbed his sister by the hands and eased her out the entry door, lowering her down until his belly leaned over the edge and he could get her no closer. "Run," he hissed as he dropped her. "Now."

The Campbell lass was already far in the distance, fleeing like a deer across the moonlit glen.

Jean stumbled forward and MacColla wasted no time leaping to the ground, landing with a grunt and rolling quickly to his feet. He sensed commotion in the castle above. The Campbell men were stirring.

"Run!" he called, clapping his hand on Jean's back. "Now, lass"—he grabbed his sister's hand and tugged—"run!"

Jean finally came out of her daze and, hiking her dress over her knees, took off with surprising speed.

MacColla ran ahead, pumping his arms and legs until he closed in on the woman. He waved his hand out to snag her dress once, twice, but she ran only faster, winding an uneven path over the grass. "*Caile mhallaichte*," he snarled.

He sprang forward then, grabbing hard around her waist, tumbling them both to the ground. MacColla wanted to catch the lass, not crush her, so he went immediately into another roll, coming to rest with her straddled over him.

He gripped her hips. Then an urge so great swept over him, he didn't question the impulse. MacColla simply ground the lass to him as the vision of her riding him filled his head.

Watching those mystical gray eyes widen at the feel of him beneath her sent satisfaction surging through his veins. Panting hard, he felt the life pumping through him, and a smile burst onto his face, flush with his triumph.

Then like a feral cat she was clawing at his cheeks, swatting, and trying to gouge at his eyes.

"You wee hellcat." MacColla ducked the blows as best he could, clutching tightly to her hip with one hand, trying to deflect her blows with the other.

"Alasdair!" It was Jean's voice, crying a warning from the shadows.

MacColla saw three men racing toward them and rolled the woman to the ground beneath him.

Grabbing her by both hands, he looked quickly to his sister. He cursed himself. Jean's safety was the only thing that should take his attention now. He couldn't let his thoughts be diverted by some mysterious Campbell clanswoman.

He looked at the woman and regretted that he had to let her go. Regretted he'd never know the name of this strange lass who'd gotten the better of him.

A Campbell captive would've been quite the spoils, and such a beautiful one all the more so. But he'd not lose sight of the most important thing: freeing his sister, seeing her safe once more.

"Och." His voice was a low grunt. The men were closing fast. He looked from the lass, to the men, and back again. A challenge was in her eyes.

"Och, God help me." Holding her arms above her head with one hand, he took her chin with the other, and crushed his mouth to hers for one last taste. He knew he needed to get his sister to safety, but he knew too that he had to press once more into that softness, feel one final lick of that heat. He pulled back and gave a quick laugh, having just missed her bared teeth.

MacColla pushed up from the woman and, grabbing Jean's cold hand in his, raced away, the Campbell castle at their backs.

He'd done it. He'd freed his sister. They had but to get to the ponies he'd tied hidden in the woods, and they'd be gone from there.

But then MacColla heard it.

A scream tore through the night, a ghastly, blood-chilling sound that stopped him dead.

Jean stumbled and fell beside him, looking up from her knees, terror in her eyes.

And then again.

It was the lass. Shrieking a sound of such horror, as if she'd been beset by demons, that MacColla's skin crawled from it.

He dragged Jean to standing and shoved her back into a run with force enough to launch her feet from the ground.

"*Ruith!*" he commanded. *Run.*

He turned, squinting to make out the figures in the darkness. The men had overtaken her. Moonlight limned their bodies, making them appear like fallen angels come seeking evil mischief from beyond. She struggled madly in their hands.

MacColla took off at a lope. Then the lass's scream broke. A hideous sound, it tore from her body until her voice grew ragged, then cracked finally into a wail of despair.

And MacColla broke into a run.

He didn't spare a thought as to the why or the how of it, but she was being attacked by her own kinsmen, and he'd not let a man get the better of any woman.

Especially *this* woman.

They had her pinned now, all atop her like wild dogs worrying a bone, and MacColla dove toward them, grabbing wildly, catching a man in his hands and peeling him up by his head, breaking his neck and shucking him away from the pile like so much garbage.

That left two on her, and, just as he was leaning down to tear away another, the lass surprised MacColla by kicking her own self free.

He was stunned, looking at her—wild-eyed, but focused. The moon cast a white bolt of light along her smooth cheek. Her full mouth parted as she breathed heavily. She caught his stare and returned it. Fearless. Proud.

The most beautiful creature MacColla had ever seen.

He felt it too late. The hands damp and hot on his calf, tripping MacColla, pulling him down before he knew what he was about. He fell hard, the deadweight of seventeen stone of muscle slamming onto the glen, and the two Campbells were on him in an instant.

Haley edged away. She was loose. She could run. *Where?*

She looked down at the scrum. The man called Alasdair fought for dominance, trying to best the odds. He had released her, leaving her to three attackers and a worse fate.

But then he'd come back.

She saw a hand—she didn't know whose—draw a knife. Haley looked behind her. The stone building at her back loomed tall in the darkness. Not a lighthouse. Not a McMansion either. *Looks like a damned Scottish tower house.*

She scanned the night. The girl stood on the horizon shivering, whimpering. Haley could run, but if Alasdair were bested, would that girl be next? She knew with certainty that the pathetic creature wouldn't survive five minutes with those men. And Haley might not like the girl, but that didn't mean she wanted to see her brutalized.

Besides, Haley could run, but she doubted she'd be able to escape these two men who clearly had a taste for blood.

One of them was on top of her kidnapper now, hands around his throat. The other one knelt, and she once again saw the flash of steel in the night.

She and her dark-haired stalker appeared to share the same enemy, which made him her ally. For the moment.

If she wanted to save her own life, she'd have to save Alasdair.

Scampering backward, she dropped to her knees, frantically combing her hands through the cold, damp grass, her eyes never once straying from the scuffle in front of her.

All the years of training with her father, and the most frustrating thing had been realizing she'd never have a shred of hope in a fight if pitting her strength against a man's. The average woman didn't, against the average man. And so Haley had learned to fight dirty.

There. The sharp edge of a stone at her fingertips. Ignoring the soil jamming under her nails, she dug, pulling the rock free. It was small, just smaller than her palm, with one end coming to a point. It was the best she could hope for.

The second man sat back on his heels, helping hold down Alasdair as he watched his friend choke the life from him. He smiled as if enjoying the show.

Which one? She weighed her options, the stone warming in her palm. Knock out the kneeling man, or distract the other? *First things first.*

Alasdair was being strangled to death. He pummeled his attacker, the brute force of his blows making his enemy sway with each hit. But the man clutched tenaciously at his neck, despite the blood that blackened his nose and eyes in the darkness.

"Alasdair!" the other woman screeched.

The attackers' attention momentary faltered, and Haley saw her opportunity.

The one choking him then.

Haley was crouched in the grass, clinging tight to her stone, its sharp point jutting from her fist like an arrowhead. She sprang, landing with a thud on the man's back, wrapping one arm tight around his neck as she brought her other down hard, slamming the rock into his temple.

"Alasdair!" the other woman screamed again, this time with a sound like hope in her voice.

She loves him.

Haley didn't have a moment to contemplate the import of that last thought. She felt the ground whooshing from the balls of her feet as the man bobbled to standing and began to thrash her arms with fierce blows.

Haley threw down her rock and hung on to her attacker, trying desperately to gouge his eyes, wrapping her legs around his waist to slam her heels down at his groin.

Alasdair had recovered quickly and was locked in a hand-to-hand battle with the one who'd been kneeling over him. Fragments of his fight pierced her consciousness. The whistle of steel slashing down to his neck. His left arm jutting over, catching his enemy's blade arm. His right swinging up, cracking the man's arm at the elbow. A grotesque wet snap sounded, and the blade flew to the ground.

The man Haley rode spun and slammed her hard to the ground. Her breath came out in a sharp squeal, and she forgot Alasdair. The man turned, pinning her, yet the only thought she could spare was the desperate desire to pull air into her lungs.

Something very wrong had happened to her ribs. The man over her seemed merely a nuisance now; pure bodily survival had become the far more acute crisis. She fought to breathe, feeling as if each inhale sucked shards of glass into her chest.

Time slowed. Darkness nagged at her, as Haley came to, then went dim, and then roused once again. And still the man was over her, until it seemed he'd always been over her, trapping her hands, grabbing at her breasts, fumbling his knees between her own.

And then, suddenly, he was gone. He'd just disappeared from over her, as if more than merely pulled away, the man had simply been eradicated from being.

She lay in the grass panting shallowly, each breath a shocking, nauseating stab. Haley brought a trembling hand up, wiping cold tears and warm snot from her face. The movement was fresh agony.

Ribs. She fought to dampen the fresh spike of adrenalin. Something was gravely wrong. *Broken?*

She tuned her senses outward. What was happening? *Focus.*

She tried to slow her breathing and her teeth ground together, biting through the shrill keening that escaped her with each exhale.

Can't breathe. A fresh spill of tears was hot on her cheeks.

She tried moving. Was able to shift, ever so slightly. *Not broken.* Fresh nausea roiled through her, and she parted her lips to breathe through clenched teeth. *Something . . . torn.*

A dull scuffling sounded at her feet. Clipped grunts. And then silence.

Haley braced, wondering if she had any fight left in her, fearing more than anything the resignation that beckoned. She didn't have to find out what had happened, where she was or with whom, when darkness was teasing her with such promise of stillness and peace.

There was movement again. She stiffened, readying herself for the inevitable.

But the hands that picked her up were gentle. She hated the whimper of pain that escaped her.

It was the black-haired man, his face close in the moonlight. And this time his eyes were soft as he looked at her.

"Alasdair . . ." Her voice was hoarse, his name neither a question nor an address on her tongue.

"Aye. I am called MacColla."

Alasdair . . . MacColla.

Her eyes shot open to gawk at this man who had taken then left her, only to turn around and save her. A fierce savage of a man.

A man who claimed the same name as a hero of old.

Chapter 5

Delusions about Alasdair MacColla? Haley's dissertation must be getting to her, thinking she'd somehow landed in old Scotland with James Graham's friend MacColla. Either that or she'd injured more than just her ribs. She blinked her eyes shut tight to expel the thought.

"Should we . . . should we leave her?" Jean's hushed voice washed over Haley where she lay, dazed, in the grass.

MacColla had somehow gotten his hands on two ponies, and they'd ridden hard through the night, with Haley doubled up in front of him.

When he finally stopped at dawn, Haley had slid gratefully to the ground, hand clutched tight to her side. She was hungry and she was dying of thirst, but all she could do for the moment was lie there.

Rather than feeling open and wide above, the sky seemed to press down on her, gradually lightening but never warming beyond monochromatic shades of gunmetal. Damp seeped into the fabric of her dress, its chill clutching her, snaking up and around her aching sides like an embrace from the grave. Her toes had lost feeling, and the mud-soaked leather of her boots shrank tight over her feet.

Still, these seemed like quaint discomforts compared to the agony she felt with each breath. Haley was relieved simply to lie there, momentarily lightening her body's pull on her rib cage. Curling into her pain, she was able to find the space in her torso for more than just shallow panting.

"Truly, Alasdair, we'll travel faster if—"

"I can hear you," Haley said to nobody in particular.

"*Wheesht*." He silenced her like a child. "Hush, Jean. The lass goes with us."

Travel faster if . . . you leave me? That's right, girlie. Please do leave me. Haley shut her eyes tight. *If only.*

She needed to get away from these people, but with such pain in her ribs, she'd never be able to outrun the man.

"Your rest is over." His voice was close. She opened her eyes to see him standing above her. "Are you ready?"

"You sure are pushing hard."

"Campbell won't rest. Nor will I."

"Aren't *you* a charmer?" she mumbled.

She ignored his outstretched hand, and MacColla made a small grunting sound. Three quick pants of air and she sat up on a sharp exhale, biting back a groan. She struggled to her knees, then her feet, and made her way to the horses.

She studied them in the morning light. They were stout little beasts, one with a mane and tail so black they seemed dyed compared to the lighter dun of its coat. The other was a shade of gray to match the drab sky.

"Where'd you get these nags anyway?" She rubbed her backside, dreading another minute of riding. Haley looked around, desperately trying to place where they could be. "I sure hope some Choate girl isn't missing her prized ponies."

"If you can jest, you can ride," he said, sweeping her up and onto the saddle.

It was the creak of leather beneath her that silenced Haley. She realized that even their horse was tacked up in period garb, with such an archaic saddle. As each step took them impossibly farther from civilization, she wondered what messed-up fantasy these two were reenacting.

Or what kind of nut job would pretend to be Alasdair MacColla. Haley glanced down at the thickly muscled legs jutting from behind her. The man sure was dressed for the part. He even had the six-foot-long, two-handed sword Mac-Colla was known for; one just like it had been tucked and waiting for him in a copse not far from that weird castle.

"Too bad," she muttered. "If you were the real Mac-Colla, you could probably tell me if James Graham were still alive."

She felt the man grow still at her back.

"What did you say?" His voice was a menacing whisper in her ear.

Not the thing to say, apparently. "Nothing," she replied quickly, thinking she might not know what they were about, but she did know that these two were dead serious about their little performance.

Anxiety curdled her stomach as much as her pain did now, wondering where they were taking her, and whether she'd be ready to fight, then flee, when the time was right.

As the hours passed, Haley tried to formulate a plan. She studied every hill and valley as they rode, thinking surely they'd soon approach a town.

She'd at first tried to track their movements, but found it impossible to place where they could be. It was odd she hadn't seen any signs of life. No cars—not even any real roads, for that matter. They must've taken her some ways out of Boston. She knew parts of Massachusetts were quite rural, but she'd never understood just how extensive it was.

The sky grew brighter, and she was able to see the land around her more clearly now. It was strangely barren. *The countryside just around Brimfield?*

Making as if to stretch, she craned her neck to take in the endless stretch of land behind them.

No. Not even close.

She'd made that drive along the Mass Pike before,

cutting through gently rolling hills whose charming farms were nowhere to be seen here.

Shifting made her realize just how stiff she was. Each step of the pony's short gait was agony. Though she refused to admit exhaustion to her captors, Haley was desperate to stop.

"Alasdair?" Though the girl's whisper was meek, it shattered what had been a slow and silent slog through the countryside.

"Jean." There was a warning in his voice that piqued Haley's curiosity.

"But I must," she whispered.

Finally. Haley chuckled low, thinking the girl probably needed to pee as badly as she did.

"Jean, can you not make it a wee spot longer? There will be Campbells surely riding in our wake. I must get you to safety. And then I've a mind to turn about and have a taste of their anger without two lasses to hold me back."

"But . . ."

"Och, fine." MacColla pulled the pony to an abrupt halt. "We break, but just for a moment, aye?"

They dismounted, and she watched as the man escorted his companion to a small thicket. Haley sneered. Of course the girl was incapable of walking the thirty yards into the trees to do her business alone.

Haley took care of herself, then sank gratefully to the grass to take inventory of her various aches and pains, noting all those parts growing numb from the damp and cold. She shifted, nudging away from a stone jabbing sharp into her backside.

The hours of endurance had given her much time to contemplate disastrous scenarios—broken ribs, a smashed spleen . . . Clearing her throat, she spat lightly into her palm and studied it. *Clear.* Part of her feared the sun might bring to light the grisly pale pink of mingled blood. But however much her ribs might feel like ragged blades in her chest, she knew there was no way anything was broken.

She wouldn't be able to ride, or even move, if something had been.

She wiped her palm on her dress, her movements slow and deliberate. In that moment, a torn something seemed no less painful to her than a broken something.

The sound of their voices gradually reemerged from the trees, coalescing into coherent snippets of conversation. Though at first their whispers had been a dense and rapidly flowing Gaelic, MacColla and Jean spoke increasingly in English.

She couldn't begin to guess who these people were or what it could mean that they spoke perfect Gaelic. Their English threw her too. It was thick and strangely accented, like no Scottish brogue she'd ever heard. Islanders, perhaps?

Just more confusing items to add to her growing list. She needed to figure out who the hell they were. At the very least, it might help her when she felt fit enough to make her escape.

Haley put her hand to her belly. Willing her diaphragm to rise, she breathed in as deeply as she could, nudging at the edges of her pain. Its acuteness had crested, dulling into something her body could reasonably handle.

"But who is she then?" he asked. "You can't be certain there wasn't another prisoner—"

"I was the only one, Alasdair."

Bickering lovers? Haley mused about the peculiar pair, wondering how a simpering girl could inspire the love of such a commanding force as this man.

She felt another small twinge of jealousy. Where were all the suitors lining up to take care of *Haley*?

And where did a girl like that meet a man like him anyway? A helpless waif and a man calling himself Alasdair MacColla. Gooseflesh pebbled her skin. *Why that name?*

And why had they taken her?

Haley retraced her steps. She'd been contemplating a gun she'd suspected had belonged to James Graham. It was a far-fetched theory, but she couldn't deny the certainty she felt in her gut. She'd discovered a weapon that could rock history as everyone knew it. Something that would prove Graham didn't really die when the history books said he did.

And then she gets abducted by a man claiming the name of none other than Graham's famous compatriot, the warrior Alasdair MacColla.

Not likely.

The two events had to be linked somehow.

A rival academic? Who else would speak such perfect Gaelic? She couldn't tamp down a shiver of excitement, thinking that this MacColla's interest only corroborated her theory.

Sensing him near, Haley turned, and was taken aback at his closeness. She mustered as great a dare in her gaze as she could, despite needing to tilt her chin up to meet his eyes.

He was handsome in the light, and it was off-putting. It'd been easy to imagine him as some mangy beast in the dark, with his soiled kilt and wild hair. The caricature had made him easy to size up, easy to place.

But the day had brought to light strong features. Large, brown eyes. A wide mouth. A rugged, square jaw. His thick, dark eyebrows exaggerated a high forehead. Wild hair hung loose from either side of a ragged part, coming to rest on wide shoulders.

He looked so . . . big. The rough weave of his shirt strained over biceps and shoulders, doing nothing to conceal the solid wall of muscle beneath. Heat surged to her cheeks, and Haley hated the traitorous and irrational response to such a conspicuous show of maleness.

To spite her own response, she forced an indifference she didn't feel, and allowed her eyes to rove the rest of him, taking in his tremendous brawn, the barrel chest, and thickly knotted calves that emerged from his kilt.

Rival academic? Yeah, right. Talk about a crazy professor type.

"Do you really need to dress up like Alasdair MacColla?"

She eyed his plaid. The muted dark greens, blues, and black had seen better days. It appeared he took a left turn at the seventeenth century and didn't look back. "Don't tell me. You're a student at Brown, aren't you?"

MacColla stared blankly. "You're a wee daftie of a lass."

"Okay, I give up." She could play along with the crazy reenactor guy. He clearly spent his weekends tossing cabers and eating venison he'd skinned with his own hands. Talk about taking his scholarship seriously. "Why a MacColla costume? I mean, everyone knows James Graham was the one you'd want to dress up as. *He* was the great hero."

The man bristled, so she just bit back a grin and went with it. "But you, you were just kind of a sidekick, right? Graham was the handsome, smart one. Weren't you more of the brawn-not-brains variety? Although"—she scanned her eyes up and down his body—"you do have the right look. You've got kind of a big-lug thing going on. I can't see *you* in the fancy velvet waistcoats."

She met his gaze again and something looking like satisfaction played on his features. He couldn't possibly think she was checking him out, right?

"*What-ever*, Mister Alasdair MacColla." She rolled her eyes. "Why don't you just tell me where you're taking me?"

Her mind whirred. She needed to figure out what was going on. He had to be another Celtic scholar, but what was he playing at? "Come on, tell me. What's your dissertation on?"

He'd surely seen the gun. She'd put money on it. "Look, if this is about the gun, we can claim the find together. Just let me go."

His eyes narrowed.

That's it. He'd seen the gun, dated it, realized it belonged to Graham, and, putting two and two together, had decided to scare her out of the equation. Anyone who'd take the name of such a famous—and famously brutal—hero of old had to be all kinds of crazy with his obsessions.

Haley rubbed her side, playing up her injury. "I think I need a doctor." Maybe that would scare him into freeing her.

Standing completely still, he simply stared, scrutinizing her.

"I won't let you have it," she finally stated baldly.

"I take whatever I want, you wee hellcat." He roved his eyes over her, giving his words a double meaning.

A shiver ran up her spine.

"It was my discovery," she replied quickly. "It's *mine*, you know. The weapon is mine."

"I know you've no weapon. Unless you've hidden it." Before she could dodge him, MacColla grabbed her close, reaching around and patting her on the rump to frisk her.

She let out a sharp squeal and watched as the light drained from MacColla's eyes. He abruptly let her go.

"Och." A hiss of breath escaped him as he visibly gathered himself. "Stop with the games, lass."

His voice grew stern. "Campbell is at our backs and I need to get Jean to safety."

She glowered. *This business about Campbell again.* "Is Robert the Bruce after us too?"

"Would that it were so," he countered with a sudden laugh. "Now, if I have the right of it, Jean's safety is *your* safety. So if you've a mind to your own hide, you'll get back up on that pony and ride."

She stared, speechless. She was going to get the hell away from them as soon as she could, of that she had no doubt.

Ride. The thought of more riding filled her with a dread so vast it felt like a physical weight in her belly.

She must've made some face, because he let out a low chuckle.

Before Haley could give him what for, MacColla surprised her by asking, "What's your name, lass?"

He was the one who'd taken *her*—wouldn't he know that already?

"Haley . . ." she hesitated.

"I see your pain, Haley." His tone was unnervingly gentle, his voice slowing to pronounce her name with care. "You need your wind back. If you're to ride anymore this day, we'll need to bind you."

"But didn't you just say we had to get out of here?"

"Aye," he smiled and cocked a brow, "I ken what I said. 'Twill take but a moment. I've no doctor at my disposal, but I myself have bound many a man."

"I'll just bet you have," she said under her breath, and he surprised her once more with a laugh.

"But," he added gravely, "I'll have your word you'll not try to claw me while I do so, my wee *caile bhorb*."

The peculiar nickname caught her off guard. A wee *what* girl? *Fierce?*

A wry smile cocked her lips before she could give it a thought. Her, a wee savage. A wisp of a laugh escaped her nostrils. Wouldn't her brothers have loved that one?

"I won't claw you," she said grudgingly, thinking what a relief it would be to have her ribs bound.

Skeptical, he raised his brows, questioning.

"You have my word." She was growing impatient with these suddenly amiable efforts. Who did he think he was to kidnap her, then think to bust out the burly charms? "Just get on with it, okay?"

He looked at her quizzically. Just when she thought he didn't understand what she said, the man unsheathed his dirk and, biting it between his teeth, proceeded to unbuckle, take off his belt, loosen his plaid, and drop the entire heavy swath of wool into a puddle on the ground. All he wore was an enormous shirt that reached to the middle of his thighs.

"What the—"

The sun was approaching midafternoon now, and it cut across the valley at MacColla's back. The sharp angle lit him from behind, making the thin linen of his shirt glow with light.

It also made it see-through.

Haley gasped, seeing the size of him through the gauzy

stretch of fabric. She turned away quickly, feeling her cheeks blaze red.

She told herself she'd seen a naked man before. Her first-year college boyfriend, to be precise. And it certainly hadn't been cause for any fireworks. If there was no magic to be had then, why should she shy away from the sight now?

Misunderstanding her uneasiness, he took the blade from his mouth and explained, "I'll need something to bind you, aye? Or were you of a mind to shred your own frock into ribbons?" Sticking the knife back between bared teeth, he unfurled the yards and yards of dingy plaid wool.

Haley realized she'd been holding her breath. Her eyes had inadvertently gone back to his shirt, and she was both a little relieved and a little disappointed to see that he'd shifted and was no longer backlit by the sun.

He took the knife and, first wiping his mouth roughly on his sleeve, began to saw long strips from the end of the plaid. The thick muscle of his thigh flexed inadvertently, and the sight of it snagged her gaze, pure instinct dragging her eyes mindlessly along the light dusting of black hair, and the solid column of muscle framed by the slit up the side of his shirt.

MacColla dropped to a squat, and, coming to herself, she quickly glanced away again. Her eyes went automatically to Jean, who was bustling about, nudging aside brush and rocks to clear a spot pristine enough to warrant her tender bottom. Haley once again tried out her best evil eye on the girl.

A throaty chuckle brought Haley's attention back to him. "Easy, lass," he said, pitching his voice for her ears alone. Then louder, he added, "Jean, love, will you fetch us some water then?"

Jean looked at him as if he'd asked her to translate something from the Greek.

"Aye, you." He nodded at her, a wide smile on his face. "You ken the word. I've a wee flask tied to the pony. We need water, and I'd have you refill it for me."

Jean rose with a high-pitched huff.

"And you, *caile bhorb*." MacColla stood and strode slowly toward Haley. Her heart gave a single sharp thump to attention as she watched that smile bleed first from his eyes and then from his lips.

He knelt just before her, placing his palm on the ground between her crossed legs. "I ken those daggers you shoot from your eyes would be caused by your injury. That it's simply your pain that I see darkening that bonny face of yours." He leaned even closer. "I ken a lass like you knows better than to wish ill upon my sister, aye?"

"*Mm-hm.*" She nodded weakly. *Sister? No kidding.* Haley experienced a curious reaction to that last bit of information. A peculiar, brief quivering on the edge of thought. Not relief, not excitement, not anticipation, just an electric flash of awareness. *Brother and sister.*

He smiled, broad and easy. Haley noticed a chipped front tooth and tried to disregard the ache in her chest from the single sudden pound of her heart.

"What's to be done then?"

"Huh?"

MacColla held the wool strips up in answer. "What's to be done? You've that frock about you. I'll need to swaddle the skin directly, or the plaid will slip hither and yon."

"Oh." Haley glanced down at her dress. "I . . . give me a moment." MacColla didn't budge, so she told him more explicitly, "Turn around."

Haley swore she saw that thick black brow flinch just before he turned his back to her. She pulled one arm, then the other, through the neck of the stretchy black knit. Despite her care, she heard the thin crackle of threads popping and frowned. So much for her favorite dress. At least she'd worn a tank top underneath.

She wondered what had become of her scarf and, with a pang, pictured the cobalt blue length of it tossed atop the storeroom table. Remembered how one of her brothers had loosened it for her at the bar. Who had it been, Colin or Conor? Their faces flashed in her mind's eye, bringing an ache to her throat. She sniffed sharply. She'd need thoughts of her family to gird her, not tear her apart.

She had to get back to them. She couldn't bear to have them worry anymore about her. She'd put them through so much before. Her whole family had been traumatized after her attack. She wouldn't put them through something like that again.

Haley tugged her dress hard to her waist, revealing a white cotton tank beneath. She'd let this man wrap her ribs. Rest awhile.

And then she'd run.

Chapter 6

He stole a glance, fascinated, as she wriggled her arms and torso through the neck of her dark dress. She shimmied and maneuvered, a look of such intense concentration on her face. It was amusing and arousing both.

The sort of shirt she'd worn underneath her gown was foreign to him. MacColla fought not to ogle, but that shirt clung to her, its white fabric looking soft to the touch, and not leaving much to the imagination.

The skin of her shoulders was pale, her collarbones delicate slopes in contrast to the firm, lean muscle of her upper arms.

MacColla distractedly rubbed his thumb along his fingertips, wondering if that ivory skin was as silky as it looked.

While she was focused on arranging the dress around her hips, he let his eyes graze her chest.

MacColla grew hard, watching as she reached her right hand across her stomach to roll the fabric down along the opposite hip.

He clenched his hands into fists, his breath suddenly shallow.

The movement crushed her arm up against the bottom of her breast, squeezing it high and tight against the white shirt. The fabric strained, revealing the barest outline of her nipple.

She folded her top up and neatly over her breasts to expose her belly. It was pale and smooth, and MacColla let out an inadvertent groan.

"Turn back around," she snapped.

His eyes whipped up to meet hers. Her voice was indignant to match her simmering gaze.

He promptly did so, using the opportunity to gather his wits. Last time he'd lost them, he'd taken her to his mouth for a taste. It would do him no good to forget himself with his very own prisoner. And a Campbell no less, he thought with disgust.

But something about the lass riled him. Intrigued him. What sort of woman was she to stand up to him as she did? He was used to all and sundry cowering before him. But there was no cowering in this woman. She merely held her chin up with a dare in her eye as if he were some ordinary crofter instead of a leader of warriors.

And then to watch the lass peel her clothes away with mingled modesty and purpose? He scrubbed his hand over his face. It was enough to send him over the edge.

"Okay."

MacColla heard that strange word again and took it to mean she was ready. Upon turning, however, he quickly realized that he was not.

She sat before him, rigidly upright, enduring what was surely extraordinary pain. And yet her bearing spoke to resilience, not defeat. MacColla had thought her a wildcat, but he saw the truth of her now. She might adopt the persona of predator, but shedding her strange garb, she sat before him a long, gorgeous swan, with pale throat and breasts that were only accentuated by her thick black hair and white undergarment.

Her shoulders were creamy and broad, but not masculine. Hands clasped in her lap, she held her arms crooked out at her sides, those smooth, firm limbs speaking to strength, but not toil.

And then his eyes went to her stomach, and a flash of pure heat stabbed him. Rather than bones or loose flesh, her belly was firm, a sweep of polished alabaster that he had to fight not to touch.

"I . . ." He fumbled with the plaid for a moment, and then noticed it. *Her neck.* MacColla sucked in a breath. And this time he did reach for her, unthinking. "Och, lass, your bonny neck."

He drew his thumb gently over her scar, a ragged, bulging line marring the otherwise perfect stretch of throat. He used the back of his hand to carefully push her hair from the skin, then traced his thumb along it once more, marveling that a thing could answer as many questions as it raised.

"How?"

He didn't need to say more than the single word. He could see in her averted gaze, in the stiffening of her spine, how this single mark defined her somehow, had been a turning point. MacColla saw true how, rather than be defeated by it, whatever tragedy had befallen her had instead scraped away the nonessential to reveal some deeper power and spirit that was the root of this woman.

"None of your business." Her voice was measured, but strained too.

He looked in her eyes, wondering at her words, and he saw a sheen of tears there. But more than her sadness, he saw her strength.

"In good time, then," he said softly.

He unrolled the fabric between them and made quick work of it, trying his best not to flinch at what muted sounds of pain she allowed to escape. MacColla leaned close, wrapping his arms around to reach behind her and back again. He worked silently, his great, thick hands fumbling to tuck fabric gingerly along the top, tugging and tightening as gently as possible.

His knuckles brushed the firm underside of her breast, and he froze. He flicked his eyes up to meet hers. What was but a moment stretched long between them, their breath held, neither choosing to look away first.

Those eyes that had at first appeared otherworldly in the dark stared at him unblinking. Gray and fathomless, spattered with black flecks like drops of ink, they were more mysterious to him now than they'd been in the shadow of Campbell's castle.

Campbell. The thought was a distant flare, recalling MacColla to himself. He had a duty to his sister. And, in taking the strange woman, he'd claimed an obligation to her too. But more so, he had a duty to his clan. These two women held him back, when what he needed to do was remember what he was truly about.

"*Haley.* Such an odd name." His voice was gruffer than he'd intended, and he saw her recoil as if struck. "What are you to the Campbell?"

The delicate thread that had stretched shimmering between them disappeared like a cobweb moving from sunlight to shadow.

This man, this whole scenario, had gone beyond confusing, past surreal, and was moving well into madness. That he kept mentioning yet another famous seventeenth-century figure eclipsed her pain and slammed her back into reality. She took a moment to focus.

"What?" she asked.

"I asked what you are to the Campbell."

She knew her history well, knew Graham and Campbell had been enemies, but what did the latter have to do with the gun?

"How about you talk first?" Haley held her body as straight as she could, trying to minimize the fresh stabbing in her ribs with a rigid spine. Stars glittered for a moment over her vision, and she was forced to swallow convulsively from a sudden wave of nausea and the saliva it brought to the back of her tongue. "I know you know about the gun."

"Gun?"

She gritted her teeth and pressed on. "What do you know about James Graham?" Her question was an accusation, and she felt the man stiffen as he tucked the last of the fabric into itself.

"What do *you* know of Graham?" He affected a cavalier tone, but Haley wasn't fooled.

"I don't think he died like people said," she replied. He went still, and Haley felt gratified. She knew it. He was some sort of wacked-out academic rival. The competition made her cocky. "In fact, I'm almost certain he didn't die when people said he did."

A single violent movement and he held her face between two viselike hands. "Who are you?" he snarled. "Are you Campbell's spy?"

His sudden movement jarred her. She flinched, and glass shattered in her chest. Haley gasped clipped breaths in and out through her pinched nostrils. "Campbell? What the . . ."

What kind of a freak show was this, where she found herself immersed in some strange flashback? MacColla, Graham, and now this insistence on Campbell too?

The hollow thunk of a flask dropping to the ground startled them. "You'd be wise not to try my brother."

Haley wrenched her face free of MacColla's grip and stared with unmitigated fury at his sister, standing hands on hips beside them. "They call him *Fear Thollaidh nan Tighean*, and he is bested by no man. And certainly by no woman."

The strange Gaelic phrase resonated in the back of Haley's mind, but she quickly shoved it aside to concentrate on the girl in front of her. *Certainly by no woman, my ass.* It was creatures like this who gave women a bad name.

"You've got me cornered." Haley made as if to concede. She needed to rest up, not rouse suspicions, if she were to eventually get away from them. "Look. I'm hurt. I'm tired. I don't know any Campbell."

She scooted back and the pain threatened, ready to explode, like a flame divining a whiff of kerosene. She

stilled, the stabbing in her chest lending truth to her charade. "I don't have the gun, if that's why I'm here. I locked
it up before you took me."

They stared at her dumbly and she chattered on. "Get
it? The gun's locked up. I don't have it. I know you want to
ride some more, but can I please just lie down and rest for a
while?"

The need for sleep had grown critical. The binding
around her chest had dulled her pain, and Haley felt the
hysteria draining from her, leaving limp, exhausted shock
in its wake. She realized her hands were freezing, and she
held them before her, watching dumbly as they trembled.

The man muttered some curse under his breath. Black
spots swam across her vision, dispersed just as quickly,
then came again, slowing and growing into a cool darkness
that swallowed her back and down.

Haley heard him issue some order to his sister, followed
at once by the snap of branches. Felt his hands on her
shoulders, then the rough ground at her back. There was
the weight of fabric over her. Then blackness.

❁

"Royalist or Covenanter, brother?"

"*Hm?*" MacColla watched the strange woman as she
slept. It would be time to rouse her soon. He was desperate
to be on his way, but he kept getting waylaid by the needs
of these two women. He should be ravaging Campbell's
lands in Argyll, not making camp.

He needed to push south, getting Jean to safe harbor
with his family in Kintyre as soon as possible. But he'd realized in frustration that the women would require a day of
true shelter, with rest and hot food, if they were to keep up
his pace.

Lately, allies bled from Campbell's control as if from a
ruptured vein, and MacColla knew of a place in Argyll
where they might find sympathetic refuge on the way.

"Fincharn Castle," his sister replied testily. The return
of his gaze over and again to the sleeping stranger seemed

to make Jean peevish, her waning patience putting questions on her tongue for which she'd normally have no concern. "I ask of the residents of Fincharn. Do we find a friend there, or a castle full of Covenanters residing in Campbell's pocket?"

MacColla spared a smile for his sister. He had to admit, she was dogged in her efforts to split his attentions from the stranger. "We find both," he said. "It was once a MacMartin stronghold, but Clan Scrymgeour holds the castle now. And though the father was a Covenanter, his son John is the one awaiting us now. He supports the king, as we do."

"And when is it we return to our own home, on Colonsay?" Her chin trembled now.

"I know not." He looked at his sister in long silence, then said somberly, "Don't fret, girl. The Campbell may have robbed our lands, but I will take from him more than that. I'll exact the heart and the spirit of all Campbells, if the cost is my own cold body."

Jean shrank, looking horrified, and MacColla laughed. "My apologies, sister." He leaned over to chuck her chin. "All you need concern yourself with is visions of joining our family in Kintyre. That's home enough for now, aye?"

He took a stick from the dirt and stoked the fire. "For the nonce, we find Royalist allies at Fincharn. And bowls full of good, hot stew, God willing."

He inhaled deeply, as if getting a lungful of air might quell his gnawing hunger. He needed to fill his belly with cooked meat for a change.

MacColla let his attention drift once more to the lass. He registered the faint *tsking* of his sister as she gave up attempts at conversation, choosing instead to stab testily at the sputtering flames.

Despite her deep sleep, the woman lay stiffly, her arms wrapped about her torso as if she could cradle the pain in her hands.

No woman had ever stood up to him as she had. Few men either, and even fewer who lived to tell about it. But rather than make him angry, her verve had excited him, kindled some long-snuffed spark back to life.

He realized he didn't even know her full name. He'd somehow neglected asking about her father's name, her clan, her origins.

But watching her sleep, he'd given it much thought. He found it curious that, as they'd fled the castle, Campbell's men had attacked her ruthlessly. And so it was unlikely she was a family member. Or, if she was, she'd somehow crossed the clan in some way.

And yet Jean claimed to have been the only prisoner held at the castle.

The woman was a puzzle. Who could she be, and more importantly, on whose side?

Her questions about James Graham alarmed him. Only a very few knew of the ruse that had spared James from the gallows. Painstaking subterfuge and smoke screens on the part of only his closest friends kept his survival a secret. That a stranger had struck at the truth was deeply troubling.

Could she be a spy for Campbell? If so, why would his men try to kill her? Was the attack on her merely a charade, some sort of trap to trick MacColla into taking her into his care?

That she was strong and determined he had no doubt. He studied her, asleep but far from peaceful. Furrows were etched on her otherwise smooth complexion, around her mouth, at her brow, her pain written on her skin. But the experience contained on her face couldn't rob her of her beauty. It perhaps even contributed to it.

Her features weren't delicate. Taken separately, they were sturdy, like her body. A square face, wide nose, full lips. Proud, unapologetic features that asserted themselves.

But, put together, those features underwent some mysterious alchemy, transformed by her luminous skin and black hair and unsettling gray eyes into some exquisitely feminine creature.

The corners of MacColla's eyes creased as he considered her.

Fierce. Robust. Yet unmistakably lovely.

In the way a lioness is all the more magnificent for her size and the power she wields.

He'd do well to fear this woman. As any wise man would such a creature.

Chapter 7

Campbell eyed the man at his left. Major Nicholas Purdon had spent time fighting on the side of the Parliamentarians and Protestants in Ireland. Average height, average build, and flat hair the color of dishwater rendered him nondescript among men, and an unimaginative nature made him a tractable one too.

Two of the traits Campbell valued most.

He nodded at Purdon to swing the bucket, and cold water doused the blood and stupor from his clansman's face. Shuffling tight past each other, they traded places.

Campbell looked down, intent on the sleeves of his ivory shirt, and creased a careful fold along each cuff. Finally ready, he looked back up and stared with disgust. The clansman's head lolled, and the only thing keeping him upright was the rope that tied him to his seat.

"You'll not die on me yet," he snarled and slapped the man. The wet smack made a sharp sound that reverberated off the cellar walls. "Tell me who took her."

"I-I told you . . ."

Another loud crack of skin on skin.

"Then tell it." Campbell bit out his words, fighting to keep his patience. "Again."

He'd returned to Inveraray only to discover that his prisoner had been rescued by MacColla with the aid of, of all things, a woman. "Tell me how it is you fools let MacColla in. Let him best you."

He'd worked so hard to capture MacColla's sister. The most valuable of all prisoners, gone like vapor in the wind. He landed another slap. "Then you let him escape. MacColla and . . ." The loose flesh of his jowls turned purple with rage. "*Two* women."

"*Unh* . . ." A strangled sound escaped the man's throat, and he stilled, seeing the terrifying calm steal over Campbell's features.

"I will ask you just once more," he said smoothly. "And then you will see what happens when my patience is tried." He pulled a dagger from the belt at his waist. Candlelight caught the superfine blade, flashed up it like lightning.

Campbell smiled to see the man eye it nervously. "You like this? I call it *the needle*." He flicked it down hard through the air, and the thin blade made a sound like a bird's chirp.

He drew it to the man's face, and the point kissed just below the clansman's eye, tugging and misshaping the delicate skin there. "Now you'll try once more to recall this other woman before you are the scrap in need of stitching."

"It was the one." The whisper came from the darkness behind him.

His hand slipped and blood trickled down his captive's face like a lone red tear.

"Finola." Campbell spun to face the witch. He'd forgotten she was there. She seemed to be always there now, watching. It chilled him. "What did you say, woman?"

"Forget not to whom you speak." She stepped from the shadows, serene, her eyes dead pools.

Campbell glared in response, schooling his features into an impassive mask.

"I am not your clansman," she warned.

Finola studied the bound man, walking a tight circle around him. He was frozen in place, except for his eyes, which rolled and jerked between his chief and the sorceress. She leaned in toward him, shutting her eyes and flaring her nostrils wide. She wore her long hair loose, and a thick hank of it slipped from her shoulder and swept toward him like a great crimson veil.

The man's whimper echoed through the chamber, and she smiled.

"I am not yours to speak to thusly." She placed a bony finger on the man's cheek. "Unlike this one." She traced the track of blood with the point of her long, yellowed nail. "You would all be wise not to forget."

The witch pursed her lips and gave the man a coy smile. A hollow tap-tapping filled the room. The sound of a thin trickle of urine dribbling to the ground. The witch shrieked a laugh and stepped back.

"He tells the truth, and I tell you, Campbell"—she spun to face him, her eyes suddenly glittering, alive with evil—"she was the one. This mysterious woman. It was she with the power to shatter the MacColla. The one I called forth."

It took him a moment to register her words. Could she be speaking the truth? He bit the inside of his cheek to silence his anger.

"I bade you bring her through time to *me*." The muscles in his legs trembled with bottled-up rage that he dare not spend on the witch. "Not to my enemy."

"I did bring her back to you, Campbell." Her voice was cavalier now, effortless. "And you were not there. I cannot pay the price for your incompetence."

Campbell chuffed, fisting and unfisting his hands in frustration. He wanted that woman, whoever she may be. And now she was with MacColla. If she had the power to destroy his enemy, did she have the power to destroy Clan Campbell as well?

He stood once more before the bound clansman. Unsheathed his "needle." Campbell scraped it lightly back up the bloody smear on the man's face, and the clansman's feet began to skitter, as if he could push his chair back and somehow flee his chief.

Purdon instinctively came to his aid and stood behind the chair, bracing it at his thighs, holding the man's shoulders in his hands.

Campbell gave him a nod. The young soldier was eager to please. And better, he appeared to be enjoying the work. The days ahead would require such men.

He looked back down at his clansman. With one swift twist of his blade, Campbell sliced the man's eye. "A reminder," he growled over the breathy, erratic screams that filled the chamber, "to take greater care the next time you stand watch."

He'd summoned this woman back in time to *him*. It was *he* who'd paid much. Risked much. Sullied himself with witchcraft. This woman was *his* property, like a misplaced weapon. And, like a lost item, he would find her and reclaim her.

And if he couldn't control her, Campbell would kill her.

Chapter 8

"When is this all going to stop?" Jean's question broke the tense silence that had accompanied them for the past couple of hours. She seemed to be finding her mettle the farther they got from Campbell's lair.

Damn straight, Haley thought, grateful that the girl had finally said something after hours of increasingly gusty and exasperated sighs.

MacColla had roused Haley far too soon, sweeping them all back into their saddles to be on their way once more.

Haley glanced around, even edgier than she'd been before. They'd entered the foothills of some sort of mountain range, and now she was totally confused. Could they be in the Berkshires?

"Yeah," Haley muttered. She also wanted to know when it was all going to stop.

" 'Tis just a wee hill."

She could hear MacColla's patience wearing thin and felt a rush of irrational satisfaction. His sister's moaning had been almost as annoying as their never-ending trail ride.

It had been slow going all afternoon, bending far up their ponies' necks to manage uphill scrabbles on scree-covered slopes, then leaning far back for skittering descents. Every movement was agony for Haley, and yet it was the girl who required coddling.

"Could be worse," he mused. "I could've taken you lasses up and over Beinn Bhreac. And faster it would've been," he grumbled, "than meandering like a snake along the belly of these valleys."

Beinn Bhreac? What the—

"Alasdair." Jean's tone was stern, and Haley smiled.

This should be good, she thought.

"I'd meant, when will this fighting stop?" The girl scrubbed at her face. Was she crying? Haley wondered just what she could be talking about.

MacColla didn't answer for a time. He rode behind Haley, and she felt him adjust, saw from the corner of her eye as he pulled his head far to the right. Felt the light tickle and tug of her hairs pulling free from the stubble where they'd snagged along his jaw.

His voice was measured when he finally replied, "It will stop when it's over, Jean. Not before."

Nice. He clearly ducked whatever question she'd been asking, and Haley couldn't believe the girl could put up with it.

Beinn Bhreac. She once more considered that strange phrase he'd said. Just what was it with him and the Gaelic? *Beinn Bhreac. Speckled hill.*

They rode along a deep valley, flanked by rocky slopes that felt way too barren for New England. Concern had become foremost in her mind, eclipsing even her injury.

The gorgeous landscape did nothing to calm her. On the contrary, the grand stretches of hill and hardscrabble foliage had an alien quality, heightening the sense of displacement that cut through her as viscerally as her pain.

Their path wound, narrowed into a thin gap, then widened again. Deep green pines studded the horizon, soaring along the hillside like a great, roughened spine. A tremendous buck crested the rise and froze, as sudden as a snapshot, captured like some sort of preposterously majestic still life.

It wasn't any Massachusetts she'd ever seen. Rocky slopes surrounded them, but they weren't the sharp, craggy peaks of the North American mountain ranges she was familiar with. These brute, rounded hills had the feel of raw rock covered by a rough green and brown quilt of tenacious vegetation.

One plant in particular dominated, coarse and low to the ground, and Haley wracked her mind, frantic to place it. Frantic to find something recognizable in this increasingly foreign landscape.

Not the Berkshires at all, more like . . .

"Aye, the heather will be even more bonny come late summer."

Heather?

"Late summer?" She heard her voice crack. "What month is it now?"

He paused for a moment, then spoke tentatively, as if to a child. "May."

May. Last thing she remembered, signs of fall had been all around. Those things that reappeared each year like clockwork. Her father's ancient Irish-knit sweater. The television tuned to a football game. Colin's trademark red and black flannel shirt. Chill wind whipping her hair in a dash along the Quad. Trees the glorious red and orange of autumn.

"May . . . Of course it is," she muttered. *Of course* it would be May. Why wouldn't it be May in this backward universe she'd landed in?

"Ho!" A man shouted at them from a distance, and MacColla froze at her back. "Alasdair MacColla," he shouted again, "as I live and breathe!"

They looked up to see someone standing on the hill above them, to the right and just slightly behind.

A *kilted* someone, with a sword at his waist and a smile on his face.

Oh good. Haley wavered in the saddle. *There's the last straw right there.* She was distantly aware of MacColla's hand steadying her waist.

"I hope we're not too late for the hammer throw," she murmured, now feeling completely unmoored. *Is everyone going to look like they're geared up for the Highland Games?* She fought to stay upright despite the blood she felt draining from her head.

MacColla either didn't hear her remark or didn't acknowledge it. His focus was on the man, now hurtling down the hill toward them, his feet galloping at a lumbering run. The dull clatter of scree echoed through the valley as the man set a small tumble of rocks sliding down with him. MacColla exploded into a sharp bark of laughter, kicking his heels to spin the pony around to face him.

"John Scrymgeour," MacColla informed his suddenly alert sister. It was just a quick aside, but the information appeared to put her at ease.

"I was told you'd been sighted in Argyll," John panted when he reached them. Thin brown hair framed a full, good-humored face. "Taking your leisure on Campbell lands? And a few other things besides, I'd wager." The man gave a questioning glance in Haley's direction.

Was this guy in on the whole kidnapping thing? If so, he seemed remarkably nonchalant about it all. Might he be able to help her? Should she beg him for help?

The man's smile faded. "I have tidings from the king."
King?

His tone was somber, and Haley felt MacColla grow wary behind her. Their pony sensed it too, and she pranced a few nervous steps to the side.

"Indeed? And so serious you are, Scrymgeour."

The man gave a single, earnest nod. Without his smile, his features appeared doughy, though no less pleasant.

"Perhaps your news would be best heard over a mug of ale. I find myself suddenly thirsty," MacColla added warily. "Ride with Jean, and we'll find ourselves by your hearth the sooner."

The girl's abrupt movement called Haley's attention to her. Two angry spots suffused Jean's cheeks, a blush that looked particularly crimson in contrast to the white-knuckled grip she had on her reins.

"Please endure just one final rise, and you'll find the valley opening up wide before us, bearing my modest Fincharn in its palm." John strode to Jean's side, giving her a gentlemanly half bow before mounting behind her. "The loch is lovely this time of year. The spring sunlight dances upon its surface like fire." He spoke for Jean's ears, adding, "My castle lies just on the eastern shore of Loch Awe."

It was all white noise to Haley, though.

Loch Awe. Great. A king and a loch.

They made good progress from there, as the hills slowly smoothed into a thick carpet of knotty green grass. The loch appeared, and nausea twinged sharp in Haley's gut. She *knew* there weren't any such bodies of water in the Massachusetts she'd seen. It was huge, stretching along a fold in the gently curving valley, and glittering as promised.

A gray building emerged in the distance, a spectral thing in the hazy light that materialized as they approached. Her queasiness became insistent, clutching at the front of her belly. Haley breathed through her mouth now as if that could curb the roiling and flipping in her stomach.

She must've faltered, or made some sound, because she felt both of MacColla's hands steadying her.

John's castle came into focus. It was a huge rectangular building constructed of dingy gray stone and studded with a few small square openings. A granite fortress, grim and nearly windowless, in the old "hall house" style of ancient castle.

Lochs, kilts, kings, and now castles.

"What's your king's name?" Her voice was a reedy whisper. "Wait. MacColla. Charles? Charles the first."

"Are you well, lass?"

She felt his hand on her shoulder, but she pulled away sharply. Swinging a trembling leg in front of her, Haley slid off the pony's back and buckled to the ground.

She heard muted chatter, then she registered the girl ranting a stream of unintelligible Gaelic.

Effortless Gaelic babbling all around.

And then the possibility came to her. But rather than the illuminating click of a bulb, Haley's sudden realization snuffed out the light. It was a boulder come crashing down, as if to seal her in a cramped, airless cave.

It was the phrase that did it. An obscure phrase that had been spoken to her. That nagged at her still. The name Jean had called her brother—she remembered it. And she knew.

Fear Thollaidh nan Tighean.

Destroyer of Houses.

Alasdair MacColla.

The Alasdair MacColla.

She ran teetering for several yards before collapsing to her knees. The weathered building loomed in the distance, mocking her, an indifferent witness to her horror. The nausea that had quivered at the edges of her belly and in the back of her throat erupted full force now, and it was as if a great, violent fist punched into her gut, hauling up everything from Haley's stomach with its clenched hand. The strain robbed her of breath, forced bile singeing into her sinuses.

The pain in her ribs made her vision waver, and a great wail escaped her. She tried to still her spasming body, tried to silence her own cries. Every movement was sheer agony.

She felt the small blip of burst blood vessels around her eyes as she retched again. And still she convulsed, as if some instinctual part of her believed she could make it all disappear by the full force of her body alone.

The violence of it made her bones creak, awoke fresh agony in her already abused ribs, and she sicked up once more from the stabbing in her torso alone.

She had the knack of sensing MacColla near, and she felt him now, standing over her, the cool cast of his shadow on her back. Knew without thought that he was leaning down toward her.

And though her heart pounded with fear, she summoned

a look of defiance. Against him, against her condition. Against the whole unreal, unfathomable, inconceivable situation.

"No!" she shouted, as she scrambled to the side, scrubbing the trails of her body's fluids from her face. "No."

One of the most brutal men in Scottish history. Somehow come for her.

She saw him, looming over her, as still as the hills at their backs. She clawed tight to her flickering consciousness and heard Jean on the edges of it. "I warned you, Alasdair. The lass is not right."

And this time instead of focusing Haley, giving her strength, Jean's distant words erased her. Unmoored her. *Not right.*

And the impermeable wall of masonry Haley had spent years stacking up and around herself became a great, towering house of cards, fluttering lightly to the ground.

Chapter 9

MacColla eased himself into the bath. The copper tub barely held him, but the water was hot and unclenched his tight muscles. He reached back to grind at the knots along the tops of his shoulders, taking pleasure in the stretch of tendons along the backs of his arms.

John had generously given them their choice of rooms, the majority of his family currently residing in their primary home in Glassary, to the east. MacColla wasn't much for luxuries, and had chosen the smaller but warmer of the rooms offered him. The hearth was big, the window faced west, and the mattress was softer than any ground he'd used as a bed these past weeks.

And still, he was tenser than he thought he had reason to be, and wondered at the strange woman who'd put him so on edge. Dunking his head underwater, he tugged his fingers through his hair, untangling the matted mass before he washed.

MacColla sat up abruptly and whipped his hair from his face. Curse his distraction, but he still hadn't pressed the issue of the woman's clan.

He'd thought she was a spy. All signs pointed to it. She'd come upon them in Campbell's own lair. A mysterious woman, strong and alone, with no ready explanations or denials on her tongue.

And, most troubling of all, she had suspected the truth of James Graham's fate.

And yet, in his heart he didn't believe it to be true. She'd seemed so . . . *innocent.* He'd thought it was merely her injury that made her appear so. But feeling her quake before him as they rode, steadying her with his own hand, he'd sensed her confusion, her vulnerability.

Some sort of scout for Clan Campbell? He couldn't give the notion much credence.

She'd trembled like a newborn foal, terrorized by the sight of Fincharn. And then she'd gotten violently ill, and he'd wondered if she weren't actually an enemy of John's clan Scrymgeour. And yet there had been no recognition between the two of them.

He felt mercy for the poor lass. Wary, but merciful.

And, oh, how he wanted her. The image of those creamy arms and shoulders stayed in his mind, taunting him. And the smooth stretch of her belly. He fantasized about pulling that strange white shirt up and over her head. He knew her breasts would be even paler and more perfect, if such a thing were possible.

MacColla shut his eyes, marshalling his body back to composure.

He'd keep her close until he could discover the truth of her origins.

And God help her if she turned out to be something she didn't appear to be.

❀

Haley paced another frantic circle around the room, dragging her hand hard along the cold stone as she went. The sharp peaks and edges of granite had made her palm raw, but she couldn't stop herself. Something had to make this experience real to her. She pressed her hand harder onto the damp rock, foisting her physical self onto this strange world, hoping her mind would follow.

She was back in time and didn't know how it had happened, just that it had. The evidence was all around her. But it was more than simply the clothes and the Gaelic. More than the godforsaken chill of the castle she now found herself in.

Haley *knew*. She felt it. Felt it in the desolation around her. An animal knowing, bone-deep and as old as man, that she could travel for miles in any direction before encountering another soul. She felt the absence of technology like a sudden silence. Felt nature around her, ascendant, all-powerful, in a way she'd never sensed it before.

Most of all, she felt small and vulnerable and terrified out of her wits.

She stopped. She needed to search again for something, anything that could be used as a weapon. She'd already noted the small candleholder on the table at her bedside. The pitcher full of water could do some damage too. And pocketing the small knife on the tray of cheese and bread had been a no-brainer. Her eyes roved the room. *There must be something else.*

She stormed to the bedside for the hundredth time. Small table with candle, pitcher, basin. She peeled the thin mattress away from the bed. It was packed tightly with straw and made a light crunching sound. There was a woven hammock beneath, attached to the wooden cot. She kicked at the base of it. The thing was too sturdy to remove a leg, and it'd be too readily noticed anyhow.

She picked at the hammock that was to be her seventeenth-century version of a box spring. It was actually a well-made thing, the rope tied off into strong, even knots and pulled over and under into a dense basket weave. Definitely something to keep in mind. Once she severed that rope, though, that was it for the bed.

Oh God, how? She dropped the mattress back into place and sat suddenly. *How?* How had she gotten there?

Her mind kept returning to the gun. And that hideous

painting. A wooden panel bearing the crude likeness of a man and a woman. The man was MacColla, she knew that now. And she was the woman, with a scar on her neck. It had been glistening with fresh blood. But whose?

That weapon and that painting were the two things that linked her to . . . *when*?

She tried to place herself in time. Tried to remember her history. When and how MacColla died. It had been on a battlefield in Ireland. He'd been betrayed, slain. She didn't recall the precise date, just that it would've been in the 1640s. The time of the Wars of the Three Kingdoms, that politically correct name for what some still referred to as the British Civil Wars.

But when, *exactly*? 1645? '46?

And why her? Why Alasdair MacColla? She tried to remember as much as she could about the man. He'd been fierce. Brave. Vicious.

Many claimed he'd invented the Highland Charge, the battlefield strategy that had brought the Highlanders so many triumphs for so many years. Fire off a musket shot, then charge, finishing off the battle with sword and targe.

Such famous MacColla victories. Such infamous Mac-Colla brutality.

He certainly was as huge as the history books said he was. She had never seen an image of the man, and thought with a shudder that the horrific wooden panel might be the only painting of him that ever existed. But his legend hadn't exaggerated his size. His power was clear in his broad chest, tremendous arms, and his thighs, solid as wood, which had cradled her as they rode as if she nestled within the branches of some great tree.

MacColla. With ties to the Highlands and to Ireland. With a bloodthirsty desire to see all Campbells in their graves.

Haley went cold. She'd appeared, somehow, in Campbell's castle. Anyone would believe *she* was a Campbell.

And then she'd asked those idiotic questions about Graham. Dread chilled her, remembering her insistence that

Graham wasn't dead. What would MacColla have thought of that? It would seem like mad chatter to him. The mad chatter of an enemy. *Oh God* . . .

She burst to her feet for one more spin around the room. *Bed, table. Two windows: no glass, openings too narrow for escape. Door: hinges? A possibility. Trunk.*

Haley dropped to her knees, opened the trunk, saw the pile of musty woolen blankets she'd already rifled through a dozen times, and quickly closed it again.

MacColla killed all in his path. And here Haley was, in his path.

She looked at her hands trembling atop the glistening blond wood. *Get ahold of yourself, Hale.* She needed to calm down if she was going to be of any use to herself.

Think logically. He hadn't harmed her. He'd actually saved her from those men.

He could have killed her a dozen times over by now. But instead he'd gently bound her torn muscles. Held her lightly on his horse. All despite the terrible things she'd said.

She looked around with fresh perspective. *A room, not a dungeon.* She didn't seem to be in any imminent danger.

The steadying breath she took sent fresh pain stabbing through her torso. *Damned injury. That's the biggest danger.*

If she were in the past, then fleeing would be certain death. Where would she go? She'd surely starve, freeze, get kidnapped, killed, or some combination thereof.

Haley put her hand to the cold stone floor and gingerly sat down to lean against the trunk.

The past. If she were truly in the past, she could solve the mystery of James Graham's fate. Haley shot up straight, her heart giving a sudden kick.

It was a dream come true for any academic. She could see for herself how it had all played out. Discover for herself if Graham had really died, or if he'd actually survived, living on in secret.

She shivered, deciding then that she needed to know.

But what about her family? They'd be beside themselves, waiting, worrying.

She looked around at her room. The pitcher and washbasin. The candle by her bedside. *The past.*

What if Graham were out there somewhere? She chafed her arms, tamping down the quiver of goose bumps along her skin.

She'd find out, then find her way home. A few weeks of uncertainty for her family, for the opportunity of a lifetime. She'd been so preoccupied with her research when she saw them at the bar, maybe they'd even assume she was just buried in her work.

But where was she? Had that strange and beautiful pistol been the thing connecting her to this time and place? Had it even been made yet?

If she'd actually landed in a Campbell stronghold, they'd likely be somewhere in Argyll.

Good Lord, will I meet Campbell too? She gasped, then gave a bemused laugh. *His* portrait came easily to mind. He'd been a wealthy and powerful man, and as unattractive as his reputation. He had other holdings, but Haley recalled the name Loch Awe now, remembered it being in the west.

She'd need a plan. She'd take her time healing, use it to suss out the world around her, see if she could pinpoint an exact place in time. She wondered if Fincharn had a library. That would be next on the agenda.

Most of all, she needed to pretend to be someone she wasn't. It struck her that she hadn't even told MacColla her last name. She replayed their meeting in her head, and sent up a silent prayer of thanks that she hadn't let any clue to her true origins slip.

For nobody could discover the truth of who she was.

She knew well that men like MacColla would think her a sorceress. Knew what that would mean in the seventeenth-century Highlands. Knew that a man like MacColla would think nothing of snapping her in two, kindling for a pyre fit for a witch.

The methodical reasoning gradually brought Haley into

focus, and the hysteria that had shaken her abated into a distant pulse.

If she couldn't tell her truth, she'd need a new truth.

She thought with sudden clarity that the best lies were embroidered with details rooted in fact.

Though she probably knew what was going on in seventeenth-century Scotland better than most of its inhabitants, Haley's grasp of Scottish Gaelic was moderate at best. Which was not good enough for her to pass as a Highlander.

But Ireland. She did know Ireland. She was a Fitzpatrick of Donegal. She knew her Irish history. Hell, she could even make a decent soda bread. She'd visited her cousins many times through the years. Enough to be able to imagine what the country had been like hundreds of years ago.

She was, and would remain, Haley Fitzpatrick. And from that moment on, she was from Ireland.

Chapter 10

I'm not a prisoner, she thought. *Not a prisoner. I'm not a prisoner.*

Though she kept telling herself MacColla hadn't placed her in a dungeon, after a few hours alone in her room, she was on edge, flinching at every distant noise and voice in the castle. She finally decided the only thing that would pacify her would be to test her theory. Prisoners, after all, weren't able to stroll about freely.

She stepped out her door, heart pounding so fiercely her chest ached from it. The stairs were situated blessedly close to her bedroom. She approached them, trod carefully down.

Haley made her way to the low-ceilinged front hallway, then to the castle's entry door. It was thick, and rounded at the top, with elaborate iron hinges. She placed her hand on the latch. The metal was cool and black.

She kept pausing, waiting for someone to stop her, but no one did.

Gathering her courage, she stepped out. The door had

swung more easily than she'd expected, and she turned to pull it shut behind her.

Breathing deeply, Haley couldn't help but smile. She hadn't realized the cloying mix of smells that filled the castle halls until the crisp air hit her lungs, the fragrance of oak and freshwater replacing the stink of mildew and meat that hung like smog in the indoor air.

Breathtaking scenery surrounded her, hills and distant peaks reaching as far as the eye could see. Drawn by the lake's lush, grassy bank and the tangle of trees growing at its edge, she strolled toward the water.

Her heart had slowed, but still it remained a low, distant hammering, echoing at the back of her mind. She fingered the small knife in the pocket of her skirts and the feel of the cold steel reassured her.

It was just a tiny thing she'd pilfered from a plate of bread and cheese. An old wooden haft attached to a short, serrated blade. She took it out and cradled it in her palm. Closed it in her fist. Her grip was tenuous on such a thin handle. As a weapon, it would be hard to hold, hard to control.

"What are you about, lass?"

She startled, and tucked her hand at her back as she spun around.

MacColla stood there, curiosity wrinkling his features. He wore the same plaid, brushed clean. His enormous sword was gone from between his shoulders, though Haley was quick to note the dagger that hung at his side.

"I thought I'd take a walk. Am I not allowed outside?"

"Aye," he said carefully. "You may go as you will. But you'd best be heedful about it. Don't stray too far." He looked up toward the foothills, then back at her. "Scrymgeour is an ally, but many are not."

Haley wasn't sure how she should respond to that, and so she didn't. MacColla simply remained standing, staring.

"What have you got there?" he asked finally.

"*Huh?*"

"Behind your back, lass. What do you hide?"

She thought about concealing her little weapon. But Mac-Colla wasn't stupid—he knew she had something. He'd probably realize eventually that she'd stolen it, and she figured she'd best just face his question head-on.

Tilting her chin high, Haley said, "It's a knife."

Bringing her hand from behind her back, she opened her fist to reveal the small wood-handled cheese knife resting on her palm.

MacColla relaxed his shoulders, appearing visibly relieved. "Planning a wee feast, is it?" Much to her annoyance, he looked like he was hiding a smile.

"I need a blade."

"You need no such thing."

"I might need to protect myself."

"Protect yourself? What are you on about?"

MacColla's gaze went to the scar on her neck and his eyes grew dark. "Is it because of that?" he asked quietly.

Haley looked away, startled by the question. Although it had defined her in so many ways, she often simply forgot that she bore such a hideous mark on her neck. Gingerly, she ran a finger over the length of it, and shrugged.

"You'd asked what happened . . ." She hesitated, not sure why she was choosing to broach the topic with him. "A man . . . two men. They attacked me."

She heard the sharp draw of his breath, and swung her head to face him. "No, not that. They got scared off. I was fine." She felt a strange need to reassure him and grazed her finger dismissively over the old wound. "Except for this."

"And so you learned how to protect yourself." He gave her a grave and, she thought, approving nod.

"And so I learned to protect myself, yes."

His eyes narrowed. The look he gave her puzzled her. Although she didn't know what it meant, she felt its impact physically. She'd been unmoored, and yet this charged stare somehow grounded her, connected her. She felt . . . understood.

And then he gave her a full-out smile. It wrinkled his

warm, brown eyes and bracketed his mouth with deep lines. Again she spotted the tiny chip in his front tooth.

Alasdair MacColla smiled for her, and a small shiver thrilled up her spine.

He nodded once more to the knife she held. "So, have you a mind to whittle your enemies to death?"

"I thought I'd practice," she said, summoning her dignity.

"Practice cutting cheese?"

She made her face hard and expressionless. Not taking her eyes from him, she spent a moment finding the knife's center of weight, balancing it across her fingertip.

Straightening her back, Haley pinched the blade between her thumb and two fingers. She turned.

Careful to keep her wrist steady, she threw it hard, overhand, grateful for the binding around her ribs that eased her movement.

The small knife spun, found its mark, its scarred wooden hilt quivering in a nearby tree. "I wanted to practice *that*."

"*Gu sealladh sealbh ort!*" MacColla strode to the tree, shaking his head as he marveled at the blade stuck more than an inch deep in the bark. He looked up at her and grinned. "Losh, woman. Where did you learn that?"

"My father." Haley returned his smile despite herself. "He taught me."

"But did he teach you how to fight with that?"

"Yes." She walked to the tree to retrieve her knife. Wiping the blade on her skirts, she added, "Fighting is mostly what he taught me."

"Show me." Skepticism pitched his words, and Haley fought the urge to hurl the blade into his bare foot.

"Love to," she said, with a challenge in her voice. She patted the fabric that was snugged comfortably tight around her torso, testing that it was secure.

He pulled his own dagger from its scabbard. Haley eyed it nervously, roughly twelve inches of glittering steel compared to her rusty little blade.

"That's not a fair fight," she said.

"It never is, aye?"

"Fine." She shrugged. Growing up with five brothers, she knew that fact all too well. "A few ground rules, though. You pull back before that thing cuts me."

"Or?" He smiled wide.

"Or I cut you back."

His laugh was broad. MacColla nodded, the smile still on his face.

She bit her lower lip. Haley had lied. She didn't know the first thing about defending herself against that size dagger.

Her father *had* shown her the basics of street knife fighting, though. It'd been the first thing he'd taught after her attack.

A forward grip, knife in the lead hand. Close the distance. Rapid diagonal slashes. Burst forward into a quick stab.

It couldn't be too different.

Hopping back lightly, she assumed her fighting posture, bouncing on the balls of her feet. MacColla's smile faded a little. He considered her, intrigued.

He surprised Haley when he took his dagger in his rear hand. She knew it was what a Highlander would do if he held a sword in his right. But instead of a broadsword, MacColla wielded only his huge hand, open and ready to swat at her knife.

"*Hm.*" The sound she made was inadvertent. Suddenly the most important thing in the world was that she put up a good fight.

He struck first, coming at her with his left in a lumbering, halfhearted attack. Clearly he thought this a lark.

Haley braced her right arm at a ninety-degree angle. As she was blocking his weak swing, she leaned back and kicked her leg straight out, catching him in the groin.

He grunted, and the smile vanished from his face. His nostrils flared, and she panicked, thinking she'd misstepped badly. She girded herself, ready to be pummeled at any moment.

But he only rubbed at his thigh, regarding her with a new and unsettling look in his eye.

He leapt toward her suddenly, and she startled with the abruptness of his attack. Skittering backward, she slammed into a tree, dropping her knife from her hand.

MacColla kicked the small blade aside, chuckling. Resting his foot on a stump, he asked, "Do you yield?"

Haley frowned. She wasn't about to yield.

She watched him resheathe his dagger. His cavalier pose put him just slightly off balance. Giving him a sweet smile, she stepped toward him.

And then she lunged. Ducking low, she went for his leg, catching his knee as she rolled to the ground.

"*Dògan!*" he barked as he toppled like a felled tree, slamming the breath from both of them.

Haley hadn't planned beyond that little maneuver and scrambled to untangle her legs from his. But he kept her pinned as he lay beneath her, his brawny thighs like vises.

He chuckled, coughed once, then, chuckling some more, slapped a hand to her bottom. "Well done, that," he muttered.

His hand didn't move from her, and Haley went rigid, unnerved by the oddly intimate position.

MacColla was breathing hard, his other hand on his belly.

And then it seemed to hit him too. She felt him grow still.

Mindful of her ribs, he placed his hands at her hips and silently rolled them both to standing.

He gave only a brusque nod before he stalked off. His plaid swirled behind him, the tail of it swaying with each long stride.

It was the swiftest and, Haley mused, possibly the only retreat Alasdair MacColla had ever marched in his life.

❈

MacColla slammed the side of his fist into a tree, then muttered a curse as he shook out his hand.

He stormed back to Fincharn, unable to think on anything else but the lass's scar. A thick twine of skin marring her otherwise perfect neck. He thought about the man who dared cut her, and irrational rage choked him.

MacColla sidestepped, lunging to slam his fist into another tree.

He didn't know how, but this strange woman had endeared herself to him. He understood what it was to have something stolen, understood the taste for revenge. He knew well what it was to suffer injury, and instead of seeking retreat, turning around to fight.

It was a warrior's impulse. He was a warrior. And he recognized the warrior in this Haley.

It touched him. Made him respect her in a way he'd not felt before. What woman lived with such courage that she'd face an enemy with naught but a cheese knife?

MacColla softened at the thought. Let a smile turn his lips.

What sort of woman indeed.

Chapter 11

"MacColla headed west." Anticipation hummed in Nicholas Purdon's voice. "My men tracked them through the passes, but lost the trail near the eastern shore of Loch Awe."

"Aye." Campbell nodded, speaking his thoughts aloud. "He'd head to water."

"My thoughts precisely." Purdon leaned back in his chair, looking satisfied. He stroked the limp brown hair at the crown of his head, brow furrowed in the way of men much impressed with their own wisdom.

Campbell eyed him, sitting to his left at Inveraray's dining table. He couldn't fault the man; Purdon had indeed done a fine job. But he had yet to bring MacColla down.

The major thought he'd succeeded, but he had much to learn. And he was wise to be looking to the Campbell for his tutelage.

Campbell spared a glance at the witch seated at the far end of the table. The flickering candlelight cast deep shadows over her sharp features. He'd thought to ignore her, and Purdon wisely followed his lead.

"You did well." Campbell raised his glass to the major.

Purdon gave a quick, gratified smile and said, "It should be a simple enough endeavor. There are but a handful of castles to search along the loch."

"Make no mistake, Purdon. You did a fine job, but your work's not yet complete." Campbell sipped his brandy, deep in thought. "You'd be wise not to underestimate my enemy. MacColla is a savage, well accustomed to dirt for a pillow. I'd not put it past him to choose a canopy of leaves to a roof over his head."

"But he travels with two women. Surely they'd not bear up for long under those conditions."

"Indeed." Campbell picked a crust of bread from the plate before him and began to toy with it. "I can't imagine the man will linger in one place for long."

Two women, he thought. Would the one they'd called forth be able to survive such circumstances?

"Witch," he called to the far end of the table. "The woman you summoned, where does she come from?"

"I know not," she replied, her tone matter-of-fact.

Campbell exchanged an irritated glance with the major. "You know not," he said flatly.

Finola shrugged and, giving her full attention to the plate before her, took a delicate spoonful of stew and began to chew slowly. Swallowing, she returned her gaze to the men. A placid, inquiring look was on her face, as if she had no idea what the problem might be.

"Are you quite done?" Campbell snarled.

"You forget your intent," Finola said calmly. "Your desire was to kill MacColla. Not this woman." She tilted her head. "When your foe wields a sword, is it the sword that you fight? Though a blade can cut the life from you, the blade is not your enemy. The one whose hand holds the weapon. He is your only enemy. To lose sight of this is to lose the battle."

"Do you threaten me, woman?" Campbell's fury boiled high in his chest. *Witchcraft.* A sport for women and fools. He'd chosen this path in error. This Finola was a weapon indeed, but one with no aim. The powers of black magic seemed haphazard, like a top set to spinning. Once put in motion, there was no way to control its course, its intent. "I ask you a question and you give me nonsense in return."

"To put a fine point on it," Purdon spoke up in tones meant to soothe, "where does MacColla ride? Does he sail for Ireland? North to the Highlands? Or first south to Kintyre?"

Finola merely giggled, a disturbingly feminine cascade of notes from high to low.

"Where is he?" Campbell shouted, slamming his hand on the table. "How powerful can your witchcraft be if you're unable to answer simple questions?"

He gestured broadly to the table, the walls. "I've fed you. You have water. Candles give fire all around. What more can you need? Cast your runes, read leaves, toss bones. I care not what you do—"

"You presume too much," she snapped, her giggling eclipsed by a severity that sent a chill through the room. Her eyes were dagger-sharp on the two men. "You cannot expect me to scry *here*." Finola looked around her in disgust.

"Oh I expect it of you." Campbell's voice was cool like glass. "You told me you were the most powerful witch in all Scotland. Now prove your worth."

They locked gazes for a long moment.

"To dare the fates so is a fool's gambit." Finola reached into her robe and pulled out a small suede pouch. She carefully tugged at the thong tying it and removed a palm-sized bundle wrapped in dark velvet.

"What is that?" Campbell asked sharply. He shoved his chair back from the table and strode to her.

His patience wore thin. She spoke of fates and portents, and yet her magic had wrought nothing but uncertainty. Though her tricks roused his curiosity, he'd soon pursue ventures bearing more empirical evidence of success. Swords, not scrying stones.

Sucking at her teeth, Finola slowly unfolded the fabric. "'Tis a *keek-stane*," she told him, her voice distant. She smoothed the velvet into a square, gently cradling the ball-shaped object into its folds. "For the scrying of visions."

Campbell leaned in to see more clearly. The ambient candlelight seemed dimmer somehow, insufficient to light this object. Squinting, he realized it was glass, the back of it painted black.

It wasn't completely rounded, as he'd thought at first. The front of the *keek-stane* was concave, and marred by a deep crack. The flaw was a black so dark, it seemed to deny the light.

Finola stroked the face of it, traced her fingers around its edge. She panted a few short breaths, and then a keening so high and so sharp screeched from her, the men clapped their hands to their ears.

Her shriek stopped suddenly. Rolling her eyes back into her head, the witch began to chant,

> *Two sights that I might see,*
> *Alasdair MacColla, come to me.*
> An da shealladh,
> *That I might see,*
> *Alasdair MacColla Ciotach MacDomhnaill,*
> *Come to me.*
> An da shealladh,
> *Two sights soar free,*
> *Alasdair MacColla mhic Gilleasbuig MacDomhnaill,*
> *Appear to me.*

Opening her eyes, Finola exhaled an impossibly long breath.

She leaned close to her *keek-stane*, clutched it between her palms. She gasped.

"What?" Campbell cried. He saw nothing but black on the face of her scrying stone. "What do you see, witch?"

Finola eased her eyes shut once more, slowly removing her hands from the glass. Tenderly, she kissed each palm.

"Beware, Campbell." She looked up at the men standing agitated beside her. "The tides have turned. I can no longer see if the woman brings MacColla's downfall—or your own."

He recoiled. Long had he suspected her witchery to be folly. But this was too much. He'd seen naught but blackness in her fool stone, and he knew now he'd been right to withhold his complete trust.

"What does that mean?" Campbell shouted, and swung his arm back to dash his cup against the hearth. "How could this foreigner, this *woman*, be a danger to *me*?"

Ignoring Campbell, she turned a hard eye to Purdon, who was visibly taken aback. "You too have much to fear."

Campbell fought to keep his hands from the witch's neck. How was he to know if she played him false? "How dare you address my man and not me? You are both in my employ. You will speak straight, woman, and speak straight to *me*."

"I know not what the vision says about you, Campbell." Finola was maddeningly placid. It smoothed the lines from her face and made her pale skin seem waxen in the candlelight. "Simply that your course is no longer a wise one."

"Then I am done with you. Done with your . . . black magic," he sputtered. "I see no use in it. Your talents are merely attempts to harness smoke. You speak the truth of reflections cast in muddy waters."

Campbell stormed away from her. He paused at the foot of the stairs and spun back to her. "You've been paid. Leave now. Your work is done."

"You neglect me at your peril." Finola's tone was like black ice on a darkened lake, its glassy surface giving lie to the roiling waters beneath.

"So be it, witch."

Chapter 12

He didn't understand it. MacColla slammed the cup onto the table, sending the amber liquid sloshing. Jean's cheeks reddened and she stared, stricken, down at her stew bowl, visibly forcing herself to chew and swallow her meal. He felt bad to have upset the lass, but he couldn't stop himself. "And you're certain he said disband?"

"Aye," Scrymgeour replied warily, "the king's letter asked that all Royalist battalions disband at once. He specifically mentioned you, Alasdair. Asking *you* to disband," he added gravely.

"Disband . . ." MacColla growled. All this talk of kings and letters. It meant nothing. The king knew nothing of Campbell. Knew nothing of MacColla's fight, of the wrongs that needed avenging.

He felt a surge of anger and frustration. The world of politics churned on, and here he sat with a glass of whisky and two lasses by his side, when what he really required was to face his enemy across a battlefield with naught but the sword at his back.

"Aye," Scrymgeour said gravely. "If you continue this

feuding with the Campbell, you'll be in defiance of the king's orders."

"Whatever my fight with Campbell, disbanding Royalist forces won't stop the king's enemies on the battlefield." He stared at Scrymgeour across the table, the weight of his glare something most men would turn from.

"I fight for Clan MacDonald," MacColla continued. "For land, for honor. These are things more ancient than the king, more ancient than Parliament, or the Covenanters, or any of the many enemies set on bringing down Charles."

MacColla was breathing hard, trying to make sense of this turn of events. He would make Campbell pay for his wrongs, and fighting was the only way. If it meant he were in opposition to the king, then so be it.

He'd sacrificed much for King Charles. Fought with James Graham against Campbell and the Covenanters, in defense of the king's own standard.

His lips twitched, face souring in anger, thinking of the countless men he'd lost. So many MacDonald clansmen, fallen.

"I'll not back down," MacColla said.

He tilted his glass once more to his lips. There'd been a day when he thought his service to Charles would be rewarded. He'd thought perhaps the king would grant him lands. A title.

But to request MacColla's submission instead?

"I'll not know what he thinks," Scrymgeour said carefully, "asking his supporters—"

"What he thinks?" MacColla interrupted, raising his voice. "He's a madman. What he thinks . . ."

Scrymgeour stiffened at such treacherous words.

Haley ventured quietly, "King Charles . . ." All heads whirled to look at her. She cleared her throat, and tried again. "King Charles thinks that if he can get you to disband, it would demonstrate to all his enemies that he's sincere in his attempts at brokering a peace."

MacColla stared at her, his eyes flat. Finally he gave her

a slow nod. "'Tis too late for a peace." And though his voice was hushed, it was cold steel. "I'll not disarm. I'll remain in arms. And if it's in defiance of king and Covenanter both, then so be it."

MacColla drank deeply then, a great swig from his glass that he swallowed back with gritted teeth. He'd thought himself isolated before. But he'd never back down from his fight with Campbell. If that made him nobody's ally, well, he wasn't in search of friends. He was hunting for enemies.

He glared around the table, challenging any who would question such a traitorous move. Scrymgeour sat at the end opposite him, nervously eyeing MacColla over the lip of his crystal tumbler.

The strange lass sat across from his sister. She was the only one at the table who returned his gaze evenly. He looked at her and met a frank stare, open but unreadable. "And you," he barked at her. "How do you know of such things? How can I be assured you're not Campbell's spy?"

She opened her mouth to speak, and he interrupted. "Tell me about this strange name of yours." MacColla picked the cup back up and poured himself another healthy two fingers of whisky.

"Haley." Her voice was even. "Haley Fitzpatrick."

"Fitzpatrick . . ." he mused. "An Irish lass, is it?"

"From Donegal," she announced, sitting a little straighter.

"Truly, now? I've known Fitzpatricks, but I've not ever heard such a strange name as *Haley*." Eyes not budging from hers, he took a big swig from his glass. "I'd know how you ended up so far from home, Mistress Haley. Or is it you were kidnapped just as my Jean was?"

Uh-oh. She hadn't thought that far into her backstory. She quickly decided a change of topic was in order.

"Now that's a funny story. My name, that is." She didn't actually know *where* her parents had gotten the name. Haley imagined her mom had heard it somewhere, liked the sound of it, and that was that. She knew she couldn't speak the truth, though, so she decided to freestyle a bit.

"My mother thought me a noisy . . . *bairn*." She knew the Scottish slang terms, and she drew on them now to embellish her story. "Strong lungs. Hale and hearty . . . *aye*?" The Scottish tic had a pleasant feel as it rolled off her tongue, and her face loosened into a smile. "And so they called me Haley."

MacColla stared silent, and just when she felt the smile begin to fade from her face, he erupted into a great laugh. He slammed his hand on the table, clinked his glass against hers. He saw that it was empty, and he quickly refilled it.

She picked up the cool, heavy cup. Waved it under her nose. Her eyes immediately teared. The stuff was one step above rotgut. She held it up to the candlelight, wondering if it would make her blind. *Great. I'll drink myself blind then I can beg for alms in front of Holyrood Palace.*

Blinking her eyes shut tight, she put the cool glass to her forehead. *Shit. Old Scotland. How the fuck . . . ?* Opening them again, she glanced around the table. Jean, nervous as ever. God forbid *she* make a peep.

Scrym . . . whatever his name was. Staring at Mac-Colla. Probably terrified MacColla would decide he didn't like him *or* his news, and tear off his head and eat it for dessert.

MacColla had been furious to hear the contents of Scrymgeour's letter from the king. Haley followed the conversation for a while, then the truly fucked-upness of her situation hit her. That she was listening hungrily to hot gossip about . . . King Charles the *first*?

She looked at the glass in her hand. *What the hell?* "*Slàinte*," she said, lifting it in his direction, then tipped it back fast, downing the contents in one burning gulp.

"*Aaaaeh*," she exclaimed, and her upper body gave a slow, comical shudder. Haley slammed the glass on the table, slid it toward MacColla, and smiled through the tears in her eyes.

She didn't want to consider the strange feeling of satisfaction that warmed her upon hearing his shocked laugh explode in response.

Haley watched him pour more whisky into her glass, vaguely aware of the uncomfortable glances exchanged between the other two at the table. The triumph she felt upon hearing Jean's chair scrape away from the table was one she didn't deny.

"Jean," Scrymgeour said earnestly. He seemed flustered by his friend's turbulent behavior, and he directed his full attentions to MacColla's sister. "May I . . ."

"Aye," the girl whispered gratefully, and Haley flashed her a broad smile.

"Please, John," Jean told him nervously.

"If you'll excuse us, Alasdair." Scrymgeour was on his feet and helping Jean from her chair in an instant. "Mistress Fitzpatrick." He nodded coolly in Haley's direction.

"Mister Scrym . . . geour." It was almost certainly the wrong title for the man, but she doubted he fully understood her anyway. The drink had burned through her like thousand-proof spirits, thickening her tongue. To make up for it, she flashed as composed a smile as she could muster, honestly hoping the effects were more drawing room than frat house.

An uncomfortable silence fell between her and Mac-Colla the moment the other two left. She wracked her brain for something to say. Mostly she wasn't ready to head back to her own room for the night. She'd need a tad more anesthetizing before she could ever fall asleep.

Besides, the issue of James Graham's death had become an obsession. And here she was, sitting with likely one of the only living men who knew the true fate of the famous war hero. Maybe if she got MacColla drunk, he'd spill the beans.

"*Uh* . . ." she floundered. "They say it was Saint Patrick who introduced the distilling of whisky to Ireland." Or so her father had claimed through the years, with a zeal that implied the sipping of his Jameson was just about divinely inspired.

"From the hand of the Almighty Himself, is it?"

It wasn't until she looked up and saw the playfulness in his eyes that she realized he wasn't serious.

"*Mhmm.*" Unsure of what to say, Haley took another big sip. Her shiver was more subtle this time, but she still had to hiss a breath out through gritted teeth. "All right. That's it." She slammed her own hand down then. "Do you have a coin or something?"

"A coin?"

"Yes, you know, money. A coin."

"I . . ." He looked hesitant.

"Oh"—she waved a hand dismissively—"my charming company is free. I just need a little help gulping this stuff down. Come on, MacColla." She acted as if she'd been slighted. "Trust me."

"Oh, I *don't* trust you, lass." His voice was cold and flat, his face unreadable, staring at her. Just when she began to feel nervous that she'd crossed a line, MacColla burst into laughter.

"Don't fash yourself." He reached across the table and pinched her chin. "Trust you I don't." He rifled through his sporran and retrieved a silver coin. "But I will listen to you, aye?" He flicked it to Haley and she caught it easily.

She fingered the cool metal between her fingers, contemplating the man before her. MacColla was clearly so much more than the one-dimensional brute history had painted him to be. She studied him. Up to that point, all she'd really registered were his strong, swarthy features, and his intensity. But his face and body were relaxed now. Though his eyes were hooded and his expression impossible to read, she imagined his features were as open as he ever let them get.

Mostly she couldn't get over how attractive he was. Big and dark and strong, with flashes of warmth that melted some secret place at her core. Haley didn't want to admit to herself that she increasingly sought those flashes, encouraged them, just to see his features soften and feel the gratifying click of his gaze with hers.

"Okay," she said quickly and a little breathlessly, "here's the deal. You have to bounce the coin into the cup. If you make it, great. If you don't, you have to drink the contents of the cup."

He stared incredulously for a moment. "Are you certain, lass?"

"What?" She looked up and saw the bemused glint in his eye. "Ohhh, I get it. You think you might beat me."

He laughed and reached for the coin, flicking it onto the table in a single motion. It clanked hard against the wood, flew up, and clattered onto the floor.

"Are *you* certain, MacColla?" She smiled and nodded at his glass for him to drink.

She reached her leg out and, pinning the coin with her foot, dragged it toward her, and then picked it up from the floor. Huffing on the silver, she made as if to polish it, holding his gaze to hers all the while.

Haley leaned over and, eyeing low along the surface of the table, shifted the glass as if she were making minute and critical calibrations.

Her preternatural skill at the drinking game Quarters had been legend around her twin brothers' Boston College dorm. She thought she might as well get something out of it. "If I make it, you have to answer a question."

"A question?" His eyes watched her hand bob up and down, warming up to her toss. "What manner of question?"

"Just"—she gently let go of the coin, which bounced back up to plunk easily into her glass—"a regular old question."

His laughter exploded through the room and he startled them both when he reached over to clap her on the shoulder. "You're a wily one."

"Thanks." Smiling at his approving nod, she slid the glass in his direction. "I'm a woman of many talents."

"Aye?" He raised his brows in question.

The double entendre made her blush. "Aye . . . what?"

"What's your question, lass?"

"Oh that. Of course." Haley wondered what she should

ask. She couldn't just up and broach the topic of James Graham right away.

While she considered, again he tried to get the coin in his glass, and failed.

Before she could think too much about it, she heard herself ask, "So what drives you, MacColla?"

"Drives me?" he asked, and downed the whisky.

"You know, what compels you?"

He shrugged as if addressing the simplest question in the world. He refilled the glass and slid it back to her. "To kill Campbell, of course."

She dropped the coin onto the table and bounced it neatly back into the cup.

Sliding it back his way, she asked, "So that's the most important thing to you? More than family even?"

He tried again and missed. He drank then gave his head a quick shake. Haley made a mental note to slow it down. She wanted to get the man drunk enough to talk about James Graham, not put him under the table.

"You misunderstand," he told her. He refilled the cup and eyed it in relation to the coin in his fingers. "My fight with the Campbell *is* about family. Clan *is* the most important thing to me."

"No, I mean . . . Here," she said impatiently, and scooted her chair nearer to his. Haley took MacColla's hand and bent his wrist slightly. "I mean a family like, you know, a wife. Are you betrothed?" She tried to ignore the warmth of his hand in hers, the broad knuckles and the thick knots of muscle at his forearm. Haley guided his arm slowly up and down, demonstrating the proper move. "Try like that."

He slammed the coin down and it popped up and hit him in the forehead. She burst out laughing, and he looked at her accusingly.

"No."

"I'm sorry," she giggled.

"I meant, no, I'm not betrothed."

"Oh." Suddenly the air felt too hot. Haley had to concentrate on keeping her tone nonchalant. "Why not?"

"It's never struck me."

"Struck you?"

"Aye." He chuckled and rubbed his thigh, evoking the place where she'd kicked him. "I can say truthfully that you're the first lass ever *to* strike me."

Haley knew she was supposed to laugh then, but somehow it didn't come.

A charged silence hung once more between them. She refilled the glass, trying to think of something to say.

He took the coin from the table and stared at it, disgruntled.

"You need to be gentler," she said finally. She took his hand in hers, adjusting his wrist even more. "You're, you're . . ." A nervous laugh escaped her. She gathered herself then added as seriously as she could, "It's like you're trying to drive the thing clear through the table. Just"—she guided his hand, and the coin bounced down and into the cup—"release it."

He drank and refilled his glass. She was acutely aware of his eyes on her as she took aim for her own turn.

Just as she dropped the coin, he said, "A simple *release*, eh?" The unexpected huskiness of his voice made her hand slip, and the coin clattered to the floor.

"Now your turn to drink, Fitzpatrick." He nudged the glass toward her, the devil in his eyes. "And it seems fair that I can now ask something of you."

"*Fitzpatrick*, huh?" A small, sad smile crooked her mouth. Her house had always been filled with a parade of her brothers' friends, all of whom had, at one point or another, called her brothers just that.

"Aye, that is your name, is it not?"

"Is that your question?"

"You ken it's not." Smiling, he nodded at her glass, indicating that she still needed to empty it.

"I know, I know." She picked up her glass, willing away the anticipatory roiling of her belly. Accustomed now to its bite, she gulped the whisky back and this time actually enjoyed the feel of its smoky fingers wending their way through her veins.

He merely stared silently at her. "I've never seen a lass able to stomach whisky."

"Well," she managed, "they do say it's 'spunkier than tea,' right?"

"Do they, then?"

"Yeah, like the song." She felt loose now. Not yet drunk, but pleasantly tipsy. She poured another dram into the cup, and, holding it aloft, she sang a line from her father's favorite Irish drinking tune. "You're sweeter, stronger, decenter, you're spunkier than tea." She let it rip, her Irish brogue blooming round and thick in imitation of her dad. "Ohh whisky you're me darlin' drunk or sohhh-ber."

He laughed again, and she laughed too, from deep in her belly, then instantly clutched her hands to her torso in pain.

"Och, easy lass." MacColla shot to his feet. He looked unsure what to do, and took up the decanter to pour more into her glass. "More of this might help the pain."

"Oh really?"

"Oh, aye, lass."

"*Uhh . . .*" Her tipsy good cheer was suddenly replaced by a searing melancholy. "It's *not* helping." The reason she wanted to get drunk in the first place slammed into her gut, as great a shock to her system as her torn muscles.

She was trapped, somehow sent back to the seventeenth century. Alone but for this man, famous for his vicious feats in battle. Alone, and with no way to get back.

"Come." His voice was so low, she wasn't entirely certain he'd spoken. And then she felt his hands. He'd moved to stand behind her, to massage the bruised muscles of her back and sides.

She'd studied those hands earlier, could picture them now in her mind's eye. The fingers, long and strong, and his palms, wide, coarse. Those huge hands spanned her back easily. Moved up and down, gently probing the tender spots between ribs until he found the source of her pain. Haley had never considered herself a small woman—she *wasn't* a small woman—and yet she felt almost delicate in that broad, muscular grip.

"I . . ." She attempted to speak, but couldn't. She had to get ahold of herself. This was entirely unexpected. *Alasdair MacColla.* Giving her a back massage? It was too much. Desperate to regain the upper hand, her voice cracked, "What can you tell me of James Graham?"

He stilled for just a moment, then continued. "I think the question is, lass, what can *you* tell *me*?"

"That he was captured."

"Aye."

"An . . . and . . ." His thumb grazed a knot. She gasped, and MacColla kneaded it slowly, tenderly. She hadn't realized how clenched her muscles had been until his fingers found the knot, released it, loosening a warm rush of blood through her torso. Her rib cage opened, and she took her first deep inhale since her injury. *Oh God, pure heaven.*

Wait. Concentrate. "And then . . . then he was paraded through the countryside."

"All know that."

She blinked her eyes for a moment, gathering her wits. The sudden openness in her chest made her light-headed. "And . . . hanged?" she ventured.

"So they say."

"*Mmhm.*" *So they say. That's just it*, she thought. *Fact? Or hearsay?*

Haley was about to probe more, when MacColla's thumb grazed the underside of her breast. It seemed innocent enough. He was intent on massaging her tight muscles. The brush was accidental. And yet, even as her muscles released, her breasts beaded tight. Her breath came short, despite the newfound openness of her lungs.

"But . . . but did anyone *see* . . ." Her breath hitched. A quick, sharp inhalation. His fingers now, rubbing along the sensitive slope just underneath her nipple.

"See what, Fitzpatrick?" His tone was no-nonsense.

Simply mild curiosity. He seemed not to have any suspicion of what she asked, or of what his touch was doing to her.

"See . . ." *Oh God.* She turned slightly. Purposefully. Angling toward him. She had to know if his touch was deliberate. God help her, she hoped it was.

"Aye?" His voice was ragged, low. Did she hear an echo of her own desire there?

A throat cleared, and MacColla was instantly apart from her. It was Scrymgeour, standing in the doorway, watching.

"I thought we could retire to my sitting room, MacColla." Scrymgeour's eyes scanned the room, and Haley wasn't sure if what she read there was judgment, curiosity, surprise, or a little of all three.

"Aye." MacColla's nod was curt. "If . . . if you'll excuse me," he told her.

Excuse him. Were his words loaded? Had he meant to touch her just then? Had she sensed his intent, or was she simply imagining it?

"Yes," she replied. "Of course."

As he left, she shuddered an exhale. The movement caused a fresh twinge, sharp along her side. But with it came focus.

And so this time, Haley welcomed her pain.

Chapter 13

"Are you trying to kill me?" Haley pulled the blanket over her face, turning her back to MacColla's sister. A drumbeat pounded in her head, and daylight brought it to a crescendo that she thought would cleave her skull.

Her eyeballs hurt, her throat was dry, her brain was scrambled, and, whatever that home-distilled whisky was, it had given her a hangover so painful she imagined surely that, if Jean only listened hard enough, she'd be able to discern the thumping in Haley's head with her ears alone.

And then there was the whole issue of safety. She tried not to consider the various technologies employed by modern distillers that made liquor fit for consumption. The concept of pasteurization had occurred to her more than once, each time bringing with it a fresh throbbing that reverberated all the way down her spine.

Jean made a small, exasperated sound, and Haley peeked tentatively out from beneath the blanket. The girl was still there, standing stricken, bearing the cup she'd brought. The white viscous liquid wavered in her trembling hand, and Haley added nausea to her list of ailments.

"Really, Jean," she croaked, "I'm grateful, but . . ."

"It always helps my brothers, aye?" She took a step closer to Haley's bed. "They call it their Morning Glory. Though I dare say, you missed the morning by a fair piece."

She ignored the sharp pang at the memory of her own brothers, shining bright in her mind's eye. How long had she been away? Would they know by now she was gone?

Oh guys . . . forgive me. Then quick on the heels of that came a bright light, an idea like a cartoon bulb flashing over her head. *Brothers.* Haley hadn't considered it before, but the best source of information could be standing right in front of her. Of course MacColla would've had brothers. She'd known of his father, knew vaguely of an older brother, but that was the extent of her knowledge. If she ingratiated herself with his sister, she might be able to learn more about the man. And in so doing, perhaps gain some insight into the fate of James Graham.

Haley grudgingly took the glass, and the smile that bloomed onto the girl's face was startling. She was downright pretty when she wasn't pulling her meek act, and the realization made it almost worthwhile.

Until she smelled the stuff in the glass.

Shuddering, she quickly foisted it back in Jean's direction. The girl merely smiled and shook her head.

"Okay," Haley conceded, "but can I at least hear what's in it?"

"Drink it first. Once you see it down, then I'll tell."

Haley scowled. Was that a smile on Jean's face? She sniffed the liquid again. A little foul and a little sweet. The worst combination.

Haley held it up to the light. Opaque, grayish white. She shrugged. What could it hurt? Her current hangover had to be about as low as a human could go.

"Bottoms up," she said, and tossed the glass back.

Her stomach clenched in revolt. The shivers she'd experienced drinking MacColla's whisky were nothing compared to the revulsion that crawled up her body now, convulsing her muscles and turning her stomach.

"Oh God." Haley wiped the tears from her eyes.
"What . . . ?"

"Eggs. Sugar. Cream. And a dram of whisky."

"Oh God, you *are* trying to kill me."

"That's what my brothers say."

Unreasonable hatred swelled in Haley. "You're enjoying this." She mustered every evil look she could and shot
them all in Jean's direction.

"Aye, and they say that too." His sister smiled again, and
Haley didn't know what to make of this new side of her.
Jean took the glass back and wiped Haley's mouth with a
rag. And Haley was so stunned, she allowed it. Jean added
saucily, "And they always manage to survive."

Haley had to chuckle then, at the unexpected verve. She
hadn't known MacColla's sister had it in her.

"I suppose you make them drink it too?"

"Oh, aye, they'd not tell *me* no."

"I . . ."

"You don't believe me." It was a statement, and Haley
realized it was true. She'd discounted Jean, and the girl had
known it. She tucked the rag at her waist and added, "Well,
not all can act as you do. Just because I don't swagger
around—"

"I don't swagger—" Haley protested.

"Because I don't swagger about like a man, doesn't
mean I can't get a man to listen to me. I dare say, my brothers mind me more than they do each other."

"Why aren't you married?" The question struck Haley
suddenly. Surely Jean was old by seventeenth-century standards.

"I was." Though her tone brooked no questions, the pain
that flickered momentarily across Jean's features was impossible to miss. "He died. I'm a widow."

"I . . . Oh. I see." And, for the first time, Haley really did
see. Jean stood before her, long black hair, delicate features. So pretty, so young. And yet, by seventeenth-century
standards, her life might as well be over. She'd go from
brother's house to brother's house, hoping for the best. And

the best would likely be finding some old widower to re-marry. Haley felt like a heel. "I'm sorry."

Jean looked at her for a long time, then finally spoke. "Aye. I see that you are. I don't ken where you come from, lass. Or who your family is to have given you such an impression of yourself." She sat on the edge of the bed, her proximity softening her words. "But you'd do well to remember, lucky you are to walk about as you do. Fighting, talking, drinking like a lad. Other lasses would, could they."

Her message was clear. Jean was speaking about herself. *She'd* walk about just as independently, if she could. *She* would speak her mind as freely.

"Yes." Haley sat up, and in the back of her mind registered that the deafening throb had abated to something approximating simply a really bad headache. "You're right, of course. I'm far from home now, though." She leaned back against the headboard. She needed an ally, and a possible good source of information to boot. "I suppose I would do well to remember that," Haley conceded. "Will you help me, then? Help me remember where I am now?"

Jean looked taken aback. Then pleased. "Oh aye." She smiled, hesitated, then reached over to finger the black fabric of the dress that Haley still wore. Though she'd bathed, she had no other choice but to put the thing back on, despite the fact that it could just about get up and walk away of its own volition. "Can I dress you first, though?"

A small smile was Haley's answer.

❈

Daylight was a flare burning through his consciousness. He'd drank too much. He'd lost control and drank too much.

MacColla rolled over in bed. Tried to push the strange woman out of his mind. Tried and failed.

Who was she? Haley Fitzpatrick, she'd said, of Donegal. The muscle in his thigh twitched with the memory of the gunshot that had almost killed him so many years ago, battling in that very county. He needed to uncover how it was this Fitzpatrick lass found herself so far from her homeland.

How she'd ended up in Campbell's castle, of all places. Was she Campbell's partner, or his prey? His thinking tended toward the latter, but how could he be certain?

Haley Fitzpatrick. With an accent and bearing like none *he'd* ever seen in Ireland.

If only he could be in a room with her without getting so distracted.

He scowled, rubbing his brow.

She'd such startling depths in those gray eyes. Physical strength and prowess like no other woman he'd ever met had. And such strange impulses. Like drinking him nigh under the table. He'd have thought her little drinking game overly masculine had she not so charmed him—and nearly unwittingly seduced him.

He curled up tight, cursing the hardness that seized him at the simple thought of it. He who normally contained his urges as good as any friar, and there he'd been, rubbing her back and even her breast with his hand, God help him.

MacColla tossed onto his back and examined the timber planks of the ceiling overhead.

It had been her questions of James Graham that had thrown him most of all. What game was she playing at? Getting him drunk, then pressing him once again on Graham's fate.

Could she be in league with the Campbell? The thought had occurred to him before, and he'd discounted it.

He'd do well not to discount anything about this one in the future.

Chapter 14

She peeked out from her bedroom, then ducked back in again. Haley had spent the day in bed and she was starving. Absolutely and completely famished. She assured herself that such a rapid recovery was attributed to rest and not to Jean's potion, but her body felt so clear and so normal, she had to wonder.

Dinner had come and gone hours ago, and the halls of Fincharn were ominously dark. She inhaled. The faint aroma of fresh bread lingered in the hall, and she wondered just how long it took for a person to die from hunger.

She tiptoed out and was immediately immersed in shadow. Her rumbling stomach nagged her, though, driving her to take another step. The kitchen wasn't too far, and she told herself she could probably feel her way there in the dark. Though the castle was silent, she knew she wouldn't be able to sleep until she had something in her belly.

The place was dreary and drafty, and a gust of cold air whooshed down the hallway and up her skirts. Tugging her plaid wrapper more tightly around her shoulders, Haley slid her foot in front of her to take another tentative step.

The scrape of her leather slipper along the flagstone sounded overly loud to her ears, which trained out into the darkness as if her sense of hearing could help her find her way.

She tapped and slid her other foot slowly in front of her, and heard the quick, quiet patter of tiny feet scuttling in response, somewhere just in front of her.

Rats. Haley sprang back into her room, cursing the shrill *meep* that burst from her lips.

She leaned against the doorjamb to catch her breath, feeling like her heart might pound out of her chest. The guttering stub of a candle on her bedside was a welcome and glorious blaze compared to the absolute blackness of the halls. She'd have taken the thing with her, if she weren't so afraid it might finally sputter out for good.

Haley shook her head. *So stupid.* She was probably skilled enough to hold her own against the worst of Boston muggers, and yet she couldn't bear the thought of a few mice scurrying about.

"I called you a hellcat . . ."

She *meeped* again, putting her hand to her chest, and spun to see MacColla's silhouette in the shadows just outside her door.

A muted laugh rumbled in his throat. "But I think mayhap you turn into a wee hell-*mouse* with the waxing of the moon."

"I'm starving," she moaned at once.

"Ah. I ken what's come to pass." He stepped into her room, and the candle cast his shadow ominously up the wall and along the ceiling. "My sister administered you her wee tonic, did she not?"

"*Ugh.*" Haley shuddered. "Did you drink it too?"

"Aye." He smiled. "The sight of it always makes me quail like a sheep at the shearing. But every time, at just about this very time, I wake up feeling as though I could spit a buck and eat it whole."

"Oh, yeah." Her mouth watered at the thought of roast anything. Knees wobbling, she dropped to sit at the side of her bed. A whole buck sounded real good at the moment. "Totally."

"Come, then." A sly grin spread across MacColla's face as he reached his hand to her.

She stared warily.

"Come now, I won't bite you. Not yet, at least." He winked, and she merely sat and stared. "Och, lass. Truly."

"Where are we going?"

"To feed you."

Haley took his hand, and pushed from her mind the sensation of it, broad and warm, enveloping hers. Instead, she followed MacColla into the blackness of the halls. Once again, the chill air swirled up her skirts and her gasp elicited more scuttling sounds from far down the hall.

"You know . . ." Haley froze, automatically grabbing his arm tight. She whispered, "I think I can wait til morning. Really. I—"

His only response was a barely perceptible chuckle as he swept her up and easily into his arms.

She gasped. Haley wasn't a small woman, and yet his effortless gesture made her feel almost delicate. Not to mention the flutter of relief and gratitude she felt at being up and away from whatever rodents might be creeping about.

But this taste of needing him brought with it a tiny stab of irritation.

"You'll fall," she hissed. "How can you see?"

"With my eyes, girl. Relax yourself, now. Your sight will adjust."

"No, I mean . . ." The staircase was narrow, and she was forced to tuck more tightly into his body. "This really isn't necessary."

But when they reached the bottom of the steps, the aromas coming from the kitchen were even stronger. "*Ohhh,*" she said dreamily. Her stomach rumbled again. "Do you think there's still food?"

"Aye, lass." MacColla stopped, but she only held tighter, finding she wasn't ready to let go quite yet. She felt secure in his arms, and the shadows along the hallway were so black and cold. He gave a little chuckle and walked on, telling her, "There's always food."

Orange and red embers warmed the hearth, casting ambient light and dancing shadows over the kitchen.

He put Haley down, leaning her against the solid butcher block in the middle of the small room.

She turned at once and began poking around. "A nice, big sandwich . . . some chips . . . maybe some ice cream . . ."

"You desire . . . cream?"

"Cream?" It took her a second to register his question. "Oh, yuck. No . . . I . . . never mind." Haley lifted the edge of a linen square and sighed, seeing a thick hunk of hard bread. "Hel-lo."

He reached over her, grabbing her hand with a small laugh, and pulled her away. "Patience. A moment, lass. A moment." He situated her once more with her back against the table. "Now," he went to a far corner, mumbling, "if I know my sister . . ."

Haley heard some rifling, then, "Ah. There's the stuff." Standing, he put his nose to a small tin and inhaled deeply. "My sister. Very predicable, aye? Her husband's mother made her a gift. Some book for ladies, with all manner of potions and receipts."

MacColla broke off a piece of something from the pan and handed it to her. "Prince bisket, lass. It has a bit of sweet that will set you to rights."

"I hadn't realized Jean was married," she said, taking the hunk of sugared biscuit from his hand. "We were talking earlier and . . . *ohhhh* . . ." Haley had taken a bite. It was still slightly warm, and she could taste the fresh butter.

"There's . . . there's *sugar* in here," she exclaimed over a mouthful of biscuit.

"Aye, lass." He raised his brows, bemused. "Have you not had sugar?"

"Well, yes, I've had sugar, but"—she paused—"where does it . . . ?"

"Come from? The West Indies." He grazed his finger playfully under her chin. "We're not so barbaric after all."

"Well, Scrymgeour isn't, at least."

Her comment silenced him, until she caught his eye and gave him a broad grin. A great laugh erupted from Mac-Colla, and something clicked inside her. The sound was rich and broad, and it made Haley want to make him laugh again.

Though he swallowed his merriment so as not to wake the entire household, he continued to watch her, a wicked light in his eye.

The history books had it all wrong, she realized. Mac-Colla had been painted as a destroyer, a two-dimensional savage. But before her stood a man who did only what he needed to do. His anger and thirst for revenge were borne from a place of joy and love, his ferocity the more intense for the depth of those feelings.

Shaking his head, MacColla took an enormous bite of biscuit, holding her gaze all the while.

Haley's mouth went dry and she swallowed hard to finish her piece. Her mind blanked, and so she simply held her hand out for seconds. "How long does this keep, anyway?" she asked, anxious to fill the silence.

"Keep?"

"Yeah, you know, how long will this stuff be good for? It's delicious."

" 'Twill last months. Aye," he said, to her incredulous look, "and when it gets too hard, Jean just breaks it up. With a hammer like."

"A hammer?" Her tone was suspicious, but he seemed completely sincere.

"Aye, a wee mallet like." He stared at her a moment. "You don't seem overly acquainted with the kitchen, lass."

Haley decided she needed an immediate change of topic. "So, back to Jean." She took a big bite, chewed for a minute, then asked, "What happened? To her husband, I mean."

And it was as if some inner light that had animated MacColla snuffed out.

"He died because of me," he told her gravely.

"You killed your brother-in-law?"

"Och, no, girl. He . . ." MacColla surprised Haley by leaning next to her on the butcher block. " 'Twas in battle. My sword broke, and—"

"You *broke* your sword?"

"Aye lass," he responded with a grim little laugh, "it happens. On the battlefield."

"*Mm-hm.*" She looked at him skeptically, inadvertently grazing her eyes over the thick brawn of his arms. She didn't think there could be that many six-foot-long, two-handed swords snapping on the battlefield. "So what did you do?"

"Not what I did. What he did. Donald. That was his name." MacColla studied the biscuit in his hand, and then tossed it back in the tin. "Donald saw my sword break. Gave me his. I was in the thick of it. Leading the men. My sword broke and then a new one appeared in my hand. I'd no time to think on it," he added quietly.

"He died, of course, Donald did." MacColla picked the half-moon-shaped shard of biscuit back up and put it in his mouth, chewing thoughtfully.

"My Jean." He shook his head. "Poor lass. What she truly wants—what she should have, aye?—is a home of her own filled with more wee ones than she can handle. Were it not for my battles . . ." He scrubbed his hand over his face. "I fight for the clan, aye? For Jean, in a way. But were it not for my fighting, she'd mayhap have a home somewhere, with a husband in her bed and a drove of bairns at her feet."

Haley imagined having kids at her own feet. She'd never considered it before, so intent was she on her academic work. Besides, she'd always figured her brothers would surely end up with over a dozen kids among the lot of them. For the first time, she thought something like that might indeed be nice, if it were with someone you loved.

"But you fight for family," she said, "and it's a good

fight. Without it, Jean wouldn't have a home anyway. Not really. Not with the Campbell to contend with."

MacColla gave her a small smile. "Are you trying to convince me?"

"No. I know." She reached to him, without thinking, gripped the plaid at his chest. "I know it's a good fight. But . . ."

"But what, lass?"

"But . . ." She looked him in the eyes. They were warm and open, and Haley marveled how much had changed in a short time. She took in the whole of him then. He'd bathed earlier, and the smell of soap clung to him, mingling with the scent of his skin, something like leather and wool and musk.

His face was scraped clean, and the dim firelight outlined his strong jaw with a golden glow. He'd washed his hair too, she could tell from the fullness of it, resting wavy and light along his shoulders.

Haley truly looked at the man before her, and she felt a sharp stabbing in her chest, some untold emotion splintering her heart in two.

She belonged at home. She missed her father and mother, her brothers. Ached with the uncertainty—of what had happened, what they were doing right now, what they must think. Most of all, she wondered just how, and when, she'd be able to go back to them once more.

And yet, she wanted to be able to stay here, with MacColla too, just a little while longer.

He watched her, waiting with those brown eyes that seemed to soften now for her, and she thought that this man had changed something deep inside her. She realized, in that moment, that he mattered to her.

Though uncertain what to say, she had the bone-deep knowledge that she needed to say something. To tell him *something*. But what, and how much?

She knew. MacColla was to die. She knew there would be a battle, that it was in Ireland. But she didn't know why or when.

He'd die and leave behind so many people who depended on him.

Would she still be there when it happened? Would he leave *her* behind?

Urgency stabbed her, turning the biscuit to stone in her belly.

She wished she remembered her history. Exactly what happened, exactly when. "Just be wary of Ireland," she told him finally.

"Of Ireland?" He looked taken aback. "What do you know of Ireland?"

"I know that it's . . . dangerous."

He laughed at her. "Dangerous?"

"I'm serious." She deflated, sagging against the counter at her back. "I assume you're going back there?"

"Aye, and soon. To gather more men for the fight."

"Just . . ." Haley wondered how to tell this man that she could predict his future, that she knew where he'd die.

She felt suddenly, unutterably sad. The sense that there might be something she could do nagged at her, that there was something she *needed* to do, but she didn't know what it was.

"Just . . . please. Please be careful, MacColla."

❋

Haley fell at once into a deep and dreamless sleep. For the first time in days, she was sated, feeling full and warm and deliciously exhausted.

She hadn't even had the wherewithal to fully undress. Or the desire. The hideous contraption that was her corset had the ironic effect of binding her injured muscles. When Jean had first laced her into it, Haley had been nearly light-headed with relief.

And so, after MacColla helped her back to her room, she'd crawled right into bed, corset and all, sighing straightaway into the mound of pillows, where she slept propped comfortably upright.

But then she was suddenly awake again. A hand was

clamped over her mouth, and for a single sleep-drenched moment, Haley thought, *she hoped*, that MacColla had come for her in the night.

She roused to skim the surface of wakefulness.

MacColla. It was a relief. He'd come to take her. He wanted her, and his wanting of her made Haley recognize how much she wanted him too.

Her body loosened at the thought. She *hadn't* imagined his intent the night before, sitting and drinking with him, his large hands so gentle on her back, massaging her. She remembered the accidental brushes in sensitive spots. Not accidents after all.

Alasdair MacColla. Come for her. It suddenly seemed the only way it could be.

But then she heard the voice. Foreign, new, more nasal than MacColla's own husky burr. "Be silent or die, bitch," the voice hissed.

Her eyes flew open. And then she felt the blade. Cold and hard, like that blade from so long ago. She inhaled sharply. Cold steel on her throat. It was the one thing in the world with the capacity to still her. The one thing capable of robbing her of all control. Haley felt the blade at her throat and froze like a small and weak thing.

Calm. Think. Two men were at her bedside, and her senses instantly startled to attention. *Darkness. Middle of the night.*

Hands seemed to be all over her. An impossible number of hands. Clamped over her mouth, gripping her arms, holding the knife to her throat.

Tears spilled, as she realized what was happening. Not MacColla at all. *Strangers.* And she was alone, her room far from the others. Scrymgeour had been so thoughtful, placing the women in rooms such a modest and decent distance from the men's.

And that was going to be her downfall.

Nobody would hear her moans, the shuffling of feet. Haley would disappear in the night, with none the wiser.

Adrenalin dumped into her veins, spiking her heartbeat

to a frenzied patter. She squealed and bit down hard. She heard a whispered curse and the hand at her mouth only clamped down harder.

Fingers tangled roughly through her hair and her body torqued awkwardly as she was dragged up and out of bed. The stiff corset that had provided her such relief twisted and jabbed into her now. Pain seared through her chest, and her terror was subsumed by a blessed wash of fury.

Haley wriggled like a mad thing then, her screams muffled by a hand that tasted satisfyingly metallic. She'd drawn blood. The thought gave her focus, and she scrambled more frantically, but the arms only grasped tighter, pulling her hard against the solid body at her back.

A coarse ripping of cloth filled the room like static. *The sheets?*

Hands clawed at her feet. She kicked, struck what she thought was a chin, then there was only air as the ground *whooshed* away from her. She jerked her body, trying to free herself from the men who held her, ignoring the now constant agony shrieking through her body.

Her writhing couldn't stop a strip of linen from being wadded into her mouth, wrapped around her face, cutting into her skin, and silencing her more effectively than any hand could.

It was easy work then, for the two men, to whisk her down the stairs and out the door. She watched Scrymgeour's castle recede in the shadows, the image wavering through the flood of her tears.

Stop. She needed to calm down, or suffocate on those tears. She needed to focus. To fight. *Think.*

This couldn't be random violence. Seventeenth-century Scotland was rife with feuding and retributions.

Who? Yet even as the question popped into her head, she knew.

Campbell.

Men invading Scrymgeour's lands in the night. Revenge aimed at a MacDonald ally, or at MacColla himself. It could only be one man.

He'd kidnapped Jean once. And now it was her being taken in the night.

They reached a copse of trees and the men dropped her feet hard to the ground. The impact jarred her, bringing with it a fresh wave of nausea. She doubled over, gulping convulsively, choking her own bile back down her throat. She tamped down the pain and tried to moderate her breathing, thinking she really would choke if she sicked up now.

The cloth in her mouth was slick, drenched with her own spit. Haley bit at it. Wrenching her chin down, her tongue pushed at the gag, trying to force it from her mouth, but it wouldn't budge.

As she caught her breath, she became aware of a stilted silence around them. The air tense with waiting.

Haley looked up and saw him. A man stood there, his eyes glued to her, fascinated.

A chill crept along her flesh. *Campbell.*

For a split second, she hoped that perhaps he'd been given short shrift by the history books. Perhaps Campbell had been a kind man. Maybe it was merely history's desire for a narrative, for good guys and bad guys, that had named him the villain.

Clouds drifted thick overhead, glowing gray in the night sky. But in that moment they parted, and a bright moonbeam cut through the trees, illuminating them in an eerie wash of light.

And she saw him clearly then, recognized Campbell from all those portraits. The jowly features paler in the moonlight than any drawing had ever portrayed.

Cruelty animated those features now. It was written at the corners of his eyes. Bracketed his thin, drawn lips.

She saw him and she knew.

He was every bit as evil as they'd said.

❦

Jean shook her hand out, then banged on the door once again. It was a solid thing and even knocking as hard as she could didn't make much of a sound. She considered kicking at it—she imagined that Haley lass would kick at it—but decided just to open it instead.

As the door swung open, she suppressed a bout of nerves. The strange woman had pinned Jean with more than one wilting glare, and despite the peace they'd seemed to reach, she wouldn't put it past Haley to come at her, claws bared and angling for a fight.

But the room was quiet. Her trepidation turned to annoyance. Was the woman still abed? She'd drank like a man, then spent the entirety of the next day in her room. Was she planning on lazing away yet another one? The attitude spoke to a certain entitlement that was new to her. Death and death alone would keep Jean in her bed for the day.

Shaking her head, she strode in, wondering what the woman's background was, that she considered the daily running of her own life—not to mention such a simple consideration as appearing for a meal—as something beneath her.

But the bed was empty.

She was gone. It was hard to imagine that she'd risen earlier than Jean that day. And even if she had, surely someone would have noted her appearance.

Confused, she wandered back into the hallway.

"What has your lovely features in such a muddle, and on such a fine morning?"

She turned to see Scrymgeour walking toward her. The man had such a pleasant countenance, always with a gentle smile and an easy manner. Even his large size felt welcoming. Rather than implying sloth, the fullness at his waist spoke to a jovial nature and a love of life that was reassuring to Jean. The sight of him brought an instant swell of relief.

"I . . . yes, Lord Scrymgeour, perhaps you can be of assistance."

"Och, please, Jean." Taking her elbow, he patted her arm. "I've told you time and again. You must please call me John."

She felt her cheeks redden, and cursed her pale skin. Casting her eyes down, she replied, "Yes, of course, John."

"Now you must tell me, how may I be of service?"

"She . . . Haley, she's gone." She nodded to the open doorway. "I came to fetch her for the morning meal, and she's not here."

"Well, surely you just missed each other?"

"No, I'd have seen her. She doesn't seem the sort to rise with the dawn." Jean hadn't intended her comment to have such sass, and Scrymgeour's answering grin embarrassed her.

"Well, then." He steered them down the hall, and the steady feel of his arm in hers warmed her. She tried not to wonder at the strangely calming effect he seemed to have on her. "Surely your brother will have some notion."

They reached MacColla's door too quickly. Scrymgeour lifted his hand to knock, and her arm felt cool where his hand had been.

"Come," MacColla called brusquely.

Scrymgeour opened the door, and Jean instinctively froze. The sight of her older brother never ceased to startle her. He'd yet to don his plaid, and he stood at his washbasin in just his linen shirt. Though it reached almost to his knees, it revealed the thick muscle of his legs and chest in a way that his plaid, wrapped about his waist and tossed over his shoulder, did not.

Jean braced. Though she had never once suffered his temper, she'd watched warily through their childhood as others had. Alasdair's great good humor blackened into fury, as sudden and mercurial as a Highland storm.

"You've not come to choke me again, is it?" He dashed the water from his face and gave a low laugh. The smile in his eyes was directed at his sister. "You forget, it's our brother Gillespie who likes your vile potions, not me."

She briefly returned her brother's smile. Like a great bear he was, and God help those who'd tempt his wrath.

"Your sister bears news of our . . . guest," Scrymgeour told MacColla.

Jean looked up at Scrymgeour, gathering strength. Though he'd let go her elbow, he still stood close by her side. She missed being in the care of a man. It felt good to remember how it was to have one speak for her at the most trying of times.

She looked back at MacColla. A strange look pinched his eyes, and Jean wondered if she wasn't seeing something protective flicker in her brother's gaze.

"Aye," she said. "Her bed is cold. I'd swear she's been gone since before dawn."

"What?" MacColla's face grew dark.

She felt Scrymgeour put his hand at the small of her back. Jean appreciated the gallant gesture, but she knew Alasdair would rather injure his own self than bring harm to his sister.

"Och," he growled, stalking to his bedside to retrieve his plaid. He remembered their time together in the kitchen. Haley's peculiar warnings of Ireland had unsettled him. "I knew something was amiss. Did she run away?"

Jean only shrugged mutely.

He shook his head impatiently. His sister would have no idea what had become of the woman. "Aye, of course you'd not know." He hastily wound the fabric about his waist. "What game does she play at?" he wondered aloud.

MacColla looked up at Scrymgeour. "Come, let's see her room then."

"Aye, perhaps there's some clue."

He stormed into the hallway, Scrymgeour's words at his back.

It was dim. There was light enough that the torches weren't lit, yet the sun had not yet reached high enough in the sky to burn off the night's cold shadows. The gray stone was cool under MacColla's bare feet. Scowling, he noted the stairway at the end of the corridor. Her room was just far enough away, just close enough to the stairs, that she could've escaped silently.

Who is she? MacColla tried to tamp down the anger he felt surging through his veins. *Where could she have gone?*

He'd been taken in by those pretty gray eyes. Had he missed some ulterior motive? She'd asked so many questions about James, had such unnerving insights about the king, about Ireland. What could her purpose be? Why trick him so, only to skulk away in the night?

He strode into her room and paced a quick circle around it. "Is anything missing, then?"

"I . . ." Jean hesitated.

"Not that I can see," Scrymgeour interjected. "There's naught much for the taking."

MacColla walked to the bedside and tore back the sheets as if he might reveal her hiding there. He tossed aside one pillow and another, and then grew utterly still. A chill ran up his back, dread filling his gut like ice.

He leaned down slowly and placed his hand on her pillow. Right beside a bloody handprint. A man-sized bloody handprint.

"God help her," he whispered.

"What?" Jean found her voice. "Alasdair, what is it?"

"The lass didn't run." He looked up at his sister, then to Scrymgeour. "She was taken."

Jean's mouth opened and shut wordlessly. She knew better than any of them what that meant.

"Campbell?" Scrymgeour asked.

"Who but?" MacColla's hand went to the back of his neck. An automatic gesture, reaching for the claymore that was usually strapped between his shoulders. His hand met only air, and he was instantly on his guard.

He'd not let Haley be taken by Campbell's dogs. The urge to find, to kill, to *destroy* the Campbell erupted anew, enraging him. Invigorating him.

"The man goes too far." Their feud was a crucible, boiling his craving for vengeance to unprecedented fury. MacColla would be damned if he'd see another of his people taken by Campbell.

Especially this woman. This woman who had been badly injured before. He'd not see Haley injured again.

"I must find her," he growled. "I leave at once. I'll track them. Find them."

"Aye," Scrymgeour said gravely. "I'll keep Jean with me."

Something flashed in MacColla's eyes as he looked from Scrymgeour to his sister. Some complicated internal calculus, a question asked and answered.

"Take her south," he responded finally. "To safety. My family waits for us in Kintyre. Take her for me, Scrymgeour."

"I will." Scrymgeour didn't appear to think then, simply reached his hand to rest protectively at the small of her back. "Leave, now," he said. "And I'll keep Jean safe in my care."

Chapter 15

"I have to"—Haley lowered her voice into an outraged hiss—"I have to, you know, *bu thoil leam fual a dhèanamh.*" Somehow saying she needed to pee in Gaelic made the task easier.

The man only gaped at her. The small fire flickered between them, casting severe shadows on his face, exaggerating his puzzlement. She sat silently, waiting stubbornly, all the while wondering at what she might have accidentally said.

She'd sat through the night, refusing to fall asleep, even though two of her three captors had dozed loudly, their backs to the flames.

Of course Campbell hadn't appeared drowsy at all, and stared at her unabashedly through the night. Haley did her best to stare a challenge right back, thinking all the while that the man likely didn't let much slip past him.

"*Tha i ag iarraidh mùin,*" Campbell growled. He didn't take his eyes from Haley, which scanned her with something between distaste and desire. Only he could make some crude remark about pissing sound menacing.

"Go then," the man announced. His use of English scorned her attempts at Gaelic. He was much younger than Campbell, in his twenties, she guessed. The dirt brown beard that covered his face like a great soiled and furry mask split into a grin.

She didn't need to fake her urgency. She really did have to go—she thought she'd burst from it—but had waited until the third man had awoken and gone off to do his own business.

The more she could better her odds, the greater her chances for escape. From what she gathered, they were riding back to that hideous castle at Inveraray. And she wasn't about to let herself be the next guest in Campbell's cellar.

Haley thrust out her hands, still bound, and raised her eyebrows. They'd untied her feet, but her hands were still tied tightly in front of her.

"No," the bearded one said flatly, as if to an impudent child.

"Come on." She raised her hands higher. "What am I going to do?" She turned to Campbell and added, "You're surely not afraid a woman could best you?"

Her gamble worked. Campbell *didn't* think a woman could best them. He nodded at the bearded man to cut her bonds, and hope flickered to life in her chest.

She creaked to standing, stiff from holding the same cross-legged position for so long on the cold ground.

"Go with her," Campbell spat. She shot what she hoped was an innocent look in his direction, and he added, "Be quick about it, girl. It's time for us to leave before your husband finds us."

"My husband?" Surely he didn't think she and Mac-Colla were married?

The bearded man snorted a laugh, and a slow smile spread across Campbell's face. Haley chalked it up to simply his version of a lewd joke.

She turned to head deeper into the trees when she heard Campbell say, "Go with her." The bearded man must've made some suggestive gesture because Campbell quickly added, "Do, and I'll punish you myself."

Haley's mind raced. She'd hoped they'd let her go alone. That she could get a bit of a head start. Then run like hell and hope for the best. But of course that would've been too easy.

She heard his shuffling feet following close behind her and mentally sized him up. He was about five-eight, five-nine tops. Not much taller than she was.

But he'd be armed. She'd seen the glint of a pistol at his waist. She imagined he probably slept with the thing strapped to him. It would take him some time to load it. Fifteen seconds, maybe.

He wasn't wearing a sword. Did he have a knife, though? That was something to consider.

She wished she'd tucked her own knife into her dress somehow. The blade wouldn't do much damage, but it would've been better than nothing.

She wondered again if he had a dagger. If she didn't manage to escape this time, perhaps she could somehow steal it. She felt her corset tight at her chest. It was stiff, unbending. She could tuck a blade away in her clothes. Maybe tear a slit along the bottom of her corset and slide it in.

The corset. Her heart kicked hard with excitement. Of course—her corset. She already had a weapon.

She was wearing it.

She'd marveled at the hideous contraption as Jean had laced her up tight. Most old corsets had ivory busks running up the front. A rib roughly two inches thick and fifteen inches long, stiff enough to hold a woman in tight.

Not so this one.

Hers had a busk all right, but it was made of steel. She'd heard of metal busks but had never seen one, and imagined it would've been cheaper than its ivory counterpart.

At the time, she had unlaced the top a bit, peeked at the buckskin that encased the steel rib. The leather was mottled dark brown, stained with some other woman's sweat.

"Give me a minute," she called to the bearded man, and thought the crack in her voice was just as well. He'd assume she was nervous for other reasons.

She brought her hands to her sternum, and dug between her breasts for the small laces that secured the busk into the front of the corset. Her fingers worked quickly, loosening, fumbling.

She glanced over her shoulder and he stood, smiling. Dark brown decay clung like moss in the crooks of his slanted teeth. It gave her focus.

Relieving herself was the first order of business. If the creep wanted to watch, let him. Turning her back firmly to him, she squatted, tucking her dress up only as far as absolutely necessary. He'd think he was getting a show, but really all he'd see was the back of her dress.

She took a moment to shudder in relief, then groped at the top of her corset with renewed concentration. She worked a finger into the narrow pocket that formed the front panel of the corset. Touched the cool edge of leather that encased her busk.

Her weapon.

She had to arch her back to shimmy it free, and she gasped with the pain the motion shot through her ribs.

"Hurry yourself, girl."

She heard him shuffle impatiently at her back.

The busk was heavy in her hand. A reassuring heft, like a length of construction rebar. She tucked it close to her chest.

Her preference would've been to pick at the stitching and pull the steel from its leather enclosure, but she had no time.

Just as well, she thought, as a plan came to her. She slid her hands to the base of the busk, as if it were a bat, and savored the weight in her grip.

A sturdy little club.

Smiling, she stood and walked briskly forward, keeping the clansman at her back.

"Ho!" Haley heard the surprise in his voice as he rushed to catch up. "Ho, girl!"

She walked faster, then faster still. If he was going to talk to her like a horse, let him try to corral her like one.

A clearing lay ahead. The trees thinned, and their leaves glowed light green from the growing sunlight.

"Ho!" His voice was angry now.

But her smile only grew broader as she broke into a jog. She needed to reach the clearing. The sound of his breath closed in, echoing through the silence of the woods.

She burst into a run, stopping just a few feet outside the edge of the grove. *Wait.*

Her father's voice came to her then, so clear, so eerily vivid as to almost break her concentration. *Wait for it.*

It wasn't until she felt him burst into the clearing that she finally spun to face him. She pivoted hard, the busk in her hands, the full force of her weight behind it. She spun and slammed it into the side of his head with a satisfying crack.

"Home run, motherfucker." Her voice was giddy, a match to the high pitch of adrenalin that trembled through her.

She came back to herself at once. She needed to run. Fast. She figured she had five minutes tops before Campbell came to see what was taking them so long.

But first . . . She knelt and grabbed the man's pistol and tugged the small leather bullet bag from his belt.

She needed gunpowder. *Where would it be?* She patted down the man as quickly as she could, hoping he was truly out cold. Then she felt it. A hard, oval bulb in his breast pocket. Using the very tips of her fingers, she peeled open his soiled and smelly coat. An uneven pocket had been stitched in as an afterthought, and the dull stopper of a brass priming flask poked out from the top.

Hurry up. She grabbed it, shoved it and the bullet bag in her corset, then stood and scanned the horizon. Hills and more hills. She'd need to go back up and over the mountain range.

Her heart sank. The gravelly hillsides and low-lying tangles of brush wouldn't provide any cover.

She rubbed her thumb distractedly over the pistol's wooden grip.

Campbell had ponies. And though they were rugged animals, there would be no way they could make it easily over the steepest peaks. She didn't know about his other clansman, but she knew she could beat Campbell in a footrace.

Fat sod. Haley broke into a run.

As she pumped her arms in the hard slog up the first slope, she came up with as many British slang terms as she could for Campbell. *Bloody porker.*

Bollocks. Wanker. Ugly shite.

Her own version of a mantra.

She switched the gun to her other hand, clutching the thick handle tight.

Catch me if you can.

❀

MacColla squatted, scanning his eyes along the terrain. Two sets of footprints had left the castle, marked clear in the dirt just outside the entrance. Men's boots, not walking in a straight line. They would've carried her, then.

He stood, inhaling sharply. It had been a mistake to stop at Fincharn. The lass had been injured, though. They'd needed to rest. Jean too. Neither would've been able to press on at the pace he'd have liked.

And now he was suffering his mistake.

Their tracks were clear enough, scuffed through gorse and scrub, headed for a distant grove on the outskirts of Scrymgeour's land.

MacColla jogged toward it. His claymore thumped against his back with each stride. Stirring him, spurring him.

He'd underestimated Campbell. Or rather, he'd underestimated what Haley meant to the man.

Who is she and what does she have to do with Clan Campbell? His own clan's sworn enemies.

She clearly wasn't a spy. He thought of that handprint on her pillow. *If blood had to be spilled in the taking of her* . . .

The thought drove him into a run.

The lass was strange. Strong and beautiful, in the guileless way of a wild creature. He felt a spark of desire whenever he saw her now. A dead man would, to glimpse those mysterious gray eyes.

He had to admit he'd wanted her from the start. Even before MacColla had known they shared a common enemy.

He reached the trees. Squatted again, then went to hands and knees looking for the traces that were harder to pinpoint in the dense undergrowth.

Snapped branches. A spot where the carpet of leaves had been disturbed to reveal the damp, dark loam beneath.

He stood, walked slowly, hands on his knees as he bent close to the ground and followed the tracks to a clearing.

A pile of dirt and ashes were all that was left of a small fire. Leaning over, he traced his fingers through the cinders. *Still warm.*

They hadn't been gone long.

He circled the camp, saw scuffs where hooves had shuffled along the rotted leaves. Three sets. Her two captors had met up with another.

Campbell? He could only hope. He yearned to fight the man. Longed for it.

MacColla's father and brother had lost years of their lives in a Campbell dungeon. Countless of his MacDonald clansmen had lost their lives fighting Campbell men, and MacColla had dreamt of the day he could take his revenge.

He found two more sets of tracks, human, and heading deeper into the trees. At one point in the trail, underbrush had been scuffed away, revealing a small patch of silt. And a single footprint.

A small, bare foot.

"Och, Haley lass," he muttered, tracing his finger along its outline.

MacColla stood and jogged again, as fast as he could while still marking the tracks. He came to a clearing, and the laugh rumbled low from his chest before he could think to keep silent.

A Campbell man, lying in the brush. Dead or near to it.

"Good girl," he whispered, grinning his relief.

She was a fighter.

He'd find her, and fight with her. Two on two.

MacColla liked the odds.

Chapter 16

Shit. Shit shit shit.

Haley cursed, and then let loose a chuckle, giddy with nerves and fear.

She'd crested the first hill and came to rest, concealed by a rocky outcropping on just the other side. Her chest was killing her. She was winded, and each heaving breath shot pain through her torso.

She thought she'd load her weapon, and wait. But she examined it now, turning it in her hands. Cursing again, she tilted it toward the sunlight. It was a pretty little pistol, made of a simple dark wood capped with steel accents that shone a dull gray in the morning's watery light.

And of course it had to be unlike anything she'd ever fired.

It was a predecessor to the flintlock. She thought of Graham's gun from the museum and gave another muted laugh. Here was her theory. Right here in her hands.

Not many flintlocks in the first half of the seventeenth century.

How the hell, she wondered, *do you fire this thing?*

She'd shot plenty of black-powder weapons for her research, but she'd never laid her hands on something like this.

She was pretty sure it was an early *snaphaunce*. They were called dog lock pistols, referring to the catch that locked the cock into the safe position. As she recalled, it was a gun used by the English soldiers.

Of course. The Campbells had sided with the Covenanters in the Wars of the Three Kingdoms. And the Covenanters often found themselves on the same side as Cromwell's Parliamentary soldiers. It made sense Campbell would have access to guns used by the redcoats.

She retrieved a bullet from the leather pouch and, saying a prayer she didn't blow her hand off, proceeded to load the weapon, carefully pouring in powder, dropping and tamping down the ball, then pouring a measure more powder in the pan.

She leaned back, and the rock at her spine felt cool. She realized she'd worked herself into a sweat. Shutting her eyes, Haley tuned her senses outward, listening for the Campbell clansman she knew would find her.

❁

Campbell put his hand to his forehead, shielding his eyes from the sun. "There." He pointed to the steepest area of the slope. A narrow stripe of dark gray spoke to scree recently displaced.

His man had been searching for tracks along the low valleys between hills, but Campbell had suspected otherwise. If the woman was canny enough to smash in the head of one of his best men, she'd not scramble hysterically into a trap.

With them on horseback, staying to the lower elevations would corner her as easily as a hare in a hole.

"Do we ride up then?"

Campbell sneered. "Neither of us is riding up that."

He puckered his lips in thought. Studied the terrain to either side, then up along the mountain.

"Off your horse," he commanded. "I'll cut her off low on the other side. You race and catch her above." He wheeled his mount around. "And one more thing, lad?"

"Aye, sir?"

"If you don't catch her"—Campbell gathered his reins in tight fists, the stout pony prancing anxiously beneath him—"don't bother coming back."

Campbell kicked his horse, galloping into the valley and toward his Inveraray Castle beyond.

❁

He tracked the horses to the base of one of the steeper slopes. He studied the rise. The gravelly hillside told a clear story. One man hiked up and another rode off.

MacColla raised his hands to the grip of his sword and leaned his head back to stare up into the glare.

Her tracks were there too, in the scree, a thick line edged by two thinner ones. Her hands and feet scuffling up the hillside. Chased.

Hissing a curse, his eyes scanned the foot of the slope, following the tracks where they headed into the valley. They were fresh. The ponies had left a trail that was easy to read, cutting a wake of broken branches and trampled leaves in the brush.

Campbell. Campbell wouldn't have climbed a mountain— not when he had a man to do it for him. It was Campbell who would've ridden off, riderless mounts beside him. Campbell who now headed in the direction of Inveraray Castle.

"By crivens," he muttered. MacColla deliberated for a moment. Looked back up the hill and down again to the valley. "Damn it and damn it to hell."

Campbell was close. Too close to ignore. And alone. That was what clinched it. MacColla could blindfold himself, tie both hands behind his back, and still he'd best Campbell in a fight.

Campbell was close, and he had to get him.

MacColla turned, looked back up the hill, staring up at

those tracks as he began to jog backward toward the valley. Away from Haley. He tried to ignore the sharp twinge in his chest.

Haley. He had to hope she'd be all right. She was a fighter. Braw, but canny too, using her brains and her strength.

"Good Christ, lass," he whispered. MacColla turned his back to her trail and took off after the Campbell. "Be safe."

He broke into a hard run, willing his physical exertion to push images of her from his mind. But those gray eyes haunted him, and he ran harder.

He would catch the Campbell and kill him.

He could come back for Haley.

He was too close to stop now.

And then he heard it. A shot cracked high above. Trees grew scant in the hills, and there was nothing to stop the sound of gunfire from echoing down to where he'd stopped, panting, deep in the valley.

And this time, MacColla's decision was an easy one.

❋

Her eyes shot open. There it was. A distant snapping of a branch underfoot.

Haley rose, tried to force calm into her trembling hands. She studied the gun. She'd shot before. But never with intent to kill.

The tang of black powder clung in her sinuses. She held the pistol in front of her, testing its weight in her hands. How much would it kick back? Would it aim truly?

She thought of James Graham's combination weapon, able to serve as a blade if the gun failed to fire. Haley quickly wiped the palm of her right hand on her dress, then brought it back to the butt. She feared her own gun might be better suited as a bludgeon than as a straight-shooting weapon.

Stepping out from behind the rock, she assumed her stance.

Another snap.

Here he comes.

She knew at once: There was no fooling this one. Haley saw his dirty-blond hair first, then the shoulders of his brown coat. He crested the rise and his eyes seemed already to be pinned on her.

The man saw the gun in her hands, and it was his laugh that stilled her trembling hands.

"Bastard," she whispered. And shot.

He recoiled, fell, and his grunt of pain was swallowed by the wide-open sky.

Exhilaration thrummed through her. But then he rose to his knees, slowly wavered to his feet, and her elation flipped into panic.

They locked eyes again and the fury twisting his face chilled her. Haley quickly ran through her options.

Could she fight him? He was injured. A hole was torn in his left shoulder, blood already staining his coat black. His left arm was useless, clenched frozen at his side.

Or she could run. Her eyes skittered behind her to the hillside below. There was no place to hide.

If his injury weren't that grave, he could catch her. Or Campbell eventually would. And then there would be two against her one.

She had to fight. He had his own pistol, but he'd never be able to load it one-handed.

Haley's eyes went to his sword. A simple broadsword, hanging at his hip. He'd only need his one hand to wield it. If he were right-handed, and she had to assume he was, he could kill her in one easy stroke.

If she was really going to fight him, she had to act now. Get close enough to render his blade useless.

She charged the man, and felt a distant shot of pleasure at seeing shock on his face for a second time.

Just a few strides and she'd reach him. His hand seemed to reach in slow motion to his sword hilt.

She needed to give it her all, or give it up.

Bracing for the agony she knew was coming, Haley leapt. She slammed into him, and the blow to her ribs was like knives slicing through her torso, dizzying her. Wrapping arms and legs about him, she clung like a monkey to the front of him.

Haley clawed tight to his injured shoulder and he grunted his own pain in her ear, his breath coming short and hot against her neck. It was an obscenely intimate pose, but she had to hug herself close enough to render his sword useless.

His right arm wriggled from under her knee and he struck at her, trying to pull her from him.

Clinging even tighter with her legs, Haley let go her right hand and pummeled a flurry of short punches directly on his wound.

She was *too* close, though, and couldn't get enough power behind her fist. Hooking her feet behind his back, she let go her other hand and went for his eyes.

Cupping his face in her hands as if ready to plant a kiss, she hooked her thumbs at the corners of his eyes and pushed back. It was a trick her dad had taught her. Snag the fingertips in, crane your opponent's neck back, and just as her father had promised, even the largest of men would fall at once, backward to the ground.

He slammed against the hillside, the impact sending rocks clattering down. She immediately scooted up his torso, bearing her full weight down to jab her elbow in his bullet wound.

Her hands clasped together under her chin, fingers interwoven for maximum force. Battering him had left traces of his blood etched in the wrinkles of her hands. It was tacky between her palms, the smell gamy and metallic in her nose and mouth.

His initial shout of pain was only a momentary triumph. She sensed him struggling beneath her, but was focused only on putting her all into grinding down on his injury, hoping he'd pass out from the pain.

She didn't sense his fist coming, slamming into the side of her face. White sparks exploded in her vision as she reeled to the side.

He kicked out from under her, scrambling to his feet, and, hopping backward a step, plowed his foot into her chin.

Darkness swallowed her for a moment, and she came to sliding slowly down the hill. Sharp rocks and gravel cut into her shoulder, and she whimpered, forcing air into her lungs.

Haley dug her heels into the slope, stopping her descent. Swiveling her head back up the mountain, she placed his location. He hobbled toward her, right hand on his bloodied shoulder, murder in his eyes.

She got to her knees. Instinctively, she ran her tongue over her teeth. The taste of blood in her mouth sickened her, and she spat onto the rocks, wiping pink and red spittle from her chin.

He let go of his shoulder and pulled his sword from its scabbard. The motion was slow to match the smile that spread over his face.

"No," she said simply. It couldn't end like this. A sword on a hillside in seventeenth-century Scotland. More than her terror, it was the sense of unreality that froze her in place.

She heard a dull thunk. Metal crunching into stone. The man in front of her hadn't moved, and it took her a moment to realize where the sound had come from.

She looked down. A dagger hilt quivered, stuck blade-first into the hillside, not one foot from her.

And then she saw him. MacColla, on a rise above, his claymore in his hands. He'd tossed her a weapon.

She saw him and she knew why he was known as *Fear Thollaidh nan Tighean*, why men feared him and called him Destroyer of Houses. He was a wild thing, in a tartan of dreary colors, his dark brow furrowed into a hard line of rage and revenge.

His sword was pointed at the Campbell clansman, but his eyes were riveted on her. Worry hardened his features and, wanting to reassure him, she pulled the dagger from the ground and gave him a small nod.

He'd heard the shot and flown up the hillside, dashing and scrambling up rocks until he saw them. He approached quietly, swiftly from the side, getting closer.

Haley was covered in blood. Alarm jolted him, pumping his heart and galvanizing his every muscle. He scanned her, looking for signs of injury, and when he found none, a knot deep in his core unraveled. Relief swelled through him, elated him.

His eyes returned to the Campbell clansman. He was bloodied; his trews were splattered with it, his face smeared. MacColla held his breath, scanning the man for some wound, then released it in a long sigh upon seeing the blackened hole at his shoulder.

His blood. Not hers.

He realized the man was wavering in his boots.

Haley. She'd done it. It had been she who'd fired the weapon.

So strong, so brave as she knelt there, her black hair lifting in the breeze. *So beautiful.* She'd stand and fight more; he was sure of it.

He smiled. She'd not have to.

He jogged straight for the Campbell, and the hollow clacking of stone on stone under his step had the man turning. But too late.

With a single, powerful swing, MacColla relieved him of his head.

Chapter 17

Tossing his sword down, MacColla fell to his knees by Haley's side, and joy shuddered through her.

She had been poised to fight—and braced for defeat. But then he'd appeared from nowhere. She'd fought, and would have fought til the end, but a hero of old had shown up and taken care of everything, and she'd been more than happy to let him.

Her modern sensibilities didn't want to think about what the implications of *that* were.

Looking at him now—black hair loose to his shoulders, the intensity of his rich brown eyes, the sweep of muted green, blue, and black plaid over his shoulder—the sight of him was so profoundly reassuring, so comforting, she had to hold herself up from collapsing to the ground in relief.

Roving his eyes over her, he rubbed his hands along her arms, her shoulders, patting her gently, searching for some injury.

"I . . . I'm fine," she said, and he stilled. MacColla took a deep breath, and though his body seemed to unclench, his gaze still wouldn't meet hers.

He slowly drew his hands to her waist, held them there for a moment, then stroked up her torso, grazing his thumbs along the sides of her breasts.

His eyes lingered on her every curve.

And instead of flaring with pain, her ribs suffused with warmth at his touch, as if the muscles could at last release, and she could be at ease.

Finally he looked up, his eyes locking with hers. And then lines etched deep at his forehead, instantly anxious to see the blood on her face where she'd been kicked. He was silent as he took the edge of his plaid, blotted her chin.

He moved his focus to her mouth.

The fabric slipped from his fingers, and MacColla stroked his thumb gently along her lower lip. He murmured tenderly, his Gaelic words too low to understand.

His face was close now, and Haley drank him in. The beautiful face that was too fierce to be conventionally handsome. The strong, Roman nose, with a high bridge that seemed to emerge directly from between his brows. Sharp cheekbones. A dusting of black stubble at his jaw.

She drank MacColla in and felt such a rush of wanting him, it was like a burst of light from within, scorching her, blinding her to all but the man before her. It raged beyond her control, this need, and she thought that it would consume her, that if it burned on untended, she might cease to exist.

"How is it I love you already, *gràdh geal mo chrìdhe*?" His voice was barely a whisper.

He cupped her face and slowly leaned in to her. His hands encompassed her, so broad and sure on her skin. She felt his breath on her mouth. Felt the brush of his lips. Then the slow give of flesh on flesh, as he gently kissed her.

Yes.

For three heartbeats, Haley was suspended. Everything stilled around her, captured frozen, a vignette in time. And she knew. *This* is what she came back in time for. *For him.*

Three heartbeats, and the embers he'd lit within her burst into wildfire.

She grabbed him then, clutched at his arms, opened her mouth to him, wrapped her hands around those thick muscles, and clung tight.

Pressing close along his chest, she tasted his growl of desire in her throat, and she thought she'd come apart. Haley clung tighter, her nails scoring into the linen-clothed skin. Wanting him, needing him, closer.

His hands were at her back, on her waist, at her breast. She sensed the bust of her gown loosening. Felt the glide of fingers along the front of her corset, loose where her busk had been. The laces tickled her, and it was agony on her sensitive skin, now attuned to the slightest shifts of flesh and fabric, aching for his hands, his mouth. He alone could soothe her.

MacColla had never imagined something like this. Never imagined someone like her. So sweet in his mouth.

She was so hard facing the world, yet so soft in his arms. So open to him.

He wanted her. More than wanted her, he would have her. Consume her. Make Haley his.

Not here. Not like this.

He slowly pulled his mouth from hers, his heart hammering in his chest. MacColla licked his lips, wet from their kiss.

They were too close to Campbell lands. He'd have her, but he'd have her away from this place.

He tore his gaze from her, swept his eyes over the barren and rocky hillside. Over the Campbell corpse that lay not twenty paces away.

Campbell was out there somewhere.

He'd have her, but it would be unsullied by Campbell filth. He didn't have his true family lands, but he did have a hearth and safe haven on Kintyre.

"Not like this, *a chiall mo chrìdhe.*" His voice was husky, words of love new and ragged in his throat. *Darling of my heart.*

Love. He'd told Haley he loved her.

MacColla pulled back. Put his hands gently on her

shoulders. Looked at her. Her black hair flying every which way. Her full nose and lean strength and strangely outspoken ways. And her eyes, ever those eyes, gray and black and beckoning him in to drown.

"Aye," he whispered, affirming to himself what he suspected to be true. *Love her.* Such an outlandish thought.

He'd a war to wage. No home to speak of. Knew nothing of this lass.

And yet here she sat, before him, his heart in her hands.

He leaned in once more and kissed her softly. He traced the hair from her face. Coarse and thick at his fingertips.

Tucking it behind her ear, he said, "Come, lass. Come with me."

❀

He hesitated at her bedroom door. Then, holding his chest high, Scrymgeour entered. His courage was rewarded by a tremulous smile from Jean. Warmth suffused his chest, and he couldn't help but beam at her in return.

He recalled his purpose and grew somber. Their enemy was close, and he had to take her away. At once.

"I've come to see if there's aught I can do. If I might be of help packing your things . . ." He couldn't help but snag his eyes in wonder at the fine edge of transparent lace that bordered her nightgown, which lay neatly folded at the foot of the bed, on loan from one of his family's old trunks.

He abruptly jammed a hand in his pocket. Renegade imaginings of her creamy skin in such a gauzy delicacy was more than his male body could endure.

"Though . . ." he stammered. "Though I suppose there's not much for you to bring." He rambled on, self-consciously, "Not much you have in the world at all, is there?"

Jean turned to him, silent, her gaze locking with his. Scrymgeour realized he'd struck at the heart of it. A young woman like her should have trunks filled with finery. Not a transient life in which she relied on the charity of strangers for something so simple as a nightgown.

"Is there more you might need?" he asked. "You'll be wanting a good cloak." He couldn't help roving his eyes the length of her, thinking there wasn't a cloak made in the world that would be bonny enough for her.

So lovely she was. And perhaps most of all because she didn't realize it. Her time in the Campbell dungeon left Jean whippet-thin, but rather than seeming gaunt, she was ever more the delicate flower, long and pale, with hair like a spill of gleaming night sky.

It was impossible for him to look at her and not be overtaken by the urge to protect her. To take Jean in his care.

"I . . . No," she said. "You've shared so much with me already."

She trembled, wavering for a moment, as if undone by his kindness.

"Oh Jean, lass." Scrymgeour went to her side, easing her down on the edge of the bed. "All that you had has been taken from you. I never told you . . . I've wanted to tell you . . . how sorry I am. For your loss. To lose a husband so young—"

Her hands knotted in her lap. "Donald was a good man." She looked down and added quietly, "Though he was still but a stranger to me."

"The loss no less devastating for it," he assured her grandly.

They sat speechless for a time. Scrymgeour considered how there was no clear place for her to turn. Many of her MacDonald clan folk had been exiled to Ireland. Though MacColla's immediate family had found safe haven on Kintyre, it wasn't their true place.

"The bloody Campbell," he muttered. The same man had torn both her home and her husband from her. *Campbell*. And now he was near.

Scrymgeour began to reach his hand out to take hers. He glanced up and his eyes were drawn to the mirror on her table. He caught sight of himself in the reflection, and the man who stared back had flesh at his belly. He saw a man with a weak chin that required reinforcement from a thick bush of brown whiskers grown about his mouth. A man with plain hair and unremarkable carriage.

The image was like a cold spill of water at his breast, and he remembered himself.

"But what if he comes for us?"

It took him a moment to register her words. It was the Campbell, of course, whom she spoke of. She'd been traumatized by her experience, and no wonder. Kidnap and imprisonment weren't something a young woman readily forgot.

"No, lass." He used the excuse to finally take her hand in his. He gave it a slight squeeze, reluctantly let her go. "He'll not get you. Ever again."

"But he . . . he was here." She fluttered her hands, gesturing to the room around them, then abruptly brought them down to wring at her skirts as if that could still their trembling. "He took Haley."

"Aye, there was likely a Campbell here, who took the woman. And your brother will save her, just as he saved you."

Her gaze rose to his, tears bright in her wide brown eyes.

And Scrymgeour knew the exact moment his heart broke.

Without thinking, he took her in his arms.

Jean tensed at the inappropriate closeness. She'd yearned for this. She had been so long alone.

Scared. Deprived. Wanting for food and light for so long in Campbell's cellars. But more profoundly, she'd been deprived for so long of the feeling of protection. Of care. Of love.

She'd ached for someone's kind touch. For John's touch, most of all.

The velvet of his coat was soft at her cheek. It was dark blue, like his eyes, deeper and calmer than any loch.

She gradually relaxed. Grew aware of the thrumming of his heart beneath her hand.

His warmth spread through her. John smelled of his pipe. Of woodsmoke and comfort.

Jean relaxed. She would let him bring her to Kintyre.

But first, she would let John bring her peace.

Chapter 18

"How did you do it?" MacColla's smile was wide as he swung his arm around her shoulder and pulled her tight. "How did you manage to clout the bearded one?"

She spied his chipped front tooth and felt an inexplicable rush of warmth in her belly. A thin triangular wedge, not immediately noticeable. She saw it and could think only that *she'd* kissed that mouth.

"My busk." Haley gave him a coy smile.

"Your . . . what is it?"

"You know." She patted her stomach. "From my corset." She grabbed his hand and pulled him uphill. "Come on. I'll show you."

Her eyes scanned the rocks all around. "Aha." Haley bent down and picked up the buckskin-wrapped length of steel from where she'd dropped it to fire the gun. She studied it, ensuring there were no signs of blood.

MacColla stared in awe as she carefully plucked at the laces between her breasts, opening the thin pocket that held the busk in place. Then, locking eyes with him, she slid the rib back in.

"You wee wildcat!" He laughed broadly and clapped her into a sudden hug. "You are something, aye? Only you would find some use for your girl clothes as a weapon." Shaking his head, he chuckled to himself.

"Now that you've reunited with your wee cudgel, we should be away from here." He scanned the horizon. Loch Awe glittered, fringed by low trees and snaking along the valley in the distance.

"I don't imagine Campbell will make the hike up," MacColla said, as he turned to face the low mountains behind them. Peak after peak reached far beyond, back toward Inveraray. "But we can't be sure he'll not return with men who will."

"But where are we going?" She shuffled to catch up to him in his sudden stride along the ridge. "What about Jean?"

He scanned along the hill he'd so wildly charged up, searching now for the best way back down. "I left Jean in Scrymgeour's care."

"Oh." She was suddenly very aware she'd been the cause of much turmoil. MacColla would've been reluctant to leave his sister. It couldn't have been an easy decision. "I'm sorry."

"Sorry?" He stopped scanning and swung his face to her. "Och, lass, you've naught to be sorry for." He was back by her side in two great strides. Tangling fingers through her hair, he rested his hand at her neck. " 'Tis I who am the sorry one. I misjudged the Campbell. And I confess, I misjudged you. It wasn't until . . . Well, I didn't know. There was no way to know Campbell would be after you with as much piss and vinegar as he'd have for one of my own clan. And for that *I'm* sorry."

"Oh . . ." She was silent for a moment, floored by the admission. Alasdair MacColla. She still couldn't get over it. *The* Alasdair MacColla stood before her, *apologizing*.

"Well?" he asked with endearing vulnerability.

"Well, what?"

"Well, do you accept my apology then?"

"No *sorry* needed." She reached up to place her hands

on his shoulders. Standing on her tiptoes, her face still couldn't reach his. "Just kiss me, MacColla."

She felt his smile on her lips.

He pulled away. "Come, we must be off now. To Kintyre."

He took her hand and led them diagonally down.

"Is that where you're from?" Haley asked, struggling to keep up with him while keeping her feet under her at the same time. He avoided the rockier spots in favor of a path that was coarse with brush, affording them thick hand- and footholds.

"Kintyre? Och, no. Though it is traditionally Clan Mac-Donald land."

MacColla was quiet for a moment, navigating a particularly steep spot. Once he was assured she had solid footing, he continued, "No, my father's home was on the isle of Colonsay. There lies the true land of my family, my Clan Iain Mor."

"But I thought you were a MacDonald."

"Aye." He looked back at her as if she were daft. "I'm a MacDonald, and what else? And though Clan MacDonald has holdings in both Ireland and Scotland, our true land is here, on Scottish soil."

"But . . ." Haley looked perplexed, and he gave her a smile.

"But what, *leannan*?" Laughing, he let go her hand to give her chin a pinch. "Don't look so confounded, lass. In any event, 'tis not my family tree that needs discussing." He raised his brows in challenge.

Taken aback, she lost her footing, and he spun to catch her. Only a short descent remained, and they made the rest of it in concentrated silence.

She'd need to tell him . . . something. *What?*

He hurtled straight down the rest of the slope, and turned to help her with her final steps.

She tried to walk on, but MacColla stopped her, his hands on Haley's shoulders. "Who are you to be such a coveted prize for the Campbell?"

"I . . ." She was breathing heavily. Focusing on the climb down had left her light-headed. Unable to think. She needed to rest for just a moment. Haley hadn't slept the night before, hadn't had any real food in some time, and it was finally all catching up with her. "Can we sit down? I need to take a break."

MacColla shook his head, disappointed in himself.

"Och, of course." He took her arm, helping her to the ground. "Of course you can rest."

Her skin was clammy in his hands, cool and damp. Campbell had been the only thing on his mind, and he'd ended up pressing her too hard. The lass had been gone for some time and likely hadn't eaten or slept—of course she needed rest. He wasn't used to dealing with women and cursed his clumsiness.

"Have you a chill?" He stood to unwind his plaid for her, but she stopped him.

"No." She tried a small laugh but it came out as a breathy exhale. "Please, there's no need to strip."

"Shall I find us some food? You need to feed yourself."

"Really, MacColla. I'm not going to expire." She gestured to the ground at her side. "I just need . . . a moment."

"It's Alasdair, lass. My Christian name." He sat next to her. "You may call me Alasdair."

"You're MacColla in my mind." She looked at him, a sidelong glance that suggested much yet said nothing. "I don't know that I could call you anything else."

His mind raced. "And how do you know of me?"

She clearly wasn't a spy for Campbell. And though he was known for his victories with Graham, he'd thought women didn't generally concern themselves with the finer points of battle.

"Tell me who you are, *leannan*. A Fitzpatrick, you say. Tell me of your family." He tentatively reached to her, paused, then put his hand lightly at the small of her back. "I'm about to bring you to the very heart of mine. I must know."

Instead of answering, she rested her chin in her hands.

Looking into the distance, she asked matter-of-factly, "What year is it?"

"*Ciod an rud?*" Her peculiar question caught him off guard. "What did you say?"

"I just wondered . . ." She turned to face him, the mystery in those gray eyes honed to a razor-sharp point. "Really, MacColla, what year is it?"

"Sixteen forty-six, though surely you—"

"Is James Graham alive?" She waved her hand. "Never mind. Don't answer that."

"Who are you to have such concerns?"

"I'm not from here."

"Aye"—he gave a small laugh—"I'd reasoned that for myself."

"No." She looked away from him again. "I mean, I'm *really* not from here."

Haley seemed so small then, so alone. He leaned closer to her, wrapped his arm tight around her shoulder. MacColla thought it best to simply wait in patient silence for whatever tale she had for the telling.

She inhaled deeply. "Well. Here goes. I'm from the future, MacColla." Haley looked at him, waiting for a response.

He just stared blankly, unsure what she was getting at.

She shut her eyes, as if bracing for something painful, then rattled quickly, "My name is Haley Anne Fitzpatrick, I'm from Boston, Massachusetts. I have . . ."

She scrubbed her face, swallowed, and tried again, her voice thickened by tears. "I've got five brothers. Danny, Colin, Conor, Gerry, and Jimmy. My dad . . ." She made a tiny, pained squeak, tightly controlled anguish keening from the cracks. "My dad's from Donegal. But he went to America the moment he finished school. He's a cop. Was. Was a cop."

She stopped for a moment, breathing hard, as if she'd just sprinted a mile.

Finally Haley continued, this time sounding numb,

wooden, "My mom's Irish too, but not fresh off the boat. Her folks were from Cork. I'm a PhD student at Harvard."

Her tone swelled again, abruptly overwrought. "Get that? *Harvard*. That's a big deal where I'm from. Celtic scholar. My focus is seventeenth-century weaponry. Isn't that a hoot?"

She babbled feverishly now, unhinged. "I was born in the 1970s. How wacked is that? Platform shoes and disco dancing. But I was too young for all that. For me it was Kool-Aid. *Star Wars*. Madonna."

She grabbed his arm, gave it a shake. "It's the *twenty-first century* where I'm from. Planes in the sky. Telephones. Video games. Not to mention hot showers." She paused, then mused wistfully, "God, hot showers seem like rocket science right about now." She looked unseeing into the distance.

MacColla finally asked, "What is it you're saying?" His voice was dangerously quiet. "I don't ken your words, *leannan*."

Leannan, she thought. He'd been calling her *leannan*. *Darling. Sweetheart.*

Lover.

Of Alasdair MacColla. So preposterous. And yet it gave her strength to see it through.

"What am I saying?" She pinned him with her gaze once more. "I'm saying this is the past. To me, you're from the past. You died. Years ago. *Hundreds* of years ago. I know about you because you're famous. Congratulations," she tossed off. "You die in Ireland. I don't remember when exactly, or how. You're betrayed, that's all I can remember." Haley raked her hands through her hair, resting her head in her hands, deflated.

"You get killed," she said softly. She looked at him, chin resting on her arm, no longer bothering to wipe the tears from her cheeks. "It all goes to shit. God, there's Culloden. The Highland Clearances. Tartans are outlawed. Swords too." She muttered, "All to shit."

He didn't understand half of what she'd said. Less than that even.

But the future?

Uncertain of what to say, he tried to make a joke of it. "Are you certain you didn't clout your own head with that wee busk of yours?"

She shot him such a look of raw pain, he felt it through his body, as gutting as any physical wound.

"Why do you keep asking of James?" His tone was gentle, and the flicker of relief he read on her face made his chest swell. Had she *feared* him? Feared his response? "Graham of Montrose," he added softly.

"Oh, I know who you mean all right. I found a weapon. I think it was *his* weapon. 'For JG, with love from Magda,' the inscription said. I mean, who else would it belong to?"

"But how does that prove—"

"I can't explain it. I just got a gut feeling about the gun, that it couldn't have been made—*wouldn't* have been made—before 1650. Here." She gestured to the gun she'd fired earlier, its long, thin barrel tucked now at his belt. "Hand me that."

She took it from his hands, plowing forward despite the bewilderment on his face. "What kind is it?"

"A pistol, lass."

She shot him an exasperated look. "Yeah, but what kind? What kind of mechanism does it have?"

He took it back from her, studied the curved wooden handle in his hands. The frizzen and flash pan, its cock and the dog catch that locked it. "It's one of the new flintlocks with the wee lock just here," he said, pointing to what was an early version of a gun safety. " 'Tis an English weapon."

"How many flintlocks have you seen before this?"

"Not many. As I ken it, they're favored on the Continent. But in the Highlands?" He shrugged. "Nay, there's none such as this here, generally speaking. You speak of guns, but my men are lucky if they find a blade in their hands."

"So what do the Highlanders shoot? When they do have a gun, I mean. What type of gun do you have?"

"You're a peculiar one, *leannan*."

Her intense focus urged him on.

"Wheel lock," MacColla replied with a sigh.

"That's it?"

"Good Christ, I thought you lassies just had a mind for frocks and hairstyles." He chucked her chin. "I'd no idea what I've been missing these years, away at war. I could've been in parlors discussing muskets and armor with the beautiful ladies."

Seeing her grave face, he just leaned back on his elbows, kicking his feet in front of him, to give it some thought. His arm remained wrapped around her, hand tucked casually at her hip.

"I once had a matchlock. But in a good Highland mist?" He shook his head. "With that wee wick on the end, och. Damp makes the gun unusable, aye? Too bloody hard to keep lit."

"Yes," she said firmly. "That was true."

"Oh," he gave a surprised chuckle. "I thank you."

Ignoring his sarcasm, she continued, "Well, this gun that I saw, Graham's gun, it was actually a combination weapon"—she waved her hand—"but that's beside the point. This pistol had a *perfect* little flintlock. The striking surface, the flash pan, all one tiny, perfect self-contained bit. You tell me how many of *those* you've seen lately."

"So what are you saying?"

"I'm saying we dated the piece to 1675 which is . . ."

"Which is after James was said to have died." Sitting up, he withdrew from her, his face solemn.

"But why should I believe you?" He kept his tone matter-of-fact. Though he didn't accept her story, neither did he discount her. Her fighting skills had already shocked him enough for one lifetime; MacColla couldn't imagine why he should be surprised she'd come at him with something even more outrageous. "What you say about this gun proves nothing."

He saw her mind working, those gray eyes staring at the

pistol she held in her hands. The pistol she'd fired as if she'd been doing it all her life.

Could it be true? She shot and fought and spoke like no other woman he'd met. Like none he'd ever heard of.

She was willful and strong. And so healthy too, that was clear. Her limbs, long and straight. Even those radiant cheeks and her bright, even smile. They spoke to a life of luxury. Of privilege.

He didn't see how to reconcile those things. That she could load and fire a gun as well as any man, and yet she had skin, luminous and fair, as if she were crafted of the finest ivory.

He'd thought she might be a spy, but could it be that she practiced some form of the dark arts? Goose bumps fanned across his skin then ebbed, like a wave washing over the sand.

"Are you . . ." His voice was hoarse, grave. "Is it that you're some sort of . . . witch?"

"What?" She laughed then. "*Me?* A witch? God no." She shook her head, and then a peculiar look darkened her features. As if she hadn't before considered such a conclusion, potential ruination narrowly averted.

A sad half smile quirked her mouth. "Are you kidding? My family? I told you, we're Irish. Irish Catholic, to put a fine point on the whole thing. I've been baptized, first communioned, confirmed . . . the whole deal."

Haley sighed deeply. She looked at him with such sadness. He wasn't sure what to do. What to think.

"You still don't believe me, do you?" she asked.

"Well . . ."

"Yeah, I wouldn't believe me either. Okay—"

"Haley—" he began.

"No, no, let me think." She knew so much about the time period. Knew about MacColla. What could she tell him to make him believe?

She wracked her mind for any tidbit from his life that she could recall. She'd taken the seminars, read her David

Stevenson. She knew famous bits of trivia that wouldn't have been so well known in his own time.

I can do this, she thought. She knew things he hadn't told her. She knew things none of his peers would've known.

She could convince him. Haley shifted, crossing her legs to face him.

"Your dad was imprisoned for years with Campbell. Wait," she said suddenly, her face blanching. "He's not still imprisoned, is he?" He shook his head and she made a mental note to try to piece together what had happened to his father, and when.

"Your brother Gillespie was with him," she continued. "There are other brothers too, but I don't know about them so much . . . " she trailed off.

That wasn't going to cut it.

MacColla just smiled at her. "Many know of Campbell's treachery against my father, *leannan*."

"There's that poet," she snapped and pointed her finger at him in excitement.

MacColla scowled.

"You know . . . what's his name?"—she tapped her fingers on her lips—"Iain Lom MacDonald! He *loved* you. Wrote all kinds of poems and songs about you."

MacColla's scowl turned into a beet red blush. He opened his mouth to speak, but she stopped him. "No, just a minute, I'm not done. He had a nickname. Now *that* wouldn't be public knowledge, would it? The Stuttering MacDonald, maybe? Bald Iain? Well, he stuttered and he was bald, and had some sort of nickname along those lines. I just can't . . ."

She raised her hand, seeing what looked like growing impatience on his face. "Wait," she pleaded. If she could only think of that nickname, surely it would be some sort of proof of *something*.

What was the poet's nickname? Nickname . . .

"Ah!" It came out as a yelp, her eyes widened. "I've got it: your father!" Haley leaned in, animated. "Your father had a nickname. *Colkitto*. It was because he was left-handed. Those close to him called him Colkitto."

He nodded silently, his eyes squinting. Whether it was from bafflement or suspicion, she couldn't tell.

"You see, in my time, for a while people . . . well, *historians* mistakenly called *you* Colkitto. They thought *you* were the left-handed one. People argued about it. But it's not your nickname, is it? Your father Coll was . . . *is* known to his closest friends as Colkitto."

She inhaled deeply, smiling in triumph.

But not MacColla. His somber face chilled her, and stole the curve from her lips.

He rose. And though he offered his hand to help Haley up, his voice was gruff when he said, "We must go. I'm expected in Kintyre. My family waits for me even now.

"Fret not, *leannan*."

MacColla began to walk, adding, "You'll soon be able to ask the man for himself."

Chapter 19

Could he believe her? They'd stopped for a brief rest, and MacColla sat, watching Haley.

The lass was in her own world, studying his sword as if it could unlock the key to the universe. She'd leapt for it the moment he pulled it from his black leather scabbard to sit.

Would he believe her fantastical story, or decide simply that she was the loveliest madwoman he'd ever met? Her crazy talk of traveling through time had confounded him. And yet . . .

"Would you call this a Gallowglass sword?" she asked.

"*Leannan*, you do have the most peculiar questions." He untied a small leather bladder from his belt and took a deep pull of water.

He wiped his mouth on his sleeve, amused and disconcerted both. "So you speak the Irish too? *Gallóglaigh*. Foreign soliders," he mused. "I've not heard that word in some time. Aye, it's got the look of an Irish sword like those the *Gallóglaigh* fought with."

He watched her return her attentions to the blade. She

ran her palm along the base of it. It was a simple design, with V-shaped lines that echoed its sharp edges. Haley slowly stroked her hand along the flat of it, dipping her fingertip in and out of the etched steel.

Hunger clutched hard and fast at MacColla's chest. He felt it smolder in his eyes and drive straight to his loins, making him rigid with want.

"How is it you make a man weak with a mere touch to his blade?" He tried to muster a smile, but could only stare, the pure craving of her pushing out all other thought.

"*Claidheamh da laihm*," he rasped. "That's what that sword is called."

"Kla . . . hi . . . dah . . . life," she pronounced slowly. "Two-hand sword."

Feeling his eyes on her, Haley glanced up, and the intensity of his gaze overpowered her. His eyes pierced her. Incinerated her.

What did MacColla think of her? Did he believe her, or think her insane?

She looked away quickly. Strangely nervous, she returned her attention to the weapon, searching for some clue to the heart of the man.

She smoothed her fingers along the guard, an unadorned span of steel in the shape of a *T*, directly over the hilt, meant to protect the bearer's hand. Thin nicks in the metal scratched her thumb, and she contemplated those strikes from other swords that had not found his flesh. She realized she was grateful.

Her finger traced down the leather grip. It was a ring-hilt, with a plain circle at the base of the pommel. Either an Irish-made sword, or with a nod to one.

She fisted her hand tight around it. The leather was smooth, from sweat and blood and use.

Haley lifted. The tip remained on the ground, but still she felt the sword's heft. It would be only seven, perhaps eight pounds. Not too much heavier than the five-pound weights she'd sometimes worked with at the gym.

She lifted the blade from the dirt. It was difficult. Eight

pounds might not be much, but stretch it into a six-foot-long sword and it was a different story. She let the tip fall to the ground.

"Your early biographers wrote that you could behead four men with a single swing."

"Ha!" He gave a resounding laugh, and the sound of it was a balm to her nerves. "Is that so?"

She shrugged innocently, a smile on her face now, and he scooted next to her to clap his arm about her shoulder and tuck her in close.

"Well, I suppose if the men were all of a height," he speculated for a moment, sounding highly amused. "And if they all stood very still for me, back to stomach. Then, aye, I could do it."

In that moment, a wave of affection for him swept her. His suddenly high spirits were irresistible. And his accent melted her. His words had come out as "verrra still," the thick brogue tripping his tongue.

She wrapped her own arm around his back, leaned close, and found herself inhaling quickly for a renegade hit of his scent. Musk and man. Closing her eyes, she shook her head at her animal response. An explosion of warmth in her belly, her body suddenly expectant, all her muscles tensed, piqued, and on alert.

Did his laughter mean he believed her? Could he believe she was from another time? She hoped desperately he did.

"We can't tarry long, *leannan*."

She sighed. Her body ached from walking. From not sleeping. Not eating. She'd been taken in the night and her feet were still bare, scratched, and sore.

Reading her thoughts, he said, "I see your weariness, and I'm sorry for it. But there's nothing to be done. We're still on Campbell land. Though some of his people rally quietly against him, we've no way to tell friend from foe."

He tangled his hand in her hair, pulled her close to kiss the top of her head. "We need to keep walking. Find horses and be away from here."

"How will we find horses?" She gestured to the grand wilderness around them. They'd traveled steadily south, as much as possible taking cover in the wooded tangles that shadowed Loch Awe. She didn't imagine they'd be running into a stable anytime soon. "We're out in the middle of nowhere."

"Don't fash your bonny head over it." He pulled her in for one last, rough hug to his side. "I've spent the better part of the season raiding this very land. I expect I'll be able to root out a pony for that sweet bottom of yours." He slid his fingers down to give her a pinch.

She made a little chirp of surprise. MacColla's grin was guileless and, Haley thought, if she didn't know better, she'd think he was quite pleased with himself.

He looked at her, his features softening, brown eyes warm as they roved over her face, taking her in.

"One more thing, *leannan*."

The naked affection she saw in those eyes startled her. Thrilled her. Scared her. "Yes?" Her voice came out breathy and slight.

"I believe you." He stroked her cheek. "I don't understand your story, but I believe it."

Tears sprang to her eyes. "Really?" Something deep in her core unspooled. She hadn't fully realized just how terrified she'd been. Terrified that he wouldn't believe her. Terrified she'd be left on her own.

But most of all, Haley had been terrified she'd misunderstood why she was sent back. Because she knew the reason now. She'd been sent back in time to him. *For* him.

"It's you," she managed. "You're why I'm here."

"Aye." Emotion tore his voice to gravel. "And I'm the reason you'll stay."

Stay. Could she? What of her family? Her life? To stay would be to forsake her old world forever.

She roved her eyes over MacColla's face. His mouth, full, with lips slightly parted, ready to take her, taste her. His eyes, in which she'd witnessed such ferocity, now vulnerable, naked with affection, only for her.

Yes, she thought. *Maybe.*

Stay.

For a while.

He kissed her then, soft and slow, and it was the rightest thing she'd ever known.

❁

"Can we swim?" Their destination was the Mull of Kintyre, and though all she knew of the place was sung by Paul McCartney and Wings, Haley was beside herself, excited to see what he claimed was a modest home in a glen by the sea.

"You're a swimmer then too?" He shook his head. "Och, you're sure to impress my father now." He raised his brows in mock gravity. "You'd be wise, however, not to call the man *Colkitto*."

Laughing, she asked again, "Well, can we?"

"Swim? Aye, you can splash about. But I dare say you'll prefer a tub of hot water to the sea. 'Tis decidedly warmer."

Oh God, a bath. Her body thrilled with it, every cell shrieking to attention. Suddenly her scalp, her back, her legs, all the parts that had been itching like mad flared into a raging prickly need for a thorough scrubbing.

"Oh." She shuddered with anticipation. "A real bath? Will we be there tonight?"

"*Leannan*"—he laughed and tousled her hair as if bemused by her silliness—"tonight? No indeed. It will take us days to get there. I'd say it's a full twenty leagues from where we stand. Or more. And there's still the matter of finding us horses."

He blew out an exhale, looking longingly at the distant lake, now only a glittering patchwork through the trees. "A boat is what we really need." MacColla turned to her. He tried to mask a smile. She saw the devil in his eye and chose to ignore it. "Kintyre is almost an island, aye? A long bit of land hanging from the mainland like a, well . . ."

"Like a . . . ?"

"Like a . . . long, thin . . . appendage dangling from the coast."

She rolled her eyes. She'd been one sister among five brothers; she caught the joke. "Okay, MacColla. I get it. It looks like a . . ."

"Peninsula," he quickly added. "It looks like . . . aye, it is a peninsula."

"Mmm-hm." Nodding her head, she bit back a grin.

"Ah," he interjected, wisely changing the subject, "I do have a story about this strapping peninsula."

She shot him a look.

" 'Twill shorten our walk," he assured her.

When she didn't protest, he began, "Kintyre didn't always belong to Scotland." He nodded solemnly, settling into his story. "Over five hundred years ago there lived a great Viking warrior."

He paused to take her elbow, helping her over a fallen log, then went on, "There'd been great fighting over who'd control the west of Scotland."

MacColla's brogue thickened, drawing out his words. "Our good King Malcolm told King Barelegs—that was the Viking's name." Raising his brows, he grinned. "And a hard name to forget, aye?"

His face lit, completely animated now, and Haley decided he'd picked up a bit of the Irish storytelling in his time away.

"Malcolm told the Viking that he could keep whichever islands he was able to sail around. Well, Barelegs asked his men to drag his boat over the narrowest stretch of Kintyre, so set was he on having the land."

"And did he do it?"

"Oh, aye," he laughed from deep in his belly, "and as the story goes, he sat proud as you please on the poop of that Viking longboat whilst his men hauled him across."

As her laugh faded, she stopped in her tracks. Watched MacColla's back as he walked on for a few paces.

Such a huge man. Six foot six, she estimated. Haley watched and admired the shift of muscles beneath his shirt, the flex of his iron calves with each step. His black hair was wild, swaying, brushing along his shoulders. And there was that tremendous sword reaching toward the ground at his back.

He was such a surprise to her.

Haley had heard of his ferocity, had seen it in his fight with the Campbells. She knew there were dark and vicious depths that she'd yet to understand.

The warrior in him scared her. Could she love a man capable of such brutality?

And yet she found she also anticipated seeing that side. God help her, she even hoped she'd see it, hoped one day she'd see Alasdair MacColla in action.

Now *her* MacColla.

A man so artlessly amused in the telling of his own stories.

And capable of such passion. With a short fuse, it lit to consume him with warrior ferocity as quickly as it had brought words of love to his mouth.

She watched his back for those few paces.

Then he turned to see where she was. They were both silent for a moment. He tilted his head. "Did you not like my tale, then?"

MacColla reached his hand out to her.

She inhaled deeply, walked forward. Haley took his hand and said, "No, MacColla, I loved your tale."

Those thick black brows of his furrowed suddenly.

"What's the matter?" she asked.

"Your feet, *leannan*." He dropped to his knees before her. "You're limping."

With his hand wrapped around her thigh to steady her, he lifted the opposite foot and drew in his breath sharply.

She put a hand at his shoulder for balance. "I'm all right."

"Why'd you not tell me? Och," he growled, and checked her other foot. "You've not the feet for such walking."

He stood and abruptly swooped her into his arms. "You're a wildcat, aye, but with such tender wee paws."

"Really, MacColla." He began to walk on and she pushed at his shoulders in a halfhearted protest. "You can't carry me all the way to Kintyre."

"I would." He guided her arms around his neck. His smile was broad as he stole a kiss from her cheek. "If you asked it."

"Well, I'm not going to ask it." She rested her head on him, her feet scissoring in the air, and she let herself enjoy the feel of it. "So what's your plan then?"

They were approaching a clearing. "My plan," he said as he set her gently down to lean against a tree near the edge of the copse, "is to see you rest here. We need horses. And, losh, but I need food."

He leaned and kissed her forehead. "Don't move, *leannan*. And please don't get yourself abducted in my absence."

He headed back into the forest. Turning, he walked backward a few steps to say, "I'll return with food and ponies, my fair lass."

MacColla spun and jogged away. Her smile grew weak.

She'd rest, and think.

And try to figure out how exactly she proposed to keep a war hero from dying.

Chapter 20

"A lass?!" Colkitto slammed his tankard onto the table and ale sloshed over the sides, puddling onto the well-scarred slab of wood. "What's my son doing mucking about the countryside with some lass?"

Jean cut her eyes to Scrymgeour. She knew her father could make even the most dauntless of men quaver, particularly when he was in his drink. But Scrymgeour sat by her side, as placid as ever, and she was grateful.

He glanced her way and she spared him a quick, shy smile. At times like this, she felt chagrined by her father's behavior. She wondered what Scrymgeour thought of them. Of her especially.

She had three brothers, four if one counted the bastard Angus, and Colkitto for a father, all of them set in their warring ways, clinging tight to a generations-long feud that she sometimes feared defined them as much as their own clan lineage.

Did Scrymgeour sit there, biding his time, waiting for his moment to be free of the lot of them?

She sat tall, marshalling her thoughts enough to answer

her father. "He's not mucking about." Jean folded her hands in her lap, a calm pose to match the smoothness of her voice. "I told you, Campbell's men took the woman. My brother simply—"

"Simply risked his own hide for some stranger?"

Jean hesitated. That had given her pause as well, though for different reasons. She hadn't liked the woman at first. Resented Haley her free and mannish ways.

But when Alasdair had discovered Haley gone, the haste with which he'd raced after her startled Jean.

She wondered if the woman might be the key to blunting her brother's desire for vengeance. His craving of it was insatiable, never-ending, razing all in his path. It was what had robbed Jean's husband from her.

"Campbell threatens even now to take back this land," her father continued. He slammed his hand down again, landing in the puddle with a dull slap.

She saw Scrymgeour bristle at the sprinkle of ale. He discretely dabbed his cheek, and mortification colored her cheeks.

Jean's mind strayed once more to her husband. Donald MacKay of Ardnacroish. He'd been a good man, she knew. A near stranger to her, but a good man nonetheless.

And then he sacrificed his sword in battle, giving it to her brother when Alasdair's own had broken. Her husband gave his sword, and so he gave his life.

It was only because of him that her brother still lived.

Jean grimaced.

She tried to take her mind from it. Faced her father, watched his mouth moving, hearing sounds yet not registering words.

The men talked of battle, always battle. She expected more from them. More from Alasdair, especially. He was smarter, more levelheaded than the rest. The only man in her family who knew how to read. Who was a visionary. A leader of men.

She wondered precisely what it was her husband had died for that day, at the Battle of Auldearn.

It had been MacColla's great victory. So great, the bard Iain Lom MacDonald sang a song to praise him. "Health and joy to the valiant Alasdair," he'd written.

She wiped her damp palms along her skirts. She should be relieved, she thought. She loved her brother, and he still lived.

But when others slept, and she knew none could hear her in the darkness, Jean wept. She mourned her loss. Resented her brother his warring ways.

She shut her eyes, hearing the men speaking as if from a distance. Her hands were clenched, clammy, the nails that burrowed into her palms the only things that kept her tears at bay.

She felt a hand snake onto her lap. Warm and firm, fingers twined with hers. Giving her a squeeze.

Unclenching, Jean opened her eyes. Glanced to Scrymgeour, stalwart by her side.

And she knew then that he wasn't simply biding his time. That he would be by her side to stay, if she wished it.

The thought gave her strength.

She tuned back into Colkitto, who roared on. "Campbell vows to take back *this very land* Clan Iain Mor so dauntonly only just carved back for ourselves."

"'Twas Alasdair who did the carving, Father," Jean said quietly. She savored her anger now, and it brought frost to her words. She would will the family to moderation, if it killed her. "And I trust he'll soon return safe," she added evenly, "with this Haley in hand."

Colkitto glared at his daughter, silent. Tensing, Scrymgeour eased his hand from hers, nearer to the dirk hanging at his belt.

Jean shot him a quick, reassuring glance.

"Och," Colkitto growled. "At ease, lad. My daughter's in no danger from me. 'Tis my son who needs a fair clouting." His eyes lit at the prospect. He and his sons sparred and tussled at every opportunity, and if Jean knew her father, he'd not miss this one.

She feared her father was forgetting what he was about.

He grew old, well past seventy now, but he'd been a warrior in his day and considered himself a warrior still.

It wasn't his body that worried her. His skin fell slack, but it hung on muscles that remained as firm as bands of iron at his arms. It was his mind that Jean had been spending more time concerned about. His wits weren't as fast or as fit as they once were.

Colkitto increasingly spent the days in his cups, bored. Lately she'd had the grim thought that he'd as soon die in battle than spend one more day in their company.

"I've already negotiated surrender of Dunyveg. I'll not—"

"That was before we were born, Father. Thirty years ago. The MacDonalds once again hold Dunyveg."

The old man let out a slow hiss. Not moving his eyes from his daughter, he shouted for his wife. "Mary! More ale!"

Jean finally let herself flinch. Would he not show a little decorum? She stole a look in Scrymgeour's direction, shame keeping her chin cast low.

Her mother glided into the room, and Jean was reminded of what a beauty she'd once been. MacColla was an unusually large man, all her brothers were, and it was a trait they could only have inherited from their mother. Though Colkitto was tall, her mother was almost of a like height, still ramrod straight and strong despite her years.

"Aye, Husband, we've ale to hand." Mary smiled, and Jean was thankful for the elegant nod she gave Scrymgeour as she refilled his cup. "There is no need to bellow like a bull. I'm only just in the other room."

She went to stand behind her husband's chair and placed a calm hand on his shoulder. "You may fashion yourself a king among men, my love," she said, taking in the unadorned walls of the humble two-bedroom cottage, "but this home is a far cry from a castle."

Face otherwise completely still, her eyes locked on Jean and she gave a sly wink.

Scrymgeour stifled a laugh, clearly shocked by Mary's impertinence.

Colkitto erupted into laughter, a thunderous sound echoing off the cold, stone walls. Her father had a broad, open-mouthed laugh, revealing teeth yellowed with age.

"To my Mary!" He lifted his newly filled cup. "Never have I known her to speak with forked tongue." He craned his head to look up at her. "You're as bonny as the day we met, *beanag*." He gave her a brusque nod before taking a deep pull of ale.

"And you, *an duine agam*," Mary replied. Reaching down, she took the cup from his lips for a sip. "I find you just as irascible."

"Aye, we drink now." Chuckling, Colkitto reached up to pat his wife on the cheek, then turned his attention back to the table. "But soon we fight. The MacDonalds have re-claimed Kintyre, and Campbell will not let it stand. Mark me, he will come at us, with blood on his mind."

Blood and more blood. It was time for the fighting to stop.

Her father's bitterness grew with each passing day. As acrid as the accursed ale that he could no longer live without.

And Alasdair. Her brother was no longer a young man. It was time for him to think on other things. A home. A wife. He had nearly four decades behind him and still no life of his own to speak of.

He'd seemed captivated by that peculiar woman.

Jean wrapped her hands around her cup. The metal was cool on her hot skin.

A shadow of a smile flickered for an instant. Perhaps the stranger named Haley would be just the one to finally turn her brother's head.

Chapter 21

Campbell cut his eyes to the right, discreetly studying the man riding beside him. He congratulated himself on a wise decision.

Major Nicholas Purdon was a solid soldier. He received orders without question and appeared to relish the slaughtering of papists and fools.

Campbell gave the young man a rare smile and urged his horse into a trot. The flat grazing lands skirting the castle was pleasant terrain, and made for an easy approach. A peculiar spot to build a fortress, to say the least. But someone else's folly was his triumph.

Triumph. He allowed himself a smile. Campbell had wanted victory. He'd tried for it with a witch, but he'd finally found it with a soldier.

With Purdon at his right and one General Leslie at his left, he had mopped the countryside of MacDonalds. Together they'd chased MacColla and his family into a corner.

And together they'd slaughtered MacColla once and for all.

"You're certain he's dead?"

"Aye," Purdon replied, "the big man is dead."

Could it be true? MacColla, dead. Campbell beamed. No MacDonald was a match for sixteen hundred of his best soldiers. Not even MacColla.

"Skipness was a rout," Purdon continued, referring to the battle Campbell's men had just fought at Skipness Castle, on the upper reaches of the Kintyre peninsula. "'Twas a long siege, but Skipness is yours." He nodded to the structure looming before them.

"I care not for the castle." Campbell pulled back on his reins and looked up. Skipness was a stout, rectangular fortress, constructed of red and yellow stone. "A dour pile of rock, is it not?"

He didn't give the major a chance to answer. He'd noticed a knot of men, studying something on the ground. And then he spotted the black boots, sticking out in an unnatural sprawl on the grass.

Campbell quickly dismounted, leaving his reins dangling.

Men surrounded the body, but Campbell could tell by the silhouette that it was a large man who lay dead on the ground.

MacColla.

Purdon caught up to him as Campbell muttered gleefully, "I care not for castles, Major, when MacColla's head is for the taking."

"And so you have it." Purdon smiled. The throng parted and the soldier gestured to the body with a flourish.

"You fool." Campbell's low curse was a snake's hiss. "This is not MacColla." He nudged the man's head with his boot, turning it side to side.

It was a tall man, with black hair, and MacColla's arrogant nose. A man who looked like MacColla. "This is his brother."

"Well . . ." Purdon began, treading very carefully. "Isn't one son of Coll Ciotach the same as another?"

Campbell answered with his silence. His hand went to

the sword at his side, and he was gratified to see a few of the men flinch.

The needle-thin steel made a satisfying whistle as he swept his blade diagonally before him. Then, in a single downward stroke, he knelt to plunge the sword in the throat of the dead MacDonald.

He stood once more, needing to wriggle his blade loose from the soil under the dead man's neck.

At last Campbell turned to the major. "No," he replied. "Not the same. Now you will find MacColla. The *real* Mac-Colla, and you will kill him. And you will kill his father. And you will kill his woman."

Campbell gazed to the southwest. Shut his eyes to the sun, low in the sky. MacColla was out there. He'd have traveled farther south. He'd be in sight of Ireland, and it would call to him.

Campbell would catch him before he could answer.

"We head south," he said, "bleeding the country of MacDonalds as we ride."

❁

The witch lay naked in the dirt, hands stretched over her head, her body an offering to the moon. She was dimly aware of the rocks that dug into her skin. Dimly aware of her thirst. But the concerns of her body were not what drove her now.

Anger thrummed through Finola's veins. She'd depleted herself, doing the Campbell's dirty work. He'd taken her energy, her time.

Most of all, he'd taken her for granted. Feeding off her with the whimsy of a child.

But it wasn't a child's game he played at.

And if Campbell didn't know that yet, she'd be the one to show him.

Chapter 22

They were closing in on the Mull of Kintyre, the scenery growing more breathtaking with every step.

And Haley was freaking out. All that natural beauty was impossible to appreciate when all she could think was, in minutes, she'd meet those people most important in MacColla's life.

Just one last stretch of lush valley separated them from his family's cottage, visible in the distance, tidy and painted a cheery white amidst so much green.

She was about to meet Colkitto. *The* Colkitto. Now *there* was a dissertation topic, she thought, incredulous.

"Breathe, *leannan*." MacColla chuckled. "You look like a wee badger with your face screwed so. If I didn't ken better, I'd think you were in pain."

She turned to see MacColla smiling wide at her. He might be amused, but she was not.

"Go ahead, laugh," she snapped. "I just wish there were some way I could subject *you* to *my* family."

A sudden twinge stabbed her throat. *My family.* What would they make of MacColla? Would she ever see them again? What could she ever tell them of this experience if she did?

She realized it would no longer be a simple thing to leave. Could she turn her back on MacColla forever? And if not, would she really choose never again to see her family?

He'd changed her. Her life would never be the same. She knew she could never take another lover now that she'd been kissed by Alasdair MacColla.

"You'll be fine, lass," he told her, mistaking the lines on her brow. He reached over and smoothed her cheek with the back of his fingers. He smiled.

His voice once again in high spirits, he added, "Though if it's Colkitto you want to win over, you might consider a wee scrap with the old man. You can show him that trick you do throwing your blade." MacColla laughed outright then, and Haley leaned over to slap the rump of his pony.

Unfortunately that sped the beast into a grudging trot, only hastening their arrival.

The door opened as they approached. A tall woman filled the doorway. She wore a simple, ruddy-colored dress, covered by an apron from the waist down. Her head was bare, and the sun shone on her gray hair. Some streaks of black remained, marbling the tight bun at the nape of her neck.

Haley drew in her breath. "Is that your—" she began, but MacColla answered her question when he leapt to the ground and, in two great strides, had the woman swept in his arms.

"Mother," she mumbled under her breath. Haley's mouth was set in a grim line. "Well, here goes nothing."

She slid from the pony. Busying herself for a minute, she stretched the life back into her legs, and then, not knowing what else to do, took and held the horses' reins, standing dumbly, waiting for it to be made clear just what she should do or where she should go.

She watched avidly as MacColla's mother held his face in her hands, chattering and exclaiming in Gaelic too rapid for her to understand. Haley spared a smile for the sight of the warrior who, despite his size and ferocity, was this mother's son.

His sister ducked out of the house from behind the two of them and headed straight for Haley. Wiping her hands on her apron, Jean gave her a nod and a surprisingly open smile.

"Welcome," she said in a muted voice. "I'm well pleased to see you. You gave my brother a fright. I'm fair certain the hounds of hell couldn't have caught him, so fast did he race from Fincharn."

Her comment gave Haley an unexpected little jag of warmth in her chest. MacColla had raced after *her*.

"I knew he'd find you," Jean added. "And I'm glad of it. I know what the Campbell is capable of," she added quietly.

It was a grave statement, and Haley wondered at what the poor girl had undergone in the cellars of Campbell's grim tower house.

An awkward silence fell between them, then Jean appeared to brighten. "But what am I thinking of?" Taking the reins from Haley's hands, she swung them back over the ponies' heads to knot them high on their necks.

"Come with me." She held out her hand. Mistaking the reason for Haley's anxiety, she added, "Don't fash yourself over the mounts. This is men's work. My brother manages the battles, let him tend the beasts as well." She gave a sly smile.

Haley took her arm, and Jean gave her a reassuring pat. "You'll be wanting to bathe. And we've a bed for you too."

It struck Haley how much of a luxury that would be.

"You'll sleep with me," Jean added, "but 'tis just the two of us."

MacColla's mother was intent on her son, and just when Haley thought she'd temporarily dodged introduction, an elegant voice announced, "Don't think you've escaped me. I'd meet the lass who's got my son in such a *fankle*."

She felt a firm hand on her shoulder and turned to face Mary MacDonald. Though her warm smile put Haley at ease, it was clear her sharp eyes missed nothing.

"Oh, I . . ." She wracked her mind for how it was one actually politely introduced themselves in the seventeenth century. Phrases like *well met* seemed a little too Shakespearean. She finally settled on saying, "I'm very pleased to make your acquaintance."

"Ah"—Mary raised her brows and shot a quick look at her son—"such fine English. No wonder my son tells me I'm not to speak to you in our own tongue."

Moving her hand to Haley's cheek, Mary studied her closely. "He also says that though your father is Irish, you have the mettle of a Highland woman." She patted her cheek as if she'd test Haley's spirit then and there.

MacColla nodded to someone in greeting, and they turned to see Scrymgeour approaching. She watched as he stole a glance at Jean, his gaze automatically drawn to her. His eyes flicked quickly away, and Haley wondered if anyone else had noticed.

The greeting he and MacColla shared was more reserved than their last had been. Haley glanced to Jean and back again, realizing that MacColla, at least, was aware of Scrymgeour's interest in her.

"What news of Gillespie have you?" MacColla asked.

Haley held her breath. She'd been so nervous about meeting his parents, she'd forgotten that a brother would likely turn up as well. She wasn't entirely certain she was prepared for it.

"No word as yet," Mary replied, her voice tight.

"Gillespie travels south even now," Scrymgeour was quick to reassure her. "I'm certain we'll see the wayward lad any day."

Haley was suddenly grateful for Scrymgeour's presence. He was polite, proper, and thoughtful as ever. She studied him while the men talked. Although he was just shy of what one would call stout, it wasn't his size that had initially struck her. He had a pleasant face, warm and open. Trustworthy.

She noticed Jean watching him too, and realized she wasn't the only one grateful for the man.

"As I understand it, you travel with Alasdair now."

It took Haley a moment to register that Mary had directed the comment to her.

"*Uh*, yes," Haley said, looking to MacColla for reassurance.

"Then you'll be soon returning to your homeland," Mary noted. "To Ireland."

Haley felt the warmth leach from her eyes. *To Ireland.* She worked to keep her lips wrenched in a smile. *Where he'll meet his death.*

"I imagine you long to see your country again."

"I . . . Yes . . ."

"It's been a long journey, Mother." MacColla's voice broke in, saving her. He was at Haley's side in an instant, his arm protectively at her back. "And I'm straight to the kitchen. I'd have some of whatever my sister has in the pot."

"She's made a fine cock-a-leekie—"

Haley heard a brief rustle from behind. MacColla's hand disappeared from her back, and she felt rather than saw him spin aside, just in time to dodge an old man leaping in to bear tackle him. Meeting air instead, the man stumbled forward, and MacColla turned to catch him before he hit the ground.

Colkitto, she presumed.

The old man stood, and showing off a mouthful of ragged teeth, bellowed with laughter.

"You're too slow for me, old man." MacColla clapped his father on the back.

This time, he was unable to dodge the quick jab Colkitto landed on his shoulder. "I'm not dead yet, boy." He glanced at Haley and back again, adding, "I see you're not either, *eh*?"

MacColla's father turned his full attention to her. "So you'd be the lass calling herself Fitzpatrick."

Anxiety prickled the nape of her neck. She knew there was a right way to answer that question, she just wasn't sure what that would be. She simply stated, "I am."

"You are," he muttered, repeating her. "Not a talkative one either, *eh*?" He eyed her up and down, nodding his approval, and Haley noticed MacColla stiffen out of the corner of her eye.

"Well, son, you've found yourself a bonny, rosy-cheeked Irish lass."

Colkitto gave her a flat stare, letting his eyes lock with hers for what felt like a very long few seconds.

Haley realized then that she'd need to do more than a knife-throwing trick to win this man over.

"They're not as feisty as the Highland lassies," Colkitto added.

"With all due respect, sir." Haley put her shoulders back to stand as straight as she could. "You've not yet met *me*."

Colkitto exploded into laughter, exuberantly shaking his head, and slapping his approval on MacColla's back. "Not met her," he mumbled, with another burst of laughter.

Haley wasn't sure what to think, though she figured it could've gone worse. Gathering herself, she shuddered an accidental sigh, and the tang of the sea filled her lungs. It drew her eyes, so vast and powerful, stretching serene across the horizon. Light winked over the peaks and valleys of its surface, calmly pitching and bobbing with no regard for any of her inner turmoil.

"*Leannan*," MacColla whispered. It had been meant for her ears alone, but she sensed Colkitto's eyes cut to her at the sound of the word. Its meaning wouldn't be lost on him. MacColla's family would know they were together. What would they think of that, of her?

"Come." He put his hand at her shoulder to guide her into the house. His touch, warm and steady, soothed her.

"Och no, Brother." Jean was quick to take her elbow, a playful challenge in her eyes. "We've need for women's time now."

Jean gave her arm an encouraging squeeze. "Come, then. I'll do up a bath for you. Between my mother and me, we'll get you set to rights."

Set to rights meant a small snack followed by a hip bath

and getting dressed in fresh clothes on loan from Mac-Colla's mother. Though the gown was a little long, Jean masterminded a way to roll it under at the waist to cinch into her apron.

"Your hair, lass," Jean *tsked*.

"It's not too bad . . ." Haley began to protest, then caught sight of herself in the mirror. What seemed like fistfuls of coarse hair had blown free from the braid she'd tucked into a makeshift bun that morning. Dark tendrils fanned around her face like a halo. "Ugh. It's like a rat's nest."

"Och, no." She guided Haley to sit on a small three-legged stool. Though Jean had a straight face, Haley could see humor light her eyes. "More like something fit for a wee bird."

A joke, she thought. *Interesting.*

MacColla's sister worked in silence, tugging a comb through Haley's hair, pausing frequently to unsnarl knots with her fingers.

Haley caught occasional glimpses of her in the mirror. Jean seemed looser now that she was near her family. There was color in her cheeks, and an ease in the way she held herself.

Her hair was finally completely smoothed, and Jean raked her fingers through it one last time. Haley shivered. Not only could she use a proper shampoo and conditioner, her scalp was sore from having her hair pulled back tight all day. The feel of it loose down her back was a delicious relief.

Jean began to separate it into thick chunks for braiding, and Haley startled them both when she abruptly said, "No."

They caught each other's eyes in the mirror.

"I mean, can I please just leave it down?" Haley asked. "Would that be all right?"

Jean's face went blank. She shrugged. "As you like."

Haley saw the girl glance at her own hair in the mirror, and she wondered if Jean just might be fantasizing about letting her own hair down.

Jean opened the door to leave, and MacColla was standing there, poised to knock.

"I . . ." He looked past his sister, locking his eyes at once on Haley. "I'd thought we could move the legs a bit. We've had a long ride. And the lands around Kintyre are exceedingly bonny."

"I . . . Yes," Haley managed. He'd washed and changed as well, and the sight of him filling the doorway, so intent on her, emptied all rational thought from her mind.

Jean gave a small shake of her head and ducked under his arm as she went out the door.

"Not as bonny as you, though, *leannan*," he said the moment his sister left. "You are a vision, your hair gleaming at your back like a loch in the moonlight."

He insisted on showing her the coastline around the Mull of Kintyre, hiking up a small cliff for a panoramic view. Though it had been a gentle rise to the top, Haley's heart lurched to see such a sharp drop over the other side and down to the beach below.

The wind whipped around them, carrying with it the smell of the sea, the cries of birds, and the faraway barking of seals.

Regretting her decision to wear it down, she held her hair knotted in one fist. Haley soon forgot the annoyance, though, when she took in the spectacular scenery around them.

"That would be Dunaverty," MacColla said, following her gaze to the castle in the distance. "A MacDonald stronghold," he added, staring solemnly at the gray and black mass perched atop a monolithic rock formation.

Almost completely surrounded by water, the gargantuan rock looked as if it'd been dropped from the sky to land at the edge of the sea.

A double rampart defended the fortress by land, reinforced by a trench hacked deep in the rocky soil. On the other side was a sheer drop to rocks and water.

The sight silenced her.

The castle had been in ruins for centuries by the time

she'd been born. None in her time had ever seen it. Not even a sketch of it.

A gust of wind howled around them, prickling Haley's skin into goose bumps.

"But look here," he said after a time. MacColla guided her chin but a fraction, leading her gaze into the far distance.

"And so there it is." MacColla leaned down to place his cheek next to hers. He pointed across the sea, to Ireland, a ghostly silhouette on the horizon. "Your homeland."

Her breath was knocked from her. "Ire—" she began, and the wind seemed to steal the rest of the word from her mouth. *Ireland. Where MacColla dies.*

"Or rather, your father's homeland," he amended, unaware of the anguish caused by the sight.

She struggled to inhale, struggled to shake the morbid premonitions that clung in her mind like cobwebs, setting her skin to crawling.

Ireland. It had always been a home for her. A place of warmth and smiling faces. Peat fires, flocks of cousins, and damp, green grass.

Riding in small, boxy cars on the wrong side of the road. The smell of cigarettes and petrol.

Getting jostled in crowded pubs, a pint of Guinness in hand. Hearing her father, sounding loud so near to her side, joining other voices in song.

"My father's homeland," she managed, agreeing. Her words were small in the wind.

Crossing her arms tight at her chest, Haley forced the feeling to pass.

Her dad's homeland. MacColla was referring to her story. They'd discussed it, discussed what to tell his family. She would rightly claim Ireland as her father's homeland. It hadn't taken long for them to agree they needed to keep the rest of her tale a secret.

All anyone needed to know was that she hailed from Ireland. That and the fact that she was Catholic would be the only points of interest to Colkitto anyhow.

She feared the questions they'd ask. Feared living in such close quarters with strangers. True strangers, around whom she had no notion of how to act, what to say, what to do.

"'Tis Antrim we're looking at. My MacDonald kinsmen are yonder." Standing behind her, MacColla wrapped his arms around her. They brushed just under her breasts and for a moment all conscious thought fled as she felt his body against hers, warm and shielding her from the wind.

Loosening, she eased her hand from her hair and relaxed her arms at her chest, savoring the feel of him.

The strong, flat belly. Thick biceps framing her arms. He'd hunched slightly, to rest his chin on her head. She felt his sporran in the small of her back and shivered to think of what lay under that kilt.

A pure, base wanting of him suffused her. She felt this man, so powerful and steady at her back, and she was desperate to keep him close. To take him, to absorb every part of him. To have him take her.

Most of all, to keep him from Ireland, a place she suddenly hated more than anything she'd ever known.

But instead they would sleep apart, she with Jean in a tiny loft at the top of a rickety spiral staircase, while he and the other men bedded downstairs, on the floor in front of the fire. The only other room, another loft belonging to Colkitto and his wife.

She didn't know what was to happen between them. They'd only shared a kiss. He'd pledged such astounding words of love, startled her with his unassuming affection, and yet she didn't know what to expect. What he'd expect of her.

"*Ist*," MacColla whispered, and she shivered at the feel of his breath in her ear. Wrapping his arms tighter, he nodded to a spot on the cliff face below. It was just a narrow crack in the rock, but the tan sprigs of old grass and debris drew the eye. "A nest, *leannan*. Do you see it?"

Haley nodded. And then her eyes adjusted. She spotted a small bobbing head, white feathers gray in the shadows. "Wait, is that a . . . a puffin?"

The bird froze, turned, showcasing a beak that looked comically like a bright orange nose.

She was waiting for his answer, wondering what the bird might be called in Gaelic, when she felt his mouth on her neck.

His tongue was hot, trailing slow, languorous kisses along her chilled skin.

Her body thrummed to life. Breath came short and blood pumped close to her skin. Trembling, she gave more of her weight to him.

"Are you mine, *leannan*?" His voice was a harsh whisper in the suddenly still air. He seemed a wild thing. Raw. Needful.

Haley felt expansive, with a swollen ache between her legs to match the stab of longing in her heart. She nodded wordlessly.

"Tonight." He smoothed aside her hair to nibble her gently, just at the base of her neck. "I will come for you."

Chapter 23

Haley spent dinner in a silent daze. Colkitto monopolized the conversation with talk of the king, of the Campbell, of Ireland. She knew she should be listening, but she was unable to focus. Her body was the only thing that claimed her attention, pushing the concerns of her mind to the far reaches of awareness.

MacColla's gaze flicked constantly to her, continually drawn to her as if she were his lodestone. And her skin flushed crimson with every glance.

He was tense, his knuckles white as he held the knife at his food. And yet MacColla wasn't still. His body seemed a cocked gun. Charged, dangerous. A weapon set to detonate.

She retired to her room. Laid awake for hours. Waiting. Anxious. For him.

Haley was nervous that Jean might awaken. Nervous he'd change his mind.

But she heard it, long after Jean had nodded off. A light scratching on the other side of the door.

Haley slipped silently from her bed. Her nightgown

glowed eerily white in the pale moonlight. She deliberated for a moment, then pulled a woolen wrapper around her shoulders.

Her heart was pounding as she padded to the door and cautiously pulled the latch.

MacColla stood there, a giant in the undersized doorway. He wore the same clothes, his faded plaid and shirt. His feet were bare and silent.

He stood unmoving, like a ghost in the darkness. His face was in shadow, the ambient moonlight picking out only select features. The bridge of his nose. The hard line of his jaw.

Haley wondered for a moment if he were an apparition. If this hadn't all been some fantasy, some figment of her imagination.

"*Tiugainn leam.*" His voice was low, rough, meant for her alone. *Come with me.*

He reached to her, his fingers limned with the silvery light of the moon. She took his hand. Let those strong fingers twine with hers, clasp her warmly. She felt the brittle bend of hair under her fingertips, a light dusting at the back of his hand.

He had to cant his body at an awkward angle to fit down the stairs, but he didn't let go of her hand. They descended in silence. Slipped out of the cottage in silence.

The grass glittered, moonlight pricking the dew into millions of tiny jewels, making it seem a magical path, cool and fresh under their feet.

They walked for a time, heading to the shore. Neither spoke, and the hushed wash of the waves on sand grew louder, floating to them on the night breeze.

Haley shivered, and he tucked her close under his arm. When he finally did speak, his voice was tentative, and she thought that perhaps MacColla was as nervous as she.

"There's a wee cove. We're not far now. I think . . ." He stopped, tilted her chin up to him. Though his eyes were dark in shadow, she felt their intensity, gazing at her. Drinking her in.

Haley held her breath, yearning to hold on to that moment in time. To keep that feeling of his eyes on her, forever tucked close.

Clearing his throat, he stroked the hair from her brow and finished, "'Tis a pretty wee cove, *leannan*. I think you'll fancy it." He stroked her cheek once with his thumb, then led them on.

They crested a small rise, and she saw it. Or rather, it was what she didn't see. The absence of land before them spoke to the sea. Her vision adjusted. The water was a glassy stretch, like black obsidian filling the horizon. A single white wash of moonlight streaked across the surface, spotlighting the low rolls of ever-moving water.

"Tread careful, lass." Putting his hand at her waist, he guided Haley over a shallow ridge of rocks, stepping gingerly up and back down the black crags.

He jumped down the last bit, his feet landing with a quiet *chuff* onto the sand. The narrow slice of beach curved before them in the shape of a crescent moon, edged by a stretch of wet sand looking like a stream of molten silver in the moonlight.

"A wee cove." MacColla turned as if to lift her down, but he froze before her. The rock she stood on brought her just slightly taller than he, their faces mere inches apart. "Just for you, *leannan*," he told her softly, his voice ragged with emotion. "All for you."

She leaned into MacColla, reaching her arms around his neck, and he lifted her easily, guiding Haley's legs around his waist.

He stepped back and she had the sensation of gravity pulling her to him, grounding her to him, as if she were more connected to MacColla than to the earth itself.

She clung tight as he headed to a dry stretch of beach, his mouth grazing over her as he walked. He stopped and dug his feet into the sand, continuing to hold and kiss her. Along her neck, to her throat, tender kisses that grew heated, then devouring, down to skim along the top of her neckline.

Haley hooked her feet behind his back, writhing tight to him, and raked fingers through his hair, desperate to bring him closer still.

He raised his head then, and intensity blazed in eyes half-lidded from want. "*A chiall mo chrìdhe,*" he whispered.

He dipped a kiss to her mouth, hungry and quick like a striking animal. MacColla pulled back again, met her gaze. "*Tha gràdh agam ort.*"

I love you.

He leaned to her once more, his mouth slow and open, to kiss her deeply, his tongue roving, tasting, exploring every part of her.

Her whole body tingled, ushering to life an explosion of sensations. She filled her lungs deep with the scent of him, of musk and the brine of the sea. The thin skin of her breasts tugged to sharp peaks, and she felt a rush from between her thighs up into the core of her, as desire raged through her, leaving a throbbing heat in its wake.

MacColla knelt then, bringing them down gradually, laying Haley slowly onto her back.

He eased over her, bearing his weight on his elbows and knees. His thick black hair swept down, bringing his scent more brightly to her, but casting his face in shadows.

Something primal roiled through her as she felt him, large and insistent, grinding against the cleft between her legs. Demanding satisfaction.

"*Leannan.*" His voice was a sigh on the wind. "I want you, *leannan.*"

His mouth found hers again. He brought his hand to her breast, chafing and pinching her through the thin nightgown. Haley moaned, shutting her eyes.

She flinched as a shock of cold rushed up her legs, then realized the slide of fabric up her thighs.

She moaned again, louder, tilting her hips to rub closer to him.

His hand fumbled for a moment as he found his way

under the rumpled hem. He reached the soft skin of her thigh. Squeezed her.

Stroked higher.

His hand found her, wet and aching for him, and she gasped. MacColla rubbed his thumb in steady circles over her, and her kisses grew frenzied as she thought she might die with want for him.

He stilled for a heartbeat, then slid his finger into her as he continued to stroke her with his thumb. He crooked his finger gently, and that merest gesture made her cry out as she came in sudden thudding waves over his hand.

A growl sounded from deep within him. He ripped the gown from her, and she heard the tiny crackle of threads as he pulled the delicate fabric free. And then he pushed roughly at his own clothing, wriggling from shirt and plaid.

Haley saw him then, and she drew in her breath. He was huge. His body was angry, ready, the full mass of him heavy on her belly.

"We"—she hesitated, her voice breathy, unsure—"you need to go slow."

"*Leannan.*" MacColla stilled. "*Mo leannan.*" A look of immeasurable tenderness swept his features, softening his brow, his mouth.

His fingers and thumb found her once more and stroked her softly. "Have you ever done this, *leannan*?"

This. He watched her, this man. Alasdair MacColla, strong and fierce, lying over her, caressing her. Adoring her.

Never this.

No man before him had brought her to the edge, stolen Haley from herself in that way, sweeping her into such ecstasy.

She wanted more of him. Wanted all of him.

"Not like this," she whispered. "Nothing like this."

"Are you ready for me?"

He was so grave, so earnest, she had to give him a tender smile. "I've been ready, MacColla."

The sound came from low in his throat, half laugh, half moan, and he eased himself closer to her. Touched his lips to hers. Brought himself to her, slick and full.

He eased in, and her body stretched tight around him. She shivered, pleasure rippling through her. Unfamiliar, unexpected waves of it roused every nerve, bringing them singing to life.

He moved slowly at first, his mouth and hands roving hungrily, and her body startled her, as once again her muscles began to clench and coil beyond her control.

Haley panted, caught her breath, came again. This time fuller, longer, her vision wavering with each pulse of her body.

She felt his name rip from her throat then, only dimly aware of how she moved, what she did. She was pure feeling, kissing him. Sucking him. Writhing beneath him.

He plowed harder. They moved in frantic unison, as if their satisfaction were something they could chase and catch.

He shouted then. "*Leannan*." And the word tore one last climax from her, from him.

Lover.

And, as Haley tucked close, her body's final spasms trembling through her, she thought, *Yes, MacColla. I am your leannan.*

❈

MacColla combed the sand from her hair, working his fingers gently through the coarse, black waves.

She was a miracle to him. *Haley.* Such a strange name, to match the woman. She was a revelation. A gift.

He'd never experienced such a thing as what they'd just shared. Had never experienced such a passion as hers.

He shifted his weight to let the moonlight hit her beautiful face full-on. So lovely, she was. Strong, fearless. Bonny and deadly. That was his *leannan*.

He smiled. He'd need to rouse her soon. It would do no

good to return after dawn, to be considered by his family over kippers and porridge.

But first MacColla thought he'd smooth the sand from her hair.

Chapter 24

"Really, Jean." Haley shuddered. She pushed the fish heads back under the boiling water with her wooden spoon. "What have you got against fish *bodies*? I'm sure they'd make a fine soup."

"You hush." The rare good humor lighting Jean's face belied the terseness of her voice. "That would be a waste of good fish. The heads make a fine *skink*. Stop your carping, or I'll make you the one to strain them out."

Haley had to look away from the pot. The steam made her eyes water, and those hideous heads kept glaring at her with glassy eyes and grim little half-open mouths that seemed poised to accuse her of something.

She watched Jean instead.

She'd seen the girl muster such backbone against her father and brother, and Haley thought her first impressions might've been off the mark. It struck her that they had more in common than she'd first thought. They both were only daughters who'd grown up in a houseful of boys. And then there was MacColla. *The girl adores her brother*, Haley thought with a smile, *so she can't be all bad*.

Using her upper arm to brush wisps of hair from her eyes, Jean finished rinsing blood from the last of the haddock heads. She caught Haley's eyes on her and *tsked*.

"Keep stirring now." Jean nodded. "That's the way. I'm about done with this one. Next we add the neeps and carrots. There's not so much of either"—she sighed and studied the modest pile of turnips on the butcher block—"but 'twill have to do. We've milk enough on hand, thanks to John."

Haley was certain that this time she hadn't imagined the look she saw flickering across Jean's face. She *knew* it. The girl had a crush on Scrymgeour.

"And does *John* like fish soup?" Haley asked innocently.

"How would I know that?" Jean asked, her voice wavering.

"Oh, I don't know." She shrugged. "You two seem to spend a lot of time together."

"No more than is seemly." Her cheeks flushed red.

"Oh no," Haley said quickly, adopting her most cavalier manner. "Not too much at all. And besides, he's quite cute. Have you noticed his hands? They're very nice."

She watched as Jean's cheeks turned from red to deep crimson, then added, "He'll make some woman a wonderful husband. What do you think? Do you think he'd be a good . . . provider? You two seem close."

"Close, is it?" Jean's chin trembled with some hidden emotion. Just when Haley thought she'd gone too far, Jean turned and pinned her with a pointed look. Wiping her hands on her apron, she announced, "All right then, we can talk of close. But keep that spoon in hand. You'll be needing to learn a good fish soup, if you're to feed my brother."

This time it was Haley who was taken off guard. "What do you mean?"

"What do I mean?" Smiling now, Jean put her hands on her hips.

"I know you've been sneaking about. And there's no need to. Slink about like a fox in the henhouse, I mean.

Though"—she tapped her finger on her chin thoughtfully—
"I suppose it'd be Alasdair the fox and you the hen, aye?"

Haley thought that she had indeed underestimated the
girl. Vastly underestimated.

"God bless you . . ." Jean laughed, a musical tinkling
that dissolved the defensive scowl from Haley's face. "But
you'll find yourself knee-deep in kettles of fish soup, if I
know my Alasdair."

Haley began to laugh too, but her smile froze on her
face. The thought of a lifetime of sharing fish soup with
MacColla didn't terrify her as much as she'd have expected. It sounded actually quite . . . nice.

"No need to gape at me like a boilt haddie." Jean nodded to the pot of boiling haddock. "A blind man could see
my brother has it for you, lass."

A sharp wail cut through the room, shattering their cau-
tious rapport. Jean didn't even spare a look for Haley before she dashed out of the room.

Haley lost a moment staring dumbly at the pot. She put
her spoon down, wondering what to do. What her place
was.

The sound came again. A thin, keening note echoing
through the chimney stones.

A single thought startled her back into the moment.
MacColla.

She put her hand to her heart. It pounded hard through
the layers of corset and dress.

Haley raced out the door and down the hall, barreling
into the common room.

Her eyes skittered over the scene until she found Mac-
Colla. It was irrational—they were all together and seemed
safe on Kintyre—but still, she felt a quick wash of relief to
see him.

His grave nod spoke both his grief and his need to have
her near.

It struck her that the room was full of people. Suddenly
self-conscious, she stopped short, backed up a step into the
doorjamb. Reaching her hands behind her, she clung to the

wood at her back, chagrined that she might have stumbled unwelcome into something that didn't concern her.

There was Jean, Scrymgeour, Colkitto, MacColla. And all eyes were on his mother. She sat on a stool by the fire, Colkitto standing at her side. Mary slumped against the belly of her husband, her hands tangled white-knuckled in the folds of his plaid.

Hers was the keening voice, repeating over and over the same word. It took Haley's ears a moment to make sense without any context. And then she realized. Mary Mac-Donald chanted, "Gillespie."

Haley saw the woman's face and knew at once. Only the most dreadful and unthinkable of tragedies would crack a façade like hers.

Somebody died.

"Gillespie," MacColla mouthed to her. "*Mo bràthair.*"
My brother.

Gillespie. This woman's son.

How would her own mother react to losing a son? Or Haley, to losing a brother?

Good God. It was all tragedy. Seventeenth-century Scotland, all unthinkable, brutal tragedy that cared not for mother, or lover. So devastating. And so commonplace.

Oh God, MacColla. Dread bloomed in her gut like a cancer, thinking of the day that could come. The day she might get news that would shatter her forever.

"Gillespie." It was Colkitto giving voice to the words nobody wanted to speak. His fury was calm, as barren, as complete as the fine sparkling of rime on pine needles. "The Campbell has killed Gillespie. And now he comes for us. For MacColla. For you, lass," he nodded to Haley.

A chill shivered through her. "How does he know about me?"

"He calls you the bride of MacColla." A voice came from the far corner, crisp and deep.

Haley's eyes adjusted to the shadows that clung to the edges of the room. A man stood there, neat and tall, with shining dark brown hair, and sharp cheekbones and jaw to match the razor edge of his gaze. "Campbell warns he will destroy MacColla's family. Will ruin MacColla, and you, most of all."

Haley decided if a knife edge had a human voice, it would sound like this man.

"I . . ." She stumbled for words, uncertain of what to make of such a threat from a stranger.

"*Leannan*." MacColla's voice was quiet, but steady, and her eyes found his. The grief she saw there broke her heart.

The mysterious man stepped from the shadows, and Haley realized he held a cane. Lifting one leg after the other, he moved with slow deliberation.

"This is Will Rollo." MacColla's face softened for an instant as he told her, "He is a friend to James Graham."

Is. Not was. She knew it. *James Graham is alive.*

It was a thrill to know she'd been right. *Graham hadn't died.* But it was a hollow victory.

She found all she cared for at that moment was Mac-Colla.

At the mention of James, Rollo swung his head sharply to MacColla, his eyes narrowed. But MacColla simply ignored him, Haley his single focus.

"Rollo." She murmured the strange name, trying to place it, trying to remember who he might have been.

"Aye, he bears news of my brother. Gillespie was killed in a siege of Skipness Castle. To the north. He's in Kintyre, lass. Campbell is in Kintyre. He slaughters his way right to us, an army at his back."

"We must fight," Colkitto growled.

"We must go." MacColla's mother finally spoke, her voice cracking as she visibly gathered her anguish, reeling it back once more, to bury it deep inside. "We have Jean to think of. We're . . ."

She hesitated, and MacColla continued for her, "We're trapped at the edge of Kintyre with naught but the sea at our backs. The Earl of Antrim has men by the thousands, waiting for us in Ireland. It's to Ireland we must go now."

There was a sharp cry. When all eyes turned to her, Haley realized the sound had torn from her own throat.

MacColla shook his head a fraction. "Would that there were a choice, *leannan*. But there's no other course. I need more men. And there are Irish confederates by the score who wait for us, eager for a taste of Campbell blood."

"Och." Colkitto pulled his wife tighter to him. "Your mother and I stay here. On Scottish soil. I'll not turn tail to Ireland. I've been driven out of my country for the last time."

"It's not—" MacColla began in a snarl.

"Och, son, I ken well. An army waits for you there. But heed me, boy. I'm an old man, and if I'm to die, it's Scottish soil will drink my blood."

"You cannot stay here." Rollo's voice cut through the room like a shard of glass, clear and deathly sharp. "You must leave Kintyre."

"To Islay, then," MacColla said to his father. "We rally a dozen men and you'll set sail for Islay."

"Ranald," his mother gasped.

"Aye, my brother is there," MacColla said. "There's a rebel stronghold at Dunyveg. Father, I need you to help hold the castle there. I'll return, with thousands at my back."

Mary delicately blotted her eyes with her fingertips. "Can I—"

"No, Mother. 'Tis not safe for you there."

Even as Colkitto flexed to pull his wife closer, Haley saw her sit just a little straighter. And it was a revelation. Mary would be accustomed to such a parting. *What life is, for these women* . . . she thought with a chill. Always saying good-bye to their men and their boys, often for the last time.

Scrymgeour spoke then, his voice warm and sure. "Mary will come with me. You both will," he said, addressing Jean. "Campbell will have left Fincharn; his attentions long directed elsewhere. He'd not suspect we'd return. We head for Loch Awe at once. Back to my home." He turned to MacColla and promised somberly, "The women will be safe there."

Scrymgeour looked to Haley, adding, "You shall come too, of course. We will all—"

"She'll do no such thing." MacColla's words resonated low and fierce, pebbling her arms into goose bumps. "Haley stays with me." His glare silenced any who would contradict him.

He intended to protect her. But Haley knew.

She looked around the room, taking in this portrait of profound grief.

The MacDonald men have begun to die.

She looked around, and she knew. It was MacColla who needed the protection now.

Chapter 25

Haley sat on the sand, not far from where she and Mac-Colla had been together. And rather than feeling warmed by the memory, it came to her on a knife's edge. Sharp and with a pang she felt as surely as steel on skin.

She had been excited, imagining what it'd be like to be intimate with him. But the reality had been so much bigger, so much more than any fantasy.

It had been both tenderness and ravaging lust. Losing herself in him was all the reassurance of coming home, with the exhilaration of setting on some new, uncharted course.

But how many more nights would they get?

She tried to savor those memories, but her eyes were continually drawn to Ireland, a long, thin band of shadow looming on the horizon like the black cloud of a coming storm.

Haley wriggled her toes in the sand, welcoming the damp chill. It grew late, and she savored the cool at her back, a peculiar craving for some physical symptom of her despair. She felt sorry for herself and would wallow in those feelings. Far from peaceful or secure, Haley would have her body chilled to the bone as well.

Fiery clouds streaked low on the horizon as the sky blazed into night. The sun came at a sharp angle, warm on her cheek. She focused on it. Anything to pull herself out of her thoughts and back into her body.

She turned her face full to the setting sun, squinting against the halo of orange winking over the sea.

Red sky at night, sailor's delight. She remembered the words her mother repeated at the sight of a particularly vibrant sunset.

Red sky in morning, sailor's warning.

Something trembled through her veins, cold, making her heart feel shallow, as if it pumped something less than blood.

They were to sail tomorrow morning.

First they would set off for Islay, with Colkitto. They'd see him off. Leave at once for Ireland. It would be good-bye to Jean, and Scrymgeour, and Mary. Good-bye to Colkitto.

She had no misconceptions of what life was in the seventeenth century. She doubted she'd ever see any of them again.

And what of her MacColla? What of this man, fated to die on an Irish battlefield?

Fate? She wondered what that meant. Wondered if the path of a human life was predestined, an unerring map of events etched in stone.

It couldn't be. How else to explain her presence in the past?

Her mind tried to wrap around it, to track the Möbius strip of her time travel. But every time she thought she had a grasp on it, tracing and tracking events in time, she'd get tangled in the paradoxes, simply ending up back where she started.

Did that mean she was able to alter history? It had to. Why else would she have been sent back? Or rather, how else *could* it be so?

Thoughts of her family flooded her mind. She didn't have to be suffering so. She could be back in Boston, sheltered and secure, surrounded by her family. She'd be safe from wars. Steeped in unthinkable luxury.

But she hadn't tried to find her way home yet. She'd chosen MacColla instead.

Would she return to her family if she had the chance? *Could* she even?

And yet she knew in that moment that she had to stay. To see it through. MacColla must not die. She had to stop it. The trouble was, events marched inexorably forward, and she had no idea how to pause it all. Redirect history.

Or how she'd even know once she did.

The taste of salt in her throat threatened tears.

"You look so melancholy, *leannan*."

His voice startled her. The intensive preparation required for these various journeys had taken his attention all afternoon. She'd thought he'd be at it still. Directing, requesting, commanding, setting all to rights for the coming days.

"You seem a gloomy wee seabird."

He stood over her, squinting against the setting sun. His plaid billowed against his legs in the evening breeze. The warm, direct light picked out the tiniest of details, warming the sand crusted atop his bare feet, highlighting the faint stubble on his face, picking deep shadows in the lines around his mouth, cocked in amusement.

The look he gave her drew the chill from her bones. It was hard to stay so wretched in the face of this big man, come to seek her out, with this smile just for her.

"But don't you need to get ready?" she asked.

"Aye. I do." He plopped heavily to the ground beside her, promptly wrapping his arm around her shoulders to tuck her close. "But I find I have other needs as well." He gave her a sly wink.

"Oh really?"

"Oh really, *leannan*."

The wanting of him sparked low in her belly, but she felt

the specter of Ireland heavy on her, staring at her from afar.

"MacColla?"

"So serious you are." He squeezed her arm. "How can I wipe the trouble from your brow?"

"Don't go."

"You know I must," he said quietly.

She was unable to speak for a time, and he sat silently by her side.

"Ireland's right there," she finally said, nodding toward the distant island. "Why don't we just sail there from here? Why do we go to Islay first?"

"You spurn my wicked intentions, asking instead after maritime matters?" MacColla laughed. "And I'd hoped you'd a question related to swordplay." He waggled his brows, amused by his own pun.

Haley frowned. She refused to take the bait.

"'Tis too dangerous to sail from here," he sighed. "The waters of the Sruth na Maoile are too unpredictable."

"The . . . Sea of Moyle?"

"Your *Gaedhealg* improves every day," MacColla said, nodding. "The only safe route to Ireland is by way of Islay. I've seen fighting men by the thousands voyage between the two, on boats made of hide and willow. They land and take the wee vessels apart again for the next man's use."

"Well," she said nervously, "we'll just take a real boat, right?"

"That is a real boat." MacColla stared grimly at her for a moment and then erupted into a deep belly laugh. "The look of terror on your bonny face." He took her chin in his cupped hand. "Stop your fretting. My father, he's a true sailor. He's got a twelve-oar birlinn that will take us safe across."

He stared out to the sea, his arm still wrapped firm around her. "We'll leave Islay on a neap tide, when the currents are weakest. 'Twill be a leisurely journey, I dare say." He chuckled. "Mayhap we can even catch us some fine haddie for a soup. Jean tells me you love a good *skink*."

He sought her gaze, but she knew the smile she gave him wasn't in her eyes.

"I see the storm in those pretty gray eyes of yours. Don't worry, *leannan*, the western waters provide some of the best sailing in the world, I'm told."

"You're *told*? Haven't you ever sailed them?"

"Och, lass, you fret overmuch." The sun winked from the horizon, and he chafed his hand along Haley's back to warm her. "A small sail and oars to hold the course will be all we need. 'Tis more pleasant by far than traveling on horseback."

"Speaking of horses," Haley said, "isn't it too risky for Jean and your mother to be setting back up through Kintyre with Campbell on the move?"

"I trust Scrymgeour to get them safe to his home. An army of men is a slow and stubborn beast. Campbell will have his eye on one thing: the MacDonald clan castle at Dunaverty. A man would have to be both deaf and blind to be caught unawares by that many soldiers on the march."

He gave her a squeeze. "No, *leannan*, they'll be fine. I've found them four sturdy ponies, and we'll pack them off with creels of grain, salt." His voice grew quiet. "We'll leave nothing of worth for the Campbell to pillage."

MacColla stroked her cheek, turning her face to him. "I crept off like a cat on the hunt to find you," he told her gently. "Our time alone will be rare now. I'd savor it without more thoughts to battles and brooding."

"Jean said we didn't need to sneak around."

"I don't sneak." Grabbing her hips, he pulled Haley onto his lap. He dragged her skirts up roughly, settling her on his crossed legs. "I said I was on the hunt." His voice was husky, as he nuzzled at her neck, up her throat, around her ear. "And I always catch what I'm after."

Wrapping her arms around him, Haley relaxed her thighs to nestle more solidly in MacColla's lap. What he'd said was right. From here on out, they'd be lucky for a few stolen moments in the dark.

She was unable to speak from the emotion that ached in her throat. And so Haley answered with her mouth.

There was no gentle easing into their kiss. It was desperate and deep, and she opened her mouth to him with the urgency of a woman starved.

He wriggled her skirts up even more, and the wool of his plaid chafed the sensitive skin of her inner thighs.

MacColla was instantly erect, and she shuddered a sigh. She needed him so badly. Feeling him pressed hard against her was such a relief.

She pulled her mouth from his to push the tartan from his shoulder and tug at his shirt. It was tucked tightly under his plaid and thick brown belt, and MacColla reached down to guide her fingers as she unbuckled him.

She was able to tug loose his shirt, and she pulled it over his head. The sight of him took her breath away. She'd only seen him in the moonlight, but here he was, half-naked before her. The gray light of the gloaming made his massive chest and its fine dusting of black hair all the more dramatic. He seemed an epic hero, sitting there with a jaw of steel and thick knots of muscle along his arms.

"The way you look at me, *leannan* . . ." His words were hushed, as if he were barely holding on. "I'd not known I could feel such wanting."

He turned his attention to her clothes, taking the fabric of her dress roughly in hand. "I need you. I need to be inside you."

She gasped. "Wait." His desire for her was a palpable thing, as strong a pull as the waves crashing just beyond.

"Careful." Haley moved his hands to her waist. "I'll do it," she whispered, her voice tremulous.

Haley reached both hands behind her to unlace the back of her gown. Her chest arched toward him and MacColla groaned. Leaning down, he put a hand to one breast and brought his mouth to the other, sucking and nibbling her through the thick fabric.

"Get this off," he growled.

She stretched and squirmed, finally loosening her top

enough for him to pull gown and chemise over her head in one sweep.

She sat naked atop him, separated only by the layers of wool still loose over his lap. Though the sun and the last of its warmth had slipped below the horizon, her skin felt hot, flushed, as though the blood coursed just beneath its surface.

"So lovely you are, *leannan*." His breath came shallow as he raked his gaze down her body and up again. "I'll still not understand what it is I did to win such beauty for my own."

He took her in more slowly then, his fingertips tenderly tracing his eyes' path.

"Your ribs," he murmured, cradling her torso gently in her hands. "They're better?"

She nodded wordlessly, unable to speak. She was still a little stiff, but that didn't matter now. Nothing mattered but them. This moment.

She brought her hands to his cheeks, and carefully pushed the hair from his face. Their eyes locked. His brown and warm on her. His features, so sharp and strong, softened, only for her.

"I love you, MacColla," she whispered. "I'm here because of you. Only you."

"I'll love you all my days," he replied huskily. His voice was fierce, and his grasp on her grew firmer. He skimmed his hands up her sides, his thumbs chafing her nipples into aching points.

He took her mouth again with his. She shut her eyes and felt as he tilted her up and back down to rest on his now naked body.

The feel of him sent a spark flashing through her. His erection was hot and smooth at her cleft, and she kissed him again, hungrily, moaning her need into his mouth.

He lifted her up, slowly easing her onto him. The physical memory of their first time still lingered inside her, the full feel of him, the wet scent and slide, and she was desperate for more.

She clutched him to her with her arms and legs, and

ground her hips down hard, begging with her body to intensify their rhythm.

He rocked into her, devouring her mouth and neck and breasts. His kisses left a trail of damp on her hot skin, a map of his passion chilled at once by the night air, and the sensation was as if he seared into her, marking her.

She grew frantic, couldn't get him close enough, and MacColla rose to his knees, pulled from her, and flipped her to kneel before him.

Haley gasped a complaint when she felt him slide out, but MacColla was immediately back inside her, from behind, so deep and so full she felt her body bursting from the joy of it. Her love for him filled her up, spilled over, overwhelmed her.

She felt a wild thing on her hands and knees before him. The sensations were almost too much to bear. Her blood raged through her, flushing cheeks and chest, throbbing between her legs, demanding release.

Her body was spinning out of control. She leaned forward, trembling as she rested her weight on her forearms. The beach was gritty and cold on her knees and at the tops of her feet. She dug her fingers into the chilled sand, trying to ground herself, but her conscious self was receding into some faraway place.

Her body rocked as he thrust into her. Her vision was fractured, registering a dreamy patchwork of images. A hand—hers, she realized—clawed into the sand.

She tilted her chin to look down along her body. Saw his hand, so large on her breast, rubbing her, chafing her, cradling her. And the sight of it shattered the last of her rational thought. She became pure feeling.

Neither spoke now. His muttered words of having her, of loving her, of keeping her, replaced now by his heavy breathing. The sound of him filled her head, echoed the wash of the waves and the short panting of her own breath.

He suffused her, so completely, her body, her mind. The rhythms of her heart and breath. MacColla filled her utterly.

She'd let her mind go, and now the last of her physical self surrendered. Her climax wracked her body, blood thrumming through her in heavy waves. She felt rapturous, as if she'd transcended her body to become some meta-physical thing exploding into space.

She heard MacColla as if from a distance. A low groan, the huff of his breath. He pumped hard and quick into her. Then a roar at her back as he found his own release.

He kissed the nape of her neck, and spoke words that felt hot on her damp skin, "You'll never forget you're mine."

Chapter 26

"You can't go to Ireland," she stated simply.

"Och, love." MacColla turned Haley to face him. They stood at the water's edge, ready to sail once more.

They'd landed safely on Islay, situated Colkitto at Dunyveg Castle. Though they'd gathered almost a dozen men for their journey, the MacDonald castle had to be ready for what protracted siege might come, and neither provisions nor weapons could be spared. Not wanting to tax the already overburdened Islay stronghold, they were to leave immediately for the northeastern coast of Ireland.

"*We* travel to Ireland," he said. "I need to gather more men. I have no choice."

"You always have a—"

"Hush," he whispered, tucking a strand of hair behind her ear. "Heed me, *leannan*. Campbell blazes through Kintyre. My clansmen barely hold Dunyveg. With disaster to the left of me and death to the right, my only choice is but to plow forward."

But Haley knew. Disaster and death lay before him as well.

MacColla looked at someone over her shoulder, and she turned to see a knot of approaching clansmen. Rollo managed stiffly, shuffling ten paces behind the group. He gave MacColla a grim nod.

That would mean all was ready. The time had come.

Heart skittering in her chest, Haley climbed into the boat. The birlinn's bench was hard beneath her, and she was forced to sit rigidly upright, her discomfort doing nothing to calm her.

She looked across the sea as they set out, focused on those few sounds that filled the air, but they only agitated her. The creak of wood as the men rowed. The small *splish* of oars dipping in and out of the water. The rhythmic slap of the sea against the hull. They approached closer to Ireland, and every noise tightened the knot in her stomach.

Hours passed with her staring sightlessly over the water, fear and uncertainty glazing her eyes. The sea was as calm as MacColla promised it would be, and the gray sky darkened so gradually, it seemed one moment it was day and the next night.

As the sky blackened, it exploded into millions of points of light. Just when she thought the vast bowl overhead might swallow her dark thoughts, she saw it. Terror shot through her. *Ireland.* It emerged from the shadows, stark and black, looming close. In that moment, she knew such hatred and fear for the place, it roiled in her stomach.

Ireland, that had once brought her such joy, now seemed an evil thing, monstrous and portentous, hovering before them like some great slumbering beast.

As they approached the shore, their boat began to bob wildly, fighting the waves that crested and broke along the sandy cove, shimmering pale in the starlight.

She inhaled sharply and looked up to the sky as if that could help tip back the fall of her tears.

Haley felt a hand on her thigh. His hand. Warm, loving. But for how long? How long until this hero of old lay cold in his grave?

She shivered.

"What will be, will be, *leannan*." She felt his fingers, strong and sure, stroking her cheek. He cupped her face, turned it toward him.

She shut her eyes tight, unable to look at him, feeling her heart breaking already at the loss of him. Tears squeezed out.

Even before her eyes fluttered back open, she knew what she'd see: love for her tempered by the single-minded drive to do what he could for his clan. She'd see his confidence, his determination that what he did was the right thing. The *only* thing.

But she knew differently. Triumph wasn't what waited for him on the shores of Ireland. It was death.

And she knew, death alone would sway MacColla from his mission.

It would be up to her to set all to rights.

She opened her eyes, studied him. Shadows blackened his brow, his mouth. He returned her gaze and she knew he'd not be the first to look away.

Haley gripped his hand, felt the give of his flesh in her nails.

She had her own mission. She couldn't lose him.

She no longer cared about James Graham, whether he lived or died. No longer cared about some foolish weapon. Studies and scholarship were meaningless now.

She knew only MacColla, and the future with him she so desperately craved.

Her father's voice came to her from far away. Those words he'd spoken at the bar, so long ago. *Our Haley knows what she needs to do.*

Flashing back to Boston, to her brothers and her father, brought pain searing through her chest. And her mother. If only she'd gotten to see her mother one last time.

But Haley knew in her heart she had a second family now. MacColla. Sitting next to her, clutching tight to her. Ready to give his own life for what he believed in. For *his* family.

There was no going back. She'd made her decision to be with MacColla.

Haley knew what she had to do. And this was it.

❀

Their spirits deflated gradually over the following weeks. They'd landed at Dundrum, in County Down, and had begun the long march south to County Cork at once.

Ireland was rocky and green, rolling endlessly before them. Haley hadn't fully believed he intended hundreds of miles of hard marching, and quickly enough to elude the Parliamentary army.

"It's a long damned way to Tipperary," she grumbled at some point on day ten. Ever since MacColla told her they skirted south of the famous burgh, she'd had the old World War I marching song stuck in her head.

"What do you cavil on about, lass?"

She looked to MacColla riding beside her. Black whiskers dusted his jaw and his shirt had seen better days, but he sat with a grin for her, as if he could will her into a better mood.

"Nothing," she said, trying to muster half a smile. Tucking the reins under her thigh, she leaned close to her horse's neck, stretching the stiff muscles in her shoulders and lower back. "It's just . . . well, when will we get there?"

"Soon now, *leannan*. A Lord Taaffe waits for us at a place called Assolas House, in Duhallow."

"Is he a Royalist?"

"Now there's a tricky question. Och, but what I'd do to scrape this from my face," MacColla mumbled, scratching at his nascent beard. "A Royalist, you ask. Well, he is and he is not. In Scotland, you've got the Covenanters sympathizing with the English Parliament on one side. And then there's the Royalists who stand with the king on the other."

"I know that."

MacColla cut his eyes to her, smiling broadly. "Aye, I suppose you do then. Well, things get a wee bit more complicated in Ireland."

Rolling his shoulders, he assessed the sun in the sky, as if control over their day's ride was a constant buzzing in the back of his mind.

He continued, "Men who are enemies in Scotland might find themselves allied in Ireland, driven by religion over clan. Here the Catholic Confederates fight to retake Protestant lands. Confederates who have a long-standing *hatred* for England and her king. Do you see? The Confederates are not naturally Royalist, aye?"

He watched her face, waiting for her to nod her understanding before he continued.

"But the king, he fancies his Catholic wife and is inclined to let we savages be." He gave a quick laugh. "While Parliament would oust both Catholics *and* king. And so two enemies have found they have much in common. Irish Catholics supporting an English monarch. My father never thought he'd see the day," he added with a chuckle.

"Will you fight?" she asked abruptly.

"If I must."

She turned her face away sharply, unable to look at him.

"*Leannan*, I've simply come for more men. I rally troops to return with me to help hold the MacDonald castle at Dunyveg. But . . ." He was quiet for a moment. "*Leannan*, look at me. Please."

"Don't," she rasped. She turned her face back to him and didn't bother to hide the angry tears that shimmered there. "You need to go back to Scotland *now*. Fight there. Not here."

"Och, Haley lass. I fight where I must. I gather men, but even now the Parliamentary army marches south. I'll not turn back to Scotland, leaving my allies to face their enemy alone. If the Munster army needs me on Irish soil, then that is where I'll stand."

They arrived two days later, and Haley's greatest fear was realized. It was as she suspected. The Munster army did indeed lay claim to MacColla.

They were welcomed at Assolas House, a lovely two-story mansion, complete with a carpet of ivy covering the gray stones of its façade and a river babbling gently beyond. The grounds were lush, featuring flowers, fruits, and a serene sweep of green lawn.

And Haley thought it hell.

She knew she needed to take control of the situation. Needed to figure out how exactly to save MacColla from himself. But reasonable solutions eluded her. The only strategy she came up with would be to knock him on the head and whisk him as far as she could from Ireland.

But she knew, he'd only come to, and come back.

They sat at dinner with Lord Taaffe, and though she told herself she should've been grateful for a meal consisting of more than just oats and hare on a spit, she couldn't muster enough of an appetite to eat.

Rollo and the others had dined earlier, leaving just the three of them to, as Taaffe had put it, "more thoroughly acquaint themselves." She wished she'd been able to dine with the soldiers, not being much in the acquainting mood.

Once inhabited by Catholic monks, the Assolas dining room featured a long, well-used table with benches on either side. Taaffe and MacColla sat directly across from each other.

And Haley saw immediately what a mess that was going to be.

Lord Theobald Taaffe was an antique. With his curled hair and fine waistcoat, he'd clearly gone straight from wealth and careful tutelage to a grand military posting.

He was broad chivalry, not blood and iron rations.

The sort of man who'd ride into battle well groomed and flanked by an attendant to carry his provisions.

Not MacColla's sort at all.

Haley watched her love's face darken through the meal, forced as he was to sit captive to Taaffe's uninformed opining.

When the man announced that he'd sent a letter to the enemy, proposing they dispatch a like number of men to fight for the purpose of recreation, MacColla's face turned purple.

"A generous gamester am I," Taaffe elaborated, "but alas, the Parliamentarians did not rise to my challenge."

"You did what?" MacColla snarled. "Is it you think you can resolve this war as though a game of dice?"

"The men have seemed dispirited of late. I'd thought a good and chivalrous challenge would rouse the blood."

"Gee," Haley muttered, astounded by the absurdity, "that's very . . . King Arthur of you."

"This is no sport we play at," MacColla said with steel in his voice. "No joust, no tilts. You'll get your fill of blood once the fighting begins. *Roused* indeed. Blood enough will spill—the sod will weep with it."

MacColla's near-growl brought her eyes to him. She saw him, truly saw him, for what he was. A blooded Highlander, eager for battle.

The flicker of humor she'd felt a moment before took a dark turn. It was this buffoon seated across from them who'd be by MacColla's side in battle.

"Ah, yes," Taaffe agreed gravely. "Bloody days are upon us. Even now we have an army of twelve hundred horse and seven thousand foot rallied. Most are encamped at Kanturk less than a league hence. The rest wait on Knocknanuss Hill. The best strategic position in Cork, I dare say."

Knocknanuss. Haley sat upright on the hard bench, her heart thumping to life.

"Though our foe marches toward us, we still strongly outnumber . . . But, dear girl"—Taaffe turned his attention to Haley—"are you ill?"

He turned to MacColla. "I beg your forgiveness, sir. How dare I speak of such dark matters before one of the fairer—"

"What did you say?" Haley interrupted.

"I fear you swoon—"

"No," she snapped. "*Where?* Where did you just say the soldiers were?"

"Why, Knocknanuss Hill, to be sure. Venture to the top, and you shall be rewarded by the finest of landscapes stretching before you."

But his words were just a drone in her ears.

Knocknanuss.

Her body buzzed with adrenalin. Why did that name strike a chord?

She'd once learned something critical, but what had it been? *Knocknanuss.* There was something that had happened in Knocknanuss.

Chapter 27

"Come on, you can tell me," Haley said, enjoying the look of discomfort on Rollo's face.

Since hearing the name Knocknanuss, she'd been upset. She finally remembered it as the site of a famous battle, but who won, and how, still eluded her. There were just too many battles from that time period; she couldn't recall them all.

But she was finding sitting and talking with Will Rollo to be a welcome diversion. She asked him again, "James Graham is alive, isn't he?"

"A crowd of hundreds would claim otherwise," Rollo replied flatly. "Graham was seen hanged, after all."

Rollo stared straight ahead, and Haley used the opportunity to study his profile. He was a large man. Not like MacColla with his massive height and brawn, but more movie-star tall, with fine, chiseled features. She eyed his sharp jaw and cheekbones, and the thick waves of chestnut brown hair skimming the nape of his neck.

Though he wasn't all ferocious Highlander, Rollo didn't

strike her as a courtly Lowland type either. He fell some-where in the middle. Sort of how she imagined James Graham.

"But MacColla all but said Graham is alive. He said you were friends. Implied that you *are* friends."

"I didn't hear MacColla say such a thing."

She would've sworn she saw a smile glimmer for a moment in his eyes.

She looked back to the dance floor, considering the question of James Graham. She realized all of her theories and speculation just didn't matter anymore.

MacColla was all that mattered now.

She scanned the room, seeking him out. He stood on the edge of the dance floor, watching dancers reel to the skirl-ing of the pipes. They might be far from Scottish shores, she thought with a grim smile, but leave it to the MacDon-alds to bring their piper wherever they went.

The set ended, and she heard someone call MacColla's name. She watched as he downed his ale in one long swal-low. A man tossed him a broadsword. He grinned, catching it easily.

The pipes shrilled to life once more, and MacColla joined two men on the dance floor.

A sword dance. Her heart thrilled at the sight of these big, glowering men, laying their swords crossed on the ground to begin one of the most ancient of rituals.

She felt so filled up at the sight of him. Glorious and ex-uberant, with a broad smile, already prancing to the music.

Someone began to slam his tankard on a table, keeping time to the music. He was joined by another, then by fists on tables and clapping hands, until a drumbeat sounded through the room.

Haley had considered MacColla to be the most magnif-icent of men. But seeing him dance she realized why songs had been written about him. Why history remembered him as more than an ordinary man. His charisma, his passion and delight, ignited the room. He was more than a man, he truly was an epic hero.

The men hopped and skipped about the blades, their arms raised high, plaids dancing with their movements.

She beamed. Such a simple and pure pleasure it was to watch him move. It thrilled through her, cutting the despair, and she knew then why the Scots turned to pipes and dance and ale, as she discovered some hidden glimmer of joy buried deep in her soul.

Her eyes cut briefly to Rollo, and she wondered what he thought of all this. His face was calm, his usual dourness replaced by some other, softer emotion. But she knew he would never be able to do such a thing as sword dancing.

The beat grew faster, and Haley clapped in time, her eyes drawn back to the men. One of them tossed off his bonnet and the crowd cheered. MacColla loudest of all. He laughed heartily, his feet moving rapidly in time, kicking and hopping over steel.

His eyes searched the crowd. He found her and grinned.

Pain sideswiped her, stabbing her in the chest, and Haley clutched her hands in her skirts. Watching him, seeing such happiness, such *life*, seared her, pulling her lungs tight, dimming her vision.

We have to get out of here. Leave Ireland.

"Don't these people realize they're at war?"

Haley didn't realize she'd spoken until she heard Rollo's reply.

"A bit of revelry is good for a soldier. Many of these men will return from battle a lifeless body on a bier." He studied the crowd, standing and cheering, clapping in time to the music. "Such diversions aren't uncommon before battle."

Diversions. The word made her think of that ridiculous Lord Taaffe. Taaffe had organized the festive evening, claiming his men were in want of diversions. Parliamentary forces were on the march, and still the man insisted on diversions.

Things between him and MacColla had been strained from the moment they'd met. This lord had coin in his coffers, and she suspected he was of a mind to buy himself a little gallantry on the battlefield.

The song drew to a close, and MacColla walked off the dance floor, slapping his fellow dancers on their backs.

He was all she saw. Another knot of men took the dancers' places, and Haley barely noticed as they arranged themselves in a circle, each holding the tip of the next man's blade.

Desperately trying to gather her emotions, she heard herself mutter to Rollo, "Only you Scotsmen would find a way to dance with your swords."

She was startled at the man's laugh. And gratified too. She turned, and it struck her how very dashing he was. Haley had never so much as seen the hint of a smile on Rollo's face. She wondered what had happened to his legs, and thought how very different his life might have been.

"Aye, Haley," Rollo agreed. "Only we Scotsmen indeed."

MacColla watched Haley where she sat. So lovely she was, despite the dark thoughts he saw continually returning to crease her brow.

He marveled. She was so fresh and bonny. The ways of women were a mystery to him. She'd appeared that evening in a clean gown, with her hair smoothed back tight. He had no notion of how women managed such things when men were unawares.

Her gown bared her neck, and the lush swell of her breasts under lace kept drawing his eyes over and over again.

MacColla felt the now-familiar madness threaten to take him, the wanting of her pushing all else from his mind. They'd not had much time together, but he knew already the taste and touch and smell of her better than any other thing.

Shutting his eyes, he imagined he could feel those breasts, firm in his hands. He knew in his soul the feel of that tight flesh and muscle, hidden under blue velvet.

They didn't have much time remaining. His hands

clenched at his sides. He and the Confederate army would strike soon, before the Protestants had a chance to move first.

Her portentous words weighed on him. He'd never let her know how much. But of choices, he had none. It was fight, and fight more, until Campbell was destroyed. If his assistance in Munster earned him more men to take back to Scotland, then all the better.

But what would become of Haley, of him? He had to hope that her presence changed the course of history somehow. That she was wrong. That he'd fight, and live to fight another day.

Opening his eyes, he drank her in with the thirst of a dying man.

She sat next to Rollo, talking easily. What did they speak of? One would never know the man was crippled, seated so. Few, in fact, would even realize his condition in battle. The man managed it well. He was a grim sort, but MacColla appreciated that. As one capable of hiding his own pain, MacColla recognized the lines on Rollo's face, knew they spoke to his discomfort.

Would she sit with Rollo all night, or come seek him out?

He watched as Rollo laughed, turned to Haley, said something that eased the tension on her face. Anger boiled suddenly hot in his belly, his mind humming with jealousy.

MacColla alone would bring his woman comfort. MacColla alone would have her by his side.

Without thinking, he strode toward the pair. The open smile she greeted him with assuaged his jealousy, but it did nothing to tamp down the fierce desire it had awoken.

"Good evening, MacColla." Rollo instinctively drew back from Haley.

"Rollo," he said in greeting, the name rough in his throat.

He turned back to Haley, reached his hand out to her, the whole of his attention only for her. He heard Rollo excusing himself, as if from a distance.

"Dance with me, *leannan*." Her hand felt so small and

cold in his. He pulled her to standing, chafing her fingers. "You're cold."

"Of course I am," she said, sounding despondent. Looking around, she added, "What do you expect? I'm sitting in a pile of stones, waiting for you to die."

He laughed then, and when he saw the outrage in her eyes, he took her face in his hands. "I'm not dead yet, my love. Come," his voice gentled. "Dance with me. It will take our minds from these dark times."

He scanned the dance floor. He didn't think much of Lord Taaffe, but this was one small instance where the man had the right of it; Haley could use a distraction just then.

"I don't know how to dance," she grumbled.

"You can fight, but you can't dance?" He tugged her toward the floor. "You'll not get away so easy as that."

They stood on the periphery, watching the current set reel around the floor. The dancers held hands in pairs, shuffling side by side, then grasped hold of the other dancers to turn in a circle, the pipes skipping out a lively tune all the while.

The song faded into another, slower one, and couples wandered from the floor to be replaced by other couples.

MacColla looked down at his woman beside him. He decided to do what he could to clear the storm from those gray eyes.

"Wha—?" Haley yelped, as he swung her onto the dance floor, silencing her with a quick kiss.

A blush rose hot on her cheeks and she looked around, making sure nobody had seen.

"So modest, are you?" he whispered in her ear. MacColla pulled her close to lead her in the dance. Wrapping one arm around her waist, he took her hand in his, savoring the press of her breasts on his chest.

"I'd not known I had such a bashful maiden for a partner." He nipped at her neck. The salt of her on his tongue shot life into his cock, and he hugged her closer to hide his hardness.

She gasped, jerking her head up to look at him.

He gave an innocent shrug. " 'Twould do no good to show all and sundry how much I want you at this very moment." Leaning back down to her ear, he added huskily, "Close those lips before I kiss them, *leannan*."

Despite her protests, Haley could dance, and well too. They moved as one, circling around and between the others in their set.

MacColla was grateful for the slower tune. It gave him an excuse to press her tightly to him. They were stomach to stomach, and each small move she made was an agony. Her every step chafed his plaid against his body, now piqued and raging hard under all that wool.

The song ended too quickly, and it took him a minute to gather himself, registering the shuffle of other dancers as the set changed.

He hugged her close for a moment more. He leaned down one last time to inhale the smell of her skin. "You are the only one on this dance floor, *mo leannan*."

She looked up at him. Saw the intensity in his eyes, and it was all for her. It felt so good to hear those words, and yet she couldn't get past this turmoil that threatened to sweep her away on a tidal wave of helplessness and fear.

Instant clarity cut through his gaze, sharp on her. "I've still not taken your mind from this, have I?"

She shook her head mutely.

"Come with me," he said, putting his arm at the small of her back.

"I know what happened the last time you said that." She tried to laugh.

"Ah. A fast learner." He stroked his hand down to quickly cup her bottom. "But it's no secret how much I want you."

The sound of his voice sent a shiver up her spine. She needed him. She would have him, keep him close for as long as she could now. Haley let him lead her to the door.

"But the others . . ." She stopped short.

"Don't fret, lass." He stretched his hands out cavalierly. "I'm just a man come to escort you back to your room."

They managed to slip away. Whether unseen or simply unhindered, it didn't matter to Haley. All that mattered was she get as much of MacColla as she could now.

Maybe her love for him would be what kept him alive. Maybe she was sent back in time to save him using her sheer will alone.

Her heart hammered in her chest, watching him carefully shut and latch the door behind them.

A funny little quiver thrummed through her. Something giddy and nervous. And she realized with wonder that, though she knew he loved her and she was sure in their love, Haley still felt awe watching him, anticipating him. She imagined she could spend the rest of her days with MacColla and never completely lose a bit of the schoolgirl crush she felt at the sight of him.

MacColla turned, and his eyes were hooded, with desire and some other dark thing. *Desperation?* she wondered. Did he hide from her his own fear of the coming days?

Emotion clenched her throat, and she vowed MacColla would live. Vowed she would do all in her power to keep him safe and alive.

The force of her drive was so violent it overtook her, made her vision waver black along the edges. She turned away, unable to look at him, fearing one look, one gesture from him would set her trembling.

Haley felt him at her back. She expected MacColla would make her turn to face him, but he didn't.

He moved so tenderly, she felt the heat of his hands before she felt his touch. As he skimmed ever closer to her, she sensed the heat of his fingers trace down her back, along her arms, hovering up the side of her throat.

MacColla finally touched her then, and though his fingers were light, like a breath on her skin, she felt burned in their wake.

She shivered, felt her body loosening, opening to him.

His hand was so large on her throat. So strong. And she was so vulnerable to him, to his strength.

She realized then how much she trusted MacColla. How completely she'd given herself to him.

His finger grazed lightly along her scar. "*Gràdh geal mo chrìdhe*," he whispered, and she heard the emotion in his voice. The pain.

He overwhelmed her. With a small whimper, she tried to turn in his arms. "Kiss me," she gasped.

She needed to face him, to see him and taste him, but his arm shot tight around her belly. "You'll wait." His voice was ragged with desire.

His arm clung tight to her like an iron band, pulling her close, his hand grazing up, seeking and finding her breast. He pushed up, fighting against the thick corset, trying to take her in his palm to knead her.

"Och," he growled, and his tender touch grew rougher. Fingers that had been light on her throat tangled now in her hair, sweeping it up, revealing her neck for his mouth and tongue.

Haley felt him grow rock hard at her back. Felt his hunger in the way he pulled her tight to him, squeezing and rubbing.

Her nipples pulled tight. The corset chafed just over them, and she moaned, desperate to be free of it. "Take it . . . take it off."

He spun her then, turning her in his arms to face him. To claim her mouth with his in a savage kiss. He filled her senses. He tasted of ale, smelled of sweat and wool. His breath filled her lungs, and she breathed him in, desperate to have him near. To make him a part of her, keeping him by her forever.

She didn't know how their clothes came off, only that they did in a frantic untangling of laces and belts, fabric and leather.

He was on top of her in an instant, on her bed, laying hungry kisses over her breasts and belly and face. He kissed her mouth once more, so deeply. She was so wet and so ready, aching with need for him. He shifted, entered her, and the world fell away.

Everything she had clung to him. Haley beckoned his tongue full into her mouth, fingers and nails clawing him even closer. Her legs wrapped tight around his back, the muscles in her core spasming tight around him, pulling him deep, and deeper still. Desperate to be his final shelter.

They came hard, amid cries and thrusts and sweat, and a great sob finally broke from Haley.

She knew what time would bring. MacColla would pull his body from hers. And the hour would come when he'd rise from her bed. And then the day when he'd step onto his last battlefield.

❀

MacColla had spent a night in heaven. Then they woke the next morning into a nightmare.

Haley had been given her own room at Assolas House, and even though he knew he needed rest, he lay tangled with her in her sheets, drifting in and out of sleep, waking to check that she was still there. To see her face once more.

She was desperate to leave Ireland. And though he must believe he'd be triumphant, her words gave him pause. What would the coming days bring?

It would be so easy, so glorious, to forsake all of it to be with her. To live only for Haley. Finding a home and hearth on some tiny western isle, where they could spend the rest of their days devoted only to each other.

He craned his head down to study her, sprawled asleep over him. Memorizing the long black lashes on her creamy skin, and the roses on those cheeks, so flushed and bonny. Her hair, wavy and black, falling every which way over his chest. The lean, strong arms that, even in sleep, clung so tightly to him.

And then the shouts came. From far away at first. Pounding on doors. Shuffling feet.

He felt her stir.

The time was coming, and a sorrow as deep as mourning speared him, unexpectedly.

The noises grew closer, louder. She awoke. Their eyes locked.

"Don't go," she whispered. Her fingers curled into him. He felt a single tear spill hot on his chest. "Don't go. You don't have to go."

He couldn't bear her protests, and so he kissed them from her mouth. She was so soft, tasting of sleep and sex. To stay would be so easy. But in this he had no choice.

"I love you, *leannan*. With my heart and soul, I love you. But you know I must do this."

Their door was next. The pounding fists. "Aye," Mac-Colla shouted. Not taking his eyes from her, he said merely, "I come."

They sat at the dining table hearing news that was far worse than they'd anticipated.

MacColla listened, and Haley watched as the passion bled from his face. A living man turned to granite.

"Dunyveg," Rollo said. "Campbell's men captured the castle at Dunyveg."

"My brother?"

"Ranald was executed the moment they took the castle." Rollo shifted slightly in his seat, the only sound in the utter silence of the cavernous room. "I'm sorry, MacColla." His words fell hollow on the stones.

Haley watched MacColla, saw clearly how he feared asking the question on everyone's minds. And so she asked it for him. "What of Colkitto?"

MacColla gave her a grateful look, and held her eyes as he weathered the news.

"Aye," Rollo rasped. "Colkitto too."

"How?" he asked, turning to his friend.

"He left the castle without asking for a promise of his safety."

"To negotiate surrender?" MacColla asked, bewildered.

"No." Rollo gave a mirthless laugh. "He exited castle walls asking for more whisky."

"Truly?"

"Aye," Rollo replied. "He must have thought himself protected. Coll was an old man, MacColla. The unspoken rules of Highland warfare don't stand with the Covenanters. These men fight without a code, without a thought to the old ways."

"It is hard to believe the great Coll Ciotach is dead," Taaffe finally said. "Such a capture was not done without tarnish to Covenanter honor."

And though MacColla's gaze was hard on him, Haley thought she heard true sadness in the man's voice, imagining that an old-fashioned sort like Lord Taaffe would be particularly distressed by such a flouting of principles.

"Whisky," MacColla muttered, shaking his head. "The old fool thirsted for more whisky."

His father was dead. Two of his brothers. And still Campbell eluded him. Still the Covenanters marched through MacDonald lands in Scotland. Parliament sympathizers razed through Ireland. Marched for them even now.

Taaffe cleared his throat. "There is more news. If you gentlemen would hear it." The man looked at Haley, as if expecting her to leave the room.

If this lord thought MacColla's woman quailed at talk of battle, the man didn't know his Haley. MacColla reached over, put his hand over hers on the table. "Speak," he said.

And even before Taaffe got out the words, MacColla knew what he would say. He knew the Parliamentary army drew close. He knew it was time.

MacColla felt the coming of battle in the air, like lightning, on his skin, in his gut. And he welcomed it.

He'd charge into it headlong. Haley's concerns were but a distant hum in the back of his brain. He'd no thought for history books now.

He knew Taaffe would be eager to disprove the rumors that abounded. Rumors that Taaffe was inexperienced. That he'd parleyed with the enemy. That the old lord would not be able, or willing, to fight.

MacColla knew these things, and he didn't care. Every man went alone into battle. Every man driven by his own demons.

MacColla had left his father and brother waiting at Dunyveg Castle. Waiting for soldiers who never arrived.

He'd redeem himself. Prove his worth. Win this war.

MacColla would avenge his family.

Chapter 28

"I'd ask if you're able to use this, but I imagine you ken better than most of my men." MacColla handed Haley a beaten-up old musket. She didn't need to look at the mechanism to know it was one of the old matchlocks. She could tell from the sheer size of the thing that it was a relic.

She'd put it at five feet long and a good fifteen pounds, likely dating from the late 1500s. Resting it butt-first on the floor, Haley squatted to take a better look. "What am I supposed to do with this?"

"Och, you'll not need it. But I'll feel better knowing you have it." He was quiet for a moment, then asked, "Truly, *leannan*, do you know how to fire it?"

"Yeah." She palmed a small leather pouch filled with shot. It was a reassuring heft in her hand, clicking like a bag of heavy marbles.

The match, though, scared her. It was a thin piece of rope that she was to keep constantly lit, sliding it into the jaw of the matchlock when the time came to shoot.

Pull the trigger and it would snap down, the match igniting the powder and firing the bullet.

And she needed to do all of that without catching herself or the powder on fire. "I can manage it," she said grudgingly.

MacColla sighed heavily. "I would that I could give you a gun suitable for a lady, with an ivory handle and in a bonny little case. But munitions are scarce. It's only because the men refuse to carry a matchlock that I can give this to you."

He picked it up, and the gun barrel slid through her hands. Tilting the musket, he sighted down the length of it. "They worry about catching themselves on fire."

"Oh great," she muttered.

He gave a humorless laugh. "When I return, I'll buy you the prettiest wee pistol in all Ireland."

"When you return, I'm going to clout you on the head and take you back to Scotland."

"Och, *leannan*." Exhaling, MacColla set the musket down. He reached to give her a hand up. "You know I must do this."

"Let me come with you."

His eyes were flat when he responded, "I've told you. No, and no again. You'll stay here. Where it's safe."

"But . . . this doesn't feel right. Battle elsewhere. If you insist on staying in Ireland, at least take the battle from Knocknanuss Hill." She couldn't recall exactly what had happened there, but every mention of the place gave her the chills.

"Nay," he whispered, tilting her face up to him. "Our enemy is on the move. Inchiquin's men march for us. Whatever I feel about this Lord Taaffe, he's chosen a decent spot from which to attack."

He cupped her chin in his hands. "This is farewell, *leannan*. Do you not have a kiss for me?"

No. It was too soon. She couldn't say good-bye. To kiss him was to part from him. Would one kiss mean good-bye forever?

Though he leaned close, the gentle touch of his hands on her face was their only contact. As if their parting had already begun.

He brought his mouth to hers and Haley felt tears spill down her cheeks. MacColla kissed her slowly. Deeply and carefully.

He didn't clutch her body to him, and even though she wanted to cling to MacColla and grab him close, Haley was grateful for the space between them. To close that gap now would snap the last fragile thread that held her together.

She was preparing herself. Getting ready for what she knew she needed to do.

He ended the kiss, and with a whispered "I love you, *leannan*," MacColla left Haley to face what might come.

Alone.

Chapter 29

The lass had been wrong. God love her, but Haley had been dead wrong. His laugh rumbled in his chest, roughened by his panting breath. The battle raged. And he triumphed.

It was a rout.

MacColla led the left side, and Taaffe the right. Though they fought on the same hill, the two flanks weren't within each other's sight.

Those of his men who had muskets had fired off a shot and then tossed away their firearms to fall on the enemy with dirk and sword.

MacColla's lips peeled into a satisfied smile. Haley told him such a thing was called a "Highland Charge," that MacColla himself had invented the strategy. It amused him greatly, for all knew the Irish had masterminded such tactics long ago. They'd fire off their arrows, toss down their bows, then barrel down in a wild onslaught like a troop of madmen.

Another round of cries erupted around him, as the men all shouted, "For God and Saint Patrick!" MacColla spun to see a fresh wave of Parliamentary foot soldiers attempting to break their left flank.

He attacked with his two-handed claymore, keeping his targe slung on his back for a modicum of protection from the rear.

It wasn't the best weapon for close hand-to-hand work, but he preferred it just the same. Somewhere in the back of his mind a memory flickered, Haley telling of his legend and how he'd used that very sword to behead so many men at once.

He'd a mind to try such a trick, if they'd only slow a bit and stand still for his blade. He laughed as he swung, and was gratified to see a knot of men turn tail at the sight.

A commotion sounded loud in MacColla's ear. He sensed a rustling. Felt a body at his back.

With a swift downward slash to an enemy collarbone, MacColla finished off the man before him and pivoted to face the disturbance behind.

Just in time to see a young man swing his targe to block an enemy thrust to MacColla's back.

The lad seemed to have the situation in hand so MacColla decided to let him finish it, watching as he thrust his dirk up into the enemy's gut, twisting hard with his arm until the man fell to his knees.

"I thank you," MacColla panted, eyeing the misshapen plaid wool on his comrade's head.

Another knot of Parliament soldiers raced toward them, and the two men spun as one, positioning themselves back-to-back against the enemy.

"What have you got on your head, lad?" MacColla swung his claymore out into a ready posture.

"I've no helmet." The boy grunted as he deflected a blade with his targe, following it with a few quick slashes from his dirk. "I'm a tinker, aye?"

"Tinker?" he panted, finishing the men before him. "What has that to do with anything?" He turned to watch the lad neatly dispatch the last of the Parliamentarians.

Smiling wide, the young man pulled the thing from his

head, revealing a frying pan snugged tightly in the fabric of his bonnet. "I fancied a helmet, so I fashioned one from an old cookpot I had about."

"Indeed." MacColla laughed, clapping him hard on the shoulder. "What's your name, tinker?"

"Robertson."

"And how many have you killed today, Robertson?"

"Nineteen."

"By Mary," MacColla muttered, shaking his head in awe. "I've killed only twenty-one myself. 'Tis a pity not all of my soldiers are tradesmen."

Still chuckling, MacColla surveyed the hill. Their work was nearly done. Many of their enemy lay dead, and an increasing number had turned and fled.

"Shall we, tinker?" he asked, gesturing down the hill.

"Oh, aye, sir." The boy took off, waggling his dirk in the air, barreling downhill and hollering, "For God and Saint Patrick!"

MacColla loped behind him, a smile broad on his face, to chase their enemy nearly one league from Knocknanuss.

❧

"I've not traveled all this way," Campbell warned, "weathering the tides, braving this land of papists and savages"—he turned and pinned Purdon with a glare—"only to see you fail."

Sensing his rider's excitement, Campbell's horse pranced beneath him. He patted the beast's neck to calm him, but the horse only took the bit in his mouth, fighting for his head.

"No, sir," the major replied at once. "The business at Skipness, with the eldest MacDonald, that was—"

"I am not interested in your excuses," Campbell snapped. "You'd do well to remember whose coin fills your coffers. It's well enough you killed MacColla's brother. But now you'll kill MacColla."

Studying the valley in the distance, he continued in a snarl, "The bastard has routed us. The sod is soaked with the blood and filth of our Parliamentary soliders. Green hills, Purdon." Campbell swept his hand before him. "Look you on these green hills kicked to bloody, muddy divots."

He rubbed the pistol at his side. *Time to die, MacColla.* Would that he could kill his enemy with his own hands. But Campbell dare not insert himself into such a melee. Although Taaffe was a disaster of a general, he had seven thousand foot soldiers in his command.

"You are my sword now, Major." He turned again to face Purdon standing eagerly by his side. "And you'll not fail me again."

Campbell didn't let the young officer respond before declaring, "MacColla roves far afield, harrying our Parliamentary footmen."

He rubbed the wooden stock of his gun, cool in his palm. "The loss of our footmen was a necessary one. Like cutting off a putrid limb to save the body." He shielded his eyes and looked far in the distance, as if he could spot his enemy from where he stood. "Our Parliamentary cavalrymen will surprise Taaffe, while MacColla's attention lies elsewhere."

"Our cavalry is posted on the enemy's reverse slope," Purdon said, swelling with anticipation. "Taaffe's Irish footmen stand like babes with those long shirts tied between their legs. When they see our horses crest Knocknanuss Hill . . ."

"Aye," Campbell chuckled. "Would that I could see Taaffe's face when a wall of horseflesh comes at him from above. He'll not see the killing blade until it presses upon his throat."

He smiled broadly. This was the moment he'd waited for. He was about to conquer the last of the MacDonalds. He'd slaughtered two brothers, captured and killed the father.

And MacColla would be the next to die.

He rubbed the thin skin of his cheeks, deep in thought. "And one more thing, Purdon?"

"Sir?"

"Be certain you kill his woman." Shaking his head, he added, "It's a pity I'll not have a chance to slay her before MacColla's own eyes."

"A pleasure, Lord Campbell," he replied, finally relaxing his features into a smile.

A distant horn sounded.

"It's time." Campbell rubbed his thigh. His desire to watch MacColla die was so great, he almost wished he were a fighting man. "Do not engage in the battle. You have other quarry."

Purdon gathered his reins in one hand, and his horse sidestepped anxiously.

"MacColla's forces will be in disarray. He'll likely be separated from his men, standing behind them. Waiting as they do what they will, he'd be standing alone, or close to it, between them and Knocknanuss Hill." Campbell chuckled once more. "He'll think the battle won."

He shot one final commanding look at the major. "Find him, Purdon. Find MacColla and show him otherwise."

The major nodded and took off like a shot, standing high in his saddle as he cantered downhill, and toward MacColla.

❀

"What do you mean he's not there?" MacColla raked his hand through his hair. He looked across the valley, scanning thickets of trees and the gentle rise of a hill beyond, as if he could spy the missing soldier from where he stood.

"Aye, sir." The young messenger fidgeted before him, crushing an already tattered bonnet in his hands. "We've scouts out seeking knowledge of Taaffe's whereabouts."

"Go back yourself," MacColla growled. He didn't understand how his counterpart could've just disappeared. The fault had to lie with the messenger. "This isn't the most challenging of tasks, boy. Taaffe will be with his men."

"But . . ." The young man looked down, unable to sustain MacColla's intense eye contact.

"Speak. And look at me as you do so."

"Aye, sir." His voice trembled. "Taaffe is not with his men. And . . . his men aren't there either. Not really. Parliament horses cover the hill. The men seem . . . well, they've retreated, sir."

"Good Christ." MacColla exhaled sharply. "Am I the only man who kens how to fight?" He studied the young man before him. "Go back. Find Taaffe. He needs to know we've beaten the Parliamentary foot. What is he thinking to retreat?"

The messenger merely stood frozen, watching him.

"Now!" he shouted, and the young man raced off.

MacColla took a moment, using his plaid to wipe dried blood off the backs of his hands and from between his fingers. The messenger had said horses. The Parliamentary army must've attacked with the full brunt of their horses. He could only imagine Taaffe had seen the lot of them and panicked.

MacColla grumbled. He couldn't believe the rich lord had squandered such a commanding victory in such a cowardly way.

He sensed movement and spun in time to see a knot of horses burst through a tangle of woods not one furlong off.

"Damn." He turned to face them full-on, quickly assessing. Four Parliament soldiers galloped straight for him.

Four men to his one.

The old proverb came to MacColla unbidden. *One magpie's joy, two's grief, three's a marriage, four's a death.*

He scowled.

His eyes darted to the right and left. He was alone and in the open. There was nothing for it. "Damn it to hell," he murmured again.

MacColla rolled his shoulders, praying his head concealed the hilt of his weapon at his back. Reaching his hands wide, he forced a smile and said, "Caught."

"Indeed." A soldier of middle years reached him first. "But"—he stretched his arm out to halt his men—"good glory, could it be?" The soldier erupted into laughter. "Men, we've captured ourselves none other than Alexander MacDonald. Though you might know him better by his Gaelic name, MacColla."

"Caught," MacColla said once more. He gave a little smile. "But not captured."

He reached behind his head and unsheathed his sword in an instant.

Horses reeled around him, and MacColla raged, slashing and spinning, and slashing some more. His steel found legs, torsos, a neck, and some good deal of horseflesh, until four horsemen were whittled to one.

He heard the click of a cocking pistol behind him and swallowed a curse.

"If you'd be so kind as to hand over your blade." It was the lead soldier, and he had the barrel of his gun lodged between MacColla's ribs.

Leannan, he thought. Her face came to him. Could this be the death she'd warned of? He'd not let it be. The soldier seemed to be offering quarter.

What was he supposed to do? Perhaps in another lifetime, MacColla might have fought him. And been shot.

He hesitated. Fight, or surrender and live? He imagined *Leannan*'s gray eyes, intent, urging him to survive.

Grimacing, he proffered his sword.

"Though you did put up a grand fight," the man added, taking MacColla's claymore. "'Twill be a tale for my children's children to tell. How their grandfather O'Grady offered the great MacColla quarter."

"I'll avail myself of your prisoner, O'Grady."

MacColla turned his head to match this new voice to the man. A fifth had joined them, and though he looked an ordinary soldier, of ordinary height and with ordinary features, MacColla saw the greedy glint of evil in his eyes.

"Major Purdon," O'Grady said in greeting. Enthusiasm brightened his voice. "We've captured the famed MacColla. I've already offered the man quarter, and will be—"

"MacColla gets no quarter." Purdon's face was flat, and

his eyes didn't sway from their prisoner. A slight twitch at the man's lips betrayed his deadly intent.

"He's my prisoner," O'Grady said dismissively. He removed the gun barrel from MacColla's back and, turning, began to lead him to his horse. "It would do me a dishonor to rescind quarter once granted."

MacColla had to credit the man's principles.

Now if he could only use this new distraction to disarm him, he'd have a chance at escape. He was eyeing the pistol held loosely in O'Grady's hand when he heard a sharp click.

"You'd be wise to halt now, O'Grady." There was another click as the newcomer pulled his musket to full cock. "Turn around."

MacColla stiffened, his mind racing. He needed to fight. Another gun was the only thing of use against a musket at this range. His hand fisted and loosened, as he contemplated O'Grady's pistol, just within his reach.

Purdon spoke again. "I'd see this MacDonald's face, watch his eyes as I watched the life bleed from his brother's."

A cold, dead chill washed over MacColla. *The man who killed Gillespie.*

Who was this bastard? MacColla began to turn, anxious now for the fight, but O'Grady's pistol was back, its barrel pressed at his ribs.

He glanced down at his captor's white-knuckled grip. The soldier was nervous, and nerves killed.

"That's right," Purdon said. "I killed your brother. What was the pup's name? Gillespie? He, at least, had the courage to face me."

Damn the pistol. MacColla flexed again, ready to pull away.

"Easy now," O'Grady said, jamming the gun harder than ever into his side. "He'll not shoot a man in the back. I offered quarter, and quarter you shall have."

"Fret not, O'Grady," Purdon said to their backs. "I'll give you credit for the capture. But the kill shall be mine."

The gunshot rang sharp across the valley. Slammed hard into MacColla's back.

He lurched forward onto his knees.

Shot. Every last facet of his body jolted to awareness. He tried to stand back up, but couldn't move.

He looked down at his belly, but saw nothing. Reaching around, MacColla fumbled his hand slowly along his waist, his side. His back.

And then his fingers found it. A ragged hole in his flesh. *Shot in the back.*

Awareness shrieked into pain. Agony seized him, radiated through his veins, blood pounding it in a steady pulse from the great, wet gash in his back.

His vision wavered black, then cleared.

Shot. The horror of it swept him like a great wave. *Dead.*

He brought his hand back and it dripped crimson with his own blood. He was going to die. Horror turned his flesh cold. The skin, already, of a dead man.

Leannan. She'd known. But still, he'd gotten himself killed. *My leannan. Left alone.*

He'd gotten himself killed. And a woman on her own? He'd killed her too, in the bargain.

He couldn't die. He had to protect her. Once again, MacColla struggled to move, but couldn't.

He sensed commotion. So slow and languorous around him, like a distant buzzing of bees. The two men moved behind him, around him, shouting. The sounds came hollow to his ears, as if from behind a pane of glass.

He tried to move his legs. To rise. He must kill these men before they found her.

Something drew his eyes. MacColla looked up, squinted against the sun. *Leannan.*

He heard a sharp, brittle noise, the sound of anguish, and realized it had escaped from his own throat. *Oh God, no.*

Haley knelt at the top of the ridge. That tremendous musket was strapped to her back.

No. His lungs squeezed. His breath grew short, the pain like lightning crackling through his veins. *Go, leannan. Go back.*

Damn this body. He needed to get up. Needed to protect her. He struggled, but still he couldn't move.

He knelt on lifeless legs, propped up like a book standing open on a table. Half dead already.

She was on the hilltop, shouting something to him.

Go. She was in danger, and he couldn't help her. The horror of it choked him. *Go now.*

He tried to pull a deep breath in. Flexed his thigh muscles, willing them to move. The stab of pain sent shards of white light skittering across his vision. The agony almost unbearable now.

They'd shoot her, and this pain would be what awaited her. *No.*

It was a nightmare from which he couldn't wake. He was dying, and he couldn't save her.

He needed to warn her, tried to gesture. But he felt buried in quicksand, frozen, sinking slowly down.

He flashed to their time on the beach. The moonlight had been silver along the wet sand. Silver on her breasts, along her thighs, on the sheen of moisture that had dampened her brow.

He felt the whole of his life summed in that single vision of her. That flash of Haley, her joy, her fire. Never again would he see her. Never again touch her in the moonlight. Even the memory, gone forever.

Clouds scudded slow over the sun, throwing her into shadow. He saw her more clearly then.

Her beautiful face. Screaming wordlessly.

Watching him die.

His throat closed on his anguish. *Oh God, my leannan.*

He coughed. Agony burst hot in his belly. Searing, blinding, unutterable pain.

His world grew gray. Stars exploded before him.

He fought to keep his eyes on her. His last sight, of her.

Oh leannan, my love. Horror faded to regret. Such regret. His veins ached, steeped in regret.

I'm sorry.

And MacColla receded into black, the world gone from him forever.

Chapter 30

Even from a great distance, Haley had been able to see, hear, and smell MacColla's battle. Musket smoke nestled in the bosom of the valley, so thick it seemed a physical thing, like steel gray cotton from which men would violently burst, only to dive back in for more. Screams echoed, hollow and faraway, as did a cacophony of explosions and the distant crashing of steel on steel.

Even the most swaybacked of ponies had been marshalled for the fight, and she'd had to sneak out, secretly following MacColla on foot. Haley raced toward that gray cloud, toward *him*. Though she could no longer see it, she knew where it was, could follow its stench, see its leaden pall hanging low over the hill. She knew she'd find it—find *him*—just over the next rise.

But for the moment, she was alone. The valley stretched empty before her, unfathomably surreal. Everyone else engaged in the fighting.

In battles of old, villagers would set up for the day to watch the bloody proceedings from a distance, and Haley now saw how that was possible. The battle was contained, holding the complete attention of every last soldier.

Where are you?

She crested the gentle rise and stopped short. Haley had her overlong musket slung on her back and it struck her shoulder blades as she dropped to her knees.

The hill was littered with the bodies of dead and blood-ied men, the smell of slaughter sweet and heavy in the air. Her stomach seized, and she slapped a hand to her mouth. Bent as her body brutally retched out every last fluid in her belly.

Shit. She wiped her mouth, and stood again, as quickly as she was able. *No time . . .*

She scanned the hill, looking for a fallen man, tall, and in dingy olive black. It sickened her, and she breathed sharply through her nose to try to keep the nausea at bay. She searched, but she didn't see MacColla among the dead, and relief shuddered through her.

Many of the bodies wore tawny coats or flaunted orange or tawny strips of cloth. *Parliamenters.*

Haley spat, wiped her mouth, and spat again. Looking far in the distance, she could see the ragged path cut by MacColla and his men.

He won. His Irish Confederates had routed the Parlia-mentary army, chased them.

Then why did she still feel so uneasy?

Hurtling downhill, she followed his path. Racing across a glen and then huffing back up the next rise, she ignored her burning lungs and the razor-sharp stitch in her side. She was suddenly certain. She needed to get to MacColla, immediately.

Reaching the top, she saw him at once. And shrieked.

"No!" she screamed, racing along the ridge, trying to make sense of what she saw.

He'd been captured. One held him, one more was be-hind.

"MacColla!" The man at his back was lifting his musket.

Sunlight glinted sharply off the metal. The whole scene was so muted, so faraway. "MacColla, watch out!"

She needed to make him hear her. *Look, turn, watch out.* Haley was stumbling downhill to him when she heard the shot crack, and she froze, watching in horror.

MacColla fell to his knees, and her heart tore from her body. Haley collapsed at the same moment, her pose mirroring his.

She needed to rise, go to him. But she was paralyzed.

He looked up then, and a sob ripped from her.

Was he watching her? She cried his name. Did he see her? *Oh God, MacColla.*

Haley hoped he saw her. But she hoped too that his last thought wouldn't be that she'd failed him. Or worse, that he'd failed her.

She teetered to standing. She needed to get to him.

He flinched, his lips moved. And Haley saw the puddle of crimson spread at his knees.

"MacColla!" she screamed.

The man at his back looked up to her position, but Haley didn't care. She could think only of MacColla.

His eyes held hers.

He wavered. MacColla fell to his belly and was still.

God, no.

Haley held her breath, and waited. She felt the slow pounding of each heartbeat. Heard it thundering, a *whoosh* and roar like the sea in her head.

She waited, but she knew.

Her MacColla was dead.

She ranted then, raving and shrieking his name as if she could call him back.

Dead. She'd followed him, but she was too late.

MacColla was dead.

"MacColla!" she shrieked again, trying to call him back.

Sobs tore from her. *Oh my God, oh my God, oh my God.* Shuddering and wailing, her body gnarled in on itself. She clawed at her chest for air, but the sobs crushed the breath from her lungs.

Oh God, MacColla.

She crumpled to the ground, her sobs slowly quieting into weeping.

She'd lost her one true love. She was alone.

She hadn't saved him. And he was gone from her, forever.

No, she thought. Panic would do her no good. She had to fight. It wouldn't be over until she herself was cold and dead.

"My condolences, love," a man shouted to her.

Oh shit.

Looking downhill, she spotted him. *His killer.* The man who'd shot MacColla in the back was climbing up the slope to her.

She looked down to the valley. The other man knelt over MacColla's body, paying no mind to what happened above.

He followed her eyes and laughed. "Shot in the back like a coward."

"Fuck you," Haley snarled, scrubbing the tears from her face. Anger was like acid in her veins, its poison curdling her sorrow into vengeance. "Fuck you," she said again, more loudly, scrambling to her knees to pull the musket from her back.

"Shit," she muttered, fumbling to remove her flint and steel from a pouch at her waist.

Struggling to hold the match and steel file in one hand, she struck the flint down, but the sparks were too weak to light the thin stretch of rope.

Laughing at her, the man broke into an uphill jog.

"Dammit, dammit." Her hands trembled. Errant memories came to her. She saw her brother's lighter in his hand, Gerry's nervous fingers flipping the silver lid of the old Zippo, open and shut. The image was too painful, too sharp to touch, and she pushed it from her mind. "Dammit," she cried, hysteria sharpening her voice.

She struck harder, and sparks flew. They landed on her hand, danced bright white on her skin, seared her. And then winked out.

The man was approaching. She opened her senses, heard

his boots scrambling up grass and rocks, felt his presence twenty feet away. She continued to struggle with the flint, but she was almost out of time.

Haley spared a quick glance. *Ten feet away.* Close to the top. Casually using his musket as a walking stick. The same musket that had killed MacColla.

Rage filled her.

He crested the hill. *Six feet.*

She tossed the flint and match down. The soldier sprinted at her, and Haley's hands wrapped tight around the base of her gun. So long and heavy in her hands.

He thought she'd be easy prey. He was wrong.

Haley sprung to her feet, swinging the musket like a windmill before her. The sheer weight of it increasing its own momentum.

It slammed into the man's arm, knocking his gun from his hand. It spiraled and slid downhill, out of reach.

She held the musket like a bat in front of her, arms trembling from the awkward weight.

"I was going to show you mercy," he said, rubbing his forearm. Fury was in his eyes. "But I think I'll have you beg for it."

She swung again, but the musket was too cumbersome and he stood too close. The man snatched the barrel and smiled.

She struggled to pull it from his grasp, letting panic get the better of her. *What am I doing?* The man would win any contest against her. She *knew* that. She needed to remember what her father had taught her.

A woman had two options. Fight dirty or run.

Haley let go and ran.

She heard him throw the musket. Heard him race after her.

She pumped her arms, felt one of her leather slippers fly off. Hiking her skirts up, she raced faster, but it was a struggle along the uneven ground.

His panting breath came louder now. He was catching her.

Fight dirty.

Haley stopped short, used her momentum as she spun, bringing the heel of her hand up hard. She aimed for his nose, but the man ducked at the last moment, and she simply grazed his forehead.

He wrenched her wrist with one hand and reached for his belt with the other. *Knife.* She spotted it hanging from his belt, tucked in an elaborate, brass-studded leather scabbard.

She couldn't let him get to his knife.

Counterintuitive, she heard her father say. The most basic principles of street fighting were counterintuitive.

Get closer.

Haley leapt for him, twining her legs around his. He still had a death grip on her wrist, so she used her free hand to strike at his eyes.

You killed MacColla.

He flinched away, but her nails found flesh, and she clawed down hard, feeling the meat of his lower eyelid and cheek warm and wet under her nails.

"Good Christ," the man screeched, and the shock in his voice girded her.

He struggled, squinting his eyes shut tight, wriggling his free hand between them to get at his blade.

"I'll kill you. Like you killed him." She hooked her thumb on the bone of his eye socket. Began to push in. "Kill you."

"Christ, bitch," he hissed, struggling to dislodge her hand. "Demon. Hellcat."

Haley reeled. *Hellcat.* Memories of MacColla cascaded rapid-fire into her mind. Of that fight so long ago when he'd called her that same name.

She faltered, and her opponent struck.

Wrenching his arm between them, he elbowed her in the belly just as he got a grip on his dagger.

She leapt off him, but he still held her wrist. *Focus or die.* Her hand was growing numb.

Break his grip. She ducked, swinging her arm up and around, and his hand automatically released her.

He was close, though. Too close for her to run.

She looked at the blade in his hand. It was a preposterously elegant little thing, with a brass horse head for a pommel.

Defang the snake, she heard her father say. *Go for the knife arm. Make your opponent lose his blade.*

Haley quickly shook life into her hands, then attacked at once. A rapid scissor strike, smacking the inside of his wrist with her right and the back of his hand with her left.

The knife flew from his grip.

He was stunned, but it lasted just a moment. The man clearly hadn't expected a fight, and he was furious.

Run. Haley turned and took off again, loping and sliding down the far side of the hill.

She heard him behind her. He was closing.

MacColla. She wanted MacColla. She wanted this all to be over.

Maybe this was it. This man would kill her like he killed MacColla, and it would all be over.

She heard a shot crack overhead and flinched. Did he have a pistol? Haley dove into a low tangle of shrubbery.

Was she shot? Her heart felt like it would burst from her chest. Was that what it felt like to be shot? Is this what MacColla had felt?

A part of her welcomed it. *MacColla.* If she were shot dead, would she see him once more?

But then her opponent shouted. Another shot was fired.

Then silence.

She heard a familiar voice, and was relieved and heartbroken both. *Not MacColla.* Haley crawled from the gorse and looked up to see Rollo.

Calm, he sat his horse at the top of the ridge as if they were a statue carved of granite. It took her mind a moment to understand what was happening.

"Come, Haley," he said. "Fast now. They approach."

Her mind kicked back into gear, and using both hands and feet, she scampered uphill, where Rollo swung her

behind him on the saddle, seating her sideways as he galloped away.

She turned to see her lover one last time. Her MacColla.
Lying dead on the field below.

❀

"I'm sorry there's not true shelter to be had." Rollo leaned
forward to stoke the fire he'd built at the mouth of the cave.

They'd ridden hard and long, reaching a rocky bit of
Irish shore. His legs were trembling by the end of it, looking like the solid and knotted branches of some tree. Haley
didn't know where on earth they were, and she was too
numb to care.

"But there's nobody I trust," he added, pounding life
into his muscles. "I'll bring us back to Scotland—"

"Where?" she interrupted, despondence giving an edge
to her voice. "I've got nowhere to go."

Home. She could go home. Could she somehow find her
way back to modern-day Boston? The thought left her hollow.

MacColla had become her home.

"I know someone who can help."

"No, Rollo," she snapped. She snatched up a bit of old
wood and used it to stab and scrape deep into the sandy
soil. "You *don't* know. You have no idea."

She was alone in the past. And Rollo thought *he* had nobody he could trust.

Her eyes darted to him. Rollo. He'd been a true friend
to MacColla. Had ridden to find her. Saved her.

She couldn't give up on MacColla. There must be some
way. But first, she had to trust somebody, and the likeliest
option, her *only* option, sat before her.

"Look, Rollo." She put her stick down and brushed her
hands on her filthy skirts. "This is going to sound crazy,
but . . ."

But, what? But . . . get this, I'm from the future!

"Never mind," she said, deflated.

"Not crazy, lass." He stared at her over the flames. Steadfast, sure. "There's another."

"Huh?"

"You were right, Haley. James Graham lives." Rollo spared her one of his rare smiles. "And he is wed to one like you."

Chapter 31

James Graham was everything Haley had ever imagined him to be. Handsome, chivalrous, strong, gentlemanly, noble, erudite.

He was also annoying the hell out of her.

She wanted to act. And *now*. But the man insisted on niceties. She knew she needed food and rest, but she'd gotten it into her head that she could save MacColla. And she wanted to figure out a plan immediately.

"Truly, lass," he said, pulling a chair from the table for her. "You must eat. We offer our assistance, and gladly, but food is the first, best help for you."

She stared at him, wrapped haphazardly in a cornflower blue plaid, with bare legs and feet. The sun had risen warm and bright that day, and all the doors and windows to their cottage were open to the breeze, rustling James's hair gently over his shoulders.

The sight of a man so casually at home stabbed her. She should have *her* man there. She should be eating breakfast with *MacColla*.

They'd arrived well after dark after a day of sailing.

Though they were on a small, barely inhabited island, it was like paradise, with a sandy beach, lush rolling hills, and strange and dramatic rocky outcroppings.

And it kindled memories of her time with MacColla on the Mull of Kintyre that were almost too painful to acknowledge.

"I'll not lift a finger for you until you have a decent meal in your belly," James said firmly.

"MacColla would want that." It was his wife Magda, speaking quietly. Haley looked at her, instantly on the defensive. But her face was so open and sincere, Haley couldn't fault her.

"All right," she muttered, sitting to let James guide her chair in. "Just a little."

Forcing herself to chew an oatcake, she stole another glance at James's wife.

Rollo told her Magda had also come from the future, and Haley had immediately recognized her as a contemporary. She couldn't put her finger on why or how. Something about her words, the way she carried herself, spoke to a different time and place.

Haley wondered if *she* stood out that much.

She'd felt instantly self-conscious in front of the woman. She was tall and pretty, with long, shining copper hair, and so effortlessly elegant despite her hugely pregnant belly.

And she was from Manhattan, of all places.

Haley swallowed hard, quickly taking a sip of water to wash down the dry lump. Only *she* would travel back in time and land with a damned Yankees fan.

Magda caught her staring. Haley felt her cheeks go red and said the first thing that came to her mind. "I have to save him."

"Haley," Rollo said somberly from across the table. "'Tis too late for MacColla. But not too late to help you find a—"

"No," Haley said more sharply than she'd intended. "I can't accept that he's dead."

James and his wife stole a glance. "There might be a way," Magda said gravely.

"Och, hen." James looked at his wife, concern plain on his face. "It could kill her."

"What way?" Haley pushed her plate away. "I'll do anything." She pinned her gaze on James, telling him, "You more than anyone must understand the need to risk your life for something, or some*one* you love."

"He does." Magda reached to place her hand over her husband's to silence him. "As I do, Haley."

Haley stared at her a moment. She felt like a heel. Of course this woman would understand more than anyone what she went through. This woman who gave up everything for the man she loved.

It was different for Haley, who spoke Gaelic, had steeped herself for years in the history of this period. But Magda? Magda, with the fancy parents and fancy job in New York City? Magda wouldn't know flintlocks from *Flintstones*.

"Come with me," Magda said softly.

Haley followed her to the only other room in the cottage. It was small and sun-drenched, with a desk, two trunks, a humble bed, and a wooden cradle waiting in the corner.

"Go ahead." Magda nodded for Haley to sit on the bed. The wooden frame creaked as she sat. The ticked mattress was thin, but more comfortable than it looked, stuffed with what felt like a mixture of feathers and straw.

Magda rifled for a moment in one of the trunks, then came to sit by her side.

"This . . ." She lovingly unwrapped a small parcel. "This is a painting of my brother." Magda held it for a moment in her hands, tenderly tracing its outline with her fingertip.

"You left your brother?" A glimmer of expectancy mingled with the sympathy in her voice. Did this woman also know what it was to leave a family of brothers?

"No." Magda pursed her lips, visibly gathering herself.

"I had a brother who left me. He died. About a year before I found James."

"Oh, I . . ." Haley thought of her own brothers. Who'd now lost their sister. "I'm sorry," she said, her voice hitching, the apology to Magda, and even more so to her own family.

"Take it." Magda thrust the painting toward her.

"What? Why? I couldn't."

"Yes." She placed it in Haley's hands. "You can. It's . . . special. A painting was what transported me back in time. I'm told this has the same powers."

"But . . . how?"

"That I don't know," Magda admitted. "But I thought . . . Well, perhaps you could go back in time again. *Before* Mac-Colla's death."

Haley sat upright, her gaze pinning Magda.

Magda continued gravely, "Of course, you could also use it to return to your own home. Your own time."

The two women locked eyes.

Magda broke the silence. "Boston, is it?"

"Don't tell me I have an accent." She attempted a smile.

"No." Shaking her head, Magda returned the look, an expression of mingled sympathy and understanding. "You mentioned Harvard."

"Oh, that." Her world seemed so far away. Things like academic success a distant and empty memory. She studied her hands in her lap. "Yeah . . . I'm a South Boston girl. Big, Irish Catholic family. You can imagine . . ." Her voice drifted off.

"You miss them."

Haley felt the tears threaten, and furrowed her face in an effort to staunch them. *Miss them?* She mustered a wordless nod. *More than anything. More than ever.*

She wanted to curl up under her mom's crocheted afghan, family all around. There'd be good-natured bickering, heated debates, and much, much laughter. Maybe an open bottle of wine shared among the women. Her mom would have a roast chicken going, or maybe a lasagna.

Something big, to feed the lot of them, filling the house with scents of warmth and comfort and home.

Miss them? Yes.

Enough to turn her back on MacColla forever?

She shuddered an inhale. "But what about you? You must miss your own family."

"Of course." Magda got a faraway look in her eyes. "But I belong here. With James."

"Don't you hate the thought . . ." Haley dashed her hands over her eyes. Her throat ached now with the effort of unshed tears. "The thought that you just . . . vanished?"

"There was a painting," Magda said in answer. "The painting, of James. The one that transported me back. I tucked it away with a note indicating it belonged at the Met, the museum where I worked. I also tucked a note away, for my parents."

"How can you know they got it?"

"Who knows? My mom was on the Met board of directors . . ." Magda shrugged. "Hell, for all I know, they could've gotten the note when I was still a kid." She gave a rueful smile. "But the painting just showed up at work one day. I have to imagine the note came with it. Was delivered with it." She took a deep breath. "I'll never know. I can hope, though."

Magda took her hand and continued, "What I do know, though, what I've learned these past months, is that, despite the wars, despite the bloodshed, people are *good*. I trust that someone would've delivered my message. Maybe even read it themselves, I don't care. But having witnessed the sacrifice that I have, the devotion and loyalty, honestly Haley, I really think my parents received my letter. And they'd want me to be happy."

"Yeah . . ." Haley cleared her throat. Scrubbed her face and tucked her hair back behind her ears. "My family would want that too. For me to be happy."

She thought of that big, loving family of hers. Her father, who positively adored and doted on her mother. Her brothers, who were beginning to pair off and begin families of their own. And she projected herself into her own future. A future in modern-day America. Empty scholarship, cold weapons, and musty books all around. Would she ever meet her life partner, there in Boston?

The moment she wondered, she knew.

She *had* met her life partner.

MacColla.

"I'll try a letter too." Haley squeezed Magda's hand tight. She was certain now. Her time and place was by Mac-Colla's side. She belonged wherever—and whenever—he was. "But . . . are you sure . . . can I really use your painting?"

At Magda's nod, Haley thanked her.

"Well, don't thank me yet. I'm not sure how this . . . works." Both women sat a little straighter, focused now.

Magda studied the painting in Haley's hands, and Haley realized what it would mean for her to give away the only likeness she had of her brother.

"There's a witch," Magda said. "You'll need to find her. I'm certain James wishes *he* could take you to her, but he can't risk being recognized."

"He's very recognizable," Haley admitted, and both women shared a tension-relieving laugh.

"As if MacColla isn't?" Magda smiled, and Haley was grateful for her use of the present tense.

"Rollo will take you," Magda continued. "She lives in the Highlands. Near Clan Cameron. I think she'll be able to help you."

"But . . ." Haley studied the painting in her hands. A handsome young man, with Magda's same regal features, and a head of bright red hair. "But this is the last image you have of your brother."

"I don't need a picture to remember Peter," Magda said, touching the edge of the painting one last time. "I don't need evidence of him when he lives on in my heart."

She wrapped Haley's hands around the miniature portrait. "You'll see. This place changes you. The simpler life becomes, the richer it grows."

Haley nodded wordlessly. "Thank you," she whispered, and gave Magda's fingers an affectionate squeeze.

"Now about that letter of yours," Magda said, smiling. She stood and walked to the desk. It was placed by the window, and a bright ray of sun shone in, illuminating the surface with hyperreal light. She took a piece of paper from a small wooden box. "My husband was a famous man. If I understand correctly, even you originally stayed back in time merely to discover if he lived or died."

Haley looked away, embarrassed.

"Oh, I don't blame you, believe me." Magda grew serious. "Write them your good-bye. I'll place it with—"

"James's sword," Haley interrupted, eyes bright. "A sword of his is famous, it's on display in a museum in Montrose. Put it with a sword, marked as his."

"Yes, I'll do that. With a request that the letter be delivered to whatever address you write, on whichever date you say. That way you won't worry as I did that they somehow got the letter, I don't know, when I was still in grade school." They shared a smile.

"It could be delivered the day after I disappear," she marveled softly.

Her gaze met Magda's. "So . . . they'd know by now. I mean, if time is a static thing, and my family is out there somewhere. The letter would be in their hands by now."

"I can't wrap my own mind around it." Magda shrugged and shook her head. "But, yes, if you think about it that way . . . By now, your family would've read your good-bye."

❀

They'd traveled for hours, hugging along a coastal inlet, finally docking in a small cove along the shore of Loch Linnhe.

The ground seemed to waver beneath her as she struggled to reclaim her land legs. Haley was stretching and stomping her limbs back to life when she sensed Rollo's abrupt movement.

She turned, amazed to see him with his pistol out, loaded, and cocked in seconds.

Haley froze, looking around. "What are you shoot—?" She swallowed back a startled yelp.

A woman stood on the bank of the lake. Gray smoke spiraled up from a small fire, as if she'd been camped and waiting just for them.

Haley darted a quick look around. They were in the middle of nowhere, vast stretches of wilderness as far as the eye could see. How is it they managed to bump into someone *here*? The woman seemed to have simply materialized from nowhere.

And why did Rollo have his gun trained on her? He, at least, seemed to have spotted the stranger straightaway.

Haley knew he was stiff from a day seated on the hard bench, but no one would ever suspect it. He stood tall, arms outstretched steadily before them, his hazel eyes turned the color of cold stone.

"Put your gun down, man." The woman sucked at her teeth and spit into the fire. "I offer you help, not harm."

The woman's nonchalance was studied. Haley thought she seemed, in fact, capable of great harm. Though she couldn't put a finger on why.

Long red hair flowed over her shoulders, marbled with a few strands of wiry gray. She was skinny, but not scrawny, her body all tendons and thin muscle. Something about her had the whiff of power.

Haley was happy to see that Rollo wasn't taking the woman's suggestion; his gun remained pointed straight at her. "The only thing you can help us with is your name," he said. "Who are you?"

"I am called Finola."

"I'm afraid I'll need more than that if I'm to lower this gun."

"You aim your foolish weapon at me as if I am your quarry." The woman peeled her lips back in an impatient snarl. "You are as a child who frolics in the water with no understanding of the depths below."

Finola spread her arms wide. Her cloak fluttered about her, and what had been a dingy gray seemed suddenly brighter, whiter than before. She, somehow taller.

Haley's knees started to buckle, and she forced herself to stand tall.

Rollo, though, didn't waver. His words resonated as he asked, "What do you play at, woman?"

Voice pitched low, she incanted, "You seek a witch, and so I stand. The star road lies at *my* command. My power, greater than hers you seek. I am strong, my enemies weak."

What the . . . Haley edged back to stand a little behind Rollo. She eyed the muscles of his back visible under the damp linen of his shirt. He was unflinching, like chiseled rock. She had to hand it to him—he still hadn't put the gun down, and it gave her courage.

"How do you know who we seek?" Haley managed.

"I *know*, girl."

"What is your clan?" Rollo stepped toward her. "You stand on Cameron lands. Are you a Cameron?"

"You ask the questions of a fool." Finola brought her arms down hard, dismissive. "Try my patience further and I'll leave you to flounder."

No. The woman had said she was a witch. What if she were the one who could help her?

"How did you know?" Haley asked, stepping out from Rollo's shadow. "How did you know I needed to . . . travel?"

"Do you not listen to what I tell you?" She glared dully at Haley. "I know of your journey. Know of your man."

Haley's breath hitched. "But . . ." Hope and fear warred in her. "Why would you help me?"

"I don't *help* you," the woman spat. "Pathetic creature." Her words came out as a hiss. The eerie green and yellow of her irises flashed, then were subsumed by black. "I help myself. Campbell has made me an enemy. There is a path whereby MacColla lives. I am merely curious to see where that path leads."

Finola turned. "But it seems you do not understand the boon you are offered." She leaned to gather a small satchel laying by the fire. "And so perhaps I take my leave."

"No," Haley said, her voice sounding more confident than she felt. "I understand what you offer. Please. Help me."

Chapter 32

Night had come too quickly, bringing with it a biting chill and the miserly half glow of a crescent moon.

Haley wanted MacColla. Missed her father, her family. What she was about to do terrified her. What if she landed in some other strange time or place? She could get stuck with no means to return.

She was desperate for a kind word, some protection, and was grateful to see Rollo's usual stoicism soften momentarily.

"I'm scared," she whispered hoarsely.

"Haley. So like that 'Frail boat of crystal in a rocky sea.'" Rollo tilted his head. He smiled quietly at her confusion, his teeth an eerie white in the black shadows. "Not my words," he said. "Drummond's. A poet."

"Quoting poetry to me?" She tried to muster some bit of good humor. "MacColla would be jealous."

"You'll see him soon, lass." Shifting his weight, Rollo brought his cane to his other hand. Grinning, he added, "You can tell him yourself how gallant you find me."

She was startled, and despite the trepidation that clutched at her chest, she laughed.

"You do the right thing," he said, growing serious. "When I look in your eyes, I can almost sense MacColla, so bright is his place in your heart. The man loved you more than reason. And it's just that sort of madness that will return you to him. I cannot imagine you landing anywhere but back by his side."

A sharp exhale announced Finola, her readiness, her impatience, and her annoyance most of all.

"Come now, or don't," she snapped. "We must work while the moon is high."

"A man is of little use when his wife's a widow, aye?" Rollo said with another smile, ignoring the witch. "So go now, dear friend. Go save MacColla."

But she didn't move, and so he reached a single hesitant finger, touching her chin gently. "You are brave in your heart, Haley Fitzpatrick. Fear not the bravery of your deeds."

It struck her that only she would remember this moment. She was traveling back to a time before, and she hoped she and MacColla would be walking a new path. One that didn't end with him dead and her standing beneath a watery moon, Will Rollo and a witch as her only company.

She was the only one who'd remember Finola's crackling fire, Rollo's kindness. And the realization made her feel even more alone.

One thought came to her, amusing her and giving her strength. Rollo's bolstering smile and kind words had betrayed him as a true friend to Haley. And though chances were good the stoic would never demonstrate as much again, she'd always have memories of this thoughtfulness as proof.

She gave him a quiet smile and, nodding, turned to face Finola.

Fire danced behind the witch, the flames blazing whiter and hotter than a bonfire should. It cast Finola's face in blackness, made her seem larger than life. Long shadows cut along the dirt, reaching toward Haley, and their blackness subsumed her feet, her calves. She wondered if the chill prickling in their wake was merely imagined.

Finola's sinewy arm stretched toward her, fingers reaching.

Haley took a deep breath. She was terrified now. But there was no other choice.

She turned her head, looking once more at Rollo. She wanted a nod, one last smile, some reassurance that this was going to be all right. But he merely locked eyes with hers, his gaze sympathetic. He'd lend her strength, but Haley was alone now. She alone could make this choice.

Flexing her fingers, she turned back to Finola and let the witch take her hand.

With a sharp inhale, the woman's head snapped back. Her face pointed to the sky, and despite the dimness of the moon, the whites of her eyes glowed eerily bright.

Haley heard humming, so low at first, it seemed to originate from inside her own head. It grew louder, and she realized the sound came from Finola.

The witch was in a trancelike state, muttering. The susurration gradually coalesced into words, growing louder and louder.

Her fingers seized, clawing Haley's skin. Haley gave an instinctive tug, but the woman's grip only tightened.

She pulled Haley to the fire.

God help me.

She could stop it all now. Live her life, find her own little island and make do from that moment on. This seemed . . . wrong. A dark thing, an evil thing.

MacColla. Turning back now would mean good-bye forever.

Haley rolled her shoulders back. *The only way.* She stepped slowly, letting Finola lead her.

Stopping before the fire, the witch dropped Haley's hand suddenly. Backed up.

And then she began to dance.

Finola whirled around, the sleeves of her robes fluttering over and through the fire as she spun like a dervish around the blaze. Nonsensical staccato sounds popped from her mouth, bits of spittle landing with a hiss in the fire. The flames licked at her cloak now, but rather than catching fire, it only glowed brighter, whiter.

The woman opened her mouth wide, a black maw in the darkness. A horrific cry erupted, a sharp, steady ululation sounding her dance around the flames.

Haley clutched her skirts in her fists. *No choice, no choice.*

The witch stopped short. Pulled something from her robes. It was the painting. Magda's painting.

She thrust it into Haley's hands. Firelight licked the edges of the portrait, illuminating the face of Magda's dead brother. He looked up at her, so innocent, with bright red hair and a slight smile curving his mouth.

Guilt stabbed her. It seemed an abomination. As if she were somehow sullying the memory of this boy. Peter, was it? An image of innocence, defiled by this witch.

She grabbed Haley's hand once more. Finola's fingers were cold now, icy and dry, the skin of her fingertips thin, like an old woman's.

Finola took Haley's hand and rubbed it over the portrait. The paint smudged with the pressure and Peter's image blurred. He was a surreal face now, still looking up at her, the memory of that once-captured innocence an indictment.

MacColla. MacColla, what am I doing?

Magda had given Haley the painting. It was her only hope. Magda had known what this meant. *No guilt. No choice.* Magda would want it this way.

Tiny splinters bit into her palm. Haley's reflex was to pull back, but Finola's grip was like steel. She intoned,

Gaoth o'n rionnaig Earraich,
Teas o'n rionnaig Shamhraidh,
Uisg' o'n rionnaig Fhogair,

Reothadh o'n rionnaig Gheamhraidh.
Wind from the Spring Star,
Heat from the Summer Star,
Water from the Autumn Star,
Frost from the Winter Star.
Hear me.

The last resonated long and low through the night.

The witch took Haley's finger and used it like an instrument, forming strange, abstract shapes along the surface.

Gooseflesh shivered along her body like ice. *What the . . .*

She stole a backward glance at Rollo, standing in the shadows, watching. The way he stiffened, putting his hand to his sword, spoke to the terror in her eyes.

I must. Haley gave him a small nod, and turned her head from him for good.

"The hero sleeps in his tomb," Finola chanted. Her hand dragged Haley's finger faster, mercilessly etching out shapes along the wooden panel. "The hero chose a path to doom."

She felt the tackiness of her own blood on its surface.

"A hero's cairn, and fates that were. The star road, to him, take her."

Even though Haley knew her head was immobile, it felt as if it whipped back and forward again. *Vertigo.*

Adrenalin kicked in, making her hyperaware of every sensation.

"Take her, take her." The witch's voice was low now. An inhuman rumbling that seemed to come from the trees all around, from the lake water, from the sky above.

"Think her on her love. Become one with stars above."

What? Was she supposed to be thinking about Mac-Colla? Finola hadn't given her instructions. She tried to speak, but her tongue was thick and dead in her mouth. *Wait.* Did she need to think something specific to go back to him?

"To dissolve into skies. To save him who dies."

The vertigo seized her again, and this time didn't let go, propelling a dull *click-click* in her head, spinning, spinning.

The flames at her back felt suddenly cold, her lungs breathing the smoke of dry ice, not fire.

Haley was chilled, her body bloodless and insubstantial, and her heart fluttered lighter and lighter, until she thought it a hummingbird set to flit from her body.

God help me.

"Take her. Take her. Take her."

❁

The humming stopped, and she sagged abruptly.

She felt sapped, saddened. She was steeped in heightened emotion, felt thick with it. *Didn't it work?*

The whirling in her head subsided and she struggled, her eyelids fluttering.

She felt hands holding her. Warm hands.

Rollo? Had she collapsed?

Haley shuddered a deep inhale. Managed to give her head a shake. Opened her eyes.

She stood before MacColla, her chin in his hands. "This is farewell, *leannan*," he told her. "Do you not have a kiss for me?"

Haley shrieked.

Chapter 33

She leapt up and into MacColla's arms, wrapping her legs around his waist, clawing her hands in his hair. She felt thick black hanks of it tug tight at his scalp, but she didn't care.

She had her MacColla back.

Haley kissed him deeply, opening her mouth wide to him, her tongue delving deep, savoring him.

She pulled away. "Laces," she said frantically, reaching behind her back to undo the bodice of her dress. "Help me. The laces."

MacColla laughed. "Oh, *leannan*." He put her down and spun her, tugging hard at the ties. She felt cool air hit her shoulders, then her back, as he pulled the gown down hard. "Had I known what a simple request would do"—he nibbled and licked along the line of her shoulders—"I'd have been asking you more politely from the start."

"Quiet," she commanded, turning to face him. "Just kiss me."

"Aye," he said huskily. His good humor was gone, leaving his eyes hungry, hooded. He took her mouth roughly with his.

Wrapping an arm around her waist, he whisked her backward. They stumbled over the long musket he'd given her, abruptly parting their kiss. "Careful," he said quickly, holding her from falling.

"Right." She glanced down and back up again. "My trusty musket," she said sarcastically.

He looked at her a moment, brows furrowed in amusement and confusion. "Och, woman, 'tis time for you to quiet yourself and kiss *me*."

MacColla seized her mouth once more. He shuffled them briskly backward, pushing her hard against the wall.

The stone was cold and rough on her naked back, and she welcomed the reminder that she was alive. That *he* was alive.

Haley tugged at his clothes, his belt and empty shoulder scabbard fell with a clatter to the ground, followed by the heavy sound of his plaid cascading to the floor.

He pushed the gown from her hips and their clothing was a tangle at their feet. Frustrated, she kicked wildly at all the layers of fabric, eliciting a husky laugh from Mac-Colla.

"Easy," he muttered, squatting down to sweep the pile away.

"Don't easy *me*," she snapped. "You have no idea."

"*Hm?*" He began to stand again, but when she tangled her fingers roughly in his hair, he squatted again, kneeling before her, a husky laugh in his throat.

MacColla slid his large hands around the backs of her thighs and gave a squeeze.

"Oh . . ." she gasped.

"*Nach tu a tha bòidheach*," he murmured. "You're so beautiful, *mo leannan*."

Haley looked down, and the sight of him, staring up at her with such pure want in his eyes, sent a shock of desire through her core. She felt herself grow wet, expansive.

"You're alive," she whispered.

She began to tremble as MacColla turned his focus to her body. His mouth hovered just above her skin, just almost kissing her. *"Cho maiseach ris a' ghrèin."* His breath was hot on her belly, her thighs.

Beauty like the sun.

She shivered, feeling those rough palms caressing her legs, stroking around to cup her ass, up her back.

"Your hands," she whispered. His fingers spanned her, so long and strong. "I missed your hands."

He brought both palms to rest on her stomach. His thumbs edged down, rubbing along the inside of her legs, tracing the V of her thighs.

Her knees buckled, and with a rasp of a laugh, he moved quickly to catch her, leaning his body in close to hold her up against the wall. Weak, Haley rested her hands on his shoulders, giving him more of her weight.

"You're alive," she murmured.

MacColla began nuzzling her, tracing his tongue along her legs and belly, nipping gently with his lips, teasing closer and closer to her cleft.

One hand held her hips firmly, the other glided up, finding her breast and kneading it. He chafed his open palm over her nipple and she drew in her breath, feeling the tender skin pulling tight. He pinched her, rolled her between his fingers.

"Yes . . ." she said softly.

His kisses skimmed closer and closer until his tongue darted for a moment between her legs, licked, and drew back out again.

"Please." Haley tightened her grip on his shoulders. "More, MacColla."

Groaning, he swooped his head back between her thighs, kissing her once, then pressing the flat of his tongue firmly against her.

His tongue laved her, sucking and flicking in a steady rhythm, until she thought the heat in her veins would catch fire.

"Mmm." It was a harsh sound, rasping low in his throat, escaping on a quavering exhale.

His thumb swiped one last time over her nipple, and

MacColla brought his hand down, using it to help support Haley's weight while he eased her legs farther apart.

He pulled away from her. The cold air on the thick dampness between her legs was a shock, and she mewled her complaint. But he tilted her hips and very quickly found her again, his rigid tongue pushing in to penetrate her.

Her knees buckled then, and MacColla caught her, wedging a shoulder beneath her knee to bear her weight. His tongue still thrusting and licking, he brought his thumb to her, steadily circling until she felt her body tightening, tensing, ready to shatter.

A sharp sound escaped her, and MacColla held her tightly as she exploded in waves over him.

Easing them both down, he lay on his back and pulled Haley to kneel astride him, slowly guiding her onto him. "So wet," he murmured, as he began to glide in and out.

His hands roved her body, teasing her breasts, caressing her thighs.

He slowed, snagged her gaze for a heartbeat. "You're too far from me, *mo chrìdhe*." MacColla slid his hands to her back and pulled her closer.

"Oh, *leannan*," he whispered huskily, kissing along her collarbones. MacColla's mouth roved down to suck each breast into a point. "So beautiful, *mo leannan*."

Haley was unable to speak, her body already burning again from within. Breathy moans escaped her, and she folded herself completely over him, chest to chest, drawing her mouth along his powerful neck, his throat, his strong chin.

He took her face in his hands and kissed her deeply. He thrust hard and fast now, and the feel of him, so thick and moving so surely inside her, replaced all thought. There was only this sensation, only this moment, only them.

Already she felt the familiar pull in her belly, building and coiling once more, and she thought her next climax might thrust her over a precipice from which she'd never return.

He pulled his mouth from hers. "Come for me," he whispered, his voice ragged in her ear.

She angled her face to his, her mouth grazing the sharp scrape of stubble at his jaw.

The taste of salt and sex destroyed the last of her control. "Yes," she cried, and the heat exploded within her, fragmenting her, consuming her.

Haley felt his arms wrapped tightly around her. Felt his fingers curled tight in her hair, clawed in the flesh of her ass. Felt him tense, grow large and spasm inside her, a guttural moan sounding his own pleasure.

MacColla stroked the sweat-damped hair from her brow. Utterly spent, they lay there unmoving, tangled with one another on the lumpy pile of clothes.

"I love you, *leannan*." He studied Haley's beautiful face, her cheeks bright from their coupling, and those long black lashes framing bottomless gray eyes. Flecked black and gray like a stormy sea, they watched him, expectantly, and for the first time in his life, MacColla felt truly seen.

" 'Tis a simple phrase from a simple man. But there it is. I love you."

Her passion never ceased to surprise him. The time for him to leave had come and gone, but he'd steal just a few more moments of this. Of her.

"I won't let you die again," was all she whispered in response.

His fingers paused. Eyes narrowed, he asked, "You mean, you believe I *will* die."

"No, MacColla. I watched you die." She twined her fingers with his and pulled them from her brow. Rolling from him to lie on her side, she said, "You died and I came back for you."

"How is it . . . ?" He didn't understand what she was telling him. But he trusted her implicitly, and so waited for understanding to dawn.

She tucked his hand at her heart, and for the first time MacColla noticed her fingertip. "What's this then?" he asked, seizing it.

Though it no longer bled, the pad of her finger shone a uniform and vivid red, as though a layer had been scraped off to reveal the tender meat just below the surface. An angry reddish brown halo already circled the injury.

"We must clean this, *leannan*." The furious desire to protect her flexed his muscles. "How did this happen?"

"That's what I'm trying to tell you," she said, giving him an impatient look.

Realizing he clutched her hand too tightly, MacColla eased his grip. He knew such a response was without merit—this was a small cut, and cuts healed. But the thought of her in any sort of pain was more than he could bear.

"You fought the battle," she rasped. "You died. A brown-haired soldier shot you in the back. Rollo helped me."

The words rattled from her, and MacColla tried to make sense of them. "Slower, lass."

"I went back in time again, to this moment, to tell you." She squeezed his hand hard. "You can't fight this battle."

"How can that be?" He studied her finger. "And what has that . . . to do with this?" he asked, rubbing her knuckle.

"I went to James Graham for help," she said, more slowly.

"Graham?" His brows raised in surprise.

"Yes."

His eyes narrowed playfully. "Is this your way to get me to betray James's true fate?"

"No." A smile flickered on her face. "My question was finally answered. I saw for myself that Graham lives."

"You say you went back in time . . . again?" Could such a thing really have happened? "Truly?"

"Yes. I met James, and Magda too. She gave me a tiny painting, of her brother, said it was a portal through time . . ." Her words drifted off. "Do you believe me?"

MacColla stared hard at her. She suddenly looked so anxious, so uncharacteristically vulnerable, her despair hinging on his response.

He remembered Magda. The woman had told him about her brother, how he'd died.

And then it struck him. There was no way Haley could've known about Magda's dead brother.

"Aye, *leannan*," he replied softly. "When have I not believed you?"

Smiling, she clutched his hand tight and continued with renewed zeal, "Rollo took me to find a witch. But a witch found us. She said she hated Campbell and would send me back to save you."

Haley let go his hand and studied the raw skin of her fingertip. "She scraped patterns on the portrait and that's what cut me. She chanted and rubbed my finger raw, and . . . well, then I was back with you."

"I see," he said quietly.

"Good. You see?" she confirmed brightly. "You can't fight."

"But I must fight."

MacColla felt her body go rigid.

Her mouth sputtered mutely for a moment. Finding her voice, she said with dangerous quiet, "What did you say?"

"Still yourself, love." He sat up, watching as the storm in her eyes grew darker.

For once in his life, he'd rely first on reason, not passion. "You tell me there's an enemy out there who'd shoot me in my back?"

At her stiff nod, he continued, "If I don't get this man now, he'll come for me another day. It may be in Ireland, mayhap in Scotland, but he will come."

Haley nodded again, reluctantly. "Yes, but—"

"We can work this through. But you have to tell me everything."

MacColla helped her sit up to lean against the wall. He draped his plaid over Haley's chest and legs.

"Fret not, *leannan*. We shall beat this blackguard at his own game."

Chapter 34

MacColla savored fighting a battle he knew he'd win. And such a commanding triumph it was. Haley had told him of his victory on Knocknanuss Hill, but he hadn't imagined such a sweet rout.

The lass had wanted to watch, and he'd flatly refused. It was only after she resorted to threats of withholding what she called her *charms* that he conceded to letting her hide in wait amidst a thick tangle of trees.

He admitted he appreciated having her musket guarding his back. It was a *decent* musket he'd given her this time, with a wheel lock and plenty of powder.

He'd considered the other ways in which he could change the day's outcome. He'd been sorely tempted to warn that fool Taaffe not to abandon his command, but he couldn't trust that the unseasoned lord might not turn tail at the last moment, and repeat history all over again.

MacColla had decided the best course would be to live out the day as he would, trying to clear his mind of all else.

It was critical he sniff out his assassin. He assumed it

would be a Campbell man. One who'd find MacColla sooner or later.

He preferred sooner.

But damned if he wasn't nettled by the wait. He'd just dismissed the messenger. Knocknanuss Hill was at his back and his soldiers were long gone, racing ahead, chasing the last of the Parliamentary soldiers.

Most men didn't know the moment of their death, yet here he stood, alone, waiting for his fate to unfold.

In an instinctive gesture, MacColla lifted his hand to touch the sword grip at his back. He'd a great affection for the weapon. *Claidheamh da laihm.* The name he'd told Haley what seemed a lifetime ago.

He looked to where she hid in the trees, praying the blade would deliver him this one last time.

Distant movement caught his eye. Four Parliamentary cavalrymen emerged, not far from where she'd taken cover.

Four men, he thought distantly, hoping there wasn't some other force at work that had already set destiny's top to spinning. *She'd said five.*

The men posed their challenge. MacColla knew: If this same scenario presented itself for him to live and relive in some mad eternity, he'd always ever make the same choice. And he slashed and spun, cutting the horsemen one by one.

He heard the click of the cocking pistol at his back. *Pistol. Not musket.*

"If you'd be so kind as to hand over your blade."

MacColla stilled. He knew the man who was left standing. He'd sized him up at once. Standard-issue honor, with boots shined and brass polished. This particular soldier didn't frighten him.

It was the mysterious fifth man who made MacColla wary, the one he predicted would appear from behind.

"'Twill be a tale for my children's children to tell," the soldier crowed. "How their grandfather O'Grady offered

the great MacColla quarter." He paused and released his
prisoner's arm. Reaching to the scabbard at MacColla's
back, the man issued a stern rebuke, "I asked for your blade,
man."

MacColla heard a rustle, and knew.

"I'll avail myself of your prisoner, O'Grady," a voice
said.

There's the bastard.

He needed to act fast. Though Haley couldn't tell him
how much time he'd have, she'd described this scenario,
these men in these very poses, and he reckoned it best not
to tease the situation out too long.

O'Grady seemed a decent enough sort. He'd offered
MacColla quarter, and MacColla felt compelled to do the
same.

"Sorry, lad," he muttered. Seizing his captor's hand
where it reached for the hilt at MacColla's back, he elbowed
the soldier hard in the gut. "You've been an honorable enemy." O'Grady doubled over, and MacColla followed with
a swift blow to the back of his head, knocking him out cold.

He spun, his claymore extended, to face his would-be
killer.

The man was disappointingly ordinary, with an unremarkable face, riding an unremarkable horse.

The musket in his grip gave pause enough, though, and
MacColla watched as his hand twitched, supporting the
long barrel.

Shaking his head, the man smiled slowly, and slid a
hand to cock his weapon.

A loud shot cracked behind him, and MacColla flinched
despite himself, so ready was he to face this man's bullet.

Haley. The lass must've emerged from her hideout. And
though her shot went wide, it was enough to spook the
man's horse.

The beast reared just as the man fired, and his bullet
skewed high off the mark.

Cursing, the man scanned the land behind MacColla,
reaching to the powder flask at his belt. Thinking better of

it, he threw his musket to the ground, jumped from the skittish horse, and stalked to MacColla.

Who stood still as granite, waiting.

"I'd know the name of the man who'd shoot me in the back," MacColla snarled.

"Purdon," he replied cavalierly, unsheathing the sword from his side. The two men began to circle each other. "Major Nicholas Purdon."

He carried a cavalry saber. A strange, foreign thing, likely brought back from the warring on the Continent. Though an elegant weapon, the ridged steel was no less sturdy for its slight curve.

Still, MacColla taunted, "That's a pretty wee sword you have there, Purdon." He stretched his claymore out farther and grinned at the sound of his joints popping. "Shall I slice your belly or take your head, do you think?"

"Such coarseness. You surprise me, Alexander Mac-Donald." Purdon tilted his head in mock contemplation. "Head or belly? You offer me two evils and no choice."

"You'll call me by my Scottish name," he growled. He repeated Purdon's words in the Gaelic and smiled. "*Dà dhiù gun aon roghainn.*" MacColla took two broad and confident strides toward him. "Two evils, no choice indeed. And so I'll do the choosing for you."

He swung his claymore down, the thick steel slamming onto Purdon's saber with a resonant clang.

Curved cavalry blades weren't made for thrusting, and Purdon slashed and slashed again, his strikes no match for MacColla.

"Head, I think," MacColla said calmly, slashing his own blade down hard. The claymore's power was in its swing, and MacColla went at the man mercilessly. Down at his head, up from his legs, down at his head. Each strike was met with a block from his opponent, forced to support his blade with two hands to withstand MacColla's onslaught.

A sideswipe at Purdon's belly nicked flesh, and Purdon gasped. Stumbled back.

MacColla went at him with renewed force, luring him

into a diagonal rhythm. Slashing up and down at angles. Up and down.

Until, with a final grunt, MacColla changed his pattern, swiping a sudden and final strike from the side, severing Purdon's head from his body.

"May you rot, bastard," he said, using Purdon's coat to wipe the blood from his blade.

Haley caught up to him not long after the Parliamentary soldier fell. She was frantic, but that didn't prevent Mac-Colla from swooping her up in an elated kiss.

"We did it, *leannan.*"

"You did it," she said, smiling and panting. She scanned the valley nervously. "But now *we* have to get out of here. Rollo should be coming along soon . . ." she muttered, then decided, "but I don't think we can wait."

She'd watched the familiar scenario play out, with a blessedly different ending. And she'd held her breath all the while. "There could be any number of other men approaching. It's anyone's guess what could happen next."

"Aye. I'm of the same mind." He gave a firm nod. Cupping her chin, he gave her one last, long look. "I've no care for my own self, but I'd have your pretty hide up and away from this place."

He turned at once to coo and beckon to Purdon's horse, trying to gather the skittish mare.

"Wait," she said suddenly. She stopped short, looking at the dead man's head with disgust. "I have an idea."

❈

"But I'm a fair spot taller than this lout was." MacColla circled round Purdon's dead body, eyeing him with disdain.

"Yeah, well . . ." Haley shrugged. "He's even shorter now."

MacColla's laugh boomed, and she flinched, automatically shifting her gaze to survey the horizon. She spared him an edgy smile, but was anxious to get out of there. They'd already lost too many minutes while she tried to convince him of her plan.

"Seriously, MacColla." She extended her hand, gesturing once more that he hand over his claymore. "People see what they want to see. If everyone thinks you're dead, it'll give us options."

"Options?" He scowled. "Well, lass, I *opt* not to leave my sword."

"We'll get you a new one. We can't stage your death without leaving that *particular* sword behind," she said, pointing emphatically to the claymore in his hand. The ring at the base of the pommel and its simple, unadorned design had a whiff of Irish to it. But the sheer size pinpointed MacColla as its owner.

"I want Campbell's neck in my hands," he groused, flexing his fingers. "Not options."

"You can't chase Campbell," she said flatly. "Don't you see? You're supposed to be dead. We can't change the course of history."

"And why not?" He shrugged. "We just did, aye?"

"Well, for one thing . . ." Haley thought about it. *For one thing, you could get yourself killed again.*

"I'm Irish," she said suddenly. "What if something we do impacts my family line?" She flashed to all the sci-fi movie clichés of people blipping out of existence. "I'd never be born."

That gave him pause. He opened his mouth to speak, then promptly shut it again.

Haley hated not giving him a choice. She knew what it meant to him to conquer Campbell. She also knew he'd not be able to sit still for long, and this would only be the first time they'd have this argument.

She had another idea. Brightening, she said, "Listen, you can still battle the Campbell."

He looked at her, interest piqued.

"Your actions will be so much more devastating if Campbell thinks you're dead."

"What are you saying?"

She gestured again for his sword, and he finally relinquished it.

"I'm saying an anonymous enemy is the most dangerous one." Haley knelt to wrap Purdon's hand around the hilt of MacColla's claymore, but froze, grimacing.

He gently shifted her aside to finish the work for her. "You'll want to turn around, lass. If I plant my sword"—he began to strip the man of his uniform boots and breeches— "I'll need to plant my plaid as well."

Turning, she continued enthusiastically, "Think how easily, and how deeply, you could penetrate Campbell lands. *The great MacColla is dead.* What have they to fear?"

She looked over her shoulder, assessing him. "You'd need to be disguised, though. You're too recognizable. Too great a hero."

"Och, *leannan*," he grumbled playfully, tying his enormous shirt between his legs.

He squeezed her bottom as he swung her up onto Purdon's horse. "Now you're just trying to flatter me."

Chapter 35

"A dark knight, you say?" MacColla chafed under the armor. Haley insisted he wear it, though he had no idea how any man could move and fight freely in such a contraption.

"Yeah, sort of like a Gaelic Bruce Wayne."

"Bruce . . . ?"

"Never mind," she said, and wriggled his steel helmet into place. "Hey, at least I didn't make you get a visor."

"Armor is for cowards, *leannan*." He pulled the helmet back off, raking his fingers through his hair. He despised the hot, constrained feel of the thing. "Can't I just grow a beard?"

"You are *so* not growing a beard," she replied quickly, snatching the helmet from him and placing it back on his head. "You can't risk being recognized. You're just lucky there's no Mylar suit I can make you wear." Waggling her brows, she stepped back to get a good look at him. "Though you'd look pretty hot in one."

"Och, I'm hot enough as it is," he grumbled.

Turning serious, she mused, "Just a vest and helmet . . . Do you think it'll be enough of a disguise?" Haley studied his face. The helmet's brim cast his features in shadow, but not so much as to hamper vision or movement.

"They all think me killed. If anything, soldiers will think they've seen a wraith. And anyhow, men well know that I'd not be caught dead battling in armor, so, aye, *leannan*. This should be quite enough." He glanced down, stomping his feet to get used to the feel of trousers and boots. "But what on earth drove you to choose red plaid for my trews?"

He glanced up, catching her as she roved an assessing look up his body.

"What?" he asked, smiling wickedly. "I see the lightning in those stormy eyes, woman. Don't tell me you've an itch for me to scratch now that I'm trussed in a couple stones of steel."

"Just admiring you, my mysterious knight."

His dramatic glower elicited a laugh from her.

"Och . . ." he grumbled, shaking his head, unable to come up with a witty enough reply.

Often did he muse that perhaps he really had died that day, and spent the past months in his own private heaven, waking to the sight of Haley in his bed every morning, and making love to her every night.

MacColla had agreed with her that he should lay low for a while. But lately he'd grown anxious. The time had come for him to return to battle.

He'd expected Haley to protest, but it was as if she'd expected the day. She met the idea ready with fully realized notions of his armor, as well as a tally of possible battles he could plunge into anonymously.

"You say this Stirling is a pivotal fight?" he asked, nestling the helmet into place.

"Well, it's one of the few Campbell battles I can recall," she said. "Stirling Castle flew the king's colors, but they fell to Campbell and the Covenanters. It was devastating. Campbell and General Leslie had thousands of soldiers posted on the outskirts of Stirling. The few hundred men of Stirling Castle had no idea what was coming and were no match for them."

"But if I strike Campbell *before* he has a chance to mobilize his men . . ."

"Exactly," she said, smiling. "The only thing is, we need to *find* him first. He'd not be one to camp with the soldiers, would he?"

"Och, that's an easy one, *leannan*. Campbell has a town residence, at Deer Park." MacColla turned to let her adjust the leather straps at his side. "The Covenanter officers would likely be near to hand. They'd also not care to camp with the foot soldiers. I say we gather ourselves some Royalists and charge the park gates."

"We'll need to get the message to Munro," she said, referring to the Highlander who led the Royalists. "A little bird told him to ready his men and wait for word."

"Very fine, my wee birdie." Grinning, MacColla rolled and flexed his shoulders against the hard armor plates. "Now let's join Campbell for his supper."

❉

She sat on a modest wooded hill, thinking of the man she'd chosen to spend her life with. And of the life she'd left behind.

Haley let the familiar bittersweet feelings sweep her, remembering those loved ones she'd left in Boston. She'd never meet her brothers' children. She'd miss watching her parents enjoy their golden years. And then she wouldn't be there when they needed help in their old age.

She could only hope they had gotten her letter saying good-bye. *Would* get her letter.

Haley's mind drifted as she waited, and her eyes roved the panorama below. Hers was the perfect vantage point, overlooking the patch of emerald glen, nestled in the center of Deer Park, which would likely be the center of the fighting.

MacColla was set to besiege what forces Campbell had at his side in Stirling. And he couldn't seem happier.

She had to smile in spite of herself, wondering why she couldn't have fallen in love with some nice seventeenth-century man of the cloth, but then again, parsons weren't her thing.

MacColla was.

She felt a warm tingling in her chest remembering the sight of him suited up for battle. He looked fierce before, but it was nothing compared to him in an armored breast-plate and helmet.

That expanse of dully glimmering metal across his chest emphasized his tremendous size, and the brim of his helmet cast his face in shadow, darkening his handsome features into a character even more threatening than MacColla had been already.

She sighed. No parson indeed.

And he was off to battle again. There was no opposing it. All she could do was ensure his weapons and armor were sound, and hope for the best.

Her eyes traced the path of the River Forth, shimmering in the distance, meandering in wide loops through the coun-tryside. The late afternoon cast everything in a cool, iron gray light, as though the sun had gone but not set.

She made out a wave of men, rushing in the far distance.

It had begun, then.

Haley tensed. Squinting her eyes, she tried to make sense of what she saw.

They had gathered only a few hundred Royalists to join the fight. But it would be enough to face the meager and disjointed forces Campbell had to hand.

A shiver crept up her spine to think of the thousands of enemy Covenanters who, even now, were posted some-where outside Stirling.

Their few hundred Royalists had to be enough to splin-ter Campbell's leadership and abort his planned attack on Stirling Castle.

And it appeared they'd be successful. Tartan-clad sol-diers hewed through knots of men as effortlessly as a farmer might clear a tract of grassland with a reaping hook.

She spotted a lone horseman peeling away from the

rest, skirting far from the fighting. He galloped toward her, in the direction of Stirling Bridge.

A portly man. The rich sherry color of his coat betrayed its finery.

Campbell. Making a cowardly escape. Why was she not surprised?

Distant shooting called her attention back to the battle.

The men were dispersing now. She could tell from the Gaelic whoops and all that plaid that the Royalists had triumphed.

That MacColla had triumphed.

Movement along a lower ridge caught her eye. Haley bristled. How had she not noticed before? She hadn't been the only person watching the battle.

A cloaked figure roamed the hillside. It looked like a woman, with a stave in her hand. A gust of wind blew back her hood and long hair spilled out, a striking red against the white mantle on her back.

Finola.

Haley blinked hard and looked again. The witch was gone.

Epilogue

Twenty-Five Years Later

MacColla leaned easily against the wall, studying the room around him. People clapped and stomped in time to the music. Flickering torchlight exaggerated their smiles, their movements. The smell of fresh ale and stew filled the air. It was a good night.

He looked down at his wife by his side. Haley was past fifty now, but she was as gorgeous and formidable a creature as she'd been on the day they met. He smiled at the memory of her feral leap from Campbell's castle into the night.

"I may never have seen the full of my clan lands restored," he told her, hugging her close, "but I've seen you dance with our son at his wedding, and that's a rare privilege indeed."

He pulled her tight to him and planted an exuberant kiss on that lovely mouth. The kiss softened. Deepened.

MacColla marveled how, with a single kiss, she was still able to make him crave her with the keenness of a lad.

He brought his hand to stroke tenderly down her neck, desperate to edge his touch just a little lower. He'd been enjoying the company of his friends just a moment before, but now all he wanted was for everyone to be gone from there so he could ravage his wife in peace.

"Hands off my mother, old man." He felt his wife's mouth smile under his. Felt his son clap him hard on his shoulder. "Come on now. Coll had his dance with mum and now it's my turn."

MacColla pulled reluctantly from his wife, trying his best to scowl at his youngest, but failing. It was those damned gray eyes. Both their sons were handsome, but Archie had inherited his mother's eyes, and it made it impossible to argue with the boy.

"Shall we, Archibald?" Haley formally raised her hand for their son to take.

She looked back to give him a wink as Archie escorted her onto the floor.

MacColla watched them dance. He spotted Coll on the floor too, taking a turn with his bonny new bride. He knew his wife missed her family desperately, and her brothers especially. He knew it didn't take away her pain, but he'd been happy to give her two of her own boys.

He studied them. Their sons might have their mother's looks, but he also saw himself in them, saw what he'd taught them about honor and strength and courage, and it made MacColla's chest swell with such joyful pride.

A father and his sons.

He may not have gotten Campbell, but MacColla's legacy was so much greater than that.

Which isn't to say he hadn't relished Campbell's demise. The man's power vanished along with his money, and twelve years had passed since his beheading.

MacColla brought his tankard to his lips and drank deep to the memory of it.

He thought again of sons and fathers. At the end of his life, Campbell's fear of his own son had grown so great, he'd sequestered himself in his own castle.

Until he was put in the Tower and sentenced to death by Charles II. His crime had been agitating against King Charles I. A son meting justice for his father.

Jean caught MacColla's eye from across the room. His sister looked like an old woman now, her black hair faded white, but she still held tight to her Scrymgeour's hand, sitting as attentively by her side as he ever did.

Though MacColla and Haley had chosen to raise their children in relative seclusion in Ireland, Jean's daughters had spent summers playing with his sons, and it pleased him.

"They're getting ready to play your song." Haley had snuck up beside him, her dance through.

"Och . . ." MacColla glowered, listening to the musicians start to play one of Iain Lom's odes to him. He took another deep pull of his ale to cleanse the taste from his throat. "I hate those."

"You can't fault them." Haley paused to listen. "You put courage into the hearts of Gaels, husband."

"You sound like one of those accursed poems."

She only smiled brightly, swaying to the tune.

Alasdair, son of handsome Colla,
Skilled hand at sundering castles,
You routed the gray-skinned Lowlanders:
And if they drank kale soup you knocked it out them.

She leaned up on tiptoe to whisper in his ear, "Maybe we can get Iain Lom to pen something about the mysterious Dark Knight. You know, something like, "A knight in dark armor is come to avenge, so that Clan MacDonald may reap their revenge."

"You've had too much ale, *leannan*."

She giggled as he smacked her on the behind.

Haley stared up at him a moment, her face growing serious.

In their life together, he'd seen her wear gowns and fire guns. And she'd been as beautiful to him in velvet and finery as she'd been fighting with her corset busk.

She'd bathed their babes then seen them into lads, offering scoldings and kisses both, always there with love and comfort. And now MacColla and Haley stood together, realizing how their sons had become men grown.

Though she still had much black in her hair, it was twined with gray, mirroring those bottomless gray and black eyes. Eyes that he'd watched, countless times, grow dark with passion. Laugh with him. Fill with tears. Brighten at the sight of him. And MacColla thought her the most exquisite woman who'd ever lived.

"Aw, hell, MacColla," she whispered. "Just kiss me."

Author's Note

I could write an entire series based on Alasdair MacColla alone. He's idolized as one of the greatest Gaelic warriors, and I was steeped in tales of his feats, his weaponry, his vast size and strength.

My primary source was David Stevenson's astoundingly thorough biography, *Highland Warrior: Alasdair MacColla and the Civil Wars*, and I could've placed a finger at random on one of its pages and landed on fodder for an excellent story. (Note: That isn't MacColla on the cover—there is no image of him that I know of.)

Although hard facts from his life are considerably spottier than from the lives of my previous heroes (we don't even know his exact date of birth), there is much adulation for him. Stories, legends, and songs abound. Truly, he is one of the best loved of all the Gaelic heroes.

He seemed to me a man full of contradictions. He was famous for his ferocity and cruelty but, digging deeper, I uncovered so many instances of mercy and humor.

My focus was the mid-1640s, a time MacColla really did spend in Campbell lands around Kintyre and the western isles, harrying Clan Campbell and wedding a woman we know nothing about.

Some basic facts about his immediate family are available, and I integrated those into my story. For example, his brother-in-law did die giving MacColla his sword, though nothing is known of what happened to Jean after her husband was killed. Scrymgeour's involvement with the family is, as far as I know, fictional. MacColla did have two sons, raised in Ireland, who both lived past seventy.

I have one major disclaimer: Because I conflated James Graham's final two battles in my previous book, my Graham timeline here is a little off. That is, although this time period found him and MacColla having parted ways, at the time of the Battle of Knocknanuss, the real Graham had not yet been executed.

Like many Gaels, MacColla was a superstitious man. He truly didn't want to fight that day at Knocknanuss, fearing a long-ago portent. There are conflicting reports on how, exactly, he was killed. His initial victory was, in fact, decisive, but Taaffe had indeed been unable to see MacColla's triumphant flank. When the unseasoned lord spotted the incoming Parliamentary cavalry, he fled.

Meanwhile, MacColla had been separated from his men, waiting for a messenger to bring word about Taaffe's whereabouts, when he was surrounded and captured. One story goes that, though a cavalryman named O'Grady offered MacColla quarter, one Major Nicholas Purdon slaughtered their prisoner. Some go so far to say that this so outraged O'Grady, he fought Purdon every year for the next seven years. Imagining that Purdon and Campbell were in league, however, was pure fabrication on my part.

In addition to these real historical events, I've woven quotes and some apocryphal stories throughout. Iain Lom MacDonald really did pen numerous adoring paeans to "Alasdair of the sharp, biting blades."

MacColla truly did meet a young tinker with a frypan for a helmet and bemoan that not more of his soldiers were tradesmen. (Though this happened at the Battle of Inverlochy in 1645, predating Knocknanuss.)

Also, MacColla did famously offer an enemy two options: hanging or beheading. The man, a Campbell of Auchinbreck, replied, *"Dà dhiù gun aon roghainn,"* or, "two evils and no choice," a phrase that has since become proverbial. (Again, this took place at the Battle of Inverlochy, so it was a different foe at an earlier time.)

And finally, as they say, you can't make this stuff up. It's believed that his father, the famous Coll, or Colkitto,

really was captured when he exited the walls of his besieged castle requesting whisky.

Please visit my website at www.VeronicaWolff.com,
where you'll discover more tales from the life of Alasdair
MacColla, warrior of the highlands.

Turn the page for a preview of the next
historical romance by Veronica Wolff

lord of the highlands

Coming soon from Berkley Sensation!

London, 1658

Not again, Will Rollo thought sourly. He'd saved his friend Ormond from many a scrape, but the Tower of London? Frowning, he pulled his cowl farther over his head. An escape from the Tower far exceeded the obligations of friendship.

He nodded to his companion, and they pulled the oars up to skim near the surface of the water, dragging the small boat to a stop. Traitors' Gate loomed just ahead, connecting the Thames to the moat that encircled the Tower complex.

"Who goes there?" The guard shouted, jangling his keys as if to stress the gravity of his position.

It was early evening, and though there were hours yet before the gate would be locked for the night, traffic at that time of day was uncommon.

Rollo's hired man shifted nervously at his side, and Rollo put his hand out, gesturing for calm. Coin bought men, but it didn't always buy composure.

Truly, he thought. *This is the last time.*

Rollo cleared his throat, trying his best to shed the Scots from his voice. "I've come wi' ale, gov'ner."

He frowned at the answering silence. He had one shot to get Ormond out and needed to think quickly.

"It's for his lordship," Rollo added. He'd grown up on the other side of the servant-lord relationship, and he knew invoking the wrath of an angry nobleman—even an anonymous one—was good for getting results. "He said I should deliver it before the gates is locked for the night, or it's all our hides."

Rollo let out a quick, sharp cough. Keeping up the false accent was a struggle and an annoyance. Ormond may thrive on these sorts of intrigues, but Rollo much preferred fighting his battles in the light of day. Preferably on horseback.

There was a pause, then a strained, "Be on your way then."

Rollo's shoulders eased. *Without question, the last,* he thought, giving the guard a nod as he rowed past.

He noted the guard's greedy eyes pause on the cask, and fought the urge to heave a visible sigh of relief. The thing was empty but for a stretch of rope over twenty fathoms long. It was his ticket in and Ormond's ride out.

Rollo spared a quick, satisfied smile. The barrel and its promise of drink had been just the thing. Only a painted French whore would've bought him swifter passage.

They cut a sharp right, rowing into the moat toward Cradle Tower, which jutted out along the southeastern side. Long ago, Edward III had built it as his own private water entrance. The days of such niceties were long gone, and Cradle Tower was now filled instead with prisoners from the civil wars. Cromwell's enemies all.

The fortress rose high above them, its beige and brown stone an ominous gray in the night's growing dark. As they glided in and toward the Galleyman Stairs, he contemplated the thin arrow slits along the façade. The small openings offered no help—he'd have to get Ormond out from above.

Even though it was his crippled legs that were stiff, Rollo rubbed his shoulder, remembering his long-ago wound. He'd been shot on the field at Philiphaugh and had been as good as dead. But it was Ormond who'd found him.

Ormond's boyish persistence that had pulled him from the field and gotten him to safety.

He rolled his shoulders, eyeing a second guard coming into view. *The last time, Ormond.*

"What have you there?" The guard was a beefy man, and it was times like this that Rollo was glad of his cane.

"Ale." He stood, his cramped legs trying to find balance in the wobbling boat. His hired man pulled them close to the stone landing, and Rollo used the cane to make his way from the craft. "For you guards, mayhap?"

Rollo tried to wrench his face into a smile, but his thoughts were only for the blood that flowed too slowly back into his limbs.

"What's this, then?" The guard laughed. "You're lame!" He shook his head in wonder. "Can't be an easy job of it, hauling ale on feeble pins."

Rollo found his footing. He tossed his cane up, catching its midpoint, and swung. He caught the guard behind his ear, and the man fell in a solid heap. "Not feeble," he gritted out.

Taking the man by the heel, Rollo dragged him under the wooden staircase. He patted down the guard's coat, plucking a ring of keys from his inside pocket.

"He'll wake," he said, returning to his companion. "But we have time."

Rollo lifted the heavy length of rope that his hired man had hauled onto the landing. "Good work. You're earning your coin and a bit besides." He looked back out to the moat, almost completely shrouded in darkness. "Be gone now," he told him. "Wait on the far side. You'll see us."

The sound of Rollo's shuffling step echoed off the dank stone as he made his ascent. The thick loops of rope cut heavily into his shoulder, but he dared not risk the noise of dragging it.

He headed straight for the end of the hall, knowing exactly where he'd find his friend. The Sealed Knot was a clandestine bunch, working anonymously to topple Cromwell and reinstate the true king. But they weren't so secretive as to watch in silence as one of their own was imprisoned. When alerted that Rollo planned on freeing his friend, an agent had sought him out, pointed him to trustworthy hired help, detailed Ormond's position, and all but escorted Rollo to the Tower.

Ormond was a nobleman, and his cell was actually quite an accommodating affair, with a settee, fireplace, and small desk. "How'd you know where to find me?" he asked the moment Rollo found the right key and slipped in.

Rollo chuckled at his friend's exuberance. Ormond's bright red hair was in a tousle, and he could use a fair spot of barbering besides, but these things only heightened the man's boyishness. Though Ormond was in his forties, Rollo expected he'd never lose his bright-eyed zeal.

"Your Sealed Knot friends seem to have much information at their disposal."

"But how?"

"Later." Rollo eyed the windowless room. They'd have to continue up, making their escape from the roof. "Let's away from here before your guard wakes sore and angry."

"Give me that." Ormond gestured to the rope.

"I can manage," Rollo said coldly.

"You never change, do you? I know better than most how well you can manage." He reached for the heavy mass. "But I've been cooped up here for weeks, and if I don't set this nervous energy to something, I swear—"

"Fine." Rollo shrugged the rope from his side. "Let's just be gone."

They made their way up a cramped spiral staircase to the rooftop. Rollo had read of a Jesuit priest who'd made this same escape not one hundred years prior, and he figured two battle-hardened soldiers could do it if a man of the cloth could. Though he did understand monks to be a feisty bunch.

"What cause do you risk your head for this time?" Rollo placed his hands on the cold stone of the battlements and peered down. The moat—and he hoped his boat—waited for them in the blackness below. "Hand me that," he said, pointing to the rope.

"The same as ever. I'll see the true Stuart king reinstated before I die." Ormond helped Rollo secure the end of the rope around one of the battlements. "Cromwell and his Parliament may have beheaded King Charles I, but they dare not behead the son. I vow, Charles II will be restored to the throne."

"They do call it a *kingdom*, after all," Rollo said dryly, tugging the rope tight, testing his knot. "There now. Who shall be first to give it a go?" He spared Ormond a smile.

"I need to tell you something, Will."

Rollo's face grew stoic once more, waiting in silence for what his friend had to say.

"Your brother." Ormond looked into the distance, weighing his words. "It's Jamie. Jamie's the one who masterminded my capture."

"I knew," Rollo inhaled sharply. "I anticipated this day. I knew when he traded wives. To go from Graham's sister to Campbell's. Aye, getting in league with Cromwell himself wasn't far behind."

"So you're not surprised?"

"There's no ill my elder brother could conceive that would give me surprise." He glanced quickly at his legs as he gave the rope one more tug. "Up and over, you."

Ormond smiled, shaking his head, and clapped his friend on the shoulder. "I thank you for this, Will."

"Aye," he muttered, watching Ormond's descent. "And it's the last time, for certain."

"Good evening, *cripple*."

Rollo turned sharply, though he knew from the voice whom he'd find. "Jamie. So happy you could join me. 'Tis a lovely wee fortress you have here. Though it does seem to have sprung a leak."

"Did you think I'd not hear you clopping about?" Jamie eyed his brother with disdain. "The years pass, and still you trudge around like a one-legged fishwife."

"Aye." Rollo smiled broadly. "The years pass, and still you talk to me as if you're the same twelve-year-old in our father's stable yard."

The hiss of Jamie's unsheathed broadsword cut through the night.

"Dear Jamie, you surprise me." Rollo laughed softly, tapping his cane lightly on the toe of his boot. "You're fighting your own battles now? Or is it that Cromwell doesn't have a sister for you to bed?"

Jamie leapt for him, but Rollo was instantly ready. Tossing his cane up, he grabbed the curve of the pistol-handled grip in one hand, pulling a tidy little sword free of its wooden sheath.

"Hiding a weapon in your walking stick." Jamie slashed hard, and their swords crossed with a sharp clang. "Not fair, little brother."

"You speak of fair?" Rollo cut his sword in the sharp diagonal slash he'd perfected in years of cavalry fighting, and his brother's blade caught it just before it bit into his shoulder. "What's not fair is destroying an innocent seven-year-old because you don't like his pony."

Jamie unleashed then, thrashing with rapid but sloppy strokes. Rollo's legs prevented him from bobbing and weaving as another swordsman might, and he suffered the onslaught, meeting each thrust with his own block and parry.

He recognized his brother's style, though, and planned to let Jamie flail himself into exhaustion. He was younger than Jamie and, ironically, it was Rollo's injury that had kept him fitter than most men, regardless of age.

Jamie bobbed forward for what he clearly thought would be a killing lunge, and Rollo saw his chance. Though he refused to kill his brother, he found he was quite eager to bruise the lout.

Rollo stepped forward, meeting Jamie's lunge. Their swords crashed, blade sliding down blade, until the brothers' hands were mere inches apart.

"You always"—jutting his foot forward, Rollo grabbed his brother's wrist and flung him over his extended leg—"make this same blunder." Jamie's sword came loose and clattered across the timber roof.

Rollo put the tip of his blade to Jamie's neck. "Don't

forget, *brother*. My injury makes me the stronger man. Or are you loath to admit that you are the cause of that strength?"

"Never." Jamie grabbed the blade in his palm, and a thin trickle of blood seeped from his fist. "You will never be the stronger man."

He rolled from beneath the sword, shouting at once for a guard.

Rollo looked for a split second at the sword in his hand, then threw it down, cursing its loss. The cane had been a fine little treasure, but he had neither the time nor the hands to spare.

He heard his brother's shouts and the scrape of his broadsword as he retrieved it.

Rollo pulled himself up between the battlements, the stone scraping his back and arms as he wriggled through. Fumbling in the dark, his hands found the rope. The rock scored his knuckles as he climbed down into the blackness below.

"Will," Ormond hissed. "Just here. Hurry now, I hear the guards rallying."

Rollo dropped the last foot, landing clumsily in the boat, and his hired man set at once to rowing them back toward Traitors' Gate.

"What are you doing?" Rollo sidled toward the empty cask, still waiting in the prow of the boat. "You were to hide."

"Someone has beat me to it." Ormond's voice had a peculiar edge.

Rollo swung his gaze to him. "You sound amused."

"Have a look-see," the hired man spoke, offering his dagger.

Rollo took the knife and pried the lid free, revealing a woman. She was curled up, fast asleep, her heavy breath echoing in the tiny chamber. "What the devil?"

He peered in. It was impossible to make out any details in the dark. "Help me," he said to Ormond. "I'll get her"—he put his hands under her arms and pulled—"you steady the barrel."

"Good Lord," Ormond said, turning his face away. "Is that her or the cask?"

Rollo grimaced at the smell of stale wine. "I think mayhap it's both?"

He laid her down gently, staring for a moment in dumbfounded silence. She was a small, fine-boned thing, with pert little features and hair that flowed long and loose down her back. The moon had risen and illuminated her face with an unearthly light, making her seem like some sort of wayward fairy princess.

Rollo spied something on her, and he carefully took her bare arm in his hand. Her skin was warm and smooth, and he couldn't help but run his thumb over the delicate bones of her hand, her fingers longer and thinner than he'd have expected.

He turned her arm to see what had stuck to her and peeled a strange card from the thin skin of her forearm. It pictured a man walking blithely along, the sun at his back and a bloom in his hand. The man in the drawing gazed up at the sky, heedless of the cliff from which he was about to step. Beneath the image was written, *The Fool.*

Rollo quickly pocketed the peculiar thing, his skin pebbling to gooseflesh.

The distant rumble of talk floated over the water from the direction of Traitors' Gate, calling him back to himself. "Hurry," he said to Ormond. "In the cask. Now."

"What of *her*?" Ormond pointed to the girl with a mix of bemusement and panic.

"I'll give her my cloak." Rollo slipped his arms from the blanket of dark wool, eyeing her strange and colorful skirt. "Something to cover the clothes she wears."

"But they'll recognize you. You can't risk so much for some drunken wench."

"What would you have me do? Drop her in the moat?" He settled the strange woman on his lap, leaning her against his neck as if she nuzzled him. "The guard's eyes will be on the lass, not me."

Ormond stared at him as if he'd lost his mind. Rollo

glared a challenge, and his friend simply shrugged, climbing awkwardly into the barrel.

"Make it fast." Rollo angled away from the guard's side of the boat, draping the woman's hair over his face. The smell of lavender filled his senses, and an unsettling feeling seized him, something visceral, striking him as both foreign and yet somehow dimly remembered. He swallowed hard, reminding himself where he was. "We approach the gate."

His hired man began whistling with affected boredom as they rowed closer, and Rollo thought the man had earned his keep.

Just as he'd predicted, the guard had eyes only for their drunken passenger. The man shot Rollo a rakish and congratulatory wink, nodding them through the Traitors' Gate and out to the Thames.

But Rollo gazed sightlessly into the distance, breathing the scent of lavender and thinking he'd wager anything that this lass was more than a mere wench.

Enter the rich world of
historical romance
with Berkley Books.

Lynn Kurland

Patricia Potter

Betina Krahn

Jodi Thomas

Anne Gracie

Love is timeless.
penguin.com

M9G0907